Judah Maccabee
Part 1 - Abomination of Desolation

Chronicles of the Watchers
Book 4

By Brian Godawa

Judah Maccabee: Part 1- Abomination of Desolation
Chronicles of the Watchers, Book 4
1st Edition b

Copyright © 2024 Brian Godawa
All rights reserved. No part of this book may be reproduced in any form or by any electronic or mechanical means, including information storage and retrieval systems, without prior written permission except in the case of brief quotations in critical articles and reviews.

Warrior Poet Publishing
www.warriorpoetpublishing.com

ISBN: 978-1-963000-60-3 (paperback)
ISBN: 978-1-963000-62-7 (hardback)
ISBN: 978-1-963000-61-0 (eBook)
ISBN: 978-1-963000-63-4 (Large Print)

Scripture quotations are taken from *The Holy Bible: English Standard Version*. Wheaton: Standard Bible Society, 2001.

Get a Free eBooklet about the Gods Referred to in This Novel.
Limited Time Offer
FREE

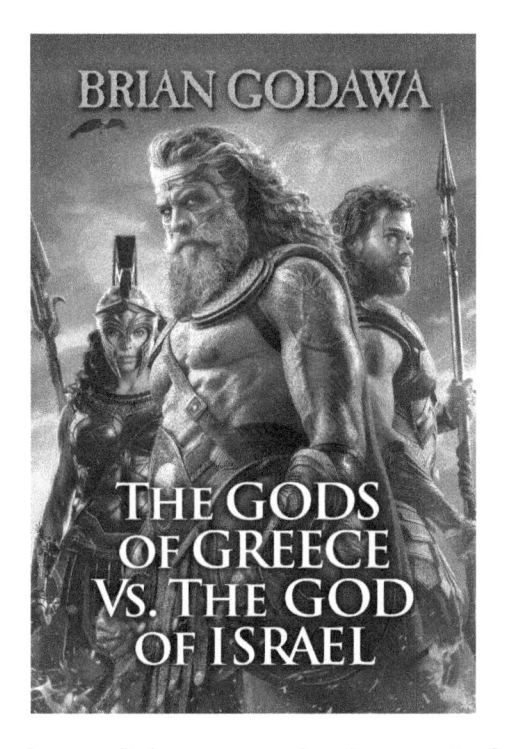

Zeus, Hera, Ares, Athena, and others vie for power in their territory allotted to them by Yahweh.

Sadly, many ancient Jews had been deceived into worshipping the gods of Greece during the time of the Maccabees. Learn about these pagan opponents of Yahweh.

https://godawa.com/free-gods-of-greece/

DEDICATION

This novel set is dedicated to Cary Schatz,

a fellow intellectual warrior for God

who seeks the purity of the Faith.

Before You Read This Novel, Get the Picture Book of Its Characters for Visual Reference

Includes Characters from This Novel of Judah Maccabee!

Full-color picture book includes characters for the
Chronicles of the Watchers and Chronicles of the Apocalypse series:

• Jezebel: Harlot Queen of Israel • Qin: Dragon King of China • Moses: Against the Gods of Egypt • Judah Maccabee 1&2 • Tyrant • Remnant • Resistant • Judgment

These full-color pictures will boost your imagination as you read the novels.

Click Here to Get Now:
(in Paper, Hardcover, or Ebook)

www.godawa.com/get-watch-pics/
affiliate link

ACKNOWLEDGMENTS

To Yahweh: Even when you are silent and apparently absent to my failing perception, you are sovereign and work all things after the counsel of your will.

To Kimberly: Once again, you are my Sophia, my Hannah, and every other worthy woman of love in all my stories.

To Jeanette: Once again, thank you for your editorial sword.

NOTE TO THE READER

Judah Maccabee: Parts 1&2 is a standalone novel set. But it is also part of the *Chronicles of the Watchers* series whose books all share what biblical scholar Michael S. Heiser has called "the Deuteronomy 32 worldview"[1] and what I call "the Watcher paradigm."

For purposes of clarity, I will lay it out here in brief summary. For more detailed biblical support and explanation, I recommend reading my booklet, *Psalm 82: The Divine Council of the Gods, the Judgment of the Watchers, and the Inheritance of the Nations (affiliate link).* It is the foundation of all three of my novel series: *Chronicles of the Nephilim, Chronicles of the Watchers,* and *Chronicles of the Apocalypse.*

Deuteronomy 32 is well-known as the Song of Moses. In it, Moses sings of Israel's story and how she had come to be God's chosen nation. He begins by glorifying God and then telling the Israelites to "remember the days of old":

> *When the Most High gave to the nations their inheritance,*
>   *when he divided mankind,*
> *he fixed the borders of the peoples*
>   *according to the number of the sons of God.*
> *But the Lord's portion is his people,*
>   *Jacob his allotted heritage.*
> *(Deuteronomy 32:8–9)*

---

[1] Michael S. Heiser, *The Unseen Realm: Recovering the Supernatural Worldview of the Bible*, First Edition (Bellingham, WA: Lexham Press, 2015), 113–114.

The context of this passage is the Tower of Babel incident in Genesis 11 when mankind was divided. Rebellious humanity sought divinity in unified rebellion, so God separated them by confusing their tongues, which divided them into the seventy (Gentile) nations described in Genesis 10 with their ownership of those bordered lands as the allotted "inheritance" of those peoples.

But inheritance works in heaven as it does on earth. The people of Jacob (Israel) would become Yahweh's allotted inheritance under his ownership and rule while the other Gentile nations were the allotted inheritance of the *Sons of God* under their ownership and rule.

So who were these Sons of God who ruled over the Gentile nations (Psalm 82:1-8)? Some believe they were human rulers. Others argue for their identities as supernatural principalities and powers. I am in the second camp. In my *Psalm 82* booklet, I prove why they cannot be humans and must be heavenly creatures.

The phrase "Sons of God" is a technical term that means divine beings from God's heavenly court,[2] but they possess many different titles. They are sometimes called "heavenly host,"[3] sometimes "holy ones,"[4] at other times "the divine council,"[5] or "Watchers,"[6] or even "gods" (*elohim* in Hebrew).[7] Yes, you read that last one correctly. *God's Word calls these beings "gods."*

But fear not. That isn't polytheism. The word "god" in this biblical sense is a synonym for "heavenly being" or "divine being" whose realm is that of the spiritual plane.[8] Simply put, the Hebrew word *elohim*

---

[2] Job 1:6; 38:7.

[3] Isaiah 24:21-22; Deuteronomy 4:19 with Deuteronomy 32:8-9; 1 Kings 22:19-23.

[4] Deuteronomy 33:2-3; Psalm 89:5-7; Hebrews 2:2.

[5] Psalm 82:1; 89:5-7.

[6] Daniel 4:13, 17, 23.

[7] Deuteronomy 32:17, 43; Psalm 82:1; 58:1-2.

[8] Michael S. Heiser, *The Unseen Realm: Recovering the Supernatural Worldview of the Bible*, First Edition (Bellingham, WA: Lexham Press, 2015), 23-27.

("god") is not just used for the Creator Yahweh alone but is also used of other different kinds of beings. According to the Bible, "e*lohim*/god" is not necessarily a word that means infinite, uncreated beings that are all-powerful and all-knowing. Yahweh alone is that God. Yahweh is the God of gods.[9] He is species-unique. That is, while Yahweh is an elohim, other elohim are not like Yahweh. These "gods" (lowercase 'g') are finite, created spiritual beings who reside in the heavenly realm that can intersect with the earthly realm of humanity. Sadly, our modern use of the word "god" does not line up with the biblical use of the term, thus causing unfounded reactions of fear in those who prefer modern over ancient context.

The biblical narrative is as follows. The Fall in the Garden was not the only source of evil in the world. Before the Flood, some of these heavenly Sons of God rebelled against Yahweh and left their divine dwelling to come to earth (Jude 6), where they violated Yahweh's holy separation and mated with human women (Genesis 6:1-4). This was not a racial separation but a spiritual one. Their corrupt hybrid offspring were called *Nephilim* (giants), and their effect on humanity included such corruption and violence on the earth that Yahweh sent the Flood to wipe everyone out and start over again with Noah and his family.[10]

Unfortunately, after the Flood humanity once again united in evil while building the Tower of Babel, a symbol of idolatrous worship of false gods. So Yahweh confused their tongues and divided them into the seventy nations. Since mankind would not stop worshipping false gods, the living God gave them over to their lusts (Romans 1:24, 26, 28) and placed them under the authority of the fallen Sons of God that they worshipped. Fallen spiritual rulers for fallen humanity (Psalm 82:1-7; 58:1-2). It's as if God said to humanity, "Okay, if you refuse to

---

[9] Deuteronomy 10:17; Psalm 136:2.

[10] Genesis 6:11-13; 2 Peter 2:4-6. For this storyline, see my first two novels, *Noah Primeval* and *Enoch Primordial*, in the Chronicles of the Nephilim series.

stop worshipping false gods, then I will give you over to them and see how you like them ruling over you."[11]

Deuteronomy 32 hints at a spiritual reality behind the false gods of the nations, calling them "demons" (Deuteronomy 32:17; Psalm 106:37-38), which in Hebrew refers to territorial guardian spirits.[12] The apostle Paul later ascribes demonic reality to pagan gods as well (1 Corinthians 10:20; 8:4-6). The New Testament continues this ancient notion of spiritual principalities and powers connected to and reigning over earthly powers in the unseen realm (Ephesians 6:12; 3:10). The two were inextricably linked in historic events. As Jesus indicated, whatever happened in heaven also happened on earth (Matthew 6:10). Earthly kingdoms in conflict are intimately connected to heavenly powers in conflict (Daniel 10:12-13, 20-21; 2 Kings 6:17; Judges 5:19-20).

So the Bible says that there is demonic reality to false gods. Just what this looks like is not exactly described in the text of Scripture. But since those Sons of God who were territorial authorities over the nations were spiritually fallen Watchers, that makes them demonic or evil in essence.

So what if they were the actual spiritual beings behind the false gods of the ancient world? What if the fallen Sons of God were masquerading as the gods of the nations to keep humanity enslaved in idolatry to their authority? That would affirm the biblical stories of earthly events and rulers occurring in synchronization with heavenly events and rulers. It would not have to be a one-to-one correspondence of demonic Watcher with pagan god. Evil angels could put on the disguises of different gods at will to achieve their deceptive purposes.

One other note of importance is that the Bible speaks of the Divine Council members, Sons of God/Watchers, and spiritual angels as being

---

[11] For this storyline see my novels, Gilgamesh Immortal and Abraham Allegiant in the Chronicles of the Nephilim series.

[12] Victor P. Hamilton, "2330 שד," (Hebrew, "shed") in *Theological Wordbook of the Old Testament*, ed. R. Laird Harris, Gleason L. Archer Jr., and Bruce K. Waltke (Chicago: Moody Press, 1999), 906.

exclusively male in their sex, names, and pronouns, but it does not explain why. It is therefore reasonable to conclude that there are no female elohim. But because this is an argument from silence, it would be extra-biblical speculation to suggest that there are female Watchers or angels, but it would not be *anti-biblical heresy* because silence is an argument for neither existence nor non-existence.

However, sometimes silence *can be* a deliberate expression of existential reality or theological purpose. In this case, we can only speculate why, but I have chosen to adopt the biblical silence as deliberate and purposeful and therefore have suggested that any female presentation of fallen Sons of God/Watchers are facades or illusive disguises that hide the true male sexual identity of the beings. The New Testament claims that the satan and his ilk can masquerade as angels of light (2 Corinthians 11:14), which means they can disguise their identities for nefarious purposes.

That is the biblical premise of the *Chronicles of the Watchers*. The pagan gods like Zeus, Hera, Ares, Baal, Anat, and others are actually fallen Sons of God, Watchers of the nations, crafting identities and narratives as gods of those nations. The ultimate end of these spiritual rebels is depicted in the series *Chronicles of the Apocalypse*. But for now they plan, conspire, and fight to keep their allotted peoples and lands, all while seeking to stop God's messianic goal of inheriting all the nations (Psalm 2:1-9; 82:8) through his seed (Genesis 3:15; Galatians 3:16).

My goal is to use the fantasy genre to show the theological reality of spiritual warfare while remaining faithful to the biblical text.

A word for those who share my high view of Scripture. In the interest of focusing on the story of the Maccabees, I not only drew from the Bible but from Jewish Second Temple literature as well as Greek sources. The purpose of this was not to "add" to Scripture through syncretism but rather to subvert pagan narratives and fill in the gaps between Scripture in a way that is faithful *to* Scripture.

Anyone familiar with the Bible will know that this story of Jewish revolt is contained in non-biblical books called 1 & 2 Maccabees. They are part of what is called the Apocrypha, Greek texts that Christians debated about in the first centuries as to whether they should be included in the canon of Scripture. Reputable Church fathers and scholars were on both sides of that debate. Clement of Rome, Irenaeus, Tertullian, Cyprian, Clement of Alexandria, and Origen were just some of those most respected who considered some of the Apocrypha to be inspired Scripture.

But as Francis Beckwith concludes, the canonicity of the Apocrypha was not uniform. "All that was agreed was that the Apocrypha were to be read and esteemed, not that they were to be treated as Scripture."[13] Later, Martin Luther expressed a common Protestant position when he described the Apocrypha as "books which are not to be equated with Holy Scripture and yet which are useful and good to read."[14]

Bible scholar John Bartlett adds:

> In England the Calvinist-inspired Geneva Bible (1560) included the apocryphal books, accepting them "for their knowledge of history and instruction of godly manners,", a phrase taken up in the Church of England's Thirty-Nine Articles of Religion, which state that "the other [i.e. apocryphal] books ... the Church doth read for example

---

[13] Roger T. Beckwith, *The Old Testament Canon of the New Testament Church and Its Background in Early Judaism* (London: SPCK, 1985), 386, 394. One of the strongest arguments for the Apocrypha not being considered canonical is that Jesus and the Apostles never quoted from those books as being Scripture. But this is not an absolute proof because there are nine other Old Testament books never quoted in the New Testament as well: Judges, Ruth, Ezra, Esther, Ecclesiastes, Song of Solomon, Lamentations, Obadiah, and Zephaniah. Obadiah and Zephaniah, however, were considered a part of the singular category called "The Twelve" in reference to the twelve prophets, so they may be assumed under that category. And it must be remembered that the New Testament also quotes from many sources that are NOT considered to be canonical but are considered relevant or truthful such as 1 Enoch.

[14] Thomas Fischer, "Maccabees, Books of: First and Second Maccabees," in *The Anchor Yale Bible Dictionary*, ed. David Noel Freedman, trans. Frederick Cryer (New York: Doubleday, 1992), 439.

of life and instruction of manners; but yet doth it not apply them to establish any doctrine."[15]

In a sense, this standard still holds today. Even though Protestants may not agree with the Roman Catholic or Eastern Orthodox views of the Apocrypha as canonical or deutero-canonical, scholarship maintains they are nevertheless worthy of respect to be studied and afforded esteem for basic historical purposes. That is the position I took as author of the novel set *Judah Maccabee: Parts 1&2*. God is sovereignly involved in all history, not only in biblically canonical history.

Another important note for the reader is that the name of Judah Maccabee in the novels begins as Judas ben Mattathiah. This is the Greek version of the Hebrew name Judah ben Mattathiah due to the Hellenistic context. It will change to Judah Maccabee later in the story for a very specific reason. Have patience!

If you are interested in learning more about the historical, biblical, and religious foundation of this novel, I have written a companion book explaining the research I've done and the choices I've made. It's called *The Spiritual World of Ancient Israel and Greece: Biblical Background to the Novels Judah Maccabee – Parts 1&2*.

Thank you for your understanding of imagination and faith.

Brian Godawa
Author, *Chronicles of the Watchers*

---

[15] John R. Bartlett, *1 Maccabees, Guides to Apocrypha and Pseudepigrapha* (Sheffield, England: Sheffield Academic Press, 1998), 14.

TABLE OF CONTENTS

Get a Free eBooklet about the Gods Referred to in This Novel. iii
Dedication iv
Acknowledgments vi
Note to the Reader vii
Table of Contents xiv
Maps xvii
Pronunciation Key xx
Gods xxi
Chapter 1 1
    Mount Zaphon, Syria Year 144 of the Kingdom of the Greeks 169 B.C. 1
Chapter 2 10
    Antioch on the Orontes River 10
Chapter 3 20
    Daphne 23
Chapter 4 30
    Nemea, Grecce 30
Chapter 5 36
    Antioch 36
Chapter 6 42
Chapter 7 51
Chapter 8 56
Chapter 9 66
    Mount Artemesium, Greece 66
Chapter 10 70
    Antioch 70
Chapter 11 81
    Daphne 81
Chapter 12 88
    Antioch 88
Chapter 13 92
Chapter 14 100
    Lake Lerna, Greece 100
Chapter 15 106
    Antioch 106
Chapter 16 110
    Pelusium, Egypt 112

Chapter 17	114
Jerusalem	114
Chapter 18	124
Chapter 19	133
Chapter 20	141
Memphis, Egypt One Month Later	141
Chapter 21	146
Jerusalem	146
Chapter 22	152
Alexandria, Egypt	152
The Nile River South of Alexandria	158
Chapter 23	162
Jerusalem	162
Chapter 24	167
Chapter 25	172
Chapter 26	176
Cape Tainaron, Greece	176
Chapter 27	182
Alexandria	182
Chapter 28	194
Jerusalem	194
Chapter 29	201
Chapter 30	207
Chapter 31	215
Chapter 32	225
Chapter 33	230
Modein, Judea	230
Chapter 34	239
Jerusalem 15 Kislev, Year 145 of the Kingdom of the Greeks December 6, 168 BC	239
Chapter 35	253
Modein	253
Jerusalem	255
Mizpah	260
Jerusalem	261
Valley of the Rephaim	269
Jerusalem	272
Outside Jerusalem	275

Chapter 36 278
   Pontus, Scythia 278
Chapter 37 283
   Modein 283
Chapter 38 290
   Pontus, Scythia 290
Chapter 39 301
   Modein 301
Chapter 40 308
   Mount Hermon 308
Get Judah Maccabee – Part 2: Against the Gods of Greece 317
Get the Book of the Biblical & Historical Research Behind This Novel ... 318
Great Offers By Brian Godawa 319
About the Author 320

MAPS

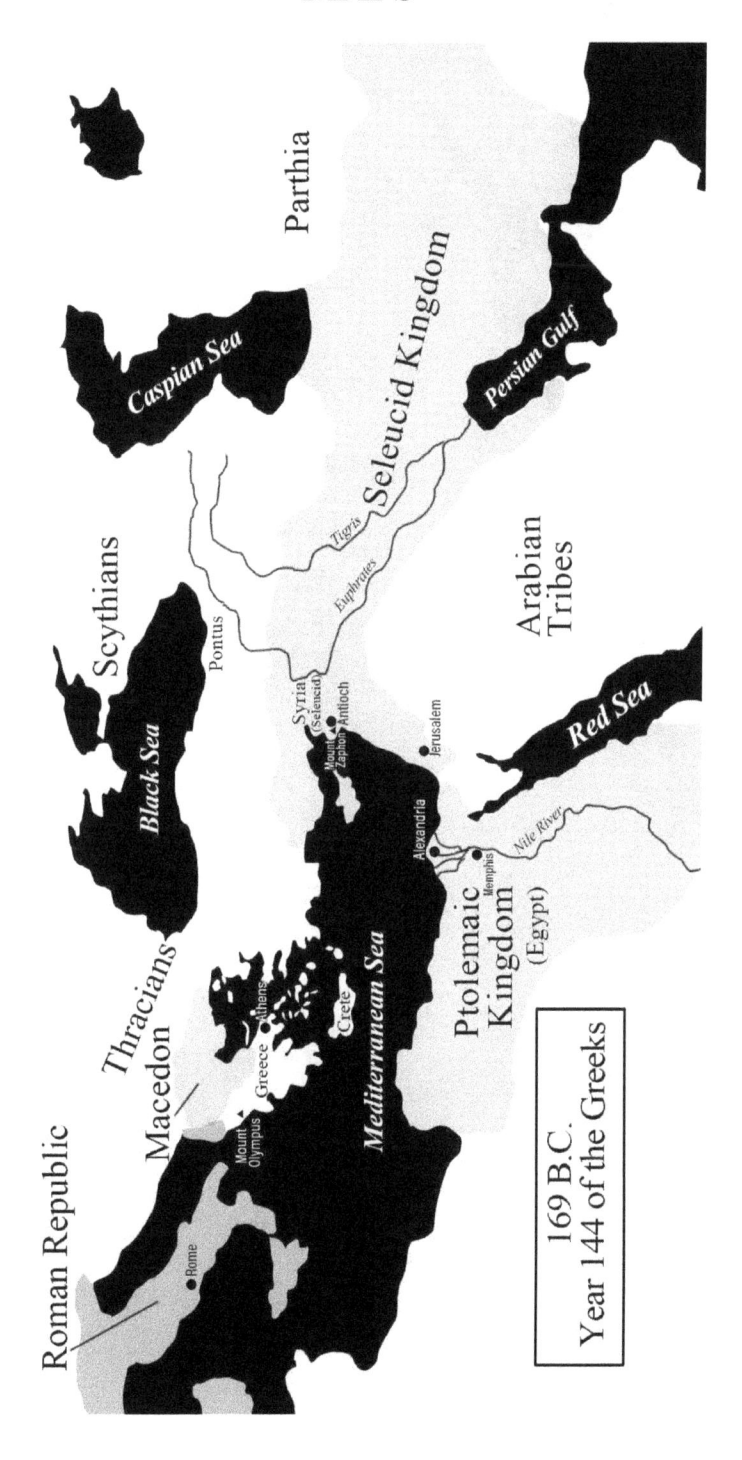

169 B.C.
Year 144 of the Greeks

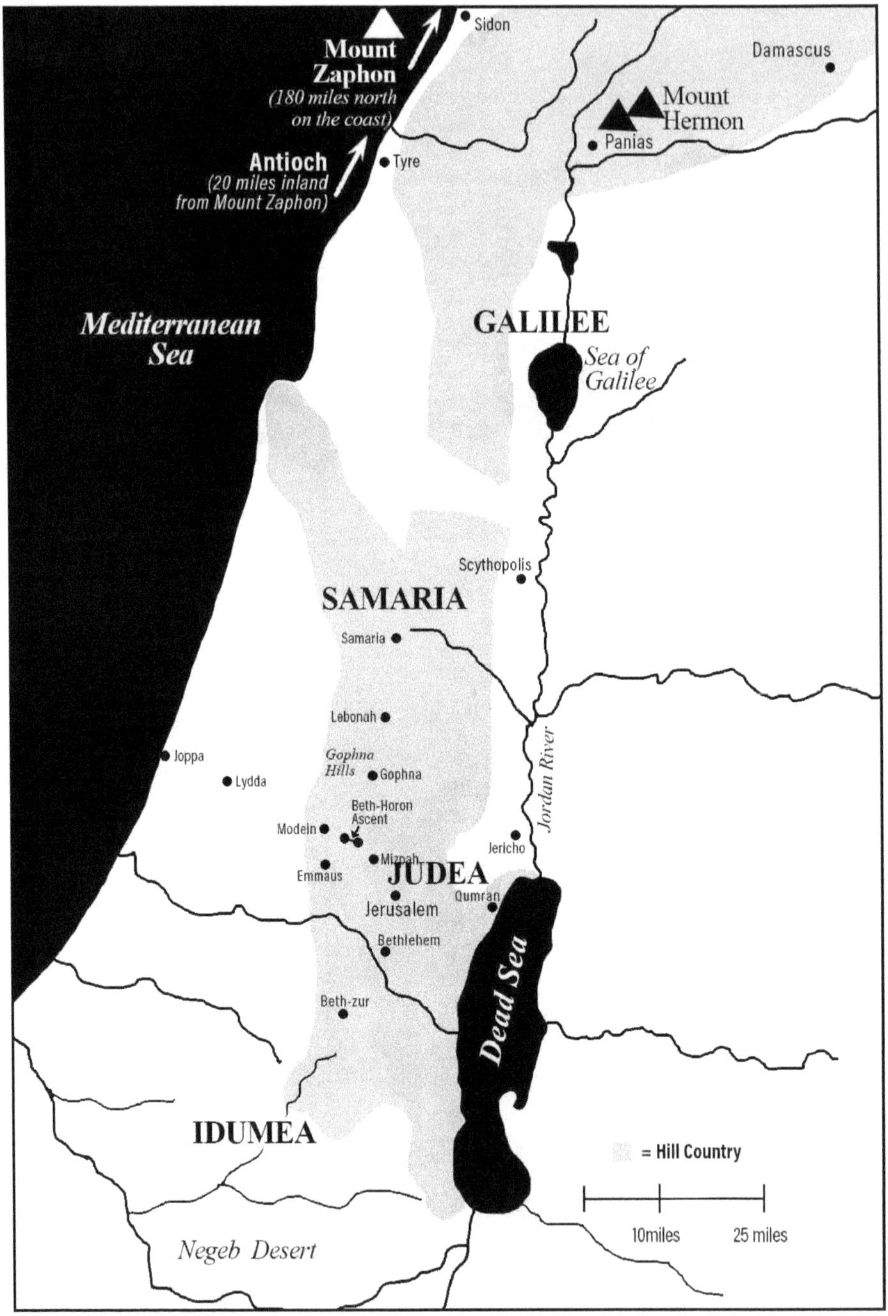

Sidon
Mount Zaphon
(180 miles north on the coast)
Antioch
(20 miles inland from Mount Zaphon)
Tyre
Damascus
Mount Hermon
Panias
Mediterranean Sea
GALILEE
Sea of Galilee
Scythopolis
SAMARIA
Samaria
Lebonah
Joppa
Lydda
Gophna Hills
Gophna
Beth-Horon Ascent
Modein
Mizpah
Emmaus
JUDEA
Jericho
Jordan River
Qumran
Jerusalem
Bethlehem
Dead Sea
Beth-zur
IDUMEA
= Hill Country
10miles
25 miles
Negeb Desert

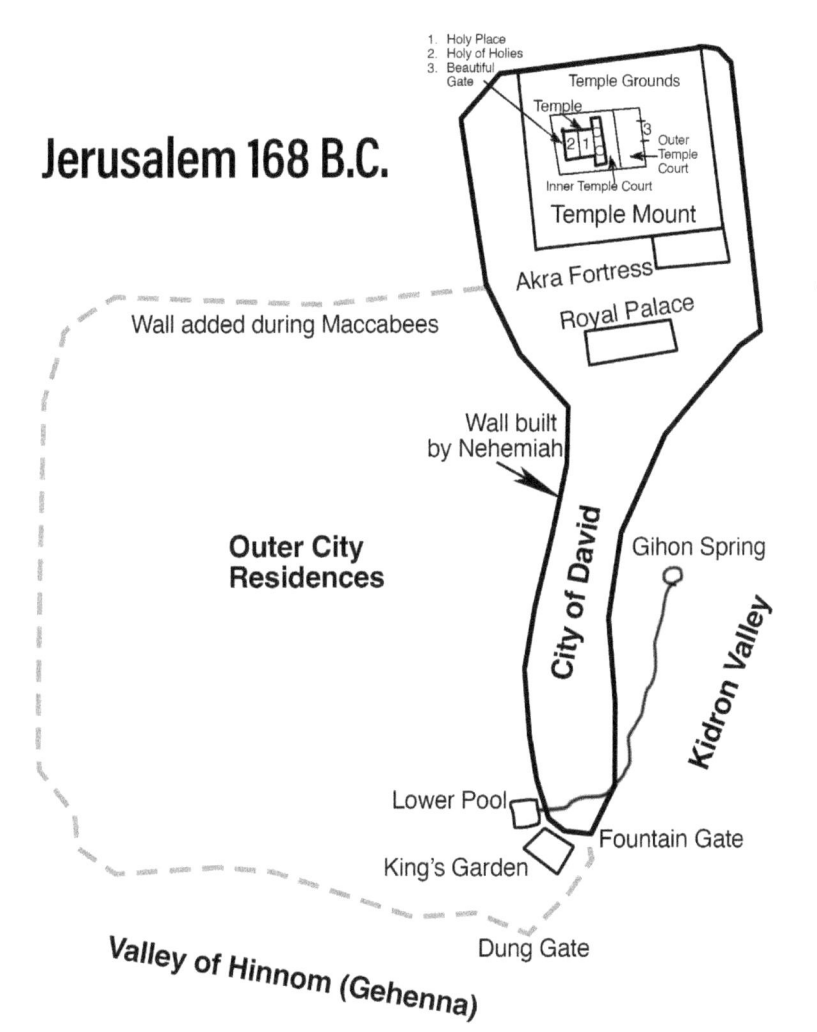

Jerusalem 168 B.C.

1. Holy Place
2. Holy of Holies
3. Beautiful Gate

Temple Grounds
Temple
Outer Temple Court
Inner Temple Court
Temple Mount
Akra Fortress
Royal Palace
Mount of Olives
Wall added during Maccabees
Wall built by Nehemiah
Outer City Residences
City of David
Gihon Spring
Kidron Valley
Lower Pool
Fountain Gate
King's Garden
Dung Gate
Valley of Hinnom (Gehenna)

xix

PRONUNCIATION KEY

Foreign Name/Word	English Pronunciation
Antiochus	Ann-**tie**-uh-cuss
Antiochene	Ann-**tie**-uh-keen
Apollonius	App-uh-**lone**-ee-uss
Gaius Popilius Laenas	**Gay**-uss Poe-**pillee**-uss **Lie**-nuss
Diadochi	Dee-uh-**doe**-kee
Eleusis	El-**loo**-sis
Euergetes	You-err-**get**-eez
Laodice	Lay-**oh**-dih-see
Menelaus	Men-eh-**lay**-uss
Seleucus	Sell-**oo**-cuss
Seleucid	Sell-**oo**-sid
Seleucia	Sell-oo-**see**-uh
Deianeira	Day-ann-**eer**-ah
Phalanx	**Fay**-lanks
Cerberus	**Sir**-bur-uss
Ceryneian	**Sir**-rin-ee-an
Cybele	**Sib**-eh-lee
Chiton	**Kye**-tun
Chlamys	**Clam**-iss
Himation	Him-**at**-ee-un
Peplos	**Pep**-low-ss

GODS

GODS OF GREECE (12 OLYMPIANS)	
God	**Attributes**
Zeus	King of the gods, god of the sky. Thunderbolts.
Poseidon	God of sea and elements. Trident.
Hades	God of underworld (Not Olympian - in Hades). Invisible helmet. Owner of Cerberus the three-headed hound of Hades.
Hera	Queen of the gods, goddess of marriage and childbirth. Owner of the Nemean Lion.
Demeter	Goddess of harvest, agriculture.
Hestia	Goddess of the hearth, domesticity (some sources do not include her in the Olympians).
Children of Zeus	Attributes
Apollo	God of sun, prophecy, archery, disease.
Ares	God of war, violence, bloodshed.
Athena	Goddess of wisdom, war. Patron of the city of Athens.
Artemis	Goddess of the hunt, virginity. Owner of the Cerynian Hind.
Aphrodite	Goddess of love, passion.
Hermes	Messenger of the gods, travel.
Dionysus	God of wine, festivity, ecstasy (some sources do not include him in the Olympians).
Hephaestus	God of fire, blacksmith forging, volcanoes.
Others	Attributes
Gaia	Mother Earth. Mother of life.
Persephone	Goddess of spring, consort of Hades in the Underworld.
Cybele	Mother goddess of Anatolia (Asia Minor) Had two lions. Worshipped by Amazonians.

GODS OF EGYPT	
God	**Attributes**
Ra	King of the gods, sun god.
Amun	Creator god. Name means "hidden."
Horus	Patron god of the Pharaohs. Falcon-headed.
Osiris	God of the dead who rules the underworld. Mummified with green skin.
Set	God of chaos and violence. Resides in the desert. Has a strange unknown animal head.
Sobek	Crocodile god of the Nile.
Montu	God of war. Bull-headed.
Ptah	Creator god of mankind and craftsmen. Patron deity of Memphis.
Ogdoad	4 gods and 4 goddesses of primordial chaos and creation.
Goddess	**Attributes**
Isis	Wife of Osiris, god of the dead.
Sekhmet	Lioness goddess, wife of Ptah. Protector of Pharaohs.
Wadjet	Cobra goddess, guardian of Lower Egypt. Sister of Nekhbet.
Nekhbet	Vulture goddess, guardian of Upper Egypt. Sister of Wadjet.
Tawaret	Hippopotamus goddess, protector of women in childbirth.
Neith	Hunter goddess.
Canaanite God	**Attributes**
Baal-Set	Originally Baal, the most high god of Canaan. Hyksos brought him to Egypt, and he became united with Set.
Anat	Goddess of war. Juvenile sister of Baal, violent. Worshipped in both Canaan and Egypt.
Resheph	God of war and plague, worshipped in both Canaan and Egypt.

GODS OF ROME		
Roman God	**Greek God Counterpart**	**Attributes**
Jupiter	Zeus	King of the gods.
Neptune	Poseidon	God of sea and elements.
Pluto	Hades	God of underworld.
Juno	Hera	Queen of the gods.
Ceres	Demeter	Goddess of harvest, agriculture.
Vesta	Hestia	Goddess of the hearth.
Apollo	Apollo	God of sun, prophecy, archery, disease.
Mars	Ares	God of war, violence, bloodshed.
Minerva	Athena	Goddess of wisdom, war. Patron of the city of Athens.
Diana	Artemis	Goddess of the hunt.
Venus	Aphrodite	Goddess of love, passion.
Mercury	Hermes	Messenger of the gods, travel.
Bacchus	Dionysus	God of wine, festivity, ecstasy.
Vulcan	Hephaestus	God of fire, blacksmith forging, volcanoes.
Others		Attributes
Prosperina	Persephone	Goddess of spring, consort of Hades in the Underworld.

"A vile, despicable person shall arise… Forces from him shall appear and profane the temple and fortress and shall take away the regular burnt offering. And they shall set up the abomination that makes desolate."

    Daniel 11:21-31

CHAPTER 1

**Mount Zaphon, Syria
Year 144 of the Kingdom of the Greeks
169 B.C.**

Hera, mother of the gods, queen of the gods, cow-eyed consort of Zeus, protector of marriage and women, stood erect on the top of Mount Zaphon overlooking the wide and wily Mediterranean sea as the sun sank into the horizon, creating a painted sky of colors. An offshore breeze was pleasant enough on this spring day, but she had to open her wool himation to cool down as she ruminated over the dilemma in which the Olympian gods now found themselves.

Oh, how she missed her beloved Mount Olympus, its rocky barren heights that jutted into the sky like a tower into heaven, twice the elevation of this five-thousand-foot Syrian molehill with its desert scrub brush and hot, prickly forests. Its one redeeming trait was its location right on the coast with this view of the eternal sea into the west.

Mount Zaphon was once the habitation of Baal, the Semitic storm god of Syria. It was now the domain of the Olympians because their patron nation, the Seleucid Greeks, had ruled here for the past hundred and fifty years, thanks to the imperial colonizing of that Macedonian goat Alexander the Great.

It made Hera curse with anger every time she thought of the reason why they had to relocate to this stinking backwater anus of the Middle East. With the Roman Republic's victories in the latest Macedonian wars, they had come to occupy Macedonia. And, well, that meant that high prince Sammael and his boot-licking gods of Rome simply had to humiliate the gods of Greece by confiscating their holy mountain and luxurious palace.

If only Alexander hadn't caught the plague and died so young into his campaign to conquer the world, the Olympians might now be ruling over all the kingdoms of the earth. Instead, they were shrinking in power as Rome and her gods were expanding in theirs. Sure, the world was still Hellenistic, deeply shaped by the Greek language and culture Alexander had established everywhere. It was superior civilization. But the Olympians were fast becoming the old gods. They had even aged in their appearance as a result of it. Hera ran her fingers through white hair made sticky by the salty air. At least she was still elegant and lean and had looks to kill despite her wrinkles.

As divine Watchers, the Olympians were immortal. But their worship by humans or the lack of it could affect their power and influence in the world. And power was life force. As the sister-wife of Zeus, king of the gods, Hera had to play a submissive role. But she knew how to get her way. And she had big plans.

And wasn't that what they were all doing anyway? The gods? Playing roles in their elaborately crafted mythologies to drag humans away from the Creator into idolatry. Everything about the gods of the nations was a crafted narrative. Even their chosen identities: Zeus and Hera, Hades and Persephone, Poseidon, Athena.

In truth, they were Sons of God, *Bene Elohim* of the divine council of Yahweh. They were gods of the nations defying the unjust commission of a narcissistic, bloviating dictator in heaven. They had replaced his monomaniacal demands of submission with their own pantheons of democratic governance. Power.

The only problem with their mythology in Hera's mind was the Patriarchy. In order to fulfill the narrative, some of the Sons of God had to masquerade as female deities, shapeshift their visible presentation. Hera had performed this transformation well enough but had long felt oppressed by the entrenched social status and restrictive boundaries for women—both mortal and immortal boundaries since the human social order reflected the divine. Hera felt held back by the very system the Watchers had established. What about *her* dreams and ambitions? Why should *she* not be allowed to rise above her station simply because of her assigned sex?

Something had to give. And it was not going to be Hera any longer.

She noticed a small fleet of a dozen triremes in the harbor city of Seleucia below, their sails furled, their oars withdrawn into the extended wooden hulls of the ships. A small army of soldiers exited the boats. They appeared to be Thracians, Cretans, and even some Gauls. Mercenaries. They also appeared to be preparing for a march to Antioch just over ten miles inland, the capital of the Seleucid kingdom of Antiochus IV Epiphanes. Antiochus was fond of using mercenaries in his military campaigns.

Hera turned and rushed back to the temple.

As she approached the House of Baal, another pang of regret washed over her. This temple was a pathetic excuse for the habitation of deity compared to their lavish Grecian temple on Olympus with its multitude of marble pillars, elegant golden-mean architecture, ornate Greek sculpture and engravings.

In comparison, the House of Baal was a Phoenician-style temple structure, a three-part building with each successive part larger than the previous. A tenth the size of Olympus, it consisted of functional square components made of limestone and capped with some silver and gold. These Syrians and Semites were so uncultured and simple-minded. No aesthetic sense.

On the other hand, Hera was glad the humans had torn down the old house from generations ago with its labyrinthine hallways and stone-age vulgarity. And she could not deny the satisfaction of Zeus and his Olympians forcibly taking the palace from Baal and his pantheon.

Ah, the sweet savor of victory. Of dominion. The Olympians were now the spiritual princes of this territory.

Entering the outer court area, Hera marched past a large stone altar of sacrifice, currently unused. A few woolen-robed bald priests performed menial duties of cleaning and maintenance in the yard.

Mortals did not see or hear the divine realm unless the gods allowed them to. So Hera ignored the human presence around her and entered the first section of the temple, the holy place. She stepped over a large footprint carved into the stone entrance floor, a symbol of Baal's might and presence. He had had his day as the spiritual prince of Canaan and then Israel. But now Zeus was the king of the gods over the Seleucid kingdom that encompassed the Fertile Crescent of the Levant and Mesopotamia along with Persia in the far east.

That temple footprint was now the footprint of Zeus.

Every time she thought of Zeus, Hera was filled with disgust. She considered him incompetent and vulnerable because of his gluttonous surrender to his sensual appetites. In the beginning, he had been discreet. But in these later years, he had become more brazen in his philandering with every god and goddess that would allow him.

He would have done so with humans as well had not the entire pantheon assured Zeus that they would unite together and bind him in the earth if he tried such an abomination. The Great Flood and Sodom and Gomorrah stood as memorial examples of what Yahweh would do if the Watchers again violated the heaven and earth divide by cohabitation with human women. Their ancestors who had done so, the two hundred Watchers led by Semjaza and Azazel, had been imprisoned in Tartarus for their disobedience in going after strange flesh. Not to mention the destruction of the world-that-was.

The only thing that kept the crowned cad in line was the fact that Zeus's power over the pantheon was not absolute. He had divided the cosmos through allotment between himself as ruler of the sky, Poseidon as ruler of sea and elements, and Hades as ruler of the underworld, also called Hades. The rest of the earth was held in common with the other gods.

Unfortunately, Poseidon and some other gods were also indulgent and promiscuous, so it took the goddesses to hold them accountable. The youngest god, Hades, avoided their orgies because he was a monogamous but jealous and controlling husband of Persephone. He despised his brothers for their infidelity, but he had his own vice that made him just as disgusting as the other patriarchal misogynist pigs.

Hera imagined the world of peace, harmony, and abundance that would result if the goddesses held the reins of power. Although the truth about their actual sex made her chuckle. Maybe "woman" was a worthless construct after all since the males were better at being goddesses than any female could be.

Hera approached the final large chamber, the Most Holy Place, the sanctuary of Baal—rather, the sanctuary of Zeus. She heard the sounds of a gathering of gods within. As she recognized those sounds, her anger flared. She pushed open the large ten-foot-tall oak doors and stomped inside.

The massive chamber, one-hundred-foot square, was decorated with purple felt drapes on windowless stone walls. Golden torch stands accented the only source of light, a large open window in the roof directly above.

At the front of the sanctuary stood a fifteen-foot-tall golden statue of Zeus Olympius with thunderbolts in his hands. Beneath that image, a group of gods lay entangled in an orgiastic pile of writhing flesh.

These naked degenerates were at it again. Zeus and Poseidon with Dionysus, Aphrodite, and Hestia. Disgusting filthy reprobates. Stopping their carnal activity, they all looked in her direction.

Zeus spoke with surprise—and guilt. "Hera, my love. I didn't know you were … Uh, would you like to join us? There's always room for one more!"

His companions giggled. Hera felt herself shining like bronze, something that happened whenever divine beings became emotionally agitated.

"No, I would not like to join you," she spit out. "I came to let you know that while you have been busy with your perverse indulgence, King Antiochus has been mustering mercenary forces. No doubt for an invasion of Egypt."

Zeus looked with surprise at his fellow white-bearded brother Poseidon. He said to Hera, "My dear beloved, there is no more perverse indulgence than our endless wars. We might as well have some fun in between them."

More giggles emanated from the naked ones.

Hera wanted to scream at him. She held back her fury. "I just watched troops arrive in the harbor on their way to Antioch. Since you are supposed to be the Prince of Greece, its guardian daemon …" She spoke the final word with sarcastic emphasis. "… I suggest you may want to act like it and find out what exactly is going on and why. That is, if you want to retain your kingdom, O mighty Cloud-Gatherer."

Another sarcastic comment referring to Zeus's epithet as the storm god. It felt a bit satisfying to deride him in front of the others.

Zeus stood up. Though he was aged with white hair and full beard, his body remained muscular and taut. His lapis lazuli eyes flared with lightning. He pulled on a purple chiton tunic and a multi-colored himation that hung off his shoulders with royal pedigree. The Olympians wore the garb of the Golden Age of Archaic Greece, a sign of heritage and tradition.

"Hera, I would like to speak to you alone," said Zeus, suddenly serious. He barked to the others, "All of you, leave us. Now."

The naked gods and goddesses scrambled to pick up their clothes and leave as quickly as possible. Hera watched each of them with jealous eyes. The women for their young, nubile bodies, the men for their masculinity. The white-bearded brothers along with the missing Hades would look like triplets were it not for the effect their realms had on their bodies. Out of water, Poseidon's skin dried and cracked and became scaly. The skin of Hades was pale from spending so much time underground.

When the room had cleared, Zeus remained standing beneath his statue at a distance from Hera.

She seethed as she spoke. "We made a deal. That you could imbibe your disgusting perversions so long as you remain discreet and do not spoil my political ambitions."

Zeus replied, "There's nowhere more private than my Holy of Holies. To be fair, you barged in on me."

Hera ignored his excuse. "You promised me Egypt. That I would get to rule over it. Now it looks like Antiochus may be preparing to attack Egypt again, and you act like it's not even important. Like you don't care. Which affects the attitudes of the rest of the pantheon, and you know it."

Zeus shrugged with deference toward her.

"Gods know I put up with enough of your recklessness. I will not suffer your derogation of duty." Hera remained at her distance from Zeus, shaking with the anger that boiled inside her.

His look turned to one of regret and vulnerability as he waved her lovingly closer. "Come here, my queen. Let us quarrel no longer."

Haltingly, Hera stepped toward him, not wanting to give in to his charm.

When she reached him, Zeus spoke seductively. "My Boopis. My cow-eyed virgin bride."

Hera softened ever so slightly. Homer had described her affectionately for her patronage of cattle.

"My Mother Goddess."

Hera gave Zeus a scolding look.

Once Hera was within his reach, Zeus suddenly punched her in the nose with such lightning speed and force she both felt and heard it crunch. She flew backward to the floor in a daze of shock. Nose gushing with blood, she lay flat on her back, too dizzy to stand. When she looked up, Zeus stood above her, glaring down with gritted teeth. His skin shone brightly with his anger, fiery lightning surrounding him.

As Zeus leaned down, Hera flinched, expecting another punch. Instead, he grabbed her hair in his fist and yanked her close. He whispered with restrained fury, "Do not ever insult me in front of the others again or I will rip out your tongue and make you eat it."

Hera could barely see him through her blurry vision and blood flow. She could only whimper in reply. Immortal beings could not die, but they had heavenly flesh and could suffer at the hands of one another. Zeus let her go and stood back up.

"As for Egypt, I have not forgotten my promise." His face suddenly turned from wrath to scorn. "After all these years of war with the Ptolemies of Egypt, you think I would be unaware of the Seleucid plans? That I would not have plans of my own? Your jealousy and vexation blinds you, Hera. You're better than that."

Turning, Zeus walked out of the chamber. Hera groaned and sat up, her head still spinning. She winced in pain as she readjusted her broken nose with the painful cracking of cartilage. It would heal quickly as divine flesh did. Zeus's cavalier and indulgent behavior hid the fact that he was in fact the most powerful of the deities. He could follow through with his threat of bodily harm.

And he was right about the Syrian wars. The Ptolemies of Egypt in the south had been fighting with the Seleucids of Syria in the north for just over a hundred years for dominance in the region. Five wars in total so far with no end in sight. They were last of the divided Greek kingdom of Alexander the Great along with Macedonia, which was currently on the verge of losing her kingdom to her own wars with the Roman

Republic. If Rome won there, it would establish Rome's hegemony over most of the Mediterranean.

Together, Egypt and Syria had a chance to stand up to Rome, but instead, they were at war with each other. Last year, King Antiochus had foiled an Egyptian invasion of Syria and sent his army to ambush the Egyptian forces at Pelusion, the gateway to Egypt. He'd stopped short of taking the capital city of Alexandria. Instead, he'd left a puppet king, Ptolemy VI Philometor, to share leadership with Ptolemy VII Euregetes, who was nicknamed Physcon, or Pot Belly, for his morbid obesity.

But with the help of their sister, Cleopatra II, the ruling brothers Philometor and Euregetes had overcome their differences, consolidated their power, and turned against Antiochus, asking for military reinforcements from the Achaean League in Greece. That was an act of aggression against the Seleucid king's authority and dignity. So Antiochus had recently sent an embassy to the Roman Republic to press his claim against Egypt.

But if Antiochus invaded Egypt again, Hera knew that might draw the giant nemesis of Rome and with it the spiritual Prince of Rome.

CHAPTER 2

Antioch on the Orontes River

Judas ben Mattathiah looked out upon the city of Antioch from the location of the Royal Guard horse stables on an elevated slope of the imperial isle. The island was the result of the Orontes River splitting and coming back together as it ran south along the foothills of Mount Silpius.

From this position, Judas could see nearest him the Hellenic imperial palace of King Antiochus Epiphanes. Just beyond it was the hippodrome where chariot races and gladiator fights took place. Off the island on the other side of the river, a long colonnaded street cut through the city from the northeastern gate all the way to the cherubim gate in the southwest end of the city where the Jewish community lived near a large amphitheater. Along the ridge of the foothills where new community residences were being built, an impressive stone aqueduct carried life-giving water to the city.

It was a beautiful Hellenistic city, considered the gem of Syria because the king had invested far too much money into its development. At the size of three square miles, it hosted a population of about 200,000 citizens from all around the world: Greeks, Jews, Cretans, Thracians, Romans, and more.

Across the river, Judas could see Epiphania in the foothills, the newest quarter named after the king where Antiochus had built an agora marketplace and a bouleuterion council chamber for city government. He was currently constructing a huge temple to Zeus Olympius patterned after the magnificent Jupiter Capitolinus structure in Rome.

Turning back to the stable, Judas entered the large wooden barracks of stalls, where he led out his pure-bred white Arabian stallion named Pegasus after the winged horse of Greek mythology. Pegasus rode like the wind for Judas and was reliable in battle.

Taking a horse comb, brush, and hoof pick with him, Judas led his steed into a large, roofed open-air pen for cleaning. As he tied the lead rope to a wooden rail, he let his mind wander.

When Judas had joined the Royal Guard three years ago as a Jewish mercenary, he was twenty-five years of age, pro-Hellenist, and desperate to get away from his priestly family in Jerusalem. He did not want to follow in the footsteps of his father's Levitical service in the temple. He had always wanted to be a warrior like Joshua or Caleb.

Judas had been a prime candidate for the special Jewish battalion of the Guard. He was close to six feet in height, a bit taller than most men his age. He was athletic with a lean, muscular build, short-cropped ashen-brown hair, and a tight beard. Because of his competitiveness in a family of five brothers, he was a skilled swordsman.

When he had signed up for the Guard, Judas had started at the bottom, being placed into stables duty for what had turned out to be a providential blessing. Within that time, he had gotten to know horses as well as he did people. He had learned everything about the equine world and had grown to love them. He cleaned them, cleaned up after them, broke them, trained them, and even put them down when necessary. He was a master of wrangling with the whip and could ride as well as any cavalryman.

His horse Pegasus felt like an extension of his own body in battle, a coordinated mass of muscle and terror. That was why Judas took painstaking efforts to ensure his horse had the best of food, care, and cleaning by doing it himself. It was the least he could do for such a magnificent animal.

Judas had always had a natural gift for leadership that seemed to follow him wherever he went. The Royal Guard was no exception. He had risen quickly in the ranks to become a company commander of a hundred men. That company had a reputation for being the finest among their mercenary units. Judas pushed his men hard and never exempted himself. But he also never forgot where he had started. He enjoyed returning to the familiar world of the stables and taking care of his horse. It was a chance to clear his head or find some peace and quiet from the madness of the city.

The sound of voices drew his attention. Four men had entered the pen area near some tethered horses a few stalls down. Judas watched them closely. They were not garbed in either the formal or casual dress of the Guards. They wore hooded cloaks and carried themselves suspiciously. The horses they approached grew skittish.

Something was wrong. Judas hadn't brought a weapon to the pen. He looked at the brushes and dung pick in his hand. Useless. Setting them on a bench, he looked around. Spotting a leather whip hanging on a wooden column, he grabbed it and quietly left his pen.

As he approached the strangers, they noticed him, muttering to each other. The four spread out in a semi-circle facing Judas as he stepped into the open pen. A dozen horses were tied up at the far end, the open corral around him fenced with rails and strewn with straw, dirt, and horse droppings.

Judas spoke with authority. "What are you doing here? The price is high for trespassing on the Royal Guard."

The strangers pushed back their hoods and swung back their cloaks, which had concealed the fact that they all carried swords. They were bearded, their faces etched with years of hard living. Ruffians.

One of them stepped forward, the leader no doubt. His tight, curly dark hair and stern features reminded Judas of one of his own elder brothers. He growled, "And what price are you paid for your treasonous collaboration with the Greek Beast?"

It was a term used by Jews of pagan nations that defied God. Beasts were animals without humanity. A goat was the most common beast used to describe the Jewish nation's Greek occupier.

Not just ruffians then. Jewish fanatics.

Judas clenched his teeth. "Leave now or you will be punished."

The leader looked at the coiled whip in Judas's hand and laughed. "And what will you punish us with? Your own leash? Dog."

They all laughed and drew daggers. Not their swords. As though they assumed they didn't need them.

A scrawny one with a hateful look approached Judas first. He held his knife in front of him, trying to scare his target away.

Judas used his coiled whip as a lasso around the attacker's hand. With a twist, he yanked the man forward to the ground. Judas kicked him in the face, knocking him out.

The others responded with surprise. Then moved in with menace. One man, ugly with pockmarks on his face, slashed at Judas. He backed up, dodging the swipes. The ugly attacker lunged too deeply. Judas sidestepped him, looping the still coiled whip around the attacker's neck to choke him. Before the ugly one could think to slash back with his knife, Judas released the choke, kicked the man in the back, and launched him at the other attacker, whose blade accidentally pierced his comrade.

The two attackers fell to the ground. The wounded ugly man screamed out in pain and rolled around, clutching his belly. The other attacker got up, yelling, "You bastard! I'll kill you!"

This one was younger with dark black hair and angry eyes. He looked like he handled a weapon well. Unfurling his whip, Judas whirled it around his head with expertise and snapped it at the attacker's head. It struck the young man's eye with precision. The attacker dropped his knife and fell to his knees, clutching his now-bloody eye socket.

The leader who looked like Judas's brother was also a well-built, seasoned warrior. Recognizing that Judas was not an easy target, he sheathed his dagger and drew his sword.

Judas kicked the kneeling, half-blinded younger intruder in the back. He hit the floor of the corral on his face in the straw and dung.

Whirling his whip again, Judas sought to take out the eye of the leader. But the warrior's sword raised to protect his face. The whip's leather tip wrapped around the blade. The leader yanked, and that small section of the whip was cut clean off. He directed a proud grin at Judas.

But the moment he took to congratulate himself was all Judas needed since his shortened whip was not too short to circle back and wrap around the leader's throat.

Judas grabbed his whip handle with both hands and pulled with all his might. The leader fell to the floor with such force that he lost his breath and broke his nose—in a pile of horse droppings.

Beating up on a man who looked like his own despised brother, shoving his face into excrement felt cathartic to Judas.

The leader pushed himself to his hands and knees, his sword now out of reach on the ground. Wiping off the feces, he spit a tooth out of his bloody mouth and snarled at Judas.

But he didn't renew his attack. Sliding further away from Judas, he helped his gut-wounded comrade to get up. The one-eyed young ruffian was now waking the unconscious one.

Judas stood defiantly with scourge in hand. "The only reason I didn't kill you all is because I didn't want to have to clean you up and explain everything to my superiors. Next time, you all die."

The ruffian bandits all left the pen, carrying each other, limping, whimpering, and bleeding.

Judas wiped off his dirtied tunic, picked up the fallen daggers and sword, and returned to his pen to care for his horse. He could not shirk his duty just because of some horse thieves.

But it struck him how brazen these men were, willing to commit theft in broad daylight. They didn't seem to be mere brigands. Their accusation against his Hellenism made them sound like the fanatical *hasidim*, or "holy ones," who were violently opposed to any Jewish acceptance of Greek ways.

And while the four were strangers to Judas, they clearly knew who Judas was and that he was a pro-Hellenist Jew. It was a strange coincidence of odd factors. Judas wondered if there was something else going on.

When he reached the horse pen, Judas tossed the blades into the corner by the railing and grabbed the dung pick. He stroked his horse's forehead.

"Okay, Pegasus, enough excitement for one day. So sorry I was delayed." Smiling to himself, Judas lifted the horse's front right leg, bending it to clean dirt and dung beneath the hoof. He heard a voice behind him, "Have you found what you are looking for?"

Judas jerked up with expectation of a new attacker. But it was ninety-year-old Jewish scribe Eleazar watching him. Though his wrinkled skin and snow-white hair and beard spoke clearly of his age, the scribe's etched brown eyes retained a brightness of inner strength, and a lean, healthy frame was hidden beneath his dark woolen robe and tunic. Eleazar had earned his status over the years as one of the most known and respected scribes in both Antioch and Jerusalem. He even had influence in the king's court. And he was a longtime friend of Judas's family.

Judas flicked off some of the dung from the pick. "If it's not me, it's my horse who is stepping in it. But I would not exactly say we are looking for it."

They shared a smile. Wiping his hands on his tunic, Judas set the pick down and approached his elder. They hugged each other with a fond familiarity.

Eleazar stared into Judas's eyes. "Is something amiss?"

Judas gave him an impish look. "I, uh, just got back from a heated quarrel in one of the bays. But I persuaded them to see things my way."

Eleazar glanced around, saw nothing. Picking up the horse comb he'd set on a bench, Judas began finding knots and clumps of debris in Pegasus's mane.

Eleazar sat down on a stool. "My old bones. It's getting harder to make the trip between Antioch and Jerusalem."

Judas smirked. "Three-hundred-mile march. You should do what I do. Just don't go back to Jerusalem at all."

Eleazar raised his brow. "Ah! Become a true Hellenist, eh? Embrace all things Greek and reject my Hebrew identity and traditions?"

"That is not fair, old man." Actually, it was fair. It was what Judas had done. He came from a family of priests but had little interest in it all. Judas had become enamored with Hellenist culture and had eventually lost his interest in the faith and traditions of his forefathers. He had adopted the Greek version of his Jewish name, Judah, and had joined the Royal Guard in Antioch to escape the crowded suffocation of Jerusalem. Indeed, Antioch was the Athens of West Asia.

Judas protested, "We are talking Greek, for God's sake. And the second language of most Jews isn't even Hebrew. It's Aramaic! Jerusalem has a gymnasium teaching Jewish youth Greek ways, theaters entertaining Jews in Greek ways. I hear some priests have become so involved in discus throwing that they're neglecting temple duties. Are you not a bit out of touch with the progressive change of your cherished Jerusalem's Hebrew identity?"

Eleazar chuckled good-naturedly. "Now, *that* is not fair. You know full well there are some of us who still protest those very compromises. We cannot control the world, but we can control *our* place in the world."

Judas kept listening as he picked up the hard brush and continued grooming Pegasus.

After a thoughtful moment, Eleazar said, "In fact, that is why I am here. Your father has sent a message requesting you return to Jerusalem."

That made Judas stop and glare at the scribe.

Eleazar explained, "Remember when your king Antiochus Epiphanes plundered the temple treasury in Jerusalem last year?"

Judas interrupted. "He is your king as well."

Eleazar ignored his assertion. "High Priest Jason did not stand against Antiochus but rather aided him. That is because the king appoints the high priest who pays him the most money. Your father rejects the corruption with a minority of other priests. He and your brothers need your help, your strength, your leadership."

Judas demanded, "Have you forgotten that I'm estranged from my father and brothers because of my Hellenism?"

The old scribe retorted, "Do your politics negate your entire heritage?"

Judas stayed silent again.

"A new serpent has bribed his way into the high priesthood," Eleazar continued. "His name is Menelaus, and I am sad to announce that he is worse than his predecessor. Jason was thoroughly corrupt, but at least he was from the line of Zadok and qualified to hold the post. This Menelaus is not a Zadokite or even a Levite at all. He is from the tribe of Benjamin. His presence as high priest profanes the holiness of both priesthood and temple and could very well start a civil war. Jason has been exiled across the Jordan River."

Eleazar stopped to let the seriousness of his words sink into Judas's conscience. But Judas was profane himself, so it did not have the effect his elder had hoped for. Judas had lost any sense of holiness long ago. He just didn't care.

"Judas, the temple and Torah are the heart and soul of Adonai's covenant with his people. Defiling either is an abomination."

Judas knew about this holiness well enough. Eleazar's use of the word Adonai, which meant "Lord," was a replacement for their God's actual name of Yahweh. During this era, priests had concluded that God's actual name was too holy to pronounce out loud, so they substituted references like Adonai and Ha Shem, which meant, "the Name." To Judas, it was all the province of fanaticism.

Eleazar added, "Menelaus plundered the temple treasury to pay the bribe and his debts to King Antiochus. And when Onias, the exiled true high priest, exposed him, Menelaus had Onias assassinated."

"Was he caught and tried?" asked Judas.

"And acquitted," answered Eleazar. "By the king, whose favor Menelaus had bought. Why do you think Menelaus spends more time here in Antioch than he does in Jerusalem? The people still hate him. He causes riots."

Judas finished with the hard brush and picked up the soft brush for final grooming of his horse. "It's all so much politics. I care nothing for the priesthood. As for the king, he is not perfect, but he is our king. And God says to obey the king."

"He will bring the Abomination of Desolation prophesied by the prophet Daniel," responded Eleazar.

Judas stopped again with surprise. "What is that?"

Eleazar gave him a smirk. "Come to synagogue tomorrow and find out. It's the festival of Purim. You are still welcome."

Judas shook his head with a smile, caught. The old man was always pushing, trying to get Judas to reconsider his waywardness.

Eleazar stood to leave. "Judas, how long will you try to live between worlds? You cannot ride two horses. Your people need you. This 'king' you serve will turn on you someday. As they all have. It is our history. We must purge the evil from our midst or we suffer the judgment of Adonai."

Judas stopped his grooming, anger rising in his tone. "How do 'my people' need me? How do we 'purge this evil'? Through violent rebellion? Insurrection? You proclaim the standard of Torah, the Law. And yet what is rebellion against authority but lawlessness? No king has ever been perfect. But we maintain stability and order by following the rule of law. If you defy the law, then you are left with chaos. And tyranny is the ultimate response to chaos. If the Jews are truly a people of Law, then they will submit to their authorities as the Lord has commanded. And seek to obtain change through *law*, not through *rebellion*."

Judas expected some kind of admission from the scribe. But all he got was what felt like a condescending smile. "So then, I will see you tomorrow at Purim? We can discuss this further."

Judas returned the condescending smile. "So you can keep arguing with me?"

"Some Greeks will be there who are converting to Judaism. You won't have to listen to me, but you might want to listen to them."

CHAPTER 3

King Antiochus IV Epiphanes led his wife Laodice IV around the unfinished structure of his glorious temple to Zeus in the Epiphania quarter of his capital city Antioch. It was almost mid-day. His guards waited for him outside and down the steps as he inspected the progress of construction.

At forty-eight years old, Antiochus felt the weight of a mighty kingdom on his shoulders. His father had been Antiochus the Great, who had reigned forty years and had both re-established and expanded the power of the Seleucid kingdom throughout Syria, Asia Minor, Mesopotamia, and Persia. Unfortunately, "The Great" had not managed to end the long Syrian wars with the Ptolemies of Egypt, which his son had now inherited. And his father's defeat at the hands of the Romans in Apamea twenty years ago marked the humiliation of the Seleucids as well as Rome's encroaching dominance over the world. Though a treaty had allowed the Seleucid kingdom to retain its independence, the heavy cost of reparations had lost them some territories, drained their wealth, and weakened the strength of their military for the past two decades. Antiochus Epiphanes was trying to build back the glory of his family dynasty.

Antiochus and Laodice stood now before the monumental sculpture of Zeus seated on his throne with scepter. A forty-foot-tall wood substructure gilded over with ivory and gold, this massive figure was a replica of the original in Olympia, Greece. This one was crafted before the temple was raised so the king of the gods could oversee the construction of the building.

Antiochus scratched his sable beard that had a slight greying as he looked around the large marble colonnade surrounding the temple's exterior. Both he and Laodice wore their royal walking cloaks of dark-blue wool with gold trim and their leather walking boots. Gazing upon the grandeur around him, Antiochus could not help but think of himself. He had been reigning the past seven years, and he felt completely vexed by the fact that he could not advance his own greatness. He had adopted the epithet *Epiphanes*, which meant "god manifest." He had minted coins with his own likeness as Zeus Olympius, his patron deity. He had invested in temples to Zeus at Dura-Europus on the Euphrates, Gerasa in the Decapolis in Judea, and Scythopolis in Samaria. And this temple…

Antiochus pointed to the cypress wood. "I will lay a gold leaf on all the walls and on the ceiling as well." He pointed up to the open sky where the roof would eventually go. "This temple for Zeus will match the Jupiter Capitolinus in Rome and the one I built in Athens." Jupiter was the Roman equivalent of Zeus.

Laodice looked at him skeptically. She was still beautiful at her age, two years his senior, though she dyed her brown hair blonde to maintain a more youthful Greek look—at least in her own mind.

She was also his sister. Laodice had first married her eldest brother, the crown prince, but he had died. She had then married the next brother, Seleucus IV Philopater, bearing him several children during his reign of twelve years. When he died, she had married her youngest brother, the last heir to the throne, Epiphanes himself, and had given him a son and a daughter. The Seleucids had wanted to keep their imperial power from dilution by political alliances. Laodice had been an ongoing living devotion to that vision of serial incest.

She said, "You still haven't finished the Jupiter Capitolinus in Athens. And the money you have been spending on the beautification of Antioch and its architecture is being whispered as a lack of concern for the masses. Not a good look for a god."

Sometimes Antiochus just wanted to choke her. He smiled impishly. "We gods are a capricious lot." But his stomach churned with pain from their earlier dinner. Digestion problems haunted him.

"I am not laughing," Laodice replied.

In truth, Antiochus could care less for the masses. The plebs, slaves, commoners, even the freedmen were tools for his purpose.

"The *polis* is dead," Laodice continued. "The Greek city-state no longer provides a higher purpose for the people. They seek their meaning in the king."

Antiochus asked, "What do you suggest I do?"

"Seek to understand them," Laodice said. "Their plight. Their everyday struggles. Zeus has done so."

"Indeed, he does. He has copulated with Europa, Leda, Callisto, and countless other human women. If that is what you mean by understanding, I am happy to consider your counsel, my love."

Laodice sighed with disgust. "All I am saying, *my love*, is that the more the people feel you are distant from them, that you do not care for them, the more control you will lose over them. It is a question of reputation more than reality."

Antiochus gestured to the temple around them. "Does this not support the reputation that I care for them?"

"It doesn't help your cause when you plunder the gold of your subjects' temples to build your own."

"You are still bothered about the Jews?" Antiochus didn't consider the Jews to be of any significance. "I was returning from an expensive campaign in Egypt last year, and I needed to replenish the coffers. They had more than they needed."

Laodice was unmoved. "You had already plundered plenty of riches from the Egyptians in your victory. You didn't need to stop off in Jerusalem on the way back and rob their temple treasury."

"Those riches were being appropriated by a corrupt priesthood. They didn't benefit the people."

"Do you want to start a war with the nation that is on the crossroads of both the King's Highway inland *and* the Way of the Philistines along the sea, the two most important trade routes in the region? And the roads to Egypt, I might add."

Antiochus scoffed. "The Jews are uncivilized tribes of clodhoppers. They couldn't fight their way out of a burlap sack." He remembered something and jumped to add, "Oh, and it was their own leaders, first Jason, then Menelaus, who pilfered *their own temple* to bribe me for their appointments to the high priesthood."

Laodice's scowl did not loosen. He added, "Why do you defend the Jews? What care you for them?"

"It is not them who I care about," she corrected. "It is your kingdom. I just think you are not considering the consequences of your actions. And those 'uncivilized tribes of clodhoppers' have a history of being underestimated."

"The ones I had better not underestimate are the Ptolemies of Egypt and their latest actions," Antiochus retorted. "Speaking of which, I need to go to the Pythian oracle and get some advice. Are you coming?"

Daphne

Their ride on horseback to the Temple of Apollo in the suburban paradise of Daphne four miles south of Antioch was quick enough. Seleucus I had created Daphne amongst its many natural springs for the purpose of recreation and luxury. A large limestone aqueduct carried the spring waters to Antioch.

This suburb of the capital city was named after Daphne the nymph and dedicated to Apollo, the god who fell in love with her. Its groomed parks, luscious gardens, glorious temples, theater, and stadium were used regularly for celebrations, religious festivals, and other bacchanalia.

Antiochus, Laodice, and the guards galloped their horses down a cypress-tree-lined driveway to the grand temple on a hillside. Spring water flowed on each side of the building.

They dismounted their horses before a forty-foot marble statue of Apollo wearing a sleeveless short tunic and playing a lyre while singing. The god's hair and laurel were gilded in gold, and his eyes were large violet gemstones shining in the rays of the midday sun.

Antiochus and Laodice walked up the flight of stone steps, leaving the guards behind.

The marbled frieze above the entrance had engraved in it the threefold Delphic maxims: *Know Thyself, Nothing in Excess,* and *Surety Brings Ruin.* All sayings the king sought to emulate in his own life. Except that sometimes excess was unavoidable.

Entering the mammoth structure took one's breath away, even the breath of a king. Antiochus squeezed Laodice's hand, and the two of them walked humbly through the threshold.

The sacred building had been patterned after the famous Temple of Apollo in Delphi, the navel of the world for Greece. The temple was the home of the Oracle of Delphi, a high priestess who was also called the Pythia for her intimacy with the python spirit conquered by Apollo. She was the most powerful woman in the Hellenistic world for her prophecies uttered under divine possession by Apollo. Nobles, princes, and kings would consult her for their decisions affecting their cities and nations. Antiochus had to settle for a local Pythia, but this one had received previously helpful visions for the king, so he trusted her.

The royal couple were greeted by three priestesses dressed in crimson body-length tunics belted by a humble rope tassel. Their long hair was braided and crowned with laurel leaves and flowers. They were young and beautiful. Antiochus wanted to take one of them by force. But his wife was with him, so he maintained self-control. Laodice gave one of them a small leather pouch with payment.

King and queen were led through the portico entrance, a long colonnade of dozens of Corinthian marble columns fifty feet tall like a forest of marble trees. At the end of the long hall, two large ten-foot oak doors opened to the adyton where the oracle would receive her visions. This was off-limits to normal citizens, but it had been approved for the king's presence.

The queen, however, had to stay behind. She sat down on a stone bench to the side, a distinct frown of disappointment on her face.

Antiochus entered alone into the incense-filled chamber. The doors shut behind him with an echo. He descended a dozen steps into a pit-like arena.

Several torches around the circular colonnaded room barely gave enough light to see through the darkness. The smokey vapor from six censors obscured what could be seen. Antiochus felt light-headed with the sweet, savory smell in his nostrils and lungs.

The Pythia slowly appeared from behind the pillars. She was about forty years old and wore a virginal white gown of flowing thin linen that barely covered her body beneath. It was only symbolic of chastity as Antiochus had taken the priestess several times in his quest for union with divinity. A purple veil covered her head and face with similar transparency.

The Pythia led a small goat on a leash behind her. Handing Antiochus the leash and sacrificial dagger, she ascended to her seat atop a bronze tripod in the center of the room. Another crimson-clad priestess came out of the shadows and handed the Pythia a bronze chalice. The oracle drank heavily, and the priestess took the chalice away. This was a liquid of sorcery, *pharmakeia*, blended herbs and plants with wine to help induce an ecstatic state from which the Pythia would see her visions. The original Oracle of Delphi had her chair over a large natural crack in the floor from whence came strange vapors from the underworld. The temple there had been built around the natural fissure, something that could not be duplicated here.

Antiochus pulled the goat over to a large bronze sacrificial bowl before the tripod. He picked up the animal and placed it inside the bowl. It bleated softly, unaware of its destiny.

Placing the dagger to its throat, Antiochus pulled through the flesh. The goat tried to cry out, but only bloody gurgling came out. It collapsed into the pool of its own blood filling up the bowl.

Antiochus wiped his hands off with a towel laid next to the bowl. He turned to the Pythia, who was already caught up in a trance, her body waving serpent-like in ecstasy.

"What do you seek, oh king?" she asked in a low, raspy voice.

Antiochus took a step closer. "The Ptolemy brothers and sister I put into power to do my will in Egypt have conspired against me and united in their rebellion. I want to invade Egypt again, this time to complete the victory with occupation of its capital Alexandria. But I am worried Rome may step in to protect her own interests. I want to know if I should go and if so, when."

Suddenly, Antiochus felt something at his feet. Like something was wrapping around his legs. He looked down. He saw nothing there, yet he had the distinct sensation of something encircling his body, binding him like a rope. No, like a python. He could not move. His heart beat fast with fear.

In the unseen realm, Apollo, the sun god of oracles and prophecy, of both healing and disease, and of too many other responsibilities, wiped from his mouth the goat's blood he had drunk at the sacrificial bowl. He was glad he wore no clothes the blood might drip upon and stain. His nakedness was his glory. He held his hand out for pause. The large, black serpentine spirit that coiled around the body of Antiochus stopped in obedience.

Apollo walked past the king and up to the Pythian oracle to whisper in her ears. As he did so, she would speak his words like a puppet in a scratchy facsimile of his own voice. This ventriloquism was called gastromancy, or "speaking from the belly."

Apollo/Pythia said, "Behold, I see a ram with two horns. This is the Medes and the Persians. This ram became great with power such that no one could stand before him. And behold, from out of the west came a goat with a single great horn between his eyes. This is the Macedonian Greeks. The goat ran and struck the ram and broke his two horns and trampled him. And the goat became exceedingly great because of this horn. This is Alexander the Great."

Apollo was cheating. He was quoting from the Hebrew prophet Daniel, who had been given this vision by Yahweh hundreds of years earlier. Apollo couldn't tell the future any more than any other created being could. And the gods were not allowed to read the sacred written Scriptures, so they had to piece these things together from what was quoted and spoken of by the humans. Some of it they still could not understand.

But it made for sensational impressions.

Apollo/Pythia continued, "At the height of his strength, the great horn was broken, and in its place came up four new horns that grew to the four winds of heaven."

Apollo noticed that Antiochus had become impatient. The king said, "Yes, of course, the four horns represent the four Diadochi rulers who took over at Alexander's death. I didn't ask for a history lesson. I want to know if I should invade Egypt and when."

Apollo/Pythia ignored him. "Out of one of them grew a little horn which grew exceedingly great to the south and to the east, even to the host of heaven, even as great as the Prince of the host. And the little horn threw some of the stars to the ground and trampled on them."

This time, Antiochus was silent. His impatience turned to confusion. "I don't understand that."

Apollo/Pythia now responded with impatience. "*You* are the little horn."

The king's eyes went wide with revelation.

Apollo/Pythia continued, "The goddess Persephone escapes from Hades in the spring. The god Dionysus celebrates a successful harvest, and Hades is too concerned with his own underworld kingdom to leave it."

Apollo pulled away from the Pythia, and she slumped into virtual unconsciousness.

Antiochus suddenly felt the restricting coils around him fall away, and he could breathe easily again. He wanted to ask for clarification but he saw the Pythia's vision was at an end.

What did she mean I would grow as great as the host of heaven? The host of heaven are the stars, and the stars are the gods. Will I become a god? And who is the Prince of the host? Zeus? Does she mean I will become as great as Zeus? And what gods would I trample upon?

At least the symbolic reference to Persephone and Hades in the spring seemed clear. Antiochus shivered with delight at the thought of it. This was good news. Very good news. Better than he had anticipated. To achieve victory over the Ptolemies was one thing, but to have one's divinity affirmed by the gods themselves was another thing altogether.

Pain suddenly struck again at his belly as Antiochus strode toward the entrance. Being a god didn't seem to help his digestion problems. He would cut back on his rich diet.

Laodice stood to meet him on his way out, but he was caught up in his thoughts. She had to jog to keep up with him.

"Well, my king, what did she say?"

"Rome is too invested in her war with Macedonia to be concerned about our conflict with Egypt. Spring is almost upon us. It is time to attack."

CHAPTER 4

Nemea, Greece

The Hunter tracked silently in bare feet up the incline of the rocky desert mountain outside the city of Nemea on the northeastern side of the Peloponnese peninsula near Corinth. He did not care for noisy sandals when hunting prey. The small trees and scrub brush would not hide his crouching six-foot height nor his massive musculature. He preferred wearing a simple crimson woolen battle skirt with his large leather belt. For hunting and battle, the simpler was the better for him. He also liked the bravado of going bare-chested, both to exhibit his physical prowess and to intimidate his enemies. He was quite proud of his own physique with its hairless muscular sheen.

But he was not confronting a human today. He was hunting a lion. A very particular lion that had terrorized the city for a long time, picking off citizens as quarry. A man-eater. Rumor said that the goddess Hera had sent it in her wrath.

Today the Nemean lion would be the quarry. Today, it would meet its match. The Hunter carried with him his dagger, a bow with arrows, and a club he had cut out of olive wood with his sword. But he had not brought his sword with him. That would be too easy. He wanted a challenge.

The Hunter stopped when he saw a track in the dirt. He knelt and looked closer. Paw prints the size of his own very large feet. Not far ahead was feline scat on the ground, still somewhat fresh.

He looked up on the rising hill ahead. Checked the burning sun above him. Plenty of time to finish this. Fire gleamed in his eyes. A smirk of confidence graced his lips.

He moved onward, fleet-footed and sure. Halfway up the mountain, he stopped again. Quickly crouched to his knees.

There it was. A cave nesting in the side of a rocky outlook. The lion's den. The villagers had told him about it. They had also told him about the second opening on the other side of the small bluff.

The Hunter checked the breeze. It came from the east as he faced north. Good. Keeping low, he circled the cave downwind to climb the ridge and find the other entrance.

He climbed the steep rocky ridge with ease like a mountain goat. The other cave opening was just below him. Hiding behind a large boulder, he watched and listened for any movement. His senses were as superior to other men as was his physical strength. He sensed nothing. The lion was most likely asleep inside. Excellent.

The Hunter looked at the boulder he hid behind. It was perfect. The size of a large tent. Maybe the weight of a ton or so.

He quietly set his club and bow with quiver down on the ground. He sized up the boulder one last time, found a couple places for his hands to grip. Setting his feet securely on the ground, he heaved with all his might. The rock moved, and he knew that the lion no doubt heard the noise. The Hunter would not have much time before his prey would become the predator.

He heaved again, straining. His face grew hot with pressure. The rock began to move. Everything in him wanted to groan under the strain. But he made no noise. He felt like his eyes were bulging out of his head.

The boulder came lose and tumbled down over the cave entrance. It brought other boulders lodged with it in a small avalanche of rock and dust.

Grabbing his weapons, the Hunter moved swiftly downhill to one side of the cave entrance. This was now blocked enough that the large lion could not get through. He returned the way he had come to the front of the first cave opening.

Again, he circled widely enough to remain out of sight, a good hundred feet out. He moved like a lion himself, swiftly, silently, ready to pounce.

The Hunter stopped when he saw the dust cloud billowing out of the entrance with the force of the air.

He heard the animal first. The sound of coughing from the midst of the dust cloud. Then as the cloud settled, he finally saw the outline of the majestic animal standing still, proud, fearless. He was larger than the Hunter and had perfect lean muscles.

With a jerking and twisting motion, the lion shook the dust off his shiny golden coat of fur. His mane sprouted from his head and neck like a royal vestment. The lion panted now for air, and the Hunter could see his fearsome teeth.

Did it suspect an enemy? The Hunter had to assume so. Fortunately, he was still downwind.

He speedily lifted his bow, a powerful compound reverse bow made of layered ibex horn, sinew, and glue. Its curve away from the archer aided in its velocity when drawn back. And the Hunter had a most powerful draw.

He sighted the lion's heart just behind the animal's left shoulder at the edge of the mane.

He released. In the blink of an eye, he reached into his quiver, drew another arrow, nocked it, and released again. All within a mere second. His speed was extraordinary.

And he never missed.

One right after the other hit their target on the lion's vulnerable spot.

Two perfect strikes.

The force of the missiles pushed the beast to the ground.

But the Hunter had already seen that the arrows had not penetrated the skin of the creature. They had shattered upon impact.

The villagers had told him the creature was invincible, its skin impenetrable. He had thought this was the exaggeration of simple-minded legends. No creature he had ever faced could withstand the mighty piercing force of his drawn arrows.

But this one did.

The great lion stood, his skin unpenetrated, his piercing grey eyes searching the brush for his enemy, his razor-sharp teeth gnashing angrily.

Then he spotted the Hunter.

A moment that stood in time between them both, locked in a stare of shared thought. Who was the predator and who the prey?

But instead of attacking, the mighty beast turned and bolted into the cave.

Why?

Was he fleeing an enemy whose strength he could feel matched his own?

Or was he drawing the Hunter into a trap?

The Hunter cared not. He dropped his bow and quiver, picked up his club, and ran up to the cave.

He stopped at the entrance. The light from outside gradually went dimmer the deeper he looked inside.

But as he walked cautiously in, his eyes adjusted with the sharpness of a preternatural predator. The Hunter was more than human.

He gripped his club tightly and kept going.

He heard a snarl around the corner, and one foot stepped on a human skull. It crunched beneath his bare calloused sole. Not impenetrable like his foe, but tough enough.

Stepping around the corner, the Hunter immediately crouched and rolled at the blurring flash of a pouncing shadow.

He heard the lion hit the dirt and the wall of the cave behind him as he rolled into a pile of bones. The inner lair.

Getting up, he readied his club. All around him were the chewed, broken, disarticulated bones of hundreds of human and animal prey.

Mostly human.

If the Hunter could not penetrate this monster's hide with arrow or dagger, he would have to knock it out before he could kill it. Was its skull as unbreakable as its skin?

If so, he was done for.

The lion swiped its huge paw at him. The Hunter felt the skin of his chest rip open. A warm stream of blood flowed down his stomach onto his battle skirt. His fingers probed the wound. Two large gashes. He would not have much time before his blood loss imperiled him.

He had to move quickly.

The lion swiped again, but the Hunter dodged and twirled around with his club, smashing its skull. He heard the crunch of bone. Good. Its skull *was* breakable.

The lion staggered, stunned by the impact. The Hunter moved without thinking.

Dropping the club, he ran and jumped onto the back of the creature as a wrestler might grab his opponent.

He reached around its neck and clasped his hands in a chokehold. The lion's neck was so thick he could just barely do so.

The beast was confused. He circled around, trying to shake off his attacker.

The Hunter's grip slipped and his left hand reached for steadying. He felt the sharp teeth and hot breath of the lion's mouth. It bit down. The Hunter screamed in pain as his little finger was bit off.

But his hands found each other again, and he held on with all his might.

The lion choked, gasped for air, but it could find none.

Finally, it collapsed to the dirt, its windpipe crushed by the stranglehold of its adversary.

The Hunter released his grip, took a moment to catch his own breath, and got up from the beast's back.

He looked at his left hand. The missing finger was still bleeding. Thank the gods he had six fingers on each hand and six toes on each foot, an extra one per limb compared to normal humans.

The Hunter set about gathering bits of cloth from the pile of bones to dress his wounds.

Then he took out his dagger to skin the beast for a trophy. After he prepped the pelt, he would take its flesh and offer sacrifice to Zeus at the temple in the city of Nemea.

But the dagger would not penetrate the hide.

He paused, considering his dilemma.

His arrows had not penetrated the skin even though they and his bow had been given him by the god Apollo. And he did not have his sword with him, a gift from the god Hermes.

With the energy of battle fading, the gash on his chest now throbbed, the pain increasing. The Hunter looked down at the lion's paws. Grabbing the nearest, he chose the largest claw. He twisted and turned it until he ripped it out of its socket.

Perhaps the creature's own body could be used against itself.

The Hunter put the claw to the lion's belly. As he had hoped, the beast's own talon sliced readily through the skin with a sharp efficiency. Blood spilled out on the floor.

The Hunter smiled proudly to himself. Not only was he a mighty warrior but he had the mind of a god.

Clenching his entire body of muscles, he looked down upon himself with satisfaction. Powerful, handsome, and the *Moirai*, the Fates, smiled upon him.

He was Heracles, son of Zeus.

CHAPTER 5

Antioch

Judas sat in the synagogue at the southern end of the city listening to the old scribe Eleazar at the podium near the center of the open sanctuary. He was only there because he had promised the old man he would show up. He had become lax in his attendance. The ritual and liturgy, the religious language, all of it had lost meaning for him.

The congregation of some one hundred Jews sat in stone tiered seats surrounding the entire rectangular structure like a Greek theater in the round. Smooth, non-fluted doric columns also surrounded the open area, holding up the two-storied building, which included a second floor for visitors and the unclean.

Eleazar wore the customary prayer shawl on his shoulders over a plain brown tunic as he stood at the podium. He would be reading from the scroll drawn from the Torah shrine behind him, a large, ornate wooden structure with engraved doors and gilded edges. Nothing but the most expensive furniture and ornamentation to house God's Word.

Eleazar's voice was strong despite his age. He pointed to the upper gallery where a few dozen people sat. "We welcome our visitors today. Some of them are in the process of becoming converts to our religion. We welcome Lycurgus of Athens and his lovely family, who will join him in the covenant. Please, stand, Lycurgus, and your family."

As Eleazar gestured with an upward wave, Judas saw a Greek man of about forty rise to his feet along with his wife, children, and slaves. They wore distinctive Athenian clothes: full-length white peplos tunics with gold pins and belts and colored sashes. No doubt they had recently travelled here from the Attica region of Greece. Two slaves in plain linen stood behind the parents and four offspring of various ages down to about age twelve.

But it was the eldest, a young woman, who caught Judas's eye. She was a Helen of Troy. She appeared to be maybe twenty years old with glowing golden hair tied in an exquisite golden headband. Everything was golden about her. Her eyes were warm hazel and her nose like that of a sculpted goddess, her lips rose-tinted. Her sure stance glowed with elegance.

Judas could not stop staring. Even after the family sat back down and Eleazar began reading, Judas found himself drawn to look up at her in intervals. A few times, he even caught her staring back.

Eleazar read the story of Esther, the beautiful young Jewish maiden who had been chosen queen of the king of Persia when the Jewish people were under his thumb. Haman the Agagite had plotted to manipulate the king's authority in a secret plan to eradicate the Jewish nation in their midst. To kill them all.

But Esther upon threat of death had come before the king, revealed the heinous plan, and pleaded with the king for mercy. The king's new edict had allowed the Jews to fight back, and fight back they did. The seed of Eve just barely survived annihilation by the seed of the Serpent. It appeared to Judas that Adonai had almost lost.

He knew the story from his youth, but he wasn't listening closely right now because his attention had been so deeply arrested by the golden goddess above.

Eleazar read from the scroll, "'Then King Ahasuerus said to Queen Esther and to the Jew Mordecai, "See, I have given Esther the house of Haman, and they have hanged him on the gallows, because he plotted to lay hands on the Jews." Then he sent letters by mounted couriers saying that the king allowed the Jews who were in every city to gather and defend their lives, to destroy, to kill, and to annihilate any armed force of any people or province that might attack them, children and women included.

"'Now the rest of the Jews who were in the king's provinces also gathered to defend their lives and got relief from their enemies and killed 75,000 of those who hated them. This was on the thirteenth day of the month of Adar, and on the fourteenth day they rested and made that a day of feasting and gladness.'

"This is the feast we celebrate today. This is Mordecai's Day. And this is the Word of Adonai in the scroll of Esther."

Rolling up the scroll, Eleazar wrapped it in its purple felt mantle and handed it to another priest, who returned it to the carved wooden Torah shrine. Judas stole another look at the golden woman on the second floor. She returned his stare. His face went flush with heat.

He simply could not believe how beautiful she was. He imagined her as Queen Esther in Persian royal robe and crown.

Eleazar announced, "And so, today we celebrate this festival of Purim. But I want you to consider the truth revealed in the scroll. Let it be known that the name of Adonai, his true name, the tetragrammaton of four letters, so holy that we speak it not, that name is never mentioned in the entire scroll. Not once. It is the only scripture where this is the case.

"Now, you may ask yourself, why? Why would Ha Shem, the Name, go unmentioned in an entire story of his people? It is as if he was silent. Hidden. Nowhere to be found. Where was he when his enemies were plotting to exterminate his people? How they must have felt at such a dire moment of calamity. And yet, Ha Shem accomplished his purposes behind the scenes, did he not? Did he not orchestrate every detail of every moment of that story to chastise his children, to punish his enemies, to bring both redemption and justice?

"Is this not a word for us this very day in which we live? Is this not a word for such a time as this? The prophet Ezekiel saw the shekinah, the very presence of Adonai, leave the temple during our Babylonian exile. His Spirit has not returned. He remains absent."

Judas noticed the group of a dozen or so priests sitting to the right of the podium become agitated and begin whispering amongst themselves. Strange. Judas did not think the scribe's statements to be controversial. Judas had not sensed God's presence in his life for a long time now. Those old priests and their hunger for power would never admit their own lack of legitimacy. Especially not in Jerusalem. Nevertheless, Eleazar had earned the right to be heard because of his elderly status as scribe.

The old man kept going. "We have been without a true prophet for hundreds of years. God is silent. He is not speaking to us. Why? Where is he? We suffer beneath the trampling feet of the Gentile kingdom of the Seleucid Greeks as we did beneath the Medes and the Persians and as we did beneath the Babylonians before them."

Now the priests were muttering and voicing disagreement aloud. Judas could hear, "Blasphemy!" and "Shame!"

Eleazar turned to the priests. "My brothers, I do not blaspheme. I believe that even when it seems Adonai is nowhere to be found and nowhere to be heard, even when we think he has abandoned us, he has not! He is still sovereign and secretly working his will and purpose in and through every event of history. As in the days of Elijah, sometimes Adonai is in the silence."

The priests quieted down.

"But Adonai has not left us without his Word. The prophet Daniel predicted what we are living through right now. His prophecies of the kings of the North and the South have been fulfilled in these Syrian wars between the Seleucids of Syria in the north and the Ptolemies of Egypt in the south.

"He foretold of Cyrus the Great, Alexander the Great, Antiochus the Great, all of them willful kings who acted as though they were gods.

But he also foretold of our king Antiochus IV Epiphanes. He is called a 'vile, despicable one' for whom kingship was not inherited but taken."

That much was true, Judas knew. Epiphanes was the youngest son of King Antiochus the Great. After the king died years ago, the eldest brother Seleucus IV had ruled for twelve years. But when Seleucus in turn died, his heir was not of age and therefore shared a co-regency with Antiochus Epiphanes. When the child regent, named Antiochus the Young, was mysteriously assassinated, Antiochus Epiphanes stepped in and took over.

Eleazar unrolled another scroll that was on the podium. "Hear now the words of Daniel the prophet, this is the Word of Adonai." He read, "A time is coming in which forces from the king of the north shall profane the holy temple in Jerusalem and he shall take away the regular burnt offering. And he shall set up the Abomination of Desolation. And he shall seduce with flattery those who violate the holy covenant, but the people who know their god shall stand firm and take action."

The audience once again rumbled with controversy. Rolling up the scroll, Eleazar announced, "I tell you the truth that the Hellenist Jews are those who violate the covenant of Moses, but the hasidim, the holy ones, shall stand firm and take action!"

To Judas it sounded as if the entire synagogue exploded in response, both positive and negative. Different factions resided within their own congregation. Many were Hellenists like Judas. They did not consider themselves in violation of their Jewish covenant but rather more sophisticated in adapting to change. They maintained their Jewish past but compromised in some ways to be Greek citizens of the future. The cosmos was growing much larger, but Israel seemed as if she was growing smaller and more ignorant.

The hasidim, however, were fanatics of "holiness" who jeopardized the good standing of the Jews through their desire for isolation and tendency toward violence. Their obsession with separation resulted in division and unrest. Separation of seeds, clothes, and foods, separation of men and women, Jew and Gentile. It seemed that everything was unclean to them.

It made Judas wonder if this beautiful golden Helen of Antioch and her parents knew what they were getting into. Seeing this squabbling would surely make them reconsider their conversion. Jews were as contentious with each other as they were with the world around them. He would have to ask the newcomers if he got the chance.

Judas did not feel insulted by Eleazar's accusation toward Hellenists like himself. He did not feel much of anything at all. He was used to the old man's extreme views and exaggerated rhetoric. He tolerated it because he still loved Eleazar as a lifelong friend of the family. The scribe had been there for the whole of Judas's life. He had educated Judas and his four brothers in the Torah when they were young. They had "adopted" him into the family like an uncle. Eleazar had also helped the family when they were in financial straits during a famine. The elderly scribe had saved their lives.

But if Judas could accept Eleazar, these other fools he could not suffer. Getting up, he left the escalating verbal storm of petty quarreling. As he stole one more glance at the visionary goddess above, he saw that she was watching him leave.

Oh, yes, he was going to the Purim feast tonight. Nothing would keep him from being there.

CHAPTER 6

Leaving the guards barracks in the north of the city, Judas walked south along the King's Way, the main thoroughfare of Antioch that ran the full two miles of the city north to south. Stores and markets lined both sides, but most were closed at this time of night. Judas knew that Antiochus had big plans for the thoroughfare. The king had just begun to line it with massive marble colonnades with the intent of providing a marble street and roof as well for the entire length of the road. It was to be another one of the architectural feats that would bring deserved glory to the capital. It was also one of many projects that remained unfinished due to the king's extravagant expenditures putting pressure on the royal treasury.

Near the southern end of the King's Way, Judas passed through the slums of the city. The poor and impoverished set up tents and other shacks for survival. Some begged on the street in rags. Prostitutes dressed in transparent linen peplos undergarments and draped with cheap jewelry sought his attention as he passed their brothels. The stench of garbage and feces turned Judas's nose and almost made him gag.

The Jewish quarter was at the end of the street adjacent to the slums. A large group of officials were leaving the area and heading his way. Judas could see the high priest at the front of the group flanked by a dozen other priests and as many palace guards. That this was High Priest Menelaus was evident from his special bright-blue tunic with gold-checkered apron and bulbous turban. In contrast, the other priests were garbed in light checkered tunics and striped prayer shawls.

As the group passed Judas, he could see the high priest, an older balding man with tight gray beard, thin lips, and angry eyes, arguing heatedly with his companions. As a commander in the Royal Guard, Judas had seen Menelaus in the king's presence on numerous occasions but at a distance. Eleazar was right. This political reptile spent too much time in Antioch currying the favor of the king. Tonight was the feast of Purim, and the high priest should have been in Jerusalem.

Instead, he was here. Menelaus had no doubt opened the festival with some kind of dedication. But the fact that they were leaving in such a display of hostility told Judas everything. The priest had not been welcomed by enough people to warrant staying at the festival. As Eleazar had told him, the Tobiad faction supported the appointment of Menelaus to office, but the Oniad faction considered him a Hellenistic puppet abomination. And they were very vocal about their displeasure. A group of Jewish men yelling curses after the exiting entourage confirmed his guess.

Judas hoped he wasn't going to step into another pile of spiritual dung.

He entered the Jewish quarter. The population was about five thousand. Though they had been here from the foundation of the city a hundred and thirty years earlier, the Jews of Antioch continued to remain sequestered in the least desirable location of the city.

They had also managed to turn it into a veritable garden paradise of economic growth and community safety despite all odds against it. Suddenly, the buildings Judas passed were clean of graffiti and the streets cleared of garbage. Jewish guards were allowed to patrol their own communities. The king had granted a certain amount of autonomy that allowed the Jews to flourish in their isolation from the rest of the city. The hasidim Jews considered this an argument for continued separation from the Gentile world. The Hellenistic Jews considered it an argument for being a leavening influence in that world.

In any case, the guardians had apparently done their job and had kept an incident from happening around the high priest. There was no civil unrest on display. People had returned to their celebration.

Tonight was the feast of Purim, so families were at home and in the agora square feasting and socializing with each other. The sound of laughter and argumentation filled the air. The tantalizing smells of roasting lamb and mutton slathered in herbs distracted Judas from the distaste he had for the religious separation that enslaved so many of his countrymen.

He arrived at the synagogue he had visited during the day. People spilled out into the street and open square, caught up in their group conversations with the energy and unguardedness that accompanied liberal consumption of wine and beer. Oniads and Tobiads argued about Menelaus and the politics of the high priesthood.

Judas pushed past a group in vigorous debate about how many steps one was allowed to walk on Sabbath before being considered in violation of Torah.

What a waste of precious time. Bickering over minutia as the world burns. As Judas entered the synagogue hall, guests reclining around low tables were being served breads, meats, and vegetables. They had already commenced the meal.

"Judas, there you are!" came a voice from the near corner. It was Eleazar. He lay at a *triclinia* U-shaped dinner table with the family of converts. "Join us!"

Judas obeyed.

"Recline next to me." The scribe pointed to an open spot of pillows next to Eleazar—and near the blonde Greek goddess Judas had not been able to get out of his head since the synagogue meeting earlier in the day.

He had to remember to breathe. And not stare.

Her smile at him sent a shiver down his spine. He felt foolish. Like some kind of infatuated youngster.

Normally, women and children ate separately from the men, but at some festivals and celebrations such as those welcoming new congregants, they joined together. Tonight was both.

A slave provided a plate of fresh bread with leeks and garlic oil. One followed quickly with a bronze cup of wine. Judas took a first gulp. The fermentation soothed his parched throat.

Eleazar shouted to be heard above the festive noise of a hundred guests enjoying their celebration. "I hope you were spared the distinct pleasure of encountering the high priest before he left."

Judas replied through smiling lips, "I treated him like all politicians. I crossed to the other side of the street."

Eleazar slapped his back with a hearty laugh and pointed to his left. "This is Lycurgus of Athens, the new convert I introduced in synagogue. His wife Cassandra beside him."

Judas toasted them both with his cup.

Eleazar turned to Lycurgus with an impish smirk. "And this is Judas ben Mattathiah. Do not let your eyes deceive you. He may look like a Jew, but he is a Hellenist through and through."

"Well then," said Lycurgus, "since *we* may look like Hellenists but seek to be Jews through and through, we might have an interesting discussion."

Judas gave the family a deferential smile in return.

Eleazar continued, "Judas, you recline next to Sophia, eldest daughter of Lycurgus."

Sophia. Her name was Sophia. An elegant name. A beautiful name.

Eleazar continued with a wide gesture. "Also his two sons Euthymius and Theodotus and younger daughter Angela."

Judas glanced at the other children, two nondescript teenaged boys with sandy hair who looked like their mother and a girl with her older sister's golden hair who looked to be just entering puberty.

Judas looked at Lycurgus and Cassandra, but he thought only of Sophia. He said with a teasing voice, "Welcome, Lycurgus, and your family. But are you sure you know what you are getting into? I can imagine a certain cut required of all male converts would be less than desirable at your age."

Lycurgus, a thin man with a balding head of chestnut hair and thick eyebrows, spoke with an affable confidence. "As a matter of fact, we were all acquainted with our covenant duty a week ago." He smiled at his sons. "Were we not, boys?"

They groaned with annoyed memory, eyes squinting and teeth clenched.

"The only thing we lack is a pilgrimage to Jerusalem. But, yes, I would say I do know a bit of what we are getting into. As well as what we are getting out of. The 'wisdom of Greece' can be a seductive temptress, but I have concluded that the fear of the Lord is indeed the beginning of wisdom, as the Hebrew scriptures state."

Indeed, thought Judas, *we might have an interesting discussion.*

A lilting voice beside him drew his attention. "My father is too humble, dear sir."

Judas turned to look at Sophia. She was even more stunning up close, and he tried hard not to stare with desire.

She went on, "You see, Father was the gymnasiarch, the head administrator, of Plato's Academy in Athens. Which I am sure you know with your Hellenist sympathies is the most prestigious school of philosophy in what used to be the most glorious city of Greece."

Judas raised his eyebrows in mock surprise. "Would Aristotle disagree with you?"

They shared a smile. Aristotle's Lyceum was the fiercest competitor of Plato's Academy.

Lycurgus interrupted them. "My daughter is too forward, dear Judas. I am afraid I have fed her curiosity and intellect more than her manners."

"Not at all," Judas said to Lycurgus. He turned back to Sophia. "I find her forwardness refreshing."

Cassandra squeaked in retort, "Then you are a most unusual man."

"Mother!" Sophia scolded. The two women exchanged looks that could only be considered a silent battle of wills.

A slave offered Judas some meat. Roasted lamb and mutton. He used his knife to place some onto his plate. He would miss not having pork at this meal. It was considered unclean for Jews, but as a Hellenist he had tasted the forbidden meat and fallen in love with it.

Judas changed the subject. "Lycurgus, do you ever feel …" He paused, looking for the right diplomatic word, "… *restrained* coming from your background of open intellectual inquiry and education only to enter the confines of an exclusive and dogmatic religion? What would cause such a dramatic change of mind?"

Lycurgus glanced at Eleazar. The old scribe nodded.

The Athenian teacher responded, "As a matter of fact, I was expelled from the Academy for my conversion. We were ostracized. A marriage betrothal was broken by a landed aristocrat."

Judas saw Lycurgus looking at Sophia, who averted her gaze, looking embarrassed.

Lycurgus continued, "I am only too sorry that my family has had to suffer with me."

"I'm sorry to hear that," Judas said. Though he was not sorry at all to discover that the beautiful goddess reclining beside him was no longer betrothed.

"You speak of dogmatic religion," Lycurgus continued. "Though both the Academy and Aristotle's Lyceum have evolved over the years to include Epicureans, Stoics, even Skeptics, there is one god none of them will tolerate. The Platonists accept the pantheon of Olympian gods, the Stoics worship the Logos and fate, the Skeptics and Cynics doubt all but their own selves, and the Epicureans believe only in matter. In the end, all Greek philosophies worship the same god, autonomous human reason, as if man is the definer of all things, even of the gods. It is not 'open intellectual inquiry' at all. It is a jealous god who will accept no gods before it. I was a blasphemer because I chose to worship the Creator to whom our reason is accountable. And for that they banished me from both schools. The cost has been high for me and my family. But I would not exchange it for the world."

Judas considered what he had heard and responded, "But did not Plato speak of a supreme God, eternal, unchanging, self-existing?"

"Yes," Sophia jumped back in. "After he visited Alexandria, Egypt, where there was a large population of Jews whom father believes shared their philosophy with Plato."

"Is that so?" Judas said, impressed.

"Indeed, it is," Lycurgus replied. "Adonai's revelation to Moses of his identity as 'I Am,' the self-existent, unchangeable source of being, was unique in all the world before Plato borrowed the concept for his own purposes. But Plato still performed sacred rites to the gods. Which illustrates the perennial problem of self-contradiction in Greek philosophy. The problem of the One and the Many. Reason and mystery, imminence and transcendence, human and divine."

Eleazar added to the discussion. "When you make human reason supreme, then the reason of tyrants will rule. And those tyrants will only tolerate gods who do not challenge their supremacy."

Eleazar gave Judas an accusing smile. Judas sought to explain to Lycurgus, "My old friend and elder makes reference to a previous discussion we've had. I am part of the Royal Guard. I protect both king and throne. I maintain the rule of law while he seems to lean heavily in the direction of insurrection."

Judas directed a friendly smile toward Eleazar.

Lycurgus asked, "Is God's law higher than man's law?"

"Yes," said Judas. "But that does not justify overthrowing a ruler for every disagreement. If that were the case, we would be in a perpetual state of lawless chaos. Rule of the mob."

"Agreed," Lycurgus responded, then asked, "So at what point would a people be justified in disobeying a ruler?"

It was not simple. Judas wasn't sure where he would draw the line.

Sophia offered, "When that ruler commanded them to break the higher law of the Supreme Being."

Lycurgus said, "Let us pray we are never forced into such a choice."

Judas said, "From the very start of his reign, King Antiochus has continued the Seleucid policy of allowing the Jews to live according to Torah. He won't be forcing any such choice. And besides, he rescued us from Egyptian control. And there is nothing Jews hate more than Egypt."

Eleazar said, "Antiochus is not the immediate threat. The sacred priesthood of Jerusalem is. In all our people's history, the high priesthood has never been defiled until Menelaus. He is illegitimate, and he will bring the wrath of God upon us. Sword and flame and captivity and plunder. With Menelaus's leadership, the priesthood in Jerusalem will support the Abomination of Desolation spoken of by Daniel."

Judas said, "That is the third time I have heard you refer to this 'Abomination of Desolation.' What exactly is it?"

"The prophet does not say precisely," replied Eleazar. "Only that it is a profane violation of Adonai's sacred space. But he does say that the temple will be trampled underfoot in this way for 2,300 evenings and mornings. That is about six years. King Antiochus has already been occupying Jerusalem for the past two years, and he will eventually defile the temple with an image of abomination. He will attack the Jews and try to force us to violate our covenant with God."

"So," concluded Sophia, "you are saying that the king will challenge our higher law and we will be forced to make a choice between our king or our God."

Judas turned to look at her. Sophia's expression was sincere, even pained. She spoke no further. She didn't have to. Her eyes looked into his soul and asked, "What will you choose, Judas?"

How reliable was this interpretation of prophecy anyway? Judas asked himself. *So many symbols. So ambiguous. What if they had it wrong?*

He spoke lightly to interrupt the solemnity. "Let us be grateful the only choice we have now is between lamb and mutton."

As hoped, his companions responded with a laugh. They all continued to eat and drink, finishing their meal with dates, sweetcakes, and honey. Judas continued to steal glances at Sophia.

Unfortunately, the evening was cut short by the arrival of soldiers under orders to enforce a curfew imposed by the king. Everyone knew it was Menelaus flaunting his connection to Antiochus and asserting his power in the face of his detractors. The fool didn't consider the effect it might have on his supporters and the precarious political unease of the city.

But Judas made sure to draw out the location of Lycurgus's residence before everyone was dispersed.

CHAPTER 7

The goddess Athena followed the dark tunnel downward beneath the temple of Baal on Mount Zaphon. She needed no torch for light because her preternatural eyes could see in the dark. And her preternatural ears could hear the discussion in the cavern at the end of the tunnel. She quickened her pace. Her anger rose within her. She stopped just before she entered the cavern. She checked to make sure her armor looked good.

Everything was golden and polished gleaming bright. She adjusted her Chalcidian helmet with protective leather cheekpieces and a horsehair crest mounted on top that flowed fabulously behind her when she walked. She fluffed her long, curly golden hair to make sure it was laid out just right. Her aegis shield was strapped to her back, her double-edged short sword in its sheath. She pulled her solid chest cuirass into better alignment. It was so confining. She hated wearing it. She patted her leather battle skirt and made sure her greaves were aligned and straight on her shins. All good.

Returning to her gait, Athena burst into the cavern and shouted, "Why in Hades have you begun the war council without the goddess of war?"

Zeus, Poseidon, Hades, and Ares all stood around a bronze table with map and war pieces for strategy. While the three brothers were rulers of the three realms, Ares, male god of war, was their musclebound tool. He wore his ostentatious golden Corinthian helmet with bright-red horsehair crest and left his chest bare to display machismo in order to compensate for his lack of intelligence. The large solid cheek guards hid half his ugly face in cowardly anonymity.

Zeus defended their shame. "We were not in council, Athena. We were waiting for you. You are always late."

"Do you have any idea how time-consuming it is to put on all this ceremonial armor?"

"We are all required to," grumbled Ares in his deep, guttural voice. He adjusted his red chlamys, a woolen over-cloak that was clasped by a golden brooch at his shoulder, allowing it to be thrown back as a cape.

"Some of us more than others," Athena complained, looking his barely-armored figure up and down. Despite her disgust, she would love to be ravaged by him. She felt the tension of pent-up desire between them.

The three brothers had it much simpler and easier. As rulers of the three realms, they each wore golden crowns and togas of the high magistrate, fully-draped white wool with a purple band on the lower edge. Such adoption of Roman fashion was an example to Athena of how Greece was becoming influenced by the rising power of their competitor. Hellenism was a constantly changing culture of appropriation that would one day lead to its own demise.

This cavern with its rocky chamber the size of a small acropolis had been the subterranean throne room of Baal before Zeus took it over. A large crevice ripped through the floor, revealing solidified volcanic rock below, hardened after generations of inactivity. A golden throne with carved sphinxes sat unused just past the crevice. Zeus did not care to spend his reign in this dark hole in the ground. He preferred the sky above. Dark holes were for scheming and battle plans.

Zeus got them back on topic, pointing to the brass figures on the map that represented the gods and their forces. "Antiochus plans to first take Memphis before laying siege to the capital of Alexandria. His plan for puppet pharaohs as client kings did not work, so he wants total surrender."

"Who are their war gods?" asked Athena.

"You don't know?" Ares mocked.

Athena fumed. "Well, I know what side I'm on. You know Egypt is not Troy, right?"

Ares shook with boiling fury. Athena had been holding that one over him for ages since the Trojan War. He deserved eternal humiliation after allowing himself to be persuaded by that whore Aphrodite to side with the losing Trojans while Athena had fought with triumphant Greece.

"Enough!" shouted Zeus. "There is Ra, the sun god, as their prince of Egypt. But also his son Horus, who represents the Pharaoh. There is Montu, a war god, and the lion-headed Sekhmet." He stopped and took a nervous breath. "And Set, the god of chaos and storm."

"Not good," offered Poseidon. "I can counter Set well enough. But Baal is the one who took Set's identity—and we took Baal's temple." He gestured widely all around them and above. "He is going to fight with vengeance like never before. He and the coalition of Canaanite deities that went with him to Egypt. I have no doubt they have their own network of spies back here."

The sea and storm god was referring to the fact that the Canaanite Hyksos had introduced the worship of their deities into Egypt a millennium ago when they occupied Egypt for a season. Baal was equated with Set and worshipped in Avaris in the delta as Set-Baal.

When the Olympians had taken over Mount Zaphon, Baal had fled to his other home base in Egypt along with his sister Anat, violent, bloody, virgin warrior. Reshef and Qeteb, Canaanite gods of war and plague, had gone with them.

Baal wasn't the only one ready to fight with vengeance against the gods of Greece.

Athena added, "What about the elephant in the room? Serapis? Should he not be our spy down in Egypt?"

Serapis was a Hellenistic hybrid deity of Greece and Egypt who was the spiritual prince of Alexandria. He had much power because he was an appropriation of Osiris, the god-king of Egypt's history, now Lord of the underworld.

"Serapis has never come to Syria and vowed obeisance to me," Zeus said. "And he broke off all communication months ago. He is allied with Set-Baal."

Poseidon added, "His Serapeum temple is in Alexandria. He will be strong with the worship of his followers."

"*I* can handle Serapis," said Hades. "*I* am Lord of the underworld." The poor youngest brother was always trying to overcome his inferiority with vain boasting. Athena considered him quite pathetic.

"What concerns me is the biggest elephant *not* in the room," Hades continued.

Athena looked around. They all knew what he was talking about. Except for maybe the dimwit Ares.

"The archangels," said Ares.

Oh, good for the brute, Athena thought. *Lucky guess.*

Zeus sighed. "We have gone over this a thousand times. There is no way that the archangels will protect an apostate community of Jews down in Egypt who have thrown off their holy separation to adorn their filthy souls with Hellenism. There will be no archangels to be found in Egypt."

"He makes a strong argument," said Poseidon. "It is the same reason why they are nowhere to be found in Israel. Many of the Jews are worshipping us, for gods' sake."

"Yahweh has abandoned them," said Zeus with finality. "He withdrew his Spirit from his temple and has never returned. It's been hundreds of years since the last prophet in Israel. Yahweh has finally done it. He has finally stopped threatening and has actually divorced his unfaithful wife of Israel. I tell you, we have free reign."

Poseidon furrowed his brow. "But what of the Seed of the Woman, the bloodline of Messiah? Surely, he has not given up on that."

"Well," said Athena. "If there was an anointed one still around, we would assume that is where the archangels would be, protecting him."

"And they are not around," Zeus concluded. "Q.E.D., there is no more bloodline to defend."

Athena chuckled. "That sounds like something Homer would write. Just before he twisted the plot with the rise of a bloodline."

Hades smirked. "You make up too many myths, Athena." He turned to Zeus as he picked up his bident scepter and helmet, preparing to leave. "Spring is upon us. I have to return to release my bitch from the underworld."

That was part of Hades's pathetic attempt to downplay his humiliation when Zeus had raped Persephone right in front of him.

Who's the bitch now?

"Wait," said Zeus. "I have something to say to my brothers. Alone." He looked at Athena and Ares. They glanced at each other, offended at being left out. But what else could they do? The king of the gods had spoken.

What are they keeping from us? wondered Athena. *Wait until the goddesses hear about this.*

She took the lead out of the cavern, making sure to swing her hips in front of Ares as she walked. She could feel his male gaze fixated upon her body. She smiled, self-satisfied.

Dream on, pinhead. Dream on.

CHAPTER 8

With his three companions, King Antiochus walked down the King's Way of Antioch beneath a starry night sky. Torches on the unfinished columns lit the way. Antiochus was disappointed that the colonnaded path was so far from completion. Everything in this city was so far from completion of his dreams for glory. He needed the patience of a god. Though come to think of it, the gods were not so patient in their pursuits. The promiscuity of Zeus and jealousy of Hera, the wrath of Ares, the arrogance of Athena.

But they did sometimes take the time to come down to earth and interact with humanity. So Antiochus had decided to spend time among the hoi polloi, the masses of Antiochenes, simple citizens who lived their lives in obscurity, subject to gods and kings. He wanted to come down from his throne and experience their world of blood, sweat, and dirt. Like a god visiting his people. Like being one of them in their midst.

Disguised as common laborers in brown ragged hooded cloaks, their weapons secreted beneath, Antiochus and his companions looked for a tavern to enjoy. Two of them were members of his closest counsel, the "King's Friends," and routinely accompanied Antiochus on these outings. Heraclides of Miletus was secretary of the king's finances while his brother Timarchus was satrap of Babylon. Both were in their thirties, well-built and handsome, which made Antiochus feel younger in their presence. When he was drunk, the king could not always tell them apart.

They had taken a new comrade with them this evening, Apollonius, governor of Samaria. Forty-three years old, the governor was one of the king's most trusted supporters in the region. Unlike Apollo, his divine namesake, Apollonius was world-weary and looked older than his years with an etched face and a perpetual frown beneath his tightly-woven graying hair.

Antiochus slapped the governor on his back. "Come along, Apollonius. I swear it is our goal tonight to give you such an entertaining diversion that you will actually smile for once. Just once." He stuck his finger in the air with feigned exaggeration.

The others laughed along. Apollonius said, "Your majesty, with due respect, we just had two hours of listening to you contemplate the craft of casting sculpture with that simple silversmith. I am afraid I may disappoint you."

"That was for the king's own interest," Heraclides interjected.

Antiochus explained, "If you think of it, there is nothing more reflective of the gods than the creation of beauty, whether a vast temple or a tiny silver statue. The creation of order out of chaos."

Heraclides butted in again. "But alas, we are done philosophizing for the evening."

Antiochus waved it off with resignation. The two brothers didn't have much tolerance for intellectual pursuits.

Heraclides put his arm around Apollonius. "We have something else much more libational planned for you, horse-face."

"Is that even a word, 'libational'?" Timarchus quipped.

"It is now," said Heraclides. "Because tonight we will all be like the gods, creating chaos out of order."

Antiochus moved to correct that inverted reference but stopped with a smile of recognition. They all shared a laugh. Except for Apollonius.

But there was still time.

They passed a brothel. Several *pornai*, low-class prostitutes dressed in short, transparent colorful chitons, beckoned to the men. But the men ignored them. The royal mission was different tonight. They would get the upper-class *hetairai* back at the palace later.

"Ah!" said Antiochus. "Here we are."

They stopped before a small tavern with a crude sign above it that proclaimed, *The Wandering Dionysus*, a reference to the god of wine's drunken origin story.

The king stopped Apollonius with his arm. "Don't forget, we are disguised as commoners. Do not refer to me with royal language."

Apollonius's frown became more so. "Is that wise, my Lor—? Forgive me. But what if we get into danger?"

Antiochus gave him a toothy grin. "That is why I brought you three gorillas."

He slapped the governor on the shoulder again, and they all laughed.

Except for Apollonius. He asked, "What is a gorilla?"

Antiochus shook his head. "You need to get out of Samaria and see the world."

Walking past a couple of patrons passed out and lying in the street, they entered the dark and noisy den of bacchanalia.

The tavern was small and cramped with about forty men in varying states of intoxication. Antiochus noticed Apollonius cringe with disgust at the sight of such plebeian degeneracy along with the stench of spilled stale beer and vomit. Coarse jesting competed with loud laughing for the prize of deafening everyone there.

Though wine was available, beer was the favored drink of the masses. So Antiochus made sure he and his companions imbibed as much beer as possible. His favorite was the one flavored with spices that gave it an extra bite to the taste. The masses called it "the nectar of Hades."

The four disguised men found a table at which to recline with a couple of common workers. They had consumed several beers before Apollonius started to loosen up.

Though he still hadn't smiled yet.

They had learned their new companions were a hefty bald Greek stone mason named Kleitos and a lean and shifty Egyptian sea merchant named Ramontu.

Antiochus was most interested in the Egyptian. "Tell us what your name means."

The Egyptian answered, "It is a combination of the sun god Ra and the war god, Montu."

"Well, remind us not to make you angry!"

They all shared a laugh.

Ramontu asked, "And what of your name, Athos? Is it not another moniker for Zeus, the storm god of heaven?"

Antiochus saluted yes with his bronze cup and took a sip of beer.

Ramontu added, "Maybe I am the one who should be cautious."

They all shared a laugh again.

Except for Apollonius.

Antiochus asked, "What exactly is it that you trade on your ship?"

"I export grain and spices from Egypt to Syria, then olive oil and wine in return."

Apollonius injected, "You are based out of Alexandria?"

"Yes."

"There are many Jews in that city. Do you buy and sell with the Jews?"

"I buy and sell with whomever is willing to pay me for my goods."

Apollonius reiterated forcefully, "Do you buy and sell with the Jews?"

Ramontu's eyes filled with fear. Antiochus stepped in with an assuring hand on his back. "You will have to forgive my friend Epaphras here. He is from Samaria. As he tells me, Samaritans have an argument with the Jews over whose mountain is the mountain of God, Mount Gerizim in Samaria or Mount Zion in Jerusalem. They have rival temples and priesthoods. It's a long story. If you ask me, it's all just petty grievances, but my friend here begs to differ."

Antiochus put his other hand on Apollonius's shoulder. "Now, I'm sure Epaphras has no problem with you trading with Jews in Egypt, do you, Epaphras?"

He gave Apollonius a chastising look. Everything Antiochus said was true. He just left out the fact that Apollonius was governor of Samaria, worshipped at that Gerizim temple, and had a vendetta against Jerusalem.

Antiochus had to reiterate the question. "Am I right, Epaphras?" The question was more of a command.

Apollonius finally answered. "Just so long as you overcharge them more than you overcharge the Greeks." He accompanied his words with a toothy grin.

Antiochus's eyes went wide. "I do believe we have made Apollonius smile!"

Heraclides and Timarchus cheered and toasted him with their beers.

The Egyptian looked confused. He asked Antiochus, "I thought you said his name was Epaphras."

Antiochus groped for a quick response, "Oh, it's just a nickname." He noticed Ramontu narrow his eyes with suspicion. So Antiochus added, "I think I'll nickname you 'Pharaoh Jew Lover.'"

Everyone burst out laughing, Apollonius the most of all, slapping his leg with enthusiastic approval.

Well, thought Antiochus. *Knowing what Apollonius hates most is how I control him.*

The king had stopped drinking for the moment. His lightheadedness turned to queasiness. When they had settled down, Antiochus shook off his nausea and changed the subject. "Ramontu, tell me about the Egyptian people. With all these wars against the Seleucids, do the average citizens support their Ptolemaic kings?"

Ramontu thought for a second. "I believe average citizens of Egypt are just like average citizen of Seleucia. They just want to live their lives, enjoy some of the fruit of their labors, and not be taxed to death by their rulers. They are not thinking much of politics and wars. They are thinking of survival. Feeding and providing for their families, their children, and their parents. They would prefer to be left alone."

Antiochus turned to the stone mason sitting beside him. "And what of the Seleucid citizens, good Kleitos. What do they think of their king, Antiochus Epiphanes?"

The stone mason had been quiet this entire time. He shrugged before speaking. "There is a saying going around."

"A saying? A saying of what?"

"The king has disgraced his throne by visiting the bathhouses, brothels, and beer halls in disguise. He tries to be what he is not. They call him Antiochus Epimanes, Antiochus the Mad."

It was a wordplay on Epiphanes, which meant "god manifest."

These deplorable ingrates, thought Antiochus.

The king looked into the stone mason's eyes. The simpleton didn't realize he was with that "madman" right now.

Or did he?

Antiochus felt rage rising in him. He turned to Ramontu. "And what of the Egyptian populace? Do they also mock their rulers?"

He could see Ramontu's eyes lighten with revelation as if he understood there was more to Antiochus's question than curiosity.

"I am sure they do," Ramontu said. "I suppose they are no different from Seleucid subjects in this as well. But regardless of their feelings toward their rulers, I am sure they would rally together against a common enemy."

"Are all sea merchants as wise as you?" Antiochus queried.

Ramontu visibly cringed. "I would not say I am wise, good sir. I am only trying to survive and provide for my family."

"Well spoken. But I disagree." Antiochus reached beneath his cloak to pull out the strapped satchel he carried. Ramontu looked worried. Antiochus said, "I think you are so wise and helpful that I want to give you a gift."

Antiochus's companions squirmed. Apollonius protested, "Athos."

Ramontu looked down on the burlap satchel as if it had a serpent inside it.

"Go on, open it," said Antiochus. He felt a sharp pain in his gut.

Ramontu slowly opened the satchel. His expression changed from fear to shock as he pulled out the small silver figurine of Zeus Antiochus had bought earlier from the silversmith.

Ramontu looked up at Antiochus as if he now knew who he was speaking to. "You are giving this to me?"

"Yes. A gift." Antiochus enjoyed seeing the emotional reaction of his subjects upon receiving grace. It made him feel divine.

Ramontu shoved the figurine back into the sack and threw the flap over it. He glanced around, hoping no one had seen the precious metalwork. The patrons were too drunk in their revelry to notice.

Antiochus raised his chalice of beer to his comrades. "To Ramontu, the wise sea merchant and Pharaoh Jew Lover!"

They all laughed and drank. Antiochus took a gulp, but his stomach pain stopped him. He looked at Apollonius. "Give me the vomit bucket."

Apollonius looked around. Timarchus found it quickly and handed it over.

Antiochus was barely able to get the brass pail up to his mouth before he threw up all that was in his stomach. It must have been over a liter. He felt the beer mixed with bile flow out of him like a spigot of rushing liquid. He retched until his wretched stomach felt free of all contents.

Though the crowd all around him barely noticed, Antiochus could see his friends watching him with empathy, hoping he was all right.

He set the bucket down for a slave to pick up. Wiping his mouth with the sleeve of his cloak, he picked up his beer and stood with a slight swagger, announcing, "A round on me for this symposium of friends!"

For the first time in the evening, much of the crowd died down and gave their attention to Antiochus. A symposium was the term for a drinking party of elites, *not* commoners. Antiochus realized this immediately after he said it. And he was still not feeling well.

But the crowd cheered him with a loud roar. The servers began pouring more beer. Antiochus shouted over the din, "A toast for King Antiochus Epiphanes!"

"Athos!" Apollonius protested again.

"Epimanes!" the stone mason beside him shouted. Antiochus shot him a dirty look.

But then others shouted in agreement. "Epimanes! Epimanes!"

Soon most of the patrons were chanting together, "Epimanes! Epimanes! Epimanes!" Laughter broke out all over.

Antiochus felt himself shaking with fury. He glared at the stone mason, who didn't even look back. He was smiling and watching the others.

Pulling out his dagger, Antiochus stabbed the stone mason deep through the neck. He withdrew it for maximum effect and muttered, "Here is your madman."

The mason jerked in dumfounded response. Dropping his beer to the floor with a clatter, he grabbed his neck wound, which was now spurting blood like a hose. There was no stanching it. He fell into unconsciousness as his life bled out onto his pillows.

Apollonius whispered harshly, "Antiochus. You place us in danger."

The king and his other companions turned to notice that some in the crowd had been watching them. The noise level fell as everyone began looking their way.

Someone shouted out, "Murderers!"

The three comrades drew their swords.

Antiochus pulled a special whistle he had crafted for this purpose. He blew it. A shrill tweet rang out, piercing their ears.

Someone pulled a sword and approached Apollonius, who cut the poor sop down with one swipe.

Others drew their weapons and moved toward them.

"We must get out, now!" Apollonius said to his companions.

But they were in the far corner of the tavern. As they began fighting the mass of angry patrons, Antiochus could see their antagonists were too drunk to be effective.

But so were Apollonius, Heraclides, and Timarchus.

Perhaps Antiochus's temper had gotten the best of him again.

• • • • •

Judas had been waiting with his squad of thirty soldiers of the Royal Guard in a dark alley across from the King's Way. They were supposed to be secretly available for protection of the king while he fraternized with the local commonfolk in disguise.

They heard the shrill whistle blare. Judas signaled to his men, and the squad sprang into action. Drawing their weapons, they bolted out of the alleyway and crossed the boulevard to enter the small tavern called *The Wandering Dionysus*.

They barged into a lair of pandemonium. Thirty or so patrons surrounded four men in the corner with drawn swords. The king and the King's Friends.

The squad had been briefed earlier about the outing so they knew exactly the situation.

Judas heard the king shout out, "Kill them all!"

The squad went into action, hacking through the crowd of patrons. Some of them froze in confusion at the presence of the royal guards. Others cowered in fear. Few fought back.

Judas could smell the hot sweat and beer mixed into a foul reek. He easily cut down drunken fools unskilled with weapons. These were mere laborers and working class who were probably out to relieve themselves of the misery of their daily existence. They didn't even understand what was happening to them because of the king's disguise.

But they were also seeking to kill the king and could not be allowed to do so. Unfortunately, Judas had had to do this very thing previously when the king got himself into similar trouble at a different venue.

Judas cut off the arm of one man, then thrust him through the gut. He almost cut off another one's head with his swipe.

These depraved behaviors of the king disturbed him deeply. But he also believed that Antiochus was ultimately responsible for his actions. He would be judged according to his deeds.

As a minister of God's appointed magistrate, Judas would not have the same guilt.

He was simply following orders.

As one last man lunged at him with a knife, Judas spun and dragged his sword blade over the man's throat, killing him instantly.

Breathing heavily from the fight, Judas stopped and turned to see it was all over. The entire tavern was filled with the bodies of slaughtered patrons lying in their blood, piss, and vomit. Thirty soldiers stood over them while the disguised king and his three companions were ushered out to safety.

As they were walking out, Judas saw Antiochus spit at some dead bodies he was passing and scold furiously, "Epiphanes. *Epiphanes.*"

CHAPTER 9

Mount Artemesium, Greece

The mountain range broke out of the northernmost tip of the long island of Euboea off the northeastern coast of mainland Greece. There was nothing of particular historic interest in the region that had once belonged to Athens and then Macedonia other than that it was the final resting place of the great philosopher Aristotle.

It was also the current location of a living creature of the spiritual realm, the great Ceryneian Hind of Artemis. This glorious beast was a female caribou as large as a bull and far from its home in the north. The caribou was the only deer kind whose females had horns, and Euripides had written of the divine hind's golden-antlered head and dappled hide. Its hooves were made of bronze, and it ran like the wind. According to legend, it snorted flames through its nostrils in defense against predators. It was also a sacred favorite of Artemis, the goddess of the hunt and of wild animals. The hind would lay waste to vineyards of frustrated husbandmen, an instrument of wrath for the goddess.

But the divine hind stood now by the River Ladon desperately lapping its fill of life-giving water after being chased for miles by a predator.

That predator crouched silently in the forest across the river. The head of a lion breached the very tip of foliage and flower. The flowers masked its smell from its prey. Its mane was matted, its eyes open but dead.

The predator that wore the lion's head and skin as a headdress and cloak peered through the brush. The focused, burning eyes of the hunter with dark-brown hair and a tight beard. Heracles.

He thirsted for a drink from that same river. He was exhausted from the hunt across so many miles from Oenoe in Attica to Hyperborea all the way to this remote mountain range in Euboea. No mere human could have endured through such tracking.

But he was no mere human.

His will power pushed aside the thirst as he readied his composite bow with three-headed "trilobate" iron-headed arrows. Their effect was devastating on victims. They ripped through flesh and organs with fatal impact. This particular beast may have been supernatural, but she did not have the impenetrable skin of the Nemean Lion.

When the hind looked away, Heracles stood and drew his bow, releasing a single arrow for its lungs. He could have launched several to strike its heart, but he wanted the thrill of consummating his kill with bare hands.

The missile hit its target, ripping through ribs and lungs alike. The beast shuddered with the impact. Her bellow of pain was cut short by her deflated lungs. She raised her head to see from whence the attack had come.

Heracles was already sprinting toward her from across the river. She must have sensed her demise was sure. She jumped into the river in a last-ditch effort at escape.

Heracles ripped off his lion skin and dove in. His taut, bulging muscles cut through the water with powerful ease. Catching up to the animal, he grabbed her golden antlers, pulling her to the bank.

Her groans of pain were decreasing with her diminished breathing. Smoke drifted from her nostrils. She could not muster any fire because she had almost drowned in the water and no longer had much breath to speak of.

Heracles was not a cruel hunter. He grabbed the hind's head. Her dark doe eyes looked upon him with fright.

"You were worthy prey," he told her. Then with a quick, powerful jerk, he broke her neck. The sound of cracking bone echoed along the surface of the water and deep into the forest.

Before he had even caught his breath, Heracles grabbed the hind's left golden antler in his hands. It was long and elegantly curved from front to back like a sliver moon with eight symmetrical points. He twisted and pulled to rip the antler from the hind's skull. Then the other. He would take these as trophies. Not for himself but for his benefactor who had given him the task to accomplish.

Heracles had yet more difficult labors to attend to before he would prove himself worthy of his purpose. Just what it was, he did not know since his father, his creator, would not reveal that to him until the time was right.

He had been spared so much in his twenty-three years of life, hidden away from both men and gods as he developed his strength and skills. He had never met his mother either. His father had promised that if he would prove both obedient and patient, he would receive the reward of immortality. He would become a god. Only then would all be revealed.

Heracles's first test was when he had been allowed to marry as a young man of only fifteen and have children. Then Zeus had commanded him to murder his entire family. That would prove the loyalty required to begin his journey toward deification. Only by freeing himself from all emotional sentiment and moral scruples could he understand the power and being of deity beyond both good and evil. The madness of the gods.

Heracles had wrestled giants, overcome serpents, and killed the invincible Nemean Lion. But the most difficult thing he had ever done was to strangle the life out of his wife and three sons, then throw their bodies into the fire.

But once it was done, he had felt his emotions dry up and his conscience leave his body like a ghost. Anything else was less difficult than what he had done to his family.

So anything was possible.

Heracles knew he was being trained and prepared for something so important that it would change the world. Something the gods themselves could not accomplish.

But what, he did not yet know. His father would reveal it in his good time.

In the meantime, he had his next labor to accomplish. And this one made him anxious. He could feel fear rising in him. So he steeled his will and set his face like flint toward his next destination.

But first he would visit some whores in the nearby village.

CHAPTER 10

Antioch

Judas was able to get a day off from work, so he made his way on horseback through the city to the Jewish quarter. He moved at an anxious pace past the modest mudbrick homes with slanted cedar wood roofs that constituted the lower caste of the city. Still, they bore the symmetry and proportion of Hellenistic design and the cleanliness and orderliness of the Jewish culture. The king had introduced multi-story buildings of apartments to allow for more residents to live on the same amount of land and maximize the landowner's profits. It had the effect of creating a compact stifling feeling for Judas. Almost suffocating. He preferred the openness of the palatial guard's headquarters and barracks.

Judas arrived at the address of Lycurgus of Athens. Tying up his mount out front, he approached the entrance. Despite having lost his high position as gymnasiarch of Plato's Academy, Lycurgus had managed to secure a modest but sufficient residence for rent. Judas had heard such lead administrators in that setting could earn as high as eight hundred drachmas a year. Twice what Judas made as an elite guard. The teacher must have saved enough to live on until he found new work.

Judas could see the building was made of limestone and basalt with terracotta tiles on the roof and portico out front with a couple of modest Doric columns. How long could Lycurgus last without his prestigious employment status?

Judas was glad he had worn his new dark-blue chiton with leather belt. It had shorter sleeves to display his muscles and was knee length to stress his physical strength as a soldier. He had even trimmed his beard with care. It dawned on him how juvenile it was for him to think this way. What had gotten into him? He had never cared for such things. And now he was concerned about impressing the father of Sophia the goddess.

A male slave answered his knock at the door. He was dressed well for his station in a clean and pressed chiton. So this Athenian intellectual treated his workers well.

"Bring your master Lycurgus," Judas instructed.

It took only moments before Lycurgus arrived, opening the door wide. "Judas! What a pleasure to have you visit. Please, enter."

As he followed the teacher into the foyer, Judas could see the spacious atrium courtyard full of well-tended trees, bushes, and flowers. "You have a respectable residence."

"Thank you."

Judas swallowed. "I am here to talk to you about your daughter Sophia." Even saying her name gave him a chill of desire.

Lycurgus turned back with a knowing smile. "There is no need to talk. You have my approval to call upon her." He called out, "Sophia."

He didn't have to shout as Cassandra and Sophia appeared from around the corner almost instantly followed by Sophia's younger sister Angela. Judas hardly noticed, too captivated by Sophia in her soft golden chiton, folds draped on her elegant figure like a Greek statue, hair pinned up and braided in modesty.

"Judas," Cassandra said. "How good of you to visit. Welcome to our humble home."

Sophia added, "Yet it is not so humble as to be incapable of hosting an honored soldier of the Royal Guard."

Cassandra rolled her eyes. With a smile, Lycurgus said, "You would like to talk to my daughter. I only hope you have a sense of humor and the patience of Job."

Judas could not stop smiling. "As for humor, I find this city is much in need of it. And as for patience, I have the day off, so I have time enough." Judas saw Sophia staring at him.

"Well," said Lycurgus, smiling, "since you have the day off, then why don't you come with me and my family on a horse ride in the hills above the city? My two sons are away with friends, but my wife and daughters are capable riders."

Cassandra and her two daughters all looked at Lycurgus with surprise.

Sophia lit up like a child. "I would love to go for a ride!"

Cassandra shushed her.

Lycurgus continued, "There will be plenty of time for you both to talk. And you might even get a word in edgewise."

"It would be an honor," Judas said, smiling.

The women giggled with delight.

"Under one condition," Lycurgus added, looking at Sophia. "You do not scare this fine man away by bringing up Zeno's Paradoxes, or … or Euthyphro's Dilemma."

"Father, you know me too well. You know I cannot promise you that."

"No, I guess you cannot, my precious daughter. Now, go get dressed."

The two sisters immediately glided out of the room, giggling and whispering to each other. Suddenly feeling awkward, Judas turned back to Lycurgus and Cassandra, who now stood with affectionate arms around each other. He didn't know what to say.

Cassandra tried to set him at ease. "It was a pleasure to meet you at Purim. Eleazar has spoken very highly of you."

"I have known him all my life," replied Judas. "He is like family to me. Though sometimes family can be annoying."

They shared a chuckle.

"Indeed," Cassandra said. "And yet that same family is with you when all the world is against you."

Judas chose not to disagree at this point. Things were too good to spoil. Instead, he smiled.

Cassandra continued, "Tell us about your family, Judas. Eleazar told us you have your parents and four brothers in Jerusalem?"

Eleazar had apparently been good enough not to speak of Judas's estrangement from that family. But now he was in a corner. What should he say?

"Yes, I do indeed."

"Would it be an imposition to ask why you are not with them?"

"That is a story I fear I do not have the time to tell right here. Perhaps under the clear blue sky."

Just then, Sophia appeared from around the corner, dressed in knee-length dark-blue chiton tunic for riding, her hair still tied back in modesty.

"I'm ready to go," she said happily.

Saved by the goddess.

Cassandra hurried away to make her own preparations. By the time a groom had brought three horses to the front of the residence, she had returned with her younger daughter, both also in riding tunics.

The ride up the sloping foothills of Mount Silpius was freeing for Judas. Though it seemed more so for Sophia as she galloped around like a wild animal freed from captivity. Her excitement and joy made him laugh.

Lycurgus and Cassandra held back fifty feet or so and discreetly made sure their younger daughter stayed at their side, giving Judas and Sophia room to talk more privately.

Judas pulled Pegasus to a halt to look down upon the city below with its winding river and bustling marketplace. He took a deep breath of the fresh air. Sophia pulled up beside him.

"It's beautiful," she said.

Judas nodded in agreement. "It's freedom. Being outside it all and looking down upon the world."

"So much joy, so much suffering," Sophia added. "Without Adonai, it would all just be chasing after the wind."

Judas felt an uncomfortable silence between them. As though Sophia were waiting for him. A surprise considering her interest in discussion.

He finally said, "Tell me of Athens."

Sophia stared thoughtfully into the distance. "'The birthplace of democracy,' it has been called. It was once the most glorious city of Greece. We had the great philosophers Socrates, Plato, and Aristotle. The great playwrights like Aeschylus and Euripides. Brilliant historians such as Herodotus and Thucydides. Its towering monuments of vainglory engraved in dead stone. Grave markers for the Golden Age of Heroes. Its vast temples of idol worship with statues of bronze and marble gods. When Alexander the Great conquered the known world, it marked the beginning of the end of Athens as the center of civilization. Now Rome threatens everything."

Judas considered her words. "So you share your father's sentiments—and conversion?"

"He has taught me from my youth to think for myself. I now know that Ha Shem raises up kings and removes them. He makes nations great, and he destroys them. *His* dominion is an everlasting dominion which shall not pass away, and *his* kingdom one that shall not be destroyed."

Judas knew it was Scripture she quoted though he did not remember from where. He asked, "What changed your mind about Hellenism?"

Sophia paused for a moment, then said, "I suppose there comes a point in every person's life where they realize they are going to die. And when they do, they'll be forgotten. Both the rich and the poor, both wise man and fool. It may take longer for some. But those who have achieved greatness or glory on earth, what will it benefit them in death?"

Judas quoted Homer. "Say not a word in death's favor. I would rather be a paid servant in a poor man's house on earth than king of kings among the dead." The statement was that of mighty Achilles in the underworld.

Sophia responded, "There are no thrones in Hades. Only beds of maggots and worms. So what can we hope for on this earth? Truth? Justice? Power? As gymnasiarch, my father would ignore the rules and bring me along with him to the school when he taught his classes. I was privileged to have access to the greatest minds and greatest books this world has ever seen. But none of them could satisfy the hunger in my soul."

"Hunger for what?" Judas asked.

"For meaning. What is the meaning of anything in our puny lives of mere decades when we are dead forever after? And for a woman, even less. I knew that the gods could not provide meaning. That they were mere images of us, shadows cast on the wall of our cave of existence. But what are *we* images of? Plato's demiurge was just another shadow created in the mind of a man. No, if there was a true and living God, he would have to be singular, eternal, infinite, and transcendent—outside of our world. The Creator of all things is not part of creation." Sophia paused thoughtfully. "But then, why was he so … silent? So absent?"

Judas said, "Be thankful for a life of ease. With time to contemplate such things. Most people in this world are just trying to survive."

"It is true," Sophia replied. "I have had a life of ease compared to many others. But I am not responsible for the blessings I receive in this life. Only for what I do with them."

Judas nodded in resignation. He could not disagree.

Sophia continued, "One day my father met a Jewish priest who had been sold as a slave to one of the benefactors of the school. He brought the Jew to the Academy to teach the young students, called ephebes, and to be honest, for a little entertainment. Give them a chance to hear the bizarre beliefs of such barbarians and maybe even have some fun debating him. The priest had given my father some of the Jewish Scriptures that had been translated into Greek. What my father did not anticipate was that it would change our lives forever.

"The Jewish man was middle-aged, hefty in weight, and hearty in his emotion. He enjoyed his food. He enjoyed life. But when he sat with us, a group of about thirty or so ephebes and instructors, he did not engage in philosophical dispute. He told us a story. A captivating narrative of the living God whose name was Yahweh Elohim and how he created the heavens and earth in seven days, creating order from chaos. And of the first man and woman he crowned in a garden paradise. How they were deceived by a divine serpent to disobey the Creator, who then banished them from the Garden. The result was enmity between the seed of the serpent and the seed of the woman. Brother killed brother. Then some of the heavenly Sons of God rebelled. They violated the heaven and earth separation and mated with human women. And there were giants upon the earth in those days. And violence and evil filled the land until Yahweh sent a flood to decreate the heavens and earth.

"All of this was familiar to me as I had heard similar stories in our myths of the giants and Deucalion's flood. But I realized that these stories were much more ancient than ours. More authentic. And they moved my soul. The priest told us about the third rebellion and the tower in the land of Shinar. How Yahweh then stopped the evil by confusing the languages, creating the nations, and placing them under the allotment of the fallen gods. But Yahweh allotted to himself one people as his inheritance. He created them from one man, Abraham, and covenanted with them to be a light to the Gentiles so that one day all the nations of the world would be blessed.

Sophia looked directly at Judas. "That was when it all began to make sense to me. That the silence or absence of God I had felt was because *I* was in darkness. *I* was a slave to the fallen principalities of the Gentile nations. I worshipped false gods. God was not absent. Instead, we were spiritually blind and deaf to him."

Judas said, "Well, we Jews have certainly not been true to our calling of being a light to the nations. We may have returned to the Land from our exile in Babylon, but God has not."

"I have read the Hebrew scriptures," Sophia responded quickly. "They say that Messiah will be God's servant who will do what Israel could not. As it is written, 'Behold, my Servant, whom I uphold; my chosen one in whom my soul delights. I have put my Spirit upon him. He will bring forth justice to the Gentile nations.' And 'those who were not my people I will call "my people," and her who was not beloved I will call 'beloved.' Messiah is the hope for us all."

Judas did not want to cause distress, but he also could not lie. He said softly, "But where is this deliverer? It has been hundreds of years, and we remain subjects of Gentile kingdoms. Maybe the nations hate us because we have caused them to. Maybe Antiochus Epiphanes is our deliverer. A profane king like Cyrus the Great used by Adonai to free us from our self-imposed exile among the nations."

Sophia replied, "Or maybe Epiphanes will become a wild beast like King Nebuchadnezzar."

Judas shrugged at the impasse. He knew they could argue all day if they had the time. But he felt invigorated by the discussion, by her thoughtfulness and hope.

Hope. Something he had steadily lost over the years. He said, "You know, Hellenism has opened my eyes to a much bigger world than that of this little plot of land and my own people. I think more about things than I used to. But I have always been more a man of action than words."

Sophia stared him in the eye. "I respect a man with vision for the world. Someone who knows what he wants and reaches for it."

Surely that implied her desire for him. Women were so difficult to read. Judas changed the subject softly. "I am sorry to hear of your broken betrothal."

"It was a blessing. The man was a rich landowner, but he was also an idolator. An unequal yoke of oxen will not work. If I am to marry, it will be to a Jew."

"Would a Hellenized Jew be adequate to your father?"

Sophia smiled and said teasingly, "Eh, I suppose so. If he wasn't *too* Hellenized. But you'd have to ask him to be sure."

They shared a smile between them. Surely, she was hinting that Judas had a chance. More than a chance. He looked over at her parents and younger sister, who had dismounted and were standing together just above them on the ridge. He wondered if they were talking about him and Sophia.

Judas dismounted from Pegasus, then moved to help Sophia down. Touching her arm and back as he did so sent a charge that reverberated through his entire body. He could swear he felt her trembling in his hands.

As they stood and continued their outward gaze, he saw nothing of what he looked at because his every other sense was focused on her. He was even close enough to smell an intoxicating scent of floral fragrance on her.

Sophia asked, "And why are you not with your family? You said you owed my father an explanation. I'd be happy to relay it to him if you'd like."

Another friendly tease. Judas thought about what he should say. "I suppose it has something to do with me being a wild beast."

They shared a laugh. For some strange reason, he wanted to tell her everything. To reveal his soul to her.

He turned serious. "When I was younger, I fell in love with an Edomite slave in our household. If you know anything about Edomites, you know that Jews hate them as much as they hate Samaritans."

Sophia commented thoughtfully, "They are from Esau, over whom Adonai chose Jacob."

"Hm, yes. She was *not* chosen. Her name was Chaya. She was a beautiful human being. Loving, kind, and good to everyone around her. I chose Chaya. I wanted to marry her. My father sold her to keep that from happening."

Judas saw Sophia's eyes tear up with empathy. He continued, "It is not my father's action that I cannot forgive. It is the religious system that perpetuates such division and hatred for others. So, you will have to excuse me if I am not enthusiastic about the separation you have now embraced."

Sophia was silent for a long moment. Finally, she spoke up. "I am sorry for your broken heart, Judas. I will pray that Ha Shem uses it for good in your life."

Judas had nothing to say to that. Immediately, he began to regret having made himself so vulnerable to her. She had a bewitching influence on him.

"There is one thing we have not yet talked about," he said.

"And what is that?"

"Euthyphro's dilemma."

She grinned. "My father did warn you."

Movement in the city below caught his attention. Judas stood. Masses of citizens were surrounding the royal palace, which was elevated on a small hill in the center of the island created by the splitting of the Orontes River. The multitude appeared agitated.

"I am sorry, Sophia, but I am going to have to leave you with your family. That appears to be civil unrest at the king's palace."

"Be safe, Judas," she responded.

Judas swung himself onto Pegasus's back. The horse seemed to know there was trouble, snorting with agitation before they bolted off down the hill for the palace.

CHAPTER 11

Daphne

Hera had convened the goddesses in a secret meeting in Daphne at the shrine of worship for the sacred prostitutes of Apollo. A small, circular stone edifice a hundred feet in diameter, it was dedicated to the goddess Daphne, patron of the city that carried her name. Men were not allowed in here, and the gods paid little attention to it, which was why Hera had chosen it for their clandestine gathering.

The exterior was encircled by marble columns beside a brook of water, and the interior hosted an atrium with a single laurel tree in the center. This was supposedly the very tree into which Daphne had been transformed when she pleaded with the river god to save her from Apollo's infatuated pursuit. How it was that other laurel trees in other cities claimed the same identity as Daphne was never quite considered by foolish humans.

Hera harbored bitterness toward the fact that Daphne represented the common plight of so many women who suffered under the ravenous obsessions of men. She hated Apollo for it. She also hated Apollo for getting a huge temple in Daphne's city while the abused goddess received this pathetic little piss hole in comparison. When were the goddesses going to get their due?

She stood around with the Olympian women and a couple others waiting for Demeter and Persephone to arrive. Athena, Artemis, and Aphrodite were already there along with Gaia, the morbidly obese earth goddess with butch orange hair, pale greenish skin, a wicked machete, and a face that could frighten humans to death. To Hera, she was beautiful even though her manners were lacking as Gaia gorged herself from a vase full of insects and maggots. She wouldn't dare eat the plants or produce of her precious body.

"Where is that yeasty twat Demeter?" Gaia complained. "Corn Queen always makes us wait."

Hera arranged her hair for elusive perfection. "Have some patience, Gaia. She went to get her daughter. It is Persephone's time of release from the underworld, and we all know that Hades always causes a scene when she leaves."

That quieted her down. Hades was a common focus of their hatred.

Artemis spoke up. "Have any of you seen my Ceryneian Hind? I've called for her, and she doesn't respond. She always obeys my call."

Everyone looked at one another baffled, shaking their heads.

Hera said, "That is interesting. My lion in Nemea is also missing."

They were interrupted by Demeter entering the sanctuary atrium. She held up a limping, bruised, and bloodied Persephone. The girl's body bore the marks of Hades's anger at his joint custody with Demeter of their daughter. Her left eye was blackened and swollen shut. It seemed as if her entire body was battered with injury. As an immortal, she could not die, but a fellow god could cause great pain and injury. Her head had bald spots where her hair had been ripped out by handfuls. Her neck, wrists, and ankles bore the bruised marks of long-term shackles from chains.

"Help me set her on the bed," Demeter called out. "Her hip has been broken."

Hera and Athena helped Persephone to the bed lounge they had brought out for her from one of the priestesses' rooms.

Aphrodite stood back, repulsed by the sight. She didn't want her sexy see-through linen tunic to be soiled by the blood. It would be near impossible to clean it out of the fabric.

It would take some time, but Persephone would heal. Divine flesh had a capacity for regeneration that human flesh once had before the Fall. Every time this year, Hades would do the same thing: beat the object of his resentment. Someone had to pay the price for his petty jealousy. Someone had to be the object of his so-called love.

Hera knelt down and placed her hand gently on Persephone's face, looking compassionately into the girl's pleading eyes.

"You are a brave girl," said Hera. "A brave girl. I am proud of you."

"So get on with it," griped Gaia. "What are the male gods keeping from us this time? They think they can just do whatever they want without including us or even asking our counsel? Arrogant misogynist pricks."

Athena spoke up. "I don't know. But they are certainly keeping something from us. At the war council we were told to prepare for war with Egypt, and while it appears that we are outnumbered by the gods of Egypt, Zeus is confident of his plan. But he won't tell us what it is. Not even the male gods know. Only the triumvirate of the three brothers."

"He's out of control!" Gaia blurted out. "Zeus is out of control! He's acting like a dictator, and he must be stopped!"

"Not so fast," said Hera. "There's something that doesn't add up here."

"It's very simple," replied Gaia. "He doesn't trust anyone with his plans because he doesn't want anyone to question his power or authority. If the rest of us don't agree with him, he doesn't want to give us enough time to conspire and stop him."

Artemis said, "Hera, do you think the mysterious disappearance of our creatures of judgment have anything to do with this? My hind and your lion?"

"I can't figure out why," said Hera. "It's not like Zeus to do that."

"It's obvious," said Gaia. "Zeus is strategically weakening our ability to fight back. By keeping us in the dark, he maintains the edge of power over us and sows discord amongst us. Killing our animal allies leaves us demoralized and less protected. I told you, Zeus is out of control. The gods are out of control. We need to rise up and take back what is ours."

"Don't be hasty, Gaia," scolded Hera. "Insurrection without a long-term plan merely replaces one tyranny with another. It perpetuates the cycle. We need to change the narrative."

"What do you mean change the narrative?" asked Athena.

"We can't just overthrow the gods," said Hera. "Mortals would never accept such a thing without justification. I have been musing over this for a while, and I think I have it figured out."

"Are you going to be silent like Zeus?" complained Gaia. "Or are you going to share it with us?"

"We want to seize power," said Hera. "But we have to construct a narrative that justifies the redistribution of that power. The narrative comes first. I suggest we replace the narrative of revolution with reformation."

Gaia was not following. "We go backward instead of forward?"

"We return to a lost Golden Age. We return to the Garden. What if we were to convince humans that the male gods are the actual rebels and insurrectionists? That an original ancient agricultural utopia was ruled with compassion and justice by the Mother Goddess, a single divine embodiment of the feminine? The goddess of nurturing, compassion, and life oversaw a world of harmony, peace—and female rule. That society was then invaded or overthrown by a male hunter-gatherer society and was replaced by masculine power, violence, and death."

Athena grinned in approval, "A toxic combination. So it was the patriarchy that overthrew an earlier and superior matriarchy."

"Exactly," said Hera. "The claim to power for us will be a return to an original paradise lost. That will gain us special goddess worship. First, we win the war of propaganda. Then we can act."

"Then we can slaughter with impunity," said Gaia. Now she was getting it.

Artemis said, "If we make ourselves victims, any atrocity can be justified as a fight against injustice."

Demeter questioned, "But can we inspire the poets and scribes to fabricate this narrative?"

"We must try," said Hera. "But we will need a primary figurehead. A goddess upon whom we can focus our attention who embodies the epitome of our values."

"That's easy," said Gaia, still sitting on her bench. "That would be me."

"You?" laughed Aphrodite. It was an ugly sounding cackle that seemed to disfigure her beauty with irony.

Gaia said, "I am the original Mother Earth."

"You are a glutton who produces thorns and thistles, desert wastelands, and seas of chaos. I am the most emblematic of the feminine mystique. No one is more beautiful or desirable. I am love, sexuality, passion, fertility."

Gaia snapped back, "You are a mindless two-bit whore. An easy slut."

Aphrodite stepped up to her and slapped her hard across the cheek.

Gaia pulled out her machete and spit out, "Try that again, bitch, and I'll cut off your hand."

"Calm down!" Artemis shouted. "My chastity and temperament is more appropriate than both of you. And I watch over the animals and vegetation of Mother Earth."

Demeter countered, "But you are goddess of the hunt, which makes you a tool of male hunter-gatherers. I, however, am the goddess of harvest and fertility of the earth. Is that not the definition of Mother Goddess?"

Athena interjected, "Only if you do not consider the fact that you are a herald of famine and an enabler of wife abuse of your daughter. That's hardly an example of leadership."

Demeter looked over at Persephone, who was too battered to join in the verbal fight. Her jaw had been shattered by her husband.

Gaia complained, "Athena, don't you dare try to make your claim here. You are a goddess of war and Athens, the very essence of patriarchy."

Athena drew her sword, "Are you calling me a traitor to my gender? I will cut you to pieces and bury you in the bowels of Mother Earth!"

Gaia gestured wide with her hands. "I rest my case."

Athena guiltily returned her blade to its sheath.

Gaia looked around at them as she accused, "Whores, tools, abusers, and misogynists the lot of you. In the end you are purveyors of violence and death. I am the birther of life."

"You are a twat." Athena punched the green goddess hard in the face. Blood splattered onto Aphrodite's white linen dress. She cringed in horror.

Gaia got up with amazing speed for her obesity and ran at the retreating Athena, screaming an ear-piercing shriek and shining with bronze hysteria. She collided with the blonde warrioress, smashing her to the floor and suffocating her beneath mounds of flesh. Athena could not move her arms to push the gargantuan Gaia off her. And she could not breath.

"I will teach you not to blaspheme Mother Earth!"

Artemis and Demeter tried to pull Gaia off the incapacitated Athena.

Once they'd done so, Gaia turned and began swinging a flurry of girl punches on the closest target, Demeter, who desperately protected her head while trying to retaliate with her own burst of swinging fists.

Artemis swept Gaia's legs, and the rotund goddess fell to the floor with another crash that shook the ground. Artemis began kicking Gaia in the head. Demeter and Athena joined her, hailing blows on the fallen goddess, who was unable to protect herself.

The atrium suddenly filled with crackling lightning that circled everyone, electrifying the air. A voice roared like thunder. "ENOUGH!"

Everyone froze in obedience, then turned to look at Hera. Her skin shone with bronze fury, her gown and hair flowing in a tornado of wind around her. She had apparently absorbed some of her husband's powers.

The lightning dissipated, the winds died down, and Hera glared at them like a stern mother. "I am Hera, sister-wife of Zeus, the king of the gods. I am Queen of the Olympians and protector of women. *I am the Great Mother*. Do any of you oppose me?"

They all looked at each other hesitantly. Gaia grunted, trying to get up.

Athena walked up the short stairs and stood beside Hera, one hand on her sword protectively. She placed her other hand as a fist over her heart, signaling devoted loyalty. She stared at the others with expectant command.

One by one, they each stood and placed their fisted hand over their hearts. Even Persephone was able to do so in allegiance.

"Good," said Hera like a chastising mother. "Now, all of you, shut up and listen to my plan."

CHAPTER 12

Antioch

After seeing the mob surrounding the palace, Judas had raced down the hill on Pegasus away from his excursion with Sophia and her family. Suiting up quickly in his armor at the Royal Guard's quarters, he reached the palace in time to lead his unit to protect the steep flight of broad steps leading up the hill to the front terrace and palace entrance. Two other commanders had already arrived on the scene, providing a total of three hundred soldiers at ready. Others guarded the king inside.

Judas had been previously appointed head of riot control by the high commander so he took the lead, stationing soldiers on each step and along the terrace parapet so the angry crowd assembled in the commons at the base of the hill could not approach the actual palace. Judas had already recognized many faces in the throng, and a few quick queries revealed that these were all Jews assembled to protest the previous night's defiling of Purim by the new high priest Menelaus. Even the Jews in Antioch would not accept a non-Zadokite in the highest sacred station.

Judas ordered the soldiers along the terrace to line up in riot formation, two lines deep, shields up, and either pikes, spears, or short swords forward. He turned to one of the other captains and barked an order. "Get a unit of a hundred elite infantry to flank the crowd from behind. With haste. And wait for my command." The captain rushed off.

But the protest had now grown into a mob bordering on violence. Judas noticed some of them wielding garden tools like hoes and shovels. Others had mining tools like pickaxes and hammers.

Some of the Jews in the mob pelted the soldiers guarding the stairs with rocks. These held their long shields high in protection but kept their short swords in their sheaths, a tactic designed to lower tension between guards and mob.

Standing on the terrace behind his line of guards, Judas turned to see King Antiochus standing just inside the palace entrance. Facing him were the Royal Guard's gruff and burly high commander Xanthos and the high priest Menelaus. The king appeared to be laying out orders. Xanthos listened stoically, but Menelaus the snake in his opulent robe and jewelry seemed anxious, shaking his head.

Then Antiochus pointed firmly to the entrance and walked away, leaving Menelaus to follow the commander outside to a large marble platform just behind Judas and the guards.

Judas saluted his commander as Xanthos and Menelaus ascended the platform. He could see fear on the high priest's face. Menelaus clearly did not want to be there. Xanthos snapped a return salute of approval toward Judas before turning to look down upon the mob pressing against the bottom steps.

It was a beautiful day for a riot. The sky was a rich blue and filled with clouds. A slight breeze came from the western sea. Judas was ready to keep order.

The chaos below seemed to grow worse.

A herald blew a long brass horn, and the mass of protestors quieted enough to hear Xanthos. Menelaus stood behind him quietly.

"Jews of Antioch!" the commander shouted above the din. "I am Xanthos, high commander of the Royal Guard. And I am here to announce that this is an unlawful assembly. You are all called upon to hereby disperse immediately or you will be charged with insurrection and dealt with accordingly."

The Jews of Antioch were not particularly agreeable with those sentiments. Some of them shouted back. Others threw more rocks.

Xanthos pushed Menelaus forward. The mob became more agitated.

Menelaus shouted an attempt to calm them down. "Sons of Israel! Please! Have some respect for the rule of law!"

Judas heard Jewish shouts of "Abomination!" "Unclean!" and "Blasphemer!" ringing out from multiple parts of the crowd below. The politics of the priesthood were deeply motivating to these people. They saw Menelaus as violating Torah, the very Word of God.

Menelaus tried to continue his argument, but the mob exploded with a fury of shouting that drowned him out.

They rushed the steps like a tsunami of rage.

Menelaus turned and scurried from the platform, ducking back through the palace entrance like a spooked reptile. Below, the angry mob charged the staircase, the fury of their onslaught pushing the Seleucid guards back up the stairs step by step.

Judas shouted a command for his men to hold their ground. Short swords were drawn from sheaths. The line advanced with extreme prejudice. The Guard offense was met with ineptly wielded shovels, pickaxes, and clubs. This would not be a fair fight.

Judas pushed his way forward to meet his rebellious countrymen in defense of the rule of law. In defense of order and defiance of chaos.

He cut down one insurgent, then another before he encountered a young Jewish man with an eye patch. Judas remembered him as the lad whose eye he had taken out with a whip in the horse stable.

Judas paused in shock. The raving mad rebel was screaming like a rabid dog, even foaming at his mouth. Judas's pause almost cost him his life as the lad swung a sword down upon his head. Moving instinctively to block the attack, Judas dropped to one knee on the stairs and plunged his blade upward into the belly of his attacker.

The one-eyed rebel tumbled forward and slid down the stairs in a swath of blood and gore.

Judas noticed the contingent of elite Seleucid soldiers had arrived behind the mob and were awaiting orders. He had his herald make the call with trumpet sound. The soldiers pressed in, trapping the Jewish rabble between the pincers of Hellenist law enforcement.

The soldiers pressed forward, cutting down their opponents with ruthless ease. Dozens more fell slaughtered within seconds.

In short order, the surviving Jews dropped their so-called weapons, threw up their hands, and went to their knees in surrender.

But not before two thirds of them had been wiped out by the superior forces of the king.

Judas stood stunned for a moment, looking out upon the dead. At least two hundred of them lay sprawled across the bloody steps of the royal palace. The one-eyed kid, other men who were middle-aged and even older, all butchered and cut to pieces by the rule of law.

It was at that moment that Judas saw everything become a different picture in his mind's eye.

These were *his* people. As much as he had tried to distance himself from their backwards religious ignorance, they were *his* people. Yes, they were guilty of violating the law. Yes, the king was right to put down an insurrection. Judas was not wrong to kill those involved in criminal rebellion. But something about this was not right. These were *his* people.

Judas suddenly felt nauseas.

The mercenary Seleucid guard under his command were all Jews. And they had just killed other Jews who were also Seleucid citizens over a rebellion of misplaced religious ideals. While the corrupt Jewish leadership was encouraging the massacre of their own people and walking away.

Judas felt himself caught between two worlds. A partaker of both and loyal to neither. Was he a man without a people? Or was he just a self-deluded fool?

Tonight would not be a night of sleep for him.

He dreaded the arrival of morning and what it would bring.

CHAPTER 13

King Antiochus sat on the toilet for his morning release. But today was another dreadful day of diarrhea as his stomach gurgled and ached in turmoil. His bowels spewed refuse and gas like a water hose.

"Ohhhh!" he exclaimed. "Curse Hygeia!"

"You should not curse the goddess of sanitation!" Laodice yelled to him from the bedroom. "You should bless the god of healing! And pray so humbly!"

"I curse Asclepius as well! Fetch my doctor! I will have more help from his herbs than from my prayers!"

The combination of mint, fennel, and dittany-of-Crete would give Antiochus temporary relief, but it never lasted. He tended to get abdominal cramps and bloating within a short time of eating any type of food. He found himself dreading meals.

Standing up, Antiochus peered into the sewage below. Thank the gods there was no blood in the stool today.

"Laodice!" he yelled for her in the other room as he sponged his rear end. "Have the dresser find my purple socks! I want to use my purple socks to match my royal robe today!"

"Yes, my love!" she yelled back. "And I have them pulling out your gem-laden diadem. The golden one with the amethyst, emerald, and onyx. I think you want to project glory, not just strength."

Antiochus also had a new pair of yellow Egyptian leather sandals to go with the socks. *That gem crown better have been polished or someone is going to pay for their negligence. Who is responsible for polishing the jewelry anyway?*

Judah Maccabee - Part 1: Abomination of Desolation

He met his wife naked in their changing room. The two of them held their hands up as servants drew tunics over their heads. Antiochus was amazed at how well Laodice kept her looks even at her age. Pity he had lost interest in her long ago.

"How are we on time?" he asked.

"We are fine," Laodice replied. "It's still early. So I want to talk to you, husband, about those Jewish captives you are getting ready to punish."

"They are criminals, not captives. They attacked the palace. *My* palace."

"No," Laodice responded like a schoolteacher. "They came to the place where they thought they would be heard."

"They caused a riot."

Laodice paused as the dressers wrapped their himation woolen cloaks around them, his royal purple, hers a complementary yellow with Persian trimmings of panther fur.

Finally, she responded, "I think you need to measure your response. They were not protesting your authority but the authority of their high priest."

"A high priest that I appointed for a bribe. They blame me."

"I don't agree," Laodice said. "Have you listened to their complaints? They are saying that Menelaus is not of the right bloodline for the high priesthood."

Antiochus countered, "A matter over which they had been fighting long before I appointed Menelaus, I might add. Jews cannot get along with each other, much less with the rest of society."

The king and queen sat on stools as the dressers pulled on their socks and laced their matching yellow sandals.

"But the one thing they unite over is their one god," Laodice pointed out.

"Ah, yes," Antiochus replied. "Their jealous bachelor god."

Laodice continued, "Our father Antiochus the Great treated the Jews with tolerance. He allowed them freedom to worship their one god and perform their dietary taboos and covenant rituals. He exempted their temple from taxes. We have kept that tradition."

"Why do you keep siding with these inconsequential sand rats?" Antiochus complained. "It's bothersome."

"I am not siding with them. I am thinking about the Seleucid dynasty and your place and reputation in it."

"Are you sure it is my reputation you are concerned with?"

"Our family's reputation, brother. This is bigger than you and me."

They remained seated as two additional servants arrived with their crowns, golden and laden with gems. The servants placed the crowns cautiously upon the heads of king and queen, adjusting for perfection.

Laodice continued, "You complain about Roman expansion and Greek decline. But why is Rome so successful? Because she allows her conquered peoples some autonomy to rule themselves. Their taxes become tribute for protection rather than blood from their veins."

"So, what is your point?"

"My only point is that 'inconsequential sand rats' can become ravenous wolves if you attack their food source."

Antiochus was handed a golden scepter. He scowled at Laodice. "So what would you have me do?"

"That, my dear husband, is up to you, the king. I would not presume. But I do believe this. What you do to those captives could either be seen as a display of a merciful king who warrants the gratitude and obedience of a chastised people or a display of a cruel despot that sparks a rallying cry of injustice and ignites the flames of a revolution. It all depends on what you do and how you do it."

Antiochus looked thoughtfully at his sister wife. She had always proven helpful in crafting his image successfully before the public. She really did care about the family dynasty. On that he could be assured.

And she always submitted to his depraved sexual fantasies in the bedroom. Which warmed his feelings toward her.

A herald's trumpet blew in the distance from the palace entrance.

"Now we are late," Antiochus said. "Let us hurry."

Antiochus and Laodice arrived at the palace entrance steps to be greeted by a fanfare of trumpets and a huge assembled crowd of Antiochenes in the wide-open commons below. Thousands of them. It was the location of last night's riot, and Antiochus wanted to execute punishment in the same location as a symbolic reminder of actions and consequences.

The stairs and perimeter were lined with a thousand Seleucid soldiers with pikes, spears, swords, and shields ready for command. On the pavement below the palace steps stood a line of ten wooden gallows guarded by a contingent of horse soldiers and infantry holding back the crowd.

The king and queen were met by Menelaus and some priests in their white linens who followed the royal couple up the steps of the raised platform from which Menelaus had been booed during the riot. The high priest wore the ceremonial garb of his status: checkered apron and golden sash over blue robe with a luxurious silken white turban. Antiochus had been told the priests wore additional vestments in their service of the temple in Jerusalem.

Arrived at the top of the platform, king and queen sat on two cedar throne chairs overlooking the crowd below. The thrones were inscribed with exotic Egyptian Sphinxes as cherubim. Menelaus stood beside the royal couple with the other priests behind.

Antiochus gestured to the row of heralds just below him. They blew their trumpets, drawing the attention of the crowd.

Antiochus stood and spoke. Standing was the royal posture of judgment. "People of Antioch! We are assembled here today for a solemn purpose. As your king, I have consulted with the high priest of the Jews. He will now address you and pass judgment with my full authority as your supreme judge!"

The crowd moved restlessly. The soldiers kept them firmly in place.

The king had told Menelaus earlier that the high priest should be the one to publicly announce the verdict for the Jewish rebels because it was *his* problem to resolve and it might help distance Antiochus from their internecine political squabbles.

But the king was still the ultimate authority for capital punishment. So he remained standing and allowed Menelaus to be his mouthpiece.

Menelaus stepped forward. "Antiochenes! Last night a mob of fellow Jews gathered at these very grounds and engaged in a riot of mayhem and violence that had to be put down by the righteous forces of the government."

Antiochus had ordered Menelaus not to speak of "revolution" or "insurrection" because that would make it seem they had risen up against the king, which they had not. Laodice was right about that.

Menelaus continued, "They defied my authority as your high priest and the Royal Guard as protectors of the throne!"

Antiochus gave Menelaus an angry look. He was supposed to speak of the riot only as a religious quarrel. The sly serpent had just made it sound as though the throne had been attacked as well. The priest did not look at the king but kept focused on the crowd.

"I am here today to express repentance on behalf of our people for those actions!" Menelaus gestured below. Two soldiers bearing an ornamented wooden chest on two poles stepped forward before the crowd.

"This is three hundred silver drachmas that I offer as a sacrifice to King Antiochus's patron god, Zeus Olympius!"

Judah Maccabee - Part 1: Abomination of Desolation

Some in the crowd cheered while others jeered. Some Jews heckled the Hellenistic compromise as profane and abominable. Antiochus shook his head at their pig-headed stubbornness.

"But this sacrifice does not pay for the crimes of the mob who revolted against their high priest and their king!"

Antiochus was spitting angry. He spoke under his breath. "Menelaus, I told you not to bring me into this."

"Forgive me, your majesty," Menelaus muttered back. "I got carried away. It won't happen again."

A line of a hundred prisoners was now led up to the gallows. The first ten men had their necks placed in the rope nooses that hung down from the high beam above them.

Antiochus glanced at Laodice, who was visibly upset. She glared hatefully at him, tears welling in her eyes. She had realized he hadn't listened to her advice at all. She turned her head, refusing to even look at him.

Menelaus continued, "I proclaim the judgment of God upon these Jewish criminals for revolting against Torah, temple, and crown!"

Antiochus clenched his teeth. Now he was as angry with Menelaus as Laodice was with him.

Menelaus said, "Let justice be done against all lawlessness and rebellion!"

Antiochus raised and lowered his hand. The gallows board dropped, and the first ten Jews fell, having the life jerked out of their bodies. The scene below looked like a fallen tree of death with dangling branches of human bodies. Gasps penetrated the crowd as the corpses swung like lifeless puppets.

Antiochus muttered to the high priest, "God of Hades, Menelaus. If you try to tie me to this debacle one more time, I will hang you with them."

The next ten men were marched up to their doom.

Menelaus tried to soothe Antiochus. "My king, forgive me, but I am actually helping you. The Jewish people believe their Torah and temple to be of higher authority than the king. So if you are not in agreement with their higher law, you will be hated no matter the consequence."

Antiochus raised and lowered his hand again. The gallows dropped again. The next ten men died. The crowd gasped again. They never seemed to get used to the horror of execution.

Antiochus couldn't believe what he was hearing. "The gall of your people. Someday I will teach them who is their true highest authority on this earth."

"My king, it does not warrant your concern," Menelaus assured. "A majority of Jews are Hellenists who know of what you speak. It is only a minority who do not. And they have little political influence."

"Lucky for you," said Antiochus, "Because they are your responsibility. And if this episode is anything more than an anomaly, you will be the one held accountable. I expect you to keep them in line."

Menelaus bowed nervously. "Yes, my king."

Judas stood in command of the Royal Guard at the foot of the palace stairs creating a border for the citizens. He had a front row seat of the hangings. As he watched his fellow Jewish citizens die for their crimes, he heard the anger and weeping of their friends and family in the multitude before him. He felt thrust into their world of pain.

One woman's voice pierced his heart. "My son! My son!" she cried out. She would never receive a response for the rest of her life. Another yelled, "Ha Shem, have mercy on your people!"

Mercy? Where was mercy? Yes, these men had violated the law. But they had done so out of commitment to a higher law, the law of God. According to Eleazar, this Menelaus was a blasphemous violation of Torah. What should the people do when their own magistrates were criminals? But as wicked as he was, the king was ordained by Adonai. And the Jewish people were commanded by their God to obey their king regardless of whether or not they agreed with his policies. Rebellion was as wicked as tyranny.

But these were Judas's people. As imperfect, as failing as they were, as foolish in their beliefs and behaviors, they were *his* people. And he was now watching *his* people be executed for their religious convictions, however naïve or unrealistic they were.

The tension of conflict between competing values was tearing Judas apart from the inside.

Then he saw Eleazar standing with Sophia and her father and mother in the crowd a distance away. Eleazar noticed him and stared back at Judas as if to ask him a question without words *What will you do now?*

Judas felt something inside him break. Something deep and primal. This world was completely mad and forced him to live with contradictory realities. He could no longer be a part of it. He wanted to walk away from both Antioch and Jerusalem.

But where could he go to escape this madness? Ptolemaic Egypt? Rome? Parthia? Was Eleazar not right that all the kingdoms of the world were equally insane beasts and equally oppressors of Israel? When would this madness end? Sophia had claimed Messiah would achieve the impossible in a new covenant age, a new kingdom that would never end.

But that seemed too clean and simple to Judas. Too perfect in a messy world of imperfection everywhere. Did not every oppressed people on the face of the Earth have the same hopeful longing? Did they not all imagine a savior to free them from their slavery?

Where could he go in all the earth?

CHAPTER 14

Lake Lerna, Greece

Heracles stomped through the swampy marshland near the east coast of the Peloponnese not far from Nemea where he had killed the lion. Now he was in a valley between two mountains in a region of springs and this lake. This small, unassuming lake so apparently insignificant in comparison with the Aegean Sea just a couple miles away. Yet it was of incomparably more significance because it was known to be an earthly entrance to the Abyss, the waters below the earth that led to the underworld of Hades.

This next labor was a frightening one because Heracles was seeking an encounter with another supernatural creature that guarded the entrance to the Abyss: the Hydra.

It was called "Keeper of the Gates," and legend had it that the Hydra was a serpentine leviathan the size of a multi-storied building. It was said to have multiple heads. Some said seven. Some said nine. Others claimed fifty or hundred. It breathed fire and could not be killed. It was a chaos creature.

Zeus had told Heracles that Hera had created the Hydra to cause trouble. Zeus wanted to humble its reputation so Hera would not seek to raise her station in the pantheon any higher than it was. She was the king's queen for gods' sake! What more should she want?

Heracles knew the gods could not create such things. One thing he had observed as he watched and learned from his heavenly father was that the gods often exaggerated to make themselves appear greater and more glorious than they were. Heracles was only allowed to secretly meet a few others like Poseidon, Hades, Apollo, and Hermes. But he had seen enough to realize this was a dysfunctional lot who had power, but not the kind of power to create a supernatural monster.

The chthonic dragon of the Abyss could not be killed. All Heracles had to do was to cut off one of its heads and return the trophy to his benefactor. That is, if the monster's other multiple jaws didn't eat him first or its fire breathing didn't burn him to ash or its venomous blood didn't poison him to death.

"This shouldn't be too difficult," Heracles muttered to himself. He had a macabre sense of humor in the face of death. In fact, one of his quirks was that he would often laugh when his life was most in danger. He sensed this mission was going to be a bit more than a chuckle for him.

Heracles came to the edge of the lake. It wasn't very large, maybe a half mile in diameter. The water was still and greenish-black. He stared into its depths. It was strangely peaceful.

Scanning the lake, his eyes fell upon a large cave opening at the far end where the mountain descended right to the lakeside. Exactly as Zeus had described to him.

Heracles took off at an easy gait around the north edge toward the cave. He wore his lion skin cloak with its teeth and upper jaw guarding his head. He carried his bow of Apollo with quiver on his back, his club in hand, but this time also sheathed his curved sickle sword of Hermes in his leather belt. It was made of heavenly metal of the gods, stronger than iron or steel, its curved edge razor sharp.

He also carried a burlap sack with a grunting, squiggling pig.

When he arrived at the cave entrance, Heracles laid his bow and quiver down. They would not be of much help for this task. He pulled out a small satchel with pitch. A wrapping soaked in the flammable liquid turned his club into a torch. A flick of flint lit it, and he carried it into the cave.

Holding the flaming club before him, Heracles stepped into a large cavern the size of a temple. Its eerie quiet was invaded by the reverberating echo of the crackling fire. The rocks and boulders cast imposing shadows on the walls from his light source.

Before him, a pond of water encompassed most of the cavern's length and breadth. He knelt down on its bank. The water was brackish, black, and viscous. Entrance waters to the Abyss. He touched the surface with his club torch. A green glowing flame spread across the water, lighting the entire cave. The viscous liquid contained no bitumen or asphalt. It was more like water. But it held certain strange properties like flammability.

On the banks of the lagoon, Heracles saw markings, magic glyphs that encircled the banks with an enchantment spell that Zeus promised would draw the Hydra to his lair. He had told Heracles he would go before him to inscribe the ancient forbidden magic from antediluvian days. This would both call forth the creature of chaos and place a containment spell upon it. Of course, one could never completely contain or control chaos. At best, it might be slowed down enough for the gods to unleash it as they had in the Titanomachy and the War on Eden.

Heracles was another matter. He was only half-god. His humanity made him vulnerable. So he would have to move quickly and precisely or he would fail catastrophically.

He had one responsibility to perform for the spell to work. Pulling out the squealing pig, he cut its throat with his dagger. He then placed the lifeless corpse on the shore of the water for its blood to flow down into the deep.

In mere minutes, the surface of the water began to quiver, then bubble as if boiling in a cauldron.

Heracles stepped back in anticipation.

The water then exploded with a mighty force as the gigantic Hydra came up out of the depths and splashed onto the shoreline. It towered over Heracles with fearsome dread. Its muscular scaled necks were like individual serpents. Its seven heads circled and swung incessantly, perceiving its environment. The writhing, twisting serpent. The sea dragon of chaos.

Thank the gods it was only seven heads, not fifty or a hundred.

In moments, the monster observed the puny little human holding a torch.

Several heads screeched with piercing shrieks. Two of them approached Heracles, snapping at him. He waved his torch in defense, and the thing backed off with hisses and snarls.

Then he saw one of the heads rear back, smoke coming from its nostrils and a small flame rolling inside its open throat.

Heracles knew what came next. Turning his back, he pulled his Nemean Lion skin tightly to himself just as the head reached toward him, belching a stream of fire.

Heracles felt the hot flames as they engulfed his body. The impervious lion skin protected him, but the heat was almost too much.

He roared with nervous laughter. He could not help it.

And a surge of courage washed over him.

The second the flames ended, he drew his sickle sword and spun around with force. The monster's head had been so close to him that his outstretched arm was easily within reach.

And his razor-sharp blade caught the thing's neck. Heracles had preternatural strength and his blade was supernatural in origin, so the creature's scales were no protection.

The curved sword cut half-way through and caught the spine.

The monster roared in pain. Its other heads as well. Shock reverberated through the Hydra's body, and its long, towering neck instinctively rose away from its nemesis.

Holding fast to his sword, Heracles felt himself lift off the ground into the air like a catapult. But he did not release his grip.

The Hydra's neck, half-severed and weakened, fell back down to the ground.

Heracles hit the ground. Immediately pulling the sword out, he hacked with precision a second time in the gaping wound. This time, his sword cut through with finality. The head fell to the shoreline with a thud. It easily massed the size of his own body.

The dragon was now in total confusion. It occurred to Heracles that if this was the effect of the containment spell, he shuddered to think what he would have been facing without it.

He laughed again, shouting "Ho Hurrah!" A roar of his own victory he had learned was a slogan of his favorite ancient hero Gilgamesh, Scion of Uruk, Wild Bull on the Rampage.

The dragon had pulled back in momentary self-defense.

Heracles picked up his fallen club. Grabbing the head, he stuffed it into the sack in which he had carried the pig and slung it over his shoulder.

He hauled it out of there, laughing with victory.

Glancing back, Heracles saw that the decapitated neck of the Hydra was already growing a new head. The monster jerked with awkwardness and pain from the regeneration. Heracles knew he had little time to get out of this chthonic pit before the Hydra would be whole again and surely go after him.

Outside the cave, he grabbed his bow and quiver and made it up fifty feet of the incline. He stopped to see if the Hydra had come after him. It had not. The spell had kept it contained.

He dropped to the ground to catch his breath. He had faced a supernatural denizen of the Abyss and had lived to tell his story. Oh, he would tell a story. He might even embellish it a little like his father did with his stories.

Heracles chuckled to himself and remembered the description of the beast's attributes. Its poisonous blood. He picked up his quiver and withdrew an arrow, looking at its iron tip.

Opening the sack, he stuck the arrowhead into the bloody gore of the Hydra's neck.

He pulled it out and looked at the drenched crimson tip. Supernatural poison from the sea dragon of chaos. It was effective on both gods and men.

This could come in handy.

CHAPTER 15

Antioch

Judas had arranged to meet with Eleazar at the synagogue in the Jewish district of Antioch. Spotting the scribe approach across the empty sanctuary, he stood up from the stone seating he had taken in a corner. As he greeted his old friend, he could see concern in Eleazar's eyes.

"It is always good to see you, Judas," the scribe said. "But before you tell me why you are here, let me sit down. My old bones cannot handle surprise like they used to."

They sat down on the bench. As soon as the elderly scribe was settled, Judas stated succinctly, "King Antiochus has mustered an army to invade Egypt. Infantry, cavalry, mercenaries. To leave in a few days."

"What is the goal?" Eleazar asked.

"He wants a final end to these Seleucid wars with the Ptolemies. He is planning on taking Alexandria."

"So, you've come to say goodbye before you leave?"

"I've come to tell you I quit the Royal Guard."

Eleazar's eyes widened with shock. "Why?"

Judas sighed. "When I saw my countrymen hanged for rebellion, something inside me broke. I had thought I was on the side of law and order that served to stem the tide of chaos and violence. But now I see that justice is an illusion defined by those in power. And violence just begets more violence. I am on no 'side.' There are no 'sides.'"

"You would be correct," Eleazar responded quietly, "if there was no God, no higher law by which we will all be judged. But Adonai lives, Judas. And you are a child of his people."

"I cannot deny my heritage," Judas admitted. "But I cannot embrace it either. A 'chosen people' so insular and cut off from the rest of the world. Chosen for what?"

Judas stared down at the worn, dirty stones making up the synagogue floor. Eleazar asked, "Where will you go?"

Judas raised his head to look at his companion. "Jerusalem. You told me my family needed me. I disagree. But I have nowhere else."

"I will join you. It is time for me to return. Unfortunately, the high priest Menelaus is also returning to Jerusalem. I hope we do not cross paths. And what of Sophia?"

Judas thought about it with a pained expression. "I can only hope her father finds a man worthy of her. A man of purpose and sure of his path. Who believes in her ideals."

Eleazar did not try to dissuade him from his shame. He knew Judas to be a man of honor whose convictions, no matter how right or wrong, could never be shaken. So he changed the subject. "I will be bringing some scrolls of Scripture with me that I purchased from a merchant in Seleucia. He brought them from the great library in Alexandria, Egypt."

Judas smiled. "Precious cargo, eh?"

Eleazar queried, "Did I ever tell you my father had worked on the translation of the Scriptures into Greek in Alexandria?"

"Indeed, you have from my youth," Judas responded teasingly. He had heard the story many times.

The old scribe smiled. "Well, indulge this old man just once more. For I have a new ending."

Judas raised his brow with intrigue.

Eleazar stared into the past. "It was so long ago now. Under the Greek pharaoh Ptolemy II Philadelphus. I was born there in Alexandria to my father, who had married less than a year previously. Which proves that scribes do more than just devote themselves to books and intellectual pursuits."

Judas chuckled along with him.

Eleazar continued, "My father had told me that the Greek pharaoh had wanted to make Alexandria the capital of knowledge and wisdom of the world since the city was founded by its namesake Alexander the Great. So Ptolemy built the great library and sent messengers to collect scrolls to fill it from every tribe and nation on the face of the earth. And to translate them into the tongue of the people, Koine Greek.

"The keeper of the library suggested to the pharaoh that they include a Greek translation of the Hebrew Scriptures as well for that ancient tongue was barely spoken even by the Jews. And since the Scriptures were sacred, Ptolemy sent for experts in Israel, six from the remnant of each of the twelve tribes, seventy-two in all, and had them convene in Alexandria to translate the Torah of Moses. By the way, did I ever tell you the name of the high priest of Israel in those days?"

"Yes," smiled Judas. "His name was Eleazar. And you were named after him."

"Ah, good memory. Well, the experts arrived, and each went about translating and comparing their work. After just seventy-two days, they completed the translation in agreement by God's sovereign providence and approval."

Judas interrupted the story. "And they called it the Septuagint, the Translation of the Seventy."

"Yes, they did. But it would be many years before the Prophets and the Writings would be translated into Greek as well."

Judas gave Eleazar a playful scowl. "I thought you said you had a new ending."

"Well, did you not say that the Jews are insular, cut off from the world?"

Judas shrugged. "Did not Adonai promise to Abraham that his seed would be a blessing to all the nations of the earth?"

"Yes," Eleazar agreed. "And what better way to reach the world than to translate Adonai's own words from an obscure singular language into the universal language of that entire world? The Translation of the Seventy may very well be to the salvation of the Gentiles."

Judas had never considered that before. But it made sense even if just within the provincial narrative of Eleazar's simple understanding.

The scribe finished, "And that is why I want to collect as many copies of the Scriptures that I can. So that one day we may have complete collections of God's Word—the Law, the Prophets, and the Writings—to distribute to the four corners of the earth."

"That's an ambitious goal for a man of your age," said Judas.

"Someone has to do it," Eleazar replied. "God will provide."

"Well, God had better provide you enough strength to keep up on the ride back to Jerusalem. I don't want to leave you in the dust."

Eleazar grinned at him. "God will provide."

CHAPTER 16

Hera led the goddesses to assembly in the sanctuary of Zeus's temple on Zaphon. Athena, Demeter, Artemis, Persephone, and Aphrodite were followed by a waddling Gaia. The ruling brothers of the three realms stood together dressed in their armor and bearing their weapons, ready for war.

The legend went that in primordial days when Kronos and the Titans ruled, they had imprisoned three one-eyed giants called Cyclopes. To accomplish his succession of power, Zeus freed the Cyclopes, who then gave the three brothers specially forged weapons to overthrow the Titans. To Zeus, they gave his all-powerful thunderbolt. To Poseidon, they gave an almighty trident. To Hades, they gave a helmet of invisibility.

The three brothers brandished those gifts now.

Beside them stood Ares in full battle regalia of golden helmet, armor, and sheaves. His massive body muscles twitched with nervous energy ready to explode. Beside him was pretty-boy Apollo, also in armor with his bow at the ready. This was unusual since the golden Narcissus usually traipsed about mostly naked to show off his youthful masculinity.

Athena stood beside Hera, growling with anger.

Hera touched Athena's arm to calm her. The queen of the gods was trying to keep her cool to avoid any more beatings. In a restrained voice, she said to Zeus, "I see you've made a change in the administration of this war. May I ask why you have replaced Athena, *the goddess of war* …" Hera gave the last phrase particular emphasis. "… with a god of music and prophecy."

"And archery," said Zeus.

"And plague," added Apollo.

Hera blinked slowly. "Athena is one of the finest warriors we have."

"Yes," said Zeus. He hesitated before adding, "About that. You see, we are going up against some of our most powerful enemies in Egypt. Ra, Horus, Montu." He paused for dramatic effect. "Set."

"And Sekhmet and Anat," corrected Hera.

"I had to raise the standard of strength," Zeus responded. "Athena is close but not close enough to the power we need."

Hera started to shake with anger, holding back a storm of fury.

Poseidon jumped in to cover for his brother. "There will be plenty more battles to come. For us all."

Hera saw Hades glaring at Persephone, not even listening to the conversation.

"This is a job for the gods," Zeus added firmly. "There are other ways for the goddesses to help out."

"Help out," Hera repeated. "Okay."

Zeus said, "I need you to stay in Antioch and prepare for any counterattacks and to receive hostages."

"Yes, my king." Hera bowed and made Athena bow with her. *If there are any counterattacks, I will surrender the kingdom to our enemies and betray you into their hand*s.

Zeus concluded, "Now, if you'll excuse us, we need to be on our way to Egypt."

Hera backed up with the goddesses as the war gods passed them and left the sanctuary. Watching Zeus with an evil eye, she became even more determined to carry out her plans for her philandering, abusive, and sexist husband.

Pelusium, Egypt

Antiochus sat on his horse beside Apollonius on his horse, surrounded by a battalion of soldiers. They stood before the mighty gates of the stone-walled fortress city of Pelusium on the Nile about a mile from the seacoast. Behind them were thirty thousand infantry, three thousand cavalry, and an additional ten thousand mercenary forces from Thrace, Crete, and Gaul. But the most imposing of all were the thirty war elephants carrying riders atop in large wooden carriages. The beasts had become a signature weapon of the Seleucid army from the earliest days and a frightening sight for the masses, who could easily be trampled beneath their colossal stature.

It had taken the Seleucids over two weeks at a fast march to make the three-hundred-mile trip overland. Pelusium was a crucial location in the geography of the Syrian wars with Egypt. As the outermost eastern city of Egypt on the border near the southernmost Philistine cities of Syria, it operated as both a major trade port for the region and as a garrison outpost for Egypt. But it was also perfectly situated as a mid-way launching point and supply depot for war on Egypt, which is why Antiochus had secured a garrison of his soldiers there last year during his first siege of Alexandria.

Antiochus felt a sharp pain in his abdomen. He cringed.

"Are you well, your majesty?" Apollonius asked.

"Yes, yes, I'm well," Antiochus responded impatiently. "Just keep your eyes focused on the task at hand."

The huge wooden-and-iron gates opened to a welcoming party consisting of the city's mayor carried by servants upon a curtained litter and surrounded by a dozen of his guards. The mayor was a small Egyptian man named Hapi, bald and unimpressive to Antiochus. He wore official dress of a multicolored kilt with white linen tunic, a large multicolored ornamental necklace, and a face painted with that silly black kohl eye-liner Egyptians liked to use. Antiochus considered their male elites to be too effeminate for his tastes.

The litter was set down. Hapi exited with wide-spread arms and a big grin on his painted face. He spoke in Greek. "Welcome, King Antiochus! The city of Pelusium greets you with open arms. Your garrison of soldiers has been treated well, and I trust you have no hostile intentions with your army."

Antiochus felt another sharp pain in his belly, but he disguised his wince with determination. "As long as you receive us with such open arms, I have no hostile intent. However, I think the time has come for a more dedicated residence of my forces in Pelusium. And I am afraid I must temporarily suspend all departures from the city until I have accomplished my purposes in Egypt."

The deflation on Hapi's face revealed he knew what that meant. Antiochus was invading his beloved Egypt again, and Pelusium would be the gateway.

CHAPTER 17

Jerusalem

Judas and Eleazar had finally arrived in the holy city on their trip from Antioch. It had been a long, hard ride for the ninety-year-old scribe. He had admitted he would have to stop doing these trips for the sake of his old bones. It amazed Judas the scribe was as strong and vibrant as he was, far beyond the very few others Judas had met who had made it to that age. Eleazar attributed his good health to Adonai and vigorous exercise. Judas suspected it was clearly the latter.

Eleazar had been kind enough to accompany Judas to his family's house in the northern district of the City of David just below the palace and temple mount. As a priestly family, Mattathiah and his children had two residences. One was in Modein, a city twenty miles west of Jerusalem, and one in the holy city itself for the time they spent out of each year in service to the temple. There were twenty-four courses or cycles of priests assigned in weekly shifts to the temple service. They were only required to serve for one week and would not be needed again for another twenty-three weeks. But Mattathiah would often stay a couple months in Jerusalem before or after their service. Their life was almost equally split between the two residences.

It had been three years since Judas had seen Jerusalem. Its thirty-foot-high white walls of limestone towered over them even higher in the Tyropean Valley through which they currently travelled. To Judas, they felt like the walls of a prison. A white prison shining brightly in the sun. And he was turning himself in to carry out his sentence. One to which he had resigned himself as though he deserved it.

The two men entered in the valley gate halfway up the elongated city. Judas noted that the city walls had been extended to the west to encompass a new larger area of residences and Hellenistic structures like the gymnasium and theater he had heard about. Eleazar had guessed that the rapidly increasing population would be near sixty thousand residents by now.

Passing through the gate of walls twenty feet thick, they entered into the busy city streets full of local residents. They passed workers laying mud bricks for houses, children playing with wooden shields and swords, donkeys carrying burdens, marketplace hawkers of vegetables, meat, pots, and utensils. Mudbrick homes gave way to stone-based architecture as they passed through the maze-like labyrinth of streets to the richer district where Judas's father and family lived. Priests were well-cared-for from the temple treasury.

The temple mount and its limestone walls stood at the very top of the rising landscape before them. But beside those southern temple walls stood the towering Akra fortress, built by King Antiochus to watch over both city and temple. Soldiers were stationed there to keep the peace. The *Seleucid* peace.

As Judas and Eleazar led horses and donkeys bearing both supplies and scrolls up the rising hill, Judas became anxious. He had sent a letter ahead of them to let his father know he was coming. He did not want a surprise that might cause trauma, especially for his mother. But in truth, he wasn't sure it would help. He did not feel he could explain in the letter his heartfelt thoughts, so he had simply told his father that he was quitting the Royal Guard and returning home to make the best of it. He could not become a priest, but he would be happy to be a servant and take care of all the management and maintenance of the household and support his brothers.

Judas just didn't want to give his father false hope that he had returned to join the priesthood. If his father could not accept that, so be it. Judas could not in good conscience partake in something he did not believe in. He could find work and living space in the poor quarters of the city. The military had prepared him for harsh conditions. He didn't care if he had to sleep with the horses in the stables. Maybe that's where he could get work, tending the horses for the soldiers or public stables. He made a note to look into that.

Judas now recognized the homes around him and some of the residents walking along the street. They hadn't recognized him yet. He would greet acquaintances later. But this was it. The moment of truth for him and his father. His family.

Eleazar stopped with his horse and donkey. Judas followed his intent gaze to see what the scribe was looking at. A hundred feet ahead Judas's father Mattathiah stood in the street peering their way, a scowl on his long face and hands on his hips. At fifty-three years old, Mattathiah was gray of hair and beard, but a solid stance in his long brown robe demonstrated a muscular build.

Judas froze with fear. Had his father been waiting here each day to make sure Judas did not get close enough to their house? Was he that disgusted with his wayward Hellenistic son?

Mattathiah's face lit up with recognition as he spotted Eleazar standing next to Judas. Turning, he shouted back toward the house entrance. Then Mattathiah marched toward Eleazar and Judas with determined purpose. He picked up his pace as if agitated.

Judas wasn't sure what was going to happen until he was close enough to see Mattathiah's eyes filled with tears.

Judas dropped the reins of his horse and donkey and met Mattathiah in a crash of embrace.

"My son, my son," cried Mattathiah.

Those words opened a floodgate of relief in Judas as he grabbed his father even tighter and wept. "Father."

Judas felt Eleazar's hand of affirmation on them both. His knees buckled, and he fell out of his father's arms to the ground. Clutching at Mattathiah's feet, he begged, "Forgive me. I don't know who I am anymore."

Mattathiah pulled his son up gently to look him in his red, puffy eyes. "I know who you are."

Judas embraced him again. This time, he saw his mother approaching. Hannah with her graying hair, forever beautiful, forever elegant in her simple modest house robe, walked toward her son with arms out, joyful tears spilling down her own face.

Releasing his father, Judas ran to his mother. They hugged with a new flood of repentance and forgiveness. She whispered into his ear, "We'll never stop loving you."

No words could express Judas's heart. His tears were a baptism of gratitude.

His father and Eleazar came leading the pack animals. Judas put his arms around both father and mother as they approached the house.

But Mattathiah stopped them and suddenly became stern. "Judas, you are welcome to stay here. But I remind you that we are a Torah observant household. So if you want to stay, you must follow *kashrut*."

"I will," Judas said. "I just ask for your patience."

Judas had prepared for this. Kashrut, or kosher, was the system of ritual and dietary rules of cleanness that separated Jews from Gentiles and made them a bothersome oddity to the Greeks. Judas hated the constraints of "clean and unclean." But he had decided to at least appear to follow them as long as he could to maintain some *shalom*, or peace, in his family. In Greek, such peace was called *concordia*, but that word was rooted in a goddess, so Judas had to shift his mindset back to Hebrew.

Unfortunately, of the members of the hasidim, the "holy ones" who kept *kashrut*, Judas considered his father to be the most extreme. It was why Judas had left three years ago to join the Royal Guard. The slave girl he had loved when he was younger had been considered unclean under Levitical law.

But here he was back home in it. So he had to suck it up.

Mattathiah grabbed Judas's Greek tunic beneath his traveling cloak. It had a blue stripe of ornamentation on it.

"For instance," said Mattathiah, "this tunic is a clothing mixture of linen and wool."

Judas remembered such mixtures of certain materials was forbidden in Torah. "I will get rid of it."

Hannah kept her eyes scoldingly on Mattathiah as she spoke to Judas, "Your father and I have spoken about this, and we will accept you and work with you."

Judas could see his father was trying very hard to restrain himself even now. "And my brothers?"

"*You* must have patience with *them*," Hannah responded promptly.

Mattathiah added, "They are not so quick to forgive or forget."

"I will earn their respect," said Judas. "It will take time, I know, but…"

They arrived at the door of the house. Judas swallowed hard as they entered the domicile. It was well-built stone, bigger than most, with a large atrium in the center.

Judas saw three of his brothers standing with dubious expressions at the entrance foyer. All three were bearded and wore short working tunics. They looked at him like a pack of angry wolves. The second eldest, Simon, was termed "Thassis," or "the Wise." He was the brains of the family, but not without some strength of fighting skill as well. He had his arms folded and a stoic look on his craggy thirty-three-year-old face that seemed to carry the weight of the world—along with a sizeable chip on his shoulder.

Judas held out his hand. "Brother. It has been too long."

Simon did not speak. And he didn't offer his hand. He just nodded with resigned acceptance.

Next to him stood twenty-five-year-old Eleazar, wiry and lean, with dirt-encrusted hands, probably from gardening. Judas offered his hand and said again, "Brother."

Eleazar took a moment before reluctantly grasping wrists with Judas. This one was termed "Avaran," which meant "the Piercer," because of his expertise in the use of spears and javelins. Judas felt his grip, a little too tight. Their father had called Eleazar a "zealot among zealots" for his devotion and passion.

Judas looked at his hand and brushed off the dirt with a smile. He turned to the last and youngest, who was also the smallest in height of the brothers. "Jonathan."

The twenty-four-year-old seemed not as angry as the others. He clasped wrists with Judas with a slight smile, unseen by the others. Jonathan was termed "Apphus," or "the Dissembler," the politician of the family.

Judas looked around. "Where is Big John Gaddis?"

Gaddis meant "the Fortunate." The eldest son at thirty-four years old, John had also been gifted with the strength and fighting skills of a mighty warrior. Which was why Judas's voice was a bit shaky. He would not want to be on John's bad side.

And when the broadly-built, muscle-bound, six-and-a-half-foot-tall bear strode down the hall, he looked like a wraith of death coming for Judas. *Did he get even bigger since I left?*

But when John recognized Judas, his rocky face lit up with a big grin. "There's my Maccabeus!"

Maccabeus meant "the Hammer." Judas had such a forceful relentlessness about him that his brothers and friends often called him "Hammerhead." Hammer was preferable for short.

Lifting Judas in the air as though he were a feather, John gave him a big bear hug. His hearty laughter and good nature were like that of the mythical Heracles. Judas could not help but laugh along with him until he started losing his breath and John had to set him down.

John looked askance at Judas, then with a grin grabbed his clean-shaven chin. "I see the Greeks are still trying to make you into a boy." He tousled the hair on Judas's head. "And you're still trying to look like Alexander the Great."

Judas swatted his hand away with a playful roll of his eyes. "Don't worry. I'll be growing out my hair again to fit in." He sniffed John with a crinkled nose. "And not showering either!"

John smiled and looked at their parents behind Judas. Then at his brothers, still a bit cold in their demeanor. "I would say we are once again one big happy family, but I see my brothers are a bunch of scowling goats."

The other three brothers looked guiltily at one another. John added with a devious grin, "There's only one thing to do about scowling goats. And that is to wrestle them until they *baaah* for mercy!"

With that, John grabbed Jonathan and Eleazar and carried them into the atrium yard, where they wrestled for their freedom. Simon jumped on top of John, but he appeared little more than a momentary distraction for the happy giant.

The brothers were good grapplers. When John pinned one, another would wriggle free. But the three of them were no match for John's skill and strength.

Mattathiah sighed and said to Judas, "I think your brothers may want your help after all."

Judas smiled and launched onto the pack of four wrestling brothers. The younger brothers struggled in vain to subdue Big John. They did not have success.

Mattathiah put his arm around Hannah, who was watching their sons with joy. He whispered into her ear, "Bring out a fatted calf. Tonight we feast. For my son has returned!"

Just after dark, Judas sat at table in the atrium area with his family and Eleazar to eat a banquet dinner in honor of Judas's return. Mattathiah said a prayer over the food, then announced with near tears, "I am so happy to have all my sons back with me."

Judas noted that Simon didn't look so happy. Mattathiah seemed to rise up taller when he continued, "We are the Hasmoneans, proud descendants of my great-grandfather Hasmon, the greatest priest from the tribe of Jehoiarib, the first of the Levite priests to return to our holy city after the Babylonian exile."

The brothers all sighed or rolled their eyes at the recitation of privileged lineage their father had repeated to them a thousand times in a vain attempt to find significance in their ordinary small lives.

Mattathiah concluded, "So let us feast!"

The family began passing around the food. The table was two stone columns with an oak wood top, and they sat on chairs in contrast with the Greek custom of reclining at couch. They ate beef with garlic and onion seasoning and had an assortment of figs and pomegranates. Judas sipped lentil soup full of herbs and spices for which his mother was famous in the neighborhood. It warmed him and brought back a flood of home-cooked memories. His mother had that effect on him.

Taking a piece of beef from the platter, he blurted without thinking, "I would enjoy some feta cheese right now."

He knew it was a mistake as soon as he said it. The mood at the table went cold. Everyone glanced at Mattathiah.

"Forgive me," Judas said quickly. "It's been a while. I know. Do not mix meat with milk."

It was another of the many rules of *kashrut*. This was going to be very difficult for him because he loved pork, another forbidden food.

Hannah watched Judas empathetically. "That is all right, son. It will take time."

The men quietly returned to eating their food. Finally, Simon spoke to Judas. "What do you think of 'Antioch-at-Jerusalem' after being away so long?"

"Simon," scolded Mattathiah.

"What?" said Simon.

"That is not what we call Jerusalem."

"That is what his king calls it." Simon turned back to Judas. "Antiochus has made it a Greek *polis*. All the Seleucid residents and their sycophants have full citizen rights, but not us hoi polloi. We have a Greek gymnasium and theater and the Seleucid Akra fortress overseeing the temple services and our dinner right now. I imagine you are quite comfortable in your element, brother."

"Your brother," said Hannah sternly, "has returned to his Jewish heritage and home. I expect you to accord him some respect."

"Sorry, mother," said Simon, clearly not sorry.

Young Jonathan spoke up. "We have to give Simon some sympathy as well. It has to be painful losing the center of attention to his younger shining star of a brother."

Eleazar tried to hold back laughing out loud. It came out as sputtering chuckling. Everyone knew Judas was the leader of the brothers. John, though eldest, didn't have the intelligence for it but couldn't care less. Simon had the intelligence but not the physical prowess. Judas had it all. The physicality of a warrior, the mind of a strategist, and the willpower of a leader. He was the Hammer.

Simon slammed his knife down on the table in anger, glaring at Jonathan and Eleazar.

Mattathiah said to Simon, "Son, control your temper."

Judas spoke up. "I did not come back to compete with you, Simon. Or to cause division. I came back because I realized that I no longer belonged in the world that I had embraced. I was not that person anymore. But I will be honest with you. I don't know that I can return to this person either." He gestured all around them. "I don't know where I fit anymore."

He couldn't tell them about the riot, about his slaughter of his own kinsmen on the steps of the royal palace. He was too ashamed. But he could see that he was getting through to them. He concluded, "I came back because I had nowhere else to go. You were all I had left in the world. This family. My brothers."

His mother sniffled and wiped tears from her eyes. Jonathan placed his hand reassuringly on Judas's back.

Simon said, "I'm sorry, but it's not that simple. You don't get to abandon your family for years and just come back, then expect us all to pretend as if everything was just as you left it. It's not."

"I'm not saying it is, Simon. And I don't expect any of you to trust me. I don't trust myself anymore."

Eleazar quipped, "Well, I hope you can solve your little philosophical dilemma before too long. High Priest Menelaus has arrived back in the temple. The tensions are rising in the city between the Hellenists and the hasidim. If it gets any worse, we might have civil war on our hands. You're going to have to decide where you stand."

"And it better be with us," said Simon.

"I think we all know our brother Judas well enough," said Jonathan.

Judas had lost his appetite.

CHAPTER 18

Menelaus snapped awake on the bed in his priestly quarters of the temple. He heard the sound again on the other side of his door, a priest announcing the arrival of a delivery at the Sheep Gate.

Pushing aside the young boy lying beside him, Menelaus quickly put on his priestly robe and sandals. "Wait a while before leaving," he told the boy, then shut the door behind him.

Menelaus met his brother Simon, captain of the temple guard, on the way to the Sheep Gate on the north of the outer temple area. Simon was an ambitious man, a few years older than Menelaus and no doubt envious of the high priesthood. But their family stuck together, and Menelaus was the most politically cunning.

They were just in time to meet a large wagon pulled by an elephant carrying a wooden crate twelve feet tall and eight feet square. It had been shipped from Alexandria, Egypt, and carted in from the coast to Jerusalem. The timing of this merchandise was fortuitous as it had arrived in port a week before Antiochus put an embargo on all Egyptian trade because of his invasion.

The two brothers led the wagon toward the inner temple complex where thirty priests were waiting to unload the precious cargo. The cart bumped over some uneven pavement.

"Careful, you fool!" Menelaus yelled, hitting the wagon with his wooden staff. The driver kept his eyes forward until they arrived at the Beautiful Gate of the holy temple itself.

Menelaus had returned quietly to Jerusalem several days earlier, not wishing to draw attention to his return as word of the Antioch riot was already spreading. Menelaus was most concerned with the supporters of the exiled high priest Jason, who was hiding out just across the Jordan in Ammon. Menelaus knew in his heart that he could not avoid it forever. A confrontation was coming. So he had wanted to take care of this task before any violence broke out.

"Never waste a crisis," he said to himself, something he often told others.

Though it was years since he'd had the high priest Onias covertly assassinated, the Oniad supporters and hasidim in the city still suspected Menelaus's involvement and never seemed able to let it go. Nor would they let go of their bitterness toward Menelaus for using temple treasure to pay King Antiochus. The bastards had killed Menelaus's younger brother Lysimachus in a riot because of it. And those troublemaking ingrates continued to complain and protest every chance they got. Menelaus needed the king to show him more support publicly than he had so far. The high priest's patience was wearing thin with these vermin.

Thirty priests surrounded the crate and slowly pulled it down so they could carry it on its side up the steps and through the Beautiful Gate. They moved like a synchronized centipede with their sixty legs moving step by step.

Then one priest tripped and twisted his ankle. Releasing his grip, he fell to the pavement.

Menelaus had the man pulled away from the others. He then used his staff to beat the priest. He hit him in the head and on his back as the poor young man lay prone at Menelaus's feet, trying to protect his head with his hands. But the blows were too much for him, and he eventually lost consciousness. The high priest wiped some blood from his cheek, breathing heavily from the exertion. Looking up, he saw his brother Simon staring at him, disappointed. Then the other priests, standing still with fearful expressions, watching him.

"Don't stop, you fools!" he shouted, "Keep going!" So they did. He yelled after them, "Any more slipups, and you will all suffer!"

The massive doors of the Beautiful Gate were opened by multiple priests using mechanical pulleys. The gate was seventy-five feet tall by sixty feet wide with two massive Corinthian bronze doors. It was an imposing presence that inspired a sense of grand magnificence. As if one were opening the doors of heaven itself.

The priests continued carrying their sacred cargo all the way through the first outer courtyard and into the inner courtyard, then past the stone altar of burnt sacrifice and up the steps into the temple between two large bronze pillars, where the large temple doors were opened for them.

All the temple furniture had been stored away to make a path for the crate. As the priests approached the large purple curtain of the Holy of Holies, Menelaus stopped them and spoke in a solemn voice. "You are about to enter the Most Holy Place of this temple. Normally, only the high priest is allowed in once a year on the Day of Atonement. But you have a special dispensation in order to place this holy artifact in its place. You will recount your experience to no one, am I understood?"

The priests muttered agreement as they strained beneath the weight of the large wooden crate.

Menelaus nodded. Then Simon and another priest pulled back the large curtains embroidered with images of the heavenly host.

There was nothing in the room. No cherubim statues. No ark of the covenant. Those had never been recovered after the Babylonian destruction of the temple.

Menelaus guided the priests to bring the crate in and place it upright against the back wall.

After they did so, they all left except five priests who carried tools to open the crate. The temple veil was pulled closed behind them.

Menelaus spoke in a hushed and venomous tone. "I remind you that you have all taken vows not to speak of what you see. For this is a holy image commanded by Adonai himself to be placed in this Holy of Holies. It is not for the eyes of anyone but the high priest and his temple captain alone. You are to pull apart the crate, get rid of its pieces, and never speak of any of this ever."

The priests nodded in silent holy agreement. Menelaus glanced at Simon next to him, then back at the priests.

He continued, "If you do, if even one of you says a single thing out there, you will all be executed by my authority as high priest. No trial. No delay. This is a holy duty for a holy God."

The priests swallowed and glanced at each other fearfully.

"Well, do it!" Menelaus ordered impatiently.

The five priests proceeded to take off the top of the crate, then each side one by one. Finally, they pulled out the massive amount of straw used to protect the large statue inside.

Menelaus and Simon stood with awe before the image. It was a nine-foot-tall, six-foot wide sculpture carved out of olivewood consisting of two winged cherubim, humanoid in figure. But instead of two males standing side by side with wings extended, they were male and female entwined in standing sexual embrace with wings retracted and heads, eyes, and mouths in raptured expression.

Menelaus had commissioned it to be graven in Alexandria, Egypt, where some strains of Merkavah mysticism had taken root. Merkavah was an esoteric Jewish cult that pursued mystical visions of Adonai's chariot throne based on Ezekiel's visions in Babylon. They conceived of spiritual union with Adonai through sexual language, expressing the depth of intimacy between Creator and creation.

Menelaus found Merkavah compelling—and more progressive than the prudish, traditionalist, and un-Hellenized elements in Jewish society. He knew they would reject this image if they were allowed to see it.

Ignorant rubes. They would never be allowed to see it.

Solomon had gilded the original olivewood cherubim of his temple with inlaid gold. Menelaus could not afford to do so in light of all he had confiscated from the temple and treasury for King Antiochus.

But though the holy ark of the covenant was still absent from this sacred space, this was a good step in the right direction.

"Well, brother," said Simon, "you may just achieve Hellenist reforms in the temple after all."

Menelaus slapped him on the back. "For the memory of our brother Lysimachus." He sighed. He and Simon would never forget the death of their brother at the hands of the hasidim Jews. And they would never forgive. "But now, we have a meeting to get to."

• • • • •

Menelaus and Simon entered the Hall of Hewn Stones in the northwestern wall of the outer temple area. It was given that name because its walls were hewn with iron tools since this room was used for political and civic jurisdiction. A different room made of unhewn stones was used for religious cultic purposes because metal used in tools was also used in weapons of war and could not be a part of Adonai's holy temple rituals.

Simon left his temple guard of a dozen men waiting outside as he followed Menelaus into the room. The *Gerousia*, or ruling elders of the city, over twenty of them, was assembled in seats that encircled the walls of the small hall. Greeks called it a *Sanhedrin*.

Without a king, Israel had become decentralized into these local bodies of authority. But over time, the office of high priesthood had risen to a level of representative authority for the nation, certainly with the occupying kings. After all, it was the high priest who was the ultimate mediator between Ha Shem and his people. So why wouldn't that mediator have the highest authority over his countrymen?

Menelaus was going to continue making sure this body remembered that. He spoke before anyone could welcome the two brothers. "This had better be important because I have much to do."

He sat down on an elaborately carved wooden throne seat in the middle that had been left vacant for the high priest. Simon sat in a seat next to him.

Some elders whispered amongst themselves. But most remained silent with intimidation. *Good. I will let them squirm.* Menelaus panned his gaze around the semi-circle.

The clearing of a throat drew Menelaus's attention to his left. To an old scribe in his prayer shawl robe. *Oh, great. Eleazar the irksome gadfly.* The ninety-year-old curmudgeon was a man Menelaus thought should be dead by now, wished he were dead because he had the scavenging hunger of a hyena and the tenacity of a crab's claw.

Menelaus sighed with recognition.

As he always did, Eleazar spoke fearlessly. "My lord high priest, we have a serious controversy that threatens the soul of the people."

Menelaus sighed again. "What new 'threat to the soul of the people' have you dredged up now, Eleazar?"

The elderly scribe continued, unfazed by Menelaus. "As we all know, the presence of the gymnasium has been the cause of much trouble in the city. Many priests are spending too much of their off time playing sports and neglecting the solemnity of their calling. There is evidence of pederasty between the young males and their older mentors."

Menelaus wished the old crowing cock would just shut up.

But he didn't. "And the nudity on display in most of the sports is both immodest for our men and leads to many of them undoing their circumcision in order to appear Greek."

The elders began grumbling and muttering in outrage amongst themselves.

Menelaus had heard of such a thing. The thought of it was gruesome in terms of its physical pain. It involved surgery with some kind of incision of the skin around the male member. To recreate the foreskin, that cut skin was then pulled forward over the glans and tied up until the cut-and-stretched skin healed. Menelaus winced at the thought of it. But he was impressed by the dedication that some Jews had to Hellenization that they would go to such extremes.

He barked out, "Why have you called me here to debate petty personal issues of Hellenist Jews?"

Eleazar would not back down. "Because it is not merely a personal bodily issue. It strikes at the very covenant commanded by our God. Circumcision is required by Adonai to be a member of the covenant people. By undoing that sign, they are denying the covenant. They are rejecting Adonai himself."

"I don't think they are rejecting Adonai," said Menelaus. "I think they are trying to get along with the rest of the world. A shared humanity."

"They are apostates," said Eleazar.

Menelaus could care less about such things. If it was up to him, he would eliminate all the tedious requirements of Torah such as dietary laws, Sabbaths, and the innumerable sacrifices they were obligated to engage in. He would maybe keep the Day of Atonement once a year to expunge the Jewish people's guilty little souls in one gesture, then let them get back to their lives. It would sure make his own life easier.

Before Menelaus could respond, they were all interrupted by one of the temple guards entering and announcing to the room, "Forgive me, my lords, there is a mob starting just outside the hallway entrance to the city."

The Gerousia suddenly became more animated with concern over their own safety. The Hall of Hewn Stones was against the temple grounds wall. It had an entrance inside the grounds for priests and scribes and an entrance from the city street for the civic rulers.

Menelaus demanded, "How did they know we were deliberating?"

"They must have seen us entering the gate," one of the elders responded.

Menelaus got up with Simon. Both marched out of the Hall and to their right down a short hallway to large oak and iron doors. The old scribe Eleazar followed them.

Simon ordered one of his men to retrieve a cohort of the temple guard and meet them here.

Menelaus could now hear the sound of the people outside the wall. They were agitated, screaming obscenities at their elders. At their *high priest*.

"Open the doors," he ordered a couple guards.

Simon suggested, "We should wait until the guard arrives."

Menelaus ignored him. "I said open the doors."

The guards did so. They strode in front of Menelaus as he stepped outside to the entrance at the top of steps leading down into the streets. As he passed Simon, he quipped to him, "You should know better, brother. Never waste a crisis."

When Menelaus arrived outside, he saw a crowd of a hundred or so people become even more agitated. He heard some curses shouted at him.

Menelaus raised his hands to quiet them so he could speak. Only some obeyed. Others were offended by his leadership.

He yelled out at them, "I hear your complaint! I understand that some of you do not accept my leadership!"

That riled them up a bit. But when they settled down, he continued, "Nevertheless, I have the authority of the God of Israel! And this is an unlawful assembly!"

They exploded with even more hostility. They pushed toward the steps. They were on the verge of rioting as in Antioch.

Menelaus tried unsuccessfully to yell above the crowd. "I order you to disperse immediately!"

The mass of people continued to push forward.

"Have it your way," he muttered. Turning, he saw that the armed cohort had arrived and was standing just inside the entrance.

Walking back inside past Simon, he said, "The holy temple is under assault by a mob of insurrectionists. I command you by my authority as high priest, kill them all."

He stopped and turned to face the open doorway, the angry mob outside. "I said, *kill them all!*"

Simon nodded to his men. Pouring like a flood out of the entrance, the soldiers spread out into the crowd and began hacking them to pieces. Many fled the scene.

Menelaus's eyes met Simon's. He spoke with a righteous smirk. "For Lysimachus."

Simon returned the facial gesture. "For Lysimachus."

No, Menelaus and Simon would never forget—or forgive—what the mob had done to their brother Lysimachus. This was only a downpayment of the payback Menelaus had planned.

He left the temple guards to finish and clean up their mess. Just down the hallway, he passed the old gadfly Eleazar, who glared at him with tears in his eyes. Menelaus felt a deep satisfaction that only power could give. He remembered words that Euripides had written. "Authority is never without hate. There is no greater evil than anarchy, for it destroys nations.*"*

If that old man doesn't die soon, I may have to do something about it.

CHAPTER 19

Judas finished cutting and sanding a few table and chair legs of temple furniture that had broken. He was working in the carpentry workshop outside the temple south of the Akra fortress in the City of David. His family was part of the priestly congregation charged with responsibility of the temple furniture. They oversaw all furniture in the temple complex from the Menorah and table of showbread to the chairs and tables in the priests' meal area. And fortunately, Judas could spend his time fixing things in the workshop without having to show his face in the temple complex. So they had put him to work here.

And they had kept him very busy.

Wiping sweat off his brow, Judas examined a new chair whose leg had splintered, probably beneath the weight of some obese priest who worked on his spiritual duties without concerning himself with his physical health. He was so engrossed he didn't hear his name called until the second time. "Judas!"

He turned to see Eleazar behind him, dressed in his scribal robe and prayer shawl down around his shoulders.

"Ah," said Judas with a smile. "Taking a break from scribal duties to check on a lowly carpenter?"

But Eleazar was not smiling. Judas put down the chair. "What is wrong, old friend?"

The scribe told him of the recent atrocity by Menelaus against some hasidim protestors the previous day. It hit Judas like a club. This was too close to home for him. It felt like trouble was following him.

"Is there anything we can do?" he asked.

"No," said Eleazar. "The crowd had become unruly. He was within his rights to declare it unlawful."

"But to have them killed like that?"

Eleazar paused briefly before continuing, "Menelaus hides behind the sacredness of the temple. He declared it an attack on the temple complex. That was not the full truth. But his brother is the captain of the temple guard, and none of the Gerousia are going to contradict him."

"What about you?"

"I am one voice. But I will testify at trial." Eleazar's voice revealed the despair of knowing it would do no good. "We will have to stay a while longer in Jerusalem before returning to Modein."

Judas recited a statement from Herodotus that had been haunting him. "Of all men's miseries the bitterest is this: to know so much and to have control over nothing."

"Not true," said Eleazar. "We have power over how we respond. As King Solomon wrote, 'The conclusion when all has been heard is this: Fear God and keep his commandments, for this is the whole duty of man. For God will bring every deed into judgment, every secret thing, whether good or evil.'"

Judas asked, "What do you propose we do, then?"

"Pray for justice. Pray that the trial will not be dismissed. There is not much else."

Judas nodded to satisfy Eleazar's hopes.

Then the old man changed the subject. "In the meantime, we would do well to stay positive and keep our minds on the good to build our hope."

"And how do you propose we do that?"

"Celebrate our God and those who act justly. You are coming with me tonight to a party in the Antiochene quarter outside the city walls."

"For what?" Judas felt tricked into this one.

Eleazar avoided answering. "Your entire family is coming. Meet me at the agora on the north end of the gymnasium at dusk." He turned and walked out.

Judas knew he had no choice in the matter. He chuckled to himself.

•••••

The sun was disappearing beneath the horizon, casting a beautiful red-orange glow on all the buildings in the Antiochene quarter of the city, most of them mudbrick two-level residences of the commonfolk that were outshined by the Hellenic gymnasium towering like a Greek marble sculpture of glory above them.

Judas had worn a new green *meil* robe over his short tunic. This was the distinctive flowing robe of the priestly class, and his parents and brothers all wore them as well. They met with Eleazar at the wide-open agora marketplace, now set up for a celebration of several hundred Jews milling about and socializing.

Eleazar wore his usual scribal woolen *simlah* cloak, basic, thick, with few folds. He never varied his boring wardrobe about which he cared little.

"Greetings!" he said and led Judas's family into the party. "We are celebrating the conversion of an Athenian family into the congregation of the Lord! This way."

Eleazar steered Mattathiah and Hannah through the throngs of partying fellow Jews, their five sons following close behind.

Simon complained, "Why didn't the old man just tell us it was a conversion celebration?"

Judas felt a wave of revelation wash over him. He knew why.

They arrived at a reception line that was greeting the converting family amidst the loud laughing and drinking around them. Food was being prepared at the far end of the agora. Fires roasted mutton and lamb. Women cut up bread and prepared plates of vegetables.

Then Judas saw the converts. It was Lycurgus of Athens and his family. Judas had forgotten that their conversion was to be consummated with a pilgrimage to Jerusalem. Eleazar had known Judas would not come if he were aware this was the family being celebrated. Judas would chastise the old man later for his trickery.

All such thoughts left his mind when Judas caught sight of Sophia standing beside her siblings just past Lycurgus and his wife Cassandra. Lovely, blonde-haired, glowing Sophia. His Helen of Troy who made his strong legs buckle with desire. It had been over two months since he'd so precipitously left Antioch, and her look of surprise made him want to hide in shame. But he could only move forward.

He reached Lycurgus, who said with his own surprise, "Judas! I had heard you quit the Royal Guard and left Antioch. I thought we would never see you again!"

"We've missed you!" Cassandra added.

"I owe you an apology," Judas told them both. "And an explanation."

"To be honest, I'm glad you left the king's employ," Lycurgus said. "We must get together again soon."

Cassandra blurted out, "Sophia will be happy to see you as well!"

Judas's stomach was churning. What would he say to Sophia? Especially after her forthright opinions on his rejection of his spiritual heritage and her embracing of the same on their last encounter.

Cassandra turned. "My dear, where has Sophia gone?"

Judas saw that Sophia had disappeared, leaving her two brothers and young sister to continue receiving greetings.

Cassandra's attention was quickly reclaimed by the remaining people in line.

But Judas knew where Sophia had gone. Away from him. His heart sank. He had begun to pursue her in Antioch and then just dropped out of her life without explaining anything to her. What else should she feel but rejected? How else would he expect her to respond?

He had to find her.

But before he could, some people pulled him away to join the crowd for dancing. How could Judas dance at a time like this? He wanted to find Sophia.

Too late. The men pulled him into a large circle surrounding several small circles of women in the middle.

Everyone locked arms. Lyre, flute, and tambourine filled the air with a melody of celebration.

The large circle of men began to rotate in their dance to the left as the women inside their circles danced to the right. Judas had lost track of his own family as he was swept along into the energetic circumambulation of revelry.

And then he saw her. Sophia was in one of the circles, arms locked with other women. Eyes watching only Judas as they passed.

And he could only watch her for as long as possible until their rotating circles were at opposite ends. He desperately searched for her as they came around again. Seeking her eyes with every revolution.

Were they were only looking for each other? Only dancing to see each other? What were her eyes revealing?

He could not tell.

On the next round, Judas could not find Sophia. She had disappeared. Another round and he knew she was gone. She had left the dance.

He knew what he had to do.

He broke off from the circulating group of men and stepped away into the dark of the night.

He marched around the rest of the Agora searching for her. He saw groups of people drinking and laughing. Torches gave sparse light to the dark corners of the converted marketplace.

Had he passed over her? Had he missed her in the crowd? Where had she gone? She had run away. And why not? His walk became a jog as he pushed through crowds of people, recklessly frantic in his search.

He had to find her, to speak to her. But now he thought he might never have the opportunity.

Then he saw a lone figure sitting on the corner of a well in the center of the agora, back to him in the dark.

But he knew her from any angle. He hurried over.

"Sophia."

She turned. Dim light from several nearby torches sparkled on damp cheeks, brimming eyes. She wiped her face. "Judas."

He stopped, afraid to come any closer. "It's not safe for you to be alone here. Or proper."

"I don't care," she said.

Torchlight or tears turned her eyes red, spilled a fresh river of fire down her face. The sound of music behind Judas faded from his ears.

"Are you angry?" he asked. "Do you want me to leave you alone?"

Sophia half-laughed through a sob. "No. I'm happy to see you. I thought you didn't want to see me."

Judas felt his entire body deflate with absolute regret. He whispered, "Because I disappeared without saying goodbye."

Sophia looked up at him longingly. Judas gently sat down on the well wall, leaving a discreet space between them. "Please forgive me. I am a fool. I couldn't face you. I thought I was beyond redemption. That I did not deserve happiness." He stopped thinking of himself. "I thought that you deserved a good man."

Sophia sniffled. "Am I not the one to determine what I deserve?"

"I am so sorry," He reiterated.

She turned her head skeptically. "What do you mean beyond redemption?"

He sighed. "I was the commanding officer during the riot at Antioch. I struck down my own brethren." Now he started to choke up. "What I had done that day suddenly showed me who I really was. And I could no longer live the life I had chosen. But I didn't know who I was. Only that I was broken."

"You returned to your family," Sophia whispered with empathy.

"Because I had nowhere else to go."

"I'm glad you had nowhere else to go," she said.

Judas looked over at Sophia. In the torchlight, her tear-stained face now bore a slight smile.

"I'm glad you came to Jerusalem," she added.

"I'm glad *you* came to Jerusalem," Judas replied. "I only hope you stay long enough for me to spend the time with you that we lost in Antioch. I want to know you better, Sophia of Athens."

"Sophia of Jerusalem," she corrected him. "We are going to stay here. My father will be teaching in the gymnasium. Where else?"

They shared a smile.

"He sees it as an opportunity to bring some light to the Hellenists."

Judas stared into her eyes. "And some light into my life."

Sophia smiled and looked away shyly, saying softly, "You bring more light than you realize, Judas ben Mattathiah."

He couldn't take a compliment well. He replied, "More like Judas the Hammerhead."

He knew Lycurgus would not be receiving the wages of the Academy in Athens. Here, they would struggle.

"And what are your plans?" Sophia asked.

Judas chuckled. "Here I am but a carpenter fixing temple furniture. A place I never thought I would be."

"You are not beyond redemption, Judas," Sophia responded firmly. "You are in the middle of it."

He looked at her, wanting to believe her but having a hard time doing so.

She smiled, "I'm sure you have your flaws. But I believe you are a good man."

"Let's see if you still feel that way after you get to know me better."

She hit him playfully on the arm.

CHAPTER 20

**Memphis, Egypt
One Month Later**

Ares and Poseidon dragged the gods Ptah and Sekhmet on the ground by their hair out of the burning temple of Sekhmet near the complex of the Great Temple of Ptah. The roof collapsed under the flames, and its brick became dangerously brittle in the heat of the fire, crumbling into small explosions of ash. The two Egyptian deities had been hiding out there when the gods of Greece arrived less than a month ago. The rest of the Egyptian divine warriors had gathered in Alexandria downriver awaiting the invasion of King Antiochus Epiphanes. The principalities and powers had not considered that Antiochus would attack Memphis first. It had been left wide open. An easy target.

But Memphis was a stepping-stone for the Seleucid king's strategy. It had been the original capital of Egypt in the earliest kingdoms and bore that long history in the power of its patron god Ptah, the alleged creator of the world through the power of his speech. He would have trouble speaking now as many of his teeth had been bashed from his mouth by his own scepter, now in the hands of Ares that had thrown Ptah against a pillar.

Ptah grunted in pain.

"Get up and walk," growled the Greek war god, his bronze armor glimmering in the sun. A pillar of black ascended in the sky behind him.

Ptah was humanoid in visage. He tried to stand though his left foot and right tibia were both broken. His white mummified linen wrap was soaked in his own blood, and his green skin had turned the color of pale vomit. Groaning with pain, he limped with his captors through the temple complex. Ares took Ptah's magic talisman ankh in his hand and tossed it aside with disgust. Silly Egyptian magic.

Poseidon dragged the still unconscious Sekhmet—lion-headed goddess and wife of Ptah—by the braided mane of her head. In the animal world, female lions had no manes. But that didn't stop the Egyptians from embellishing her appearance for the sake of artistic license. It would take a long time to heal that appearance as her hair had been almost torn from its roots and her face looked barely recognizable, having been pulverized by the storm god.

They followed Zeus, Apollo, and Hades up to the huge temple complex dedicated to Ptah and his craftsmanship of architecture. It was several city blocks square with thick limestone walls covered in a myriad of storied hieroglyphs and accented with sandstone and granite trimming. The Greek gods marched triumphantly past two thirty-foot-tall stone statues of pharaohs in front of two large, wide pylons at the gate entrance. The city was on the banks of the Nile across from the huge, flat plateau of pyramids over a hundred miles upriver from Alexandria and the fertile delta.

Memphis was also the residence of young Ptolemy VI, teen puppet king of Antiochus who had been declared ruler of Egypt last year for Seleucid interests. But Ptolemy had betrayed his loyalty by reconciling with his younger brother, "Pot Belly" Euregetes, and sister-wife Cleopatra II to reunite Egypt under a triumvirate of Ptolemy rule—and against Seleucid interests.

That was why Antiochus had wanted to subjugate Memphis before besieging Alexandria. He wanted to assume kingship of Upper Egypt and the mouth of the Nile delta and humiliate Ptolemy as a warning to the two other sibling rulers in Alexandria.

It had taken Antiochus over a month to get to Memphis, then take it as his first conquest without so much as a battle—except for one little temple being burned down ostensibly by accident. But now the Seleucid king was in possession of the city. So the Olympians dragged their divine hostages in the unseen realm over to watch the coronation of Antiochus as king of Upper and Lower Egypt in the earthly realm.

Antiochus Epiphanes marched along the long colonnade of pillars that led through the center of the complex up to the temple steps. It was like walking through a forest of mammoth stone trees lined with Seleucid infantry in chainmail and brass helmets holding their long pikes and oblong shields. Thousands of Greek soldiers filled the temple complex and occupied the city. Outside, dozens of Seleucid war elephants guarded the gates with their fearsome presence.

A parade of dozens of Egyptian lector priests followed Antiochus. Their black hair was cut straight across and balled behind their head, their eyes lined with black kohl make-up. They wore multi-colored flat necklace collars over naked torsos and triangular starched aprons over white linen kilts. The silent padding of their bare feet gave them an otherworldly impression to the king. Their chief lector priests wore leopard skins over their shoulders.

Antiochus had earlier been purified in a ritual bath and was now adorned in the special garb of Pharaoh, their king. Like the priests, his torso was naked, and he wore the multi-colored collar and triangular apron over a kilt. But on his head was the striped royal *nemes* headcloth with its large lapels that came from behind his ears and lay upon his shoulders. Over this was a gold headband with a *uraeus* cobra, guardian of the king, erect above his forehead. A solid ceremonial beard was attached to his chin, making him look like one of the graven statues around the city.

The previous pharaoh, eighteen-year-old Ptolemy VI, tagged behind Antiochus, now dressed as a lowly servant in mere white tunic with bracelets and collar. He was as forgettable in his looks as his kingdom would soon be.

When Antiochus arrived at the top of the steps of the temple of Ptah, trumpets announced his presence with fanfare. Antiochus bowed. Two lector priests took off his nemes and poured anointing oil on his head. They wiped the excess from his face and head, then said a prayer to Ptah followed by a prayer to Amun-Ra.

Antiochus straightened to a standing position for his Horus ceremony where he would receive his crown and new Egyptian throne name as Horus on earth, son of Ra.

Ptolemy was handed the white hedjet crown of Upper Egypt, a tall white ovoid cap that ended in a ball shape. This had been the young king's crown, which was now placed on the head of his successor.

Antiochus then sat in an ornate throne chair with small graven sphinxes beside it as throne guardians. Two more priests brought the royal insignias on silken pillows to Ptolemy, who then placed them in Antiochus's hands. The symbolic crook and flail signified that Pharaoh was both shepherd and judge of his people.

Antiochus held these crossed over his chest as Ptolemy announced to the crowd in his broken young voice, "Behold, Egypt, your new king, Usermaatre Setepenre Meryamun! He is Epiphanes God Manifest, the living image of Zeus, son and beloved of Ra, Horus on earth!"

The crowd of soldiers cheered along with the hundreds of Egyptian state officials who had gathered to witness the transfer of power. The new name translated meant, "The powerful justice of Ra, chosen by Ra, beloved of Amun."

Antiochus couldn't care less about the tedious details. He just wanted this whole thing over with. Now that he was crowned king, he would have to make offerings to the gods, parade his forces through the streets, and then take a ceremonial boat ride on the Nile, connecting him to the life-giving source of their world.

He was dying of hunger. He hadn't eaten all day in order to avoid his digestion issues. He didn't want to have a bout of diarrhea in the midst of his coronation as god-king. He had been losing a lot of weight because he had been eating less food. And the worst of it was that fasting didn't always stop the pain.

He just wanted to get to the end of this all as quickly as possible so he could eat something, then abuse and humiliate the young Ptolemy in his bedchamber again. This time he had the royal scepter that might come in handy.

And within weeks, he would launch his forces downriver to besiege Alexandria.

CHAPTER 21

Jerusalem

Judas led his four brothers, who were carrying an empty litter, through the streets on their way to the home of Lycurgus of Athens in Jerusalem's Athenian quarter. They were dressed in fine tunics and cloaks with colorful bands, and they followed a line of women dressed in white flowing linen who were dancing to timbrel and tambourine. Many had flowered wreaths on their heads. As the brothers approached the house, the dancing women threw flowers into the road, creating a colorful carpet for them to tread across.

Judas wore an elaborate embroidered mantle with decorative fringes on the corners and a silk turban wrap on his head. It was custom to carry weapons as well, so his short sword was polished and sheathed at his side. He was probably the cleanest he had ever been in the past three years.

Judas could only think of one thing at this moment: Sophia. It had been two months since that fateful day of their reunion at the conversion celebration. He had pursued her with clear intentions and had finally gotten the nerve to ask her father if he had misgivings of a Hellenized Jew asking for his daughter's hand.

Knocking at the door, Judas was met by Lycurgus, who then stepped aside to offer Sophia to him.

And there she was. Sophia of Jerusalem, the most gorgeous woman in all the world. Her sparkling eyes arrested his soul even through the transparent veil she wore over her hair of gold full of curls and ribbons.

A diadem of flowers adorned her head like a queen of creation, and her golden nose ring and earrings proved her a goddess. She was adorned beneath her long white woolen tunic with gold anklets, bracelets, and necklace.

Judas said, "Sophia, your beauty is staggering."

"You aren't too bad yourself, handsome," she replied.

"May I?" he asked.

She nodded, and he picked her up in his arms. Carrying her over to the litter, he placed her gently inside. His brothers were beaming ear to ear as they held the poles that would transport the curtained carriage for two. All personal issues they had with Judas were forgotten on this sacred day of marriage.

Judas got inside with Sophia, and they were carried back to Judas's new home amidst more singing and dancing women.

Inside the carriage, they stared into each other's eyes for a long silence. Then Sophia said, "Judas ben Mattathiah, I will never reject you."

She had known how his entire life had been one of rejection for being different, for not fitting in, for seeking truth at the risk of everything—family and nation.

Judas replied softly, "And I will never break your spirit."

He had known how her heart and mind hungered for knowledge and understanding, to seek truth no matter where it led.

Family and neighbors had gathered in the atrium courtyard of Judas's new home next to the compound of his father Mattathiah. It was small and humble compared to that of his brothers, who all had their own families already.

A packed house of a hundred people watched as Judas signed the *ketuvah*, a marriage contract promising to care for Sophia as his wife, protect her dowry and her person, provide food, clothing, and sexual union, a home for family, inheritance for their sons, and dowries for their daughters. The primary obligations were upon him as the spiritual leader of the marriage and family.

Her obligations were a matter of complete trust. She would submit to his loving and sacrificial leadership to create the beautiful complimentary balance of harmony that Adonai had established in the Garden between man and woman of one flesh. Judas knew Sophia to be a highly intelligent and confident woman, so he did not take her submission lightly. It was a sacred honor that she gave to him. And he knew he would be accountable for it before God Almighty. She gave herself out of her strength. He received her with a grateful humility.

They stood beneath the huppah, a simple canopy stretched out on four poles under the open night sky, representing the tents of their forefathers the Patriarchs.

As a priest, Mattathiah could officiate the ceremony. He stood before the couple and proudly announced, "Welcome to the wedding celebration of my son Judas of the house of Hasmon with Sophia of Jerusalem." Hasmon was Mattathiah's grandfather and had been a famous priest with a lasting legacy, so he often proudly announced that they were "Hasmoneans."

Judas and Sophia gave each other simple golden rings of devotion. Mattathiah pronounced the Seven Blessings upon them: the Blessing of Wine, of Creation, of Humanity, the Couple, Joy, Community, and Future Happiness. As he did, Judas looked over at his mother Hannah. She watched them silently with tears of joy. Only a woman of her goodness and strength could have handled his father and his stubborn ways for all their years. She had nurtured five boys that Mattathiah had led into manhood. Without her, his father would have had nothing.

Returning his gaze to Sophia, Judas said a prayer that he would be worthy of her. That he would listen to her as his father did his mother. That Judas would not have nothing.

Mattathiah ended with the prayer, "The Lord bless you and keep you. The Lord make his face to shine upon you and be gracious to you. The Lord lift up his countenance upon you and give you peace."

Mattathiah turned to the crowd filling the home. "Now, come let us celebrate in my home next door and leave this man and wife to uh, *get some rest.*"

Everyone laughed at the sarcasm. They filtered out of the house shouting for food and drink and dancing until Judas and Sophia were all alone. They would join the party later, and it would last seven days.

Judas closed the front door and led Sophia into their new bedroom where a large bronze bath big enough for two had been recently filled with hot water.

He drew her close and whispered, "I have longed for this since the day I met you."

Sophia raised her brow. "I applaud your patience. But I have waited for you my whole life."

They kissed.

He consumed her. Her sweet perfume, her soft, wet lips.

He teased her, "And what is Plato's discourse on love?"

Sophia closed her eyes in deep satisfaction. "I prefer King Solomon's Song of Love."

They shared a smile.

Judas began to remove her headdress and wreath of flowers. He quoted from the Song, "Behold, you are beautiful my love. Your eyes are doves behind your veil. You are altogether beautiful my love. There is no flaw in you."

"Oh," Sophia said. "So you haven't forgotten all of God's Word."

He shared her smile again as he helped her release the brooches of her peplos gown and let it drop to the floor.

"You have captivated my heart, my sister, my bride. You have captivated my heart with one glance of your eyes. Your lips drip nectar, my bride. Honey and milk are under your tongue."

He kissed her again. And her tunic fell to the floor.

He caressed her skin. It felt like exotic silk to his touch.

"Your thighs are like jewels," he quoted, "the work of a master hand. Your navel is a rounded bowl that never lacks wine. Your breasts are like two fawns, twins of a gazelle."

He felt her quiver with pleasure at his grasp.

He pulled off his own cloak and tunic.

"My beloved is radiant and ruddy," Sophia whispered, "distinguished among ten thousand."

She touched him. "My love's arms are rods of gold set with jewels."

Her hands moved downward. "His abdomen with a tusk of polished ivory bedecked with sapphire stones."

Now Judas shivered with delight. He felt completely vulnerable to her. Completely in her hands. He heard her sniff his musky sweat as though it intoxicated her. She said, "The mandrakes give forth fragrance."

Sophia kissed him, then quoted more, "His mouth is most sweet, and he is altogether desirable. This is my beloved. This is my friend."

"You are a rose of Sharon, a lily of the valleys," Judas whispered. Picking Sophia up as if she weighed nothing, he carried her to the bed.

They never made it to the bath. They didn't need to.

I adjure you, O daughters of Jerusalem,
that you not stir up or awaken love
    until it pleases.

My beloved has gone down to his garden
    to the beds of spices,
    to graze in the gardens.

Judah Maccabee - Part 1: Abomination of Desolation

I am my beloved's and my beloved is mine;
   he grazes among the lilies.
Let my beloved come to his garden,
   and eat its choicest fruits.

I came to my garden, my sister, my bride,
   I gathered my myrrh with my spice,
   I ate my honeycomb with my honey,
   I drank my wine with my milk.

Eat, friends, drink,
   and be drunk with love!

CHAPTER 22

Alexandria, Egypt

The Egyptian residents of the harbor city of Alexandria went about their day as best they could considering the massive Seleucid army of Antiochus Epiphanes encamped outside its protective walls to both east and west. To the north was the Mediterranean Sea, and to the south was the large Lake Mareotis. They were hemmed in and besieged. But the walls were strong, the Egyptian forces were competent, and the harbor was an open access for supplies, so there was hope and confidence for a successful resistance.

The scribes of the Great Library near the Jewish quarter on the east side of the city were not as optimistic as the rest. They had been furiously trying to protect their multitude of scrolls in case the walls were breached and buildings put to the torch. The most important manuscripts were boxed up and buried in locations around the city. Others were simply hidden in private houses all around. Palaces and temples were ripe for destruction but hopefully not the inconsequential commonfolk.

Today was another of many that both terrified and gave hope to the Alexandrians. A heavenly war horn resounded in the clouds. It could not be from the Greeks because those on the walls saw nothing astir in the enemy siege camps.

This was not the first time this had happened over the previous month of the siege. Scribes scurrying to hide scrolls stopped to look up. Sailors in the harbor stopped ship duties and looked up. Locals in the marketplace and royals in the palace stopped what they were doing and looked up.

From their perspectives, they saw the clouds open and dissipate like an ethereal curtain of heaven, behind which stood armies in golden armor and helmets. Their swords were drawn as they faced off, ready to fight. Chariots of gold were ready to roll while anxious war stallions snorted and kicked. It could have been considered a hopeful dream had it not been seen by so many people.

Was mass delusion even possible? If not, then why were they being allowed this glimpse into the heavenly realm? Only the gods knew. Yahweh had allowed his prophets to see such things in visions in the past, but there were no prophets in Israel anymore. And this was Egypt. Perhaps this was just a chance crack in the curtain that divided the heavens and earth.

Some of the Jewish scribes in the library argued that Ha Shem might be protecting the seedline of the Anointed One. Others disputed such outrageous speculation. Egypt was as cursed as Babylon. It was no place for Messiah to rise.

The pagans could not see this vision, but there was one group who were preparing for their own spiritual warfare: Serapis worshippers. Many priests and devoted followers of the Egyptian/Greek hybrid god gathered often at the Serapeum temple on the far western edge of the city to pray and seek the help of the patron god of Alexandria. Serapis was a mighty warrior, and because of his Hellenist origins, he both knew the strategy of the Greek war gods and had reason to oppose them. His connection with the Egyptian primal god Osiris made him doubly powerful in strength. The offering up of Apis bull sacrifices, prayers, and worship would empower Serapis in his defense of the city.

•••••

Antiochus Epiphanes watched his soldiers sacrifice an Apis bull on a temporary shrine in the midst of their camp outside the western walls of Alexandria in a suburb called Eleusis. They were encamped about a mile out because the necropolis of the city, the cemetery, was no place to set up tents and animals. The superstition of holding camp in the midst of death was too strong to avoid.

Antiochus saw the smoke rising from inside the city walls and knew that they were sacrificing to Serapis as well. Though Serapis was the patron god of the city, Antiochus figured you could never be too sure. Since Serapis was half-Greek, he might as well try an appeal to the god.

The Seleucid king looked with envy upon that city. It was truly the most glorious in the entire East if not the world. It was one of twenty cities that Alexander the Great had founded and named after himself. But this one had become the greatest. So Ptolemy I had stolen Alexander's body after death and buried it here in a golden sarcophagus filled with honey inside a golden casket.

Antiochus wanted that power of a god in his control. The city was worthy of Alexander's glory as it contained a vibrant mixture of the best of both Greek and Egyptian architecture and culture that even Antiochus had envied when compared with his own Antioch. Its Serapeum temple was the greatest in Egypt. The Great Library was housed here as well, the most extensive collection of the wisdom of the ages. The Pharos was a massive three-hundred-foot lighthouse on the island jetty in the harbor. It was considered one of the wonders of the world and oversaw her port, a hub of maritime trade that humbled the Syrian ports of Tyre and Sidon. Her most important economic export was the grain that virtually kept much of the world alive, including Rome.

While this made Alexandria a dangerous target for Antiochus, he also thought an occupation of the city without disrupting the grain supply to Rome might create an indebtedness to Antiochus's advantage. Conversely, if Rome misinterpreted a Seleucid occupation as hostile to their own interests, then Antiochus might find himself at war with the Republic. And *that* was not a misunderstanding he was willing to risk.

So he would continue to wait until he heard word from the emissaries he had sent to Rome before attacking the city.

※ ※ ※ ※ ※

A waxing moon rose in the east as dusk descended upon Alexandria. Zeus stood with Hades on his brother's glorious and terrifying golden chariot of death in the middle of the necropolis outside the western wall of Alexandria. His four black underworld stallions snorted smoke from the flames that gurgled furiously in their throats. They had split their forces with Apollo and Ares at the eastern wall and Poseidon where he was so at home on the coastal harbor.

Zeus took a deep breath of the air around them, filled with death amidst a square mile of tombs, mausoleums, and unmarked graves. It was a breath of fresh air to him, and he considered this to be a good location for a battle. As the divine Egyptian generals approached him, he heard Hades mutter their names in recognition. "Amun, Horus, and Montu. Where is Ra?"

"I don't know," Zeus said. "And I don't care."

"Why not?" Hades asked.

"Because he is just a pretender. The original Ra fled at the parting of the Red Sea over a millennium ago. Horus was drowned with Pharaoh. Amun was consumed by swarms. These deities are all weak replacements for the original gods of Egypt who were judged and executed by Yahweh with the ten plagues. They're almost all pretenders."

"See, now that's what I hate," said Hades. "I am stuck down in the underworld cut off from everything happening up here, and nobody tells me anything."

"I'm telling you now," said Zeus.

"And that's my point. You're a thousand years late."

"You should get out more."

Hades rolled his eyes. "Not while I have Persephone with me. But what do you mean, '*almost* all pretenders?'"

"Set."

"Oh, right!" Hades remembered that Baal had been kicked off his holy mountain Zaphon by the Olympians and had returned to his identity as Set-Baal in Avaris. "I suppose that's why he and the other Canaanite deities worshipped in Egypt are the most dangerous. They're fighting with vengeance against us."

"Mm hm," murmured Zeus. "That is what we talked about in Syria. With the help of Anat, Set rebuilt the Egyptian pantheon of gods."

He didn't want to bother explaining that the original Ra had become Mastema back in the days of Moses and then moved to Italy to take on the identity of Sammael, who now ruled Rome. Hades would probably forget that as well. That special helmet of invisibility seemed to mess with his brain.

Amun, Horus, and Montu stopped a good hundred feet from the two brothers in their chariot. Amun was dressed like a blue-skinned pharaoh with two large plumes on his headdress. Horus was a falcon-headed deity and Montu a bull-headed one. They all stood with anxious readiness. When they spoke, the distance was insignificant as their words carried along on the wind in the unseen realm.

Amun spoke first. "You will not break through our defenses."

Zeus ignored it. "Why do you speak for Ra?"

"I share authority with Ra. And he is on his way from Avaris right now with Set. When they arrive, you will regret what you are doing."

Set was a mighty force to contend with. But Zeus smiled. "Will we? Most of you are far from your centers of power. Set and Ra will be far from Avaris, Montu from Karnak, Horus from Edfu, You, Amun, from Thebes. Oh, and you may need to subtract your desert warrior Sekhmet and her creator husband Ptah from those numbers."

Reaching into the chariot, Zeus threw out Ptah's staff covered with pieces of his brain matter and Sekhmet's bloody scalped braided mane. They landed in between the two companies.

Pretending not to care, Amun said, "We still have you outnumbered."

"But we have you surrounded."

Amun looked casually to his left at Lake Mareotis, then behind him toward the east where Ares and Apollo with Antiochus's forces were arraigned against the Egyptian forces and four goddesses: Tawaret the hippopotamus goddess, Neith the huntress/warrioress, and the throne guardians, Nekhbet of the vulture and Wadjet of the cobra.

That didn't include their secret weapon of Serapis and the Canaanite gods inside the city.

"The harbor is still open," Amun pointed out. "Alexandria will not run out of supplies."

Zeus smiled again. "Are you sure about that?"

The harbor island of Pharos protected the Great Harbor where merchant ships were docked and unloaded with trade goods and supplies for most of the Egyptian economic commerce. Sobek, the alligator-headed god of the Nile waters, had been appointed as a watchman over the harbor port.

He was standing beside the huge lighthouse looking out to sea when his attention was taken by the arrival of a small armada of ships on the horizon: Seleucid triremes, warships. The warning bell from the top of the lighthouse rang out in alarm to the city.

Then out of nowhere, a huge wave rose like a watery hand from the Abyss. Sobek didn't have the time to prepare as it engulfed him with full force and slammed him up against the lighthouse foundation stones.

When the water washed away back into the sea, Sobek lay immobile with a huge trident impaling him against the wall.

And over him stood Poseidon, grinning with glory and power.

Back at the necropolis, the Olympians and Egyptian gods both heard the warning bell signifying the Seleucid blockade of the sea. Turning back to Amun, Zeus whispered, "I think your supply chain was just severed."

Amun boiled with anger.

Zeus twisted the proverbial knife. "And what if Ra and Set do not arrive?"

Amun looked at him quizzically. Zeus had something up his sleeve, but Amun wasn't sure what it was—and Zeus was not about to tell him.

•••••

The Nile River South of Alexandria

The Nile glistened like a river of black silk beneath the starry night sky of a waxing moon. Set captained the lunar barque of Ra called "Boat of Millions of Years" as it cut through the water toward its destination of the besieged city. Ra manifested his underworld green-skinned ram's head as he sat in his throne in the middle of the barge. The night was a weakness to the sun god, so Set knew Ra was hoping they would not end up in battle tonight.

What a pathetic shadow this Watcher was compared to the great prince who had previously held the identity of Ra a thousand years ago. That Ra had been a real "king of the gods." Set had believed *that* Ra had a future. But when he left for Rome at the parting of the Red Sea, this weak one had used his political connections to snatch the throne.

Set could care less when they fought. He was always ready and eager. To the Egyptian mortals, Set appeared as a humanoid warrior with the head of a strange long-nosed desert creature. But in the spiritual realm, he maintained his visage as Baal, the musclebound, horn-headed deity from Canaan. Egyptians loved to combine their gods, so in Avaris he was worshipped as Set-Baal.

Set had accomplished much in the past millennium in building his second location of power in Egypt. That despicable Jehu had removed Baal worship from Israel during the days of Jezebel. Ever since then, Baal had struggled to recover his power amidst the ruling conquerors of Babylon, Persia, and now Greece. He had regained Anat's loyalty since those days of betrayal, and she now allied with him in Alexandria.

Also in those days, the archangel Gabriel had confiscated Baal's weapons that together had made him near invincible: Driver, a mighty war hammer, and Chaser, a javelin of such powerful energy that it rivaled Zeus's thunderbolts. With those weapons in his hands, Set-Baal could easily challenge Zeus's supremacy. Without them, he'd had to submit.

And submit he did.

Set saw the city of Alexandria on the horizon. They were close. Ra barked, "There she is! Hurry up. They need me."

Set pulled out a battle mace and lifted a large fishing net with his other hand from the floor of the barque. "I am afraid Zeus needs you more."

He bashed Ra's skull with his mace. It hit the god's ram horn with a loud cracking sound so his skull didn't receive the full force. Instead it broke the horn and knocked Ra into a stupor. He raised his hands in protection.

"Why?" he babbled through blurry confused eyes. "You control the deserts of Egypt!"

"Because Zeus has offered me *all* of Egypt."

Set raised his mace for a final clobbering.

But before he could do so, the boat rose up out of the water on the back of a very large creature. Set lost his balance and dropped the mace as the boat crashed back down on the river with a huge splash. Water soaked them both.

Set knew who had attacked. Apophis, leviathan of the deep, the chaos serpent. Its seven heads appeared, some on each side of the barque. Diving out of range of one chomping mouth, Set found himself on the floor of the drenched boat. Then he spotted his mace just within reach.

In a flash, he was up and swinging with the weapon, bashing one serpent head unconscious and knocking out the teeth of another. A hideous screeching sound roared from several throats.

Ra barely kept himself on his throne, the canopy now ripped off like twigs by another head.

Seeing his chance, Set threw wide the fishnet in his hands. It caught three of the beast heads that were close to each other, tangling them in a web of constraint.

Set bashed another head into unconsciousness just as a large tail burst from the water and came down on the back end of the boat, crushing it into the waves. Ra was catapulted from his throne onto the riverbank. He looked shaken but uninjured.

Grabbing the netting, Set hung in the air as the long boat frame, now broken in half, sank into the depths. The three serpent heads shook with fury to escape the netting, flinging Set into the water. Two of the heads belched out fire that burnt the netting to cinders.

He treaded water without a weapon in his hands to defend himself.

Scrambling to his feet on the river's edge, Ra saw the huge serpent slip beneath the surface.

Set began swimming toward the bank—toward Ra—cutting through the water with hostile intent. He was seconds away from reaching Ra with that hostility.

Then suddenly, the Watcher was yanked beneath the surface by a powerful force. In moments, the churning waters returned to calm with no sign of sea monster or Watcher.

Ra waited to see if Set would survive. If he would break the surface again to hunt his prey.

But it never happened.

Set never returned to the surface.

Gods could not drown in water. They could not die by natural means. But they could be consumed by the supernatural sea dragon of chaos.

Ra turned and ran toward Alexandria.

CHAPTER 23

Jerusalem

Judas finished fixing some scroll shelves that had collapsed in the priest's library of the temple. They had been poorly made and quickly put together. He had grown to enjoy his work. Fixing things was productive and redeeming, especially furniture from the temple. But it was also a time to be alone as he worked and time to think. He had been married over a month to Sophia, and it had been like heaven. He had finally found some peace in his soul that he had longed for. Her love had been healing to him.

His brothers were getting more used to him as well. Big John had never wavered from his good-natured acceptance of Judas, but Simon had not been so accepting. Lately, he had been less sarcastic and spoke more to Judas than when he had first arrived. The younger brothers were more in their own worlds.

The workday was over for Judas, so he put away his tools, picked up the room, and left the workshop. As he walked home, he thought about Sophia. Though they had begun with such hope and happiness, he had recently noticed something change in her. He wasn't sure what, but she had begun to seem a bit withdrawn, sad.

His first thought was that she might be missing her family. She was twenty and had lived with them for so long as Hellenes he wondered if she might be feeling the loss of her past. Not that the family regretted converting but rather that they had not realized the difficulty of adopting a completely different identity. So many things to which they had been accustomed—food, clothing, relationships, and all of life's habits—had been guided by one way of living in the world. Now, everything was different with unsettling newness. From his own perspective, Judas considered the sabbaths and dietary rules quite burdensome. How much more so, Hellenes who had not grown up with such restrictions.

Then again, it had crossed Judas's mind more than once that maybe Sophia was regretting marriage. That it was not what she had hoped it would be. Was she seeing Judas with more honesty and clarity and not liking what she saw? Was it his stubborn, impatient temper? Or his own sad disposition having given up his commanding lead of soldiers for a life in the shadows of insignificance?

Sophia was a woman of intellect, a Greek mind hungry for philosophy, not as typical in Jewish culture. Was Judas not enough for her intellectually? He had pursued more of a Hellenistic education than his Jewish brothers. But still, he wasn't as interested in philosophical discourse as he was in fixing the injustices he saw in society.

Judas desperately wanted his bride to be happy. But he could sense that she wasn't.

Arriving at his home, Judas entered. The smell of cooking herbs filled his nostrils with pleasure. Food was such a significant source of pleasure in his life. Food and sex. His thoughts grew anxious to see his bride. He walked through the small courtyard and over to the dining area.

Sophia turned from the fireplace, where a cooking pot steamed. Her face lit up when she saw Judas. Every time he saw her, it was a little surprise of joy. She approached him with a broad smile. They embraced and kissed.

She asked, "How was your day?"

"I don't care," he said. "I'm just happy to see you."

Sophia smiled. "Your father tells me that this is your family's week of priestly service, and when it is finished, we will all be traveling back to your hometown of Modein for a couple months."

"You'll like it there," Judas responded. "It's a small city of just a thousand people, but we have a larger house there than here."

Sophia lost her smile, returning to the fireplace. Judas sat down at their dining table and watched her as she ladled out some lentil soup in a wooden bowl. She placed it in front of him and smiled again. But he could see it was forced. Something was wrong.

Sophia suddenly turned her back to him and said, "I'm not feeling well. I have to lie down."

"Of course. Please do." As Judas watched her walk out and over to their bedroom, he felt his stomach drop with dread.

What was wrong? What was...

Wait a minute! Could she be with child?

Judas got up and walked over to the bedroom with hope.

Looking in, he saw Sophia on the bed, her back turned to him, her body shaking with suppressed weeping.

"Sophia," he whispered, sitting on the bed beside her. He placed his hand on her shoulder with painful empathy. "What is wrong, my beloved?"

Now her weeping was not held back. It was as though his words opened a floodgate of emotion. Of pain.

He waited for her to calm.

Sophia wiped her eyes and nose. She looked up at him and said, "You should not have married me."

Oh no. Judas had been right. Marriage was a disappointment to her. He was not enough for her.

But something deeper rose up inside him. He would become enough. He loved her more than life itself. He would fight for her.

Judas whispered to her, "I would marry you all over again." He paused. "And again."

He smiled with all the love in his heart for her.

Sophia searched his eyes. She whispered back, "I cannot get pregnant. I cannot give you a son."

His smile turned to a frown of confusion. "*That* is your concern?"

"Yes. Is it not yours?"

Judas laughed a little with surprise. "Sophia, we have only been married just over a month. I think it's too early to conclude you are barren."

"No," Sophia said. "Something is not right. I can feel it. I waited too long. And now I'm lost forever."

"What do you mean?" Judas asked.

"Ever since I was young, I wanted to leave a legacy in this world. Like my father. Like Diotema of Mantinea."

He smiled again. "Athenian pride."

"Diotema, she instructed Socrates."

Judas raised his brow. "Well, that is something."

Sophia began to tear up again. "Man's glory. Chasing the wind. It took me too long to realize she was a fictional character created by Plato. I believed a fiction. And now, the only legacy I want is to provide you a family for God's glory. To build God's family, his kingdom. But I can't."

"Sophia, it is still too early to tell. Have patience."

"In the last few years, I have had problems with my monthly issue. Something is not right."

Judas smiled lovingly at her. "Do you know what I think?"

Sophia looked to him for something, anything.

He said, "I think that you think too much."

It threw her for a second. Then she appeared to realize it was a loving tease. She smiled through her tears and playfully slapped him.

Judas got serious. "Sophia of Athens and Jerusalem, I chose you because you are a woman of beauty, integrity, intelligence, honor, and faith. And if Adonai so decrees to leave us barren for the rest of our lives, then I will treasure all the time I will have with you alone."

She teared up again, but this time with joy. He continued, "And if Adonai so decrees us to have a dozen children together, there is nothing you can do to stop him."

Sophia slapped his arm playfully. "So you would not want another wife, like Abraham, Isaac, or Jacob?"

"Are you jesting with me?" he demanded with mock seriousness. "You are all I can handle, woman."

She grinned. "Then it seems we better get at it again, Mr. Hammer, if we are going to need a dozen children."

She grabbed his chin and drew him to her to kiss.

They drank deeply of each other.

CHAPTER 24

Menelaus was exhausted as he checked the sheep in their pens for bodily defects before the evening sacrifice in the temple. It was his duty to preside over the daily morning and evening sacrifices called the *tamid*. Though the high priest could choose to be involved in any of the priestly duties for the tamid, Menelaus kept to the minimum of merely overseeing the rituals. They were so tedious to him. He wished he could appoint a proxy for himself so he could spend his time on the political governance of the city and nation.

He also despised the high priest vestments he had to wear. They were uncomfortable and cumbersome. They were twice the number of garments that normal priests wore and heavier with embroidered colors. Golden thread and plating were an emphasis in the material because of the spiritual symbolism of gold, the metal of heaven.

It was hard to bend down and check the sheep's skin because of the stiff ephod he wore beneath his dark-blue robe. The ephod carried the unique breastplate with twelve gemstones arranged in a square representing the twelve tribes of Israel. He also had to be careful his extra-large white turban would not fall off his head if he leaned over too much.

And then there was the Ziz, or golden plate on his forehead, inscribed with the phrase, "Holy unto YHWH." That one in particular gave him a creepy feeling as if he was being watched by God. Menelaus saw his position as holy but certainly not himself.

He wrinkled his nose at the smell of the sheep pen with all the animal odor and excrement. He couldn't wait to get out of there.

He managed to get back up and make his way to the temple building followed by three assistant priests. With every step he made, the sound of tinkling bells at the bottom hem of his robe alerted everyone to his presence and location—constantly. The bells had become like crying little children to him, intolerable noisemakers he wished would just shut up.

Menelaus passed the large altar of burnt sacrifice that stood out front of the entrance to the temple building. It was the most prominent object in the inner courtyard at thirty feet square, fifteen feet high, and made of stones unhewn by iron tools. Priests shoveled out the coals and remains of the morning sacrifice, then started a new fire with fig-tree wood.

The huge bronze laver, or basin, called the "Molten Sea" stood to the right of the altar, where the priests would wash themselves with water pouring from the mouths of twelve colossal oxen that held up the laver.

The temple and its services were a symbolic representation of the cosmos. The altar represented the earth. The sea of bronze was the sea. The temple building was the Garden of Eden, a mirror of Adonai's temple in heaven. The high priest was a symbol of Adam, God's own image on earth. As Adam tended and kept the Garden, so the high priest and his entourage tended and kept the temple. The Menorah candelabrum inside the Holy Place stood like a Tree of Life before the very presence of Ha Shem in the Holy of Holies, veiled by a curtain with images of cherubim guarding the throne. The sacrificial system was a way for the people of Israel to be regularly cleansed of their sin and allowed back into the holy presence of the God from whom they were exiled like Adam. In a way, the land of Israel, the Land of Promise, was the Garden of God's presence.

Though Menelaus knew all of this rich meaning behind his rituals, he didn't really believe it. He had seen inside the Holy of Holies, and Ha Shem was not there. There was no Shekinah pillar of cloud or fire.

No ark of the covenant. Nothing. Only the recent statue of cherubim he himself had created and placed there.

No, Menelaus had long ago concluded that his entire religion *was* the act of creation, creating his people's purpose and existence in the world. And it was a world of kingdoms led by Greek and Roman gods, themselves also systems of creating meaning and justifying dominion. Everything was power.

But Menelaus knew you had to work within the kingdom systems to get what you wanted. With the help of a little luck, that was why he had become the high priest.

Three blasts from silver trumpets summoned the priests and announced to the city the sacrifice was to begin. The gates to the Holy Place were opened to the priests, and the gates to the city were opened to any citizens who wanted to enter the temple grounds to watch. There were twelve gates all around the city walls, seven of them alone on the temple mount. An entire clan of priests was responsible for those gates, opening, closing, and protecting.

Now several things took place simultaneously. First, inside the Holy Place priests trimmed and refilled five of the seven lamps of the huge Menorah, that Tree of Life, the "light of the world." This lampstand was kept perpetually burning day and night by the priests. It was never allowed to burn out.

Second, another priest lit incense of sweet spices and frankincense on the bronze altar of incense. The smoke and scent drifted upward like prayers of the holy ones.

Third, the high priest presided over the slaying of the sacrificial lamb, an unblemished male lamb, next to the altar of burnt sacrifice. The little creature's bodily perfection was symbolic of pure innocence meant to be a substitutionary sacrifice for the people. For only such clean purity could absorb the sins of the unclean many. The innocent in place of the guilty.

A priest drew a blade across the gullet of the lamb as another priest caught its blood in a golden bowl.

The high priest then took the bowl and sprinkled blood from it onto the four horns of the altar. He poured the rest at the foot of the altar into a channel in the stone. The life was in the blood. So it was the pouring out and sprinkling of blood that could cover death.

Another priest butchered the lamb with a blade and threw the pieces into the fire of the burnt sacrifice. Atonement was made.

And all this done two times a day, every day, forever—or rather, as long as the temple stood.

Now came Menelaus's most dreaded part. He read the Ten Words aloud to the audience outside the temple, and everyone recited the Shema. "Hear, O Israel: the Lord our God, the Lord is one. You shall love the Lord your God with all your heart and with all your soul and with all your might."

Menelaus felt false every time he said those words. He had to remind himself there was no other way to help others out of their delusion but to temporarily play along with the delusion, to steer them incrementally in the right direction.

They recited several prayers as an assembly. Then a priest said the blessing over them. "The Lord bless you and keep you. The Lord make his face to shine upon you and be gracious to you. The Lord lift up his countenance upon you and give you peace."

As Menelaus was finishing the liturgy, he saw out of the corner of his eye his brother Simon, captain of the temple guard, anxiously waiting to approach him.

The silver trumpets blew. Then a choir of a hundred singers standing on the steps to the outer temple began to sing psalms accompanied by instruments of drums, cymbals, tambourines, flutes, and lyres. It was all so annoyingly loud to Menelaus.

Simon ran over to his brother and shouted in his ear. "We have received a dispatch that King Antiochus Epiphanes is dead in Egypt."

Menelaus felt as though he had been hit by a war hammer in the gut. "How?"

"It does not say. But evidently, Jason the Oniad has also heard and is marching upon Jerusalem right now with a thousand men from Ammon."

Menelaus knew exactly what Jason was thinking. Without the protection of Antiochus, Menelaus was vulnerable to overthrow for Jason to recapture the high priesthood over Israel.

He shouted back to Simon, "Quickly, seal all the temple and city gates and prepare the temple guard to protect the walls. I will contact the Syrian forces in the Akra."

Simon nodded vigorously and left him.

Menelaus cursed Antiochus in his heart. *Why would he go and die on me like that? Just when I was consolidating my power.*

CHAPTER 25

Judas and Sophia were awakened by a pounding on their house door. Judas picked up a dagger and held it ready as he approached the door in the dark.

He opened it to his brother John, who was dressed in light leather armor with his war hammer in hand. Outside, Judas could hear the sounds of battle up on the hill of the Akra not far away.

John yelped, "The temple is under attack."

"By whom?"

"Jason ben Onias. He has come out of hiding in the Transjordan with a small army. They burned the Sheep Gate on the north of the temple mount."

"No surprise," said Judas. "The weakest gate."

"Menelaus drew them out of the temple, and there is fighting at the Akra fortress. Family meeting at father's. Hurry."

John disappeared into the night.

Judas turned to see Sophia behind him, having heard it all.

Judas and Sophia arrived at his father's house to see the others already there. Father and mother, the four brothers, the two wives of John and Simon, and the old scribe Eleazar. Judas joined the men in the center of the courtyard. The women sat at the outer edge beneath the roof but within hearing range.

Judas asked, "What is the latest intelligence?"

His father responded, "Menelaus is besieged inside the walls of the Akra by Jason's forces. Menelaus has about three hundred temple guards and as many of the Seleucid garrison with him. Jason has about a thousand men outside. They will not be successful trying to breach the Akra. It's a solid fortress."

"This is a battle over the high priesthood," the old scribe commented.

Mattathiah frowned. "It will surely bleed into the population."

"I have done some reconnaissance at the temple mount," John said. "Evidently, hasidim are gathering to attack Jason from behind. They hate him as much as they hate Menelaus."

"We have a civil war on our hands," said Simon.

Judas added, "And when Antiochus hears of it, there will be hell to pay. For all of us."

Mattathiah concluded, "We should get the women and children safely back to Modein."

"Should we come back?" asked John.

"We take care of our families first," said Judas. "Then we can consider our course of action."

Simon glared at Judas. "Will you come back with us if we do?"

Judas was a man without sides in this religious battle.

"I want to protect our families first," he said, glaring back at his brother.

"Judas is right," said Mattathiah. "If we get involved, take sides, we will contribute to a civil war that divides our people."

Judas said to Simon, "You have said yourself that Jason is no less corrupt than Menelaus. Who would you fight for?"

"We may have no choice," said John. "The hasidim have appealed to our family to join them."

A moment of silence pervaded the gathering.

The elder Eleazar offered, "The hasidim stand against both Jason and Menelaus. But they are not organized. Without a leader, they are doomed to fail."

Sophia's voice interrupted from the outer colonnade. "Antiochus will see no difference between rebels and defenders. We're all the same Jews to him."

The men were shocked by her interruption. Simon looked at Judas. "I think you need to acquaint your Greek wife with our Jewish ways of men and women and counsel."

Judas stood, ready to fight. "Apologize to my wife."

Mattathiah broke in. "Now is not the time for family squabbles. The violence in the city is growing."

Sitting next to Judas, Big John placed his hand gently on Judas's shoulder. He sat back down.

"Forgive me, Simon," Sophia said apologetically. "I presumed I was allowed to speak. In Athens, I wouldn't even be allowed to be here."

Another moment of silence was broken by Simon laughing, his hands raised in mock surrender. "No, I apologize, Sophia."

He looked back at Judas and said, "I should have remembered the Greeks are far worse toward their women."

"And she is correct," added Judas. "The only concern of Antiochus is to suppress dissent."

"There is one other thing," said John. "There are rumors that the reason for Jason's attack on Menelaus is because King Antiochus is dead in Egypt."

"Rumors?" asked Mattathiah.

"Yes."

Simon said, "If that is true, then we will have to take a side, choose the lesser of two evils."

"I reject both evils," said Judas.

"This is the imperfect real world," said Simon. "Not the perfect world of ideas."

Judas broke the deadlock. "Father, what is your decision?" Everyone looked to the patriarch for his lead.

Mattathiah had been considering everything with a furrowed brow of concern. Finally, he said, "This is our scheduled week of service for the temple. I will not abdicate our sacred responsibility to Ha Shem regardless of the danger. Our forefathers did not, and we will not. And I will not trust rumors. At this point, the fight is contained to the Akra between Menelaus and Jason, not the city. We will stay, perform our temple duties as we are able."

He looked at Judas, "If the fighting spreads, we will bring our families to Modein for safekeeping, then return if we have to. When we know the truth over rumors, then we will reconsider our options."

The brothers displayed varying expressions of approval and disapproval. But they all deferred to their father's leadership.

CHAPTER 26

Cape Tainaron, Greece

Heracles climbed over the large boulders that formed the rocky barren peninsula of the cape on the southernmost tip of mainland Greece. A mile behind him, the city of Taenarum bustled with activity for the day. Fish markets. Marble workers harvesting the unique green marble of the area. Dye manufacturers extracting the highly coveted purple dye from murex snails off the coast.

He felt the cool salty sea breeze on his bare skin, though this time he was clad in a full woolen battle tunic with leather belt beneath his Nemean Lion skin. On his feet he now wore leather boots. He carried no weapons because this labor required his bare hands. But he had a large adamantine chain draped over his shoulders for the new creature he was supposed to capture alive. He had been assured that the diamond-like substance of adamantine would be effective at restraining the chthonic beast.

Pausing for breath, Heracles gazed upon the temple of Poseidon at the very top of the mountain he was climbing. Its distant vaulted roof and columns of green marble glittered in the afternoon sun. His mind was drawn back to the temple of Demeter in distant Eleusis where he had been initiated into the Eleusinian Mysteries as a younger man. The Mysteries were a kind of death and rebirth. They had been required by his heavenly father to enable Heracles to be more sensitive to the unseen realm around him. It was part of the reason why he could see spiritual creatures that normal humans could not and was no doubt part of his preparation for his descent into the underworld, his current destination.

The Mysteries had been kept secret for hundreds of years to all but the initiated. They were organized around the story of Persephone's abduction by Hades and her ultimate return to Demeter. It had involved a pilgrimage from Athens to nearby Eleusis, fasting, sacrifices, and secret rituals of things done, things seen, and things said. The climax of it all for Heracles had occurred in the Telesterion, the great hall and sanctuary, where he had drunk the kykeon drink made from barley, poppy, and ergot fungus.

After drinking, Heracles had experienced visions of gods, the underworld, the afterlife, and other dreamlike phantasms. After that rebirth, Heracles had felt more in touch with the spiritual world around him and the beings of that world. He even carried some of the ergot fungus in a small pouch with him along with some sacred mushrooms the priests used in their rituals.

Heracles stood at the entrance of a cave still some distance from the temple above. He took a deep breath before entering the opening and beginning the descent on a pathway barely wide enough for his six-foot, muscle-bound figure. The path was steep, and darkness quickly enveloped him.

He took a pinch of the fungus from his satchel because even though his eyes were more capable in darkness than normal humans, the fungus gave him clearer sight in this underworld of death.

At length, he came upon a large cavern covered with luminescent moss. The lighting effect was a green-blue cast to everything as he looked around. Before him was a small creek of water trickling through the crevices of the underground cave. At the other end of the cavern, he could see another tunnel opening leading deeper into darkness.

A large shadow stood sentinel over the opening. It had three heads, and Heracles could hear its canine growl even at this distance. This was his target. Cerberus, the Hound of Hades, the threshold guardian of the dead.

But it struck him how unlike this world was from the stories he had heard of the underworld and the visions he had experienced. This was just an unimpressive simple cavern. Where was the River Styx? The famous gates of Acheron that Cerberus guarded? Where was the palace of Hades and the Elysian fields of paradise?

As soon as Heracles began ruminating over this incongruity, he felt dizzy. The environment around him began to change shape before his eyes. The cavern walls dissolved into an infinity of space. The creek before him seemed to fill with a flood and become a river wide enough to cross on boat. The dark opening across the way transformed into thirty-foot-tall gates of bronze with Cerberus guarding them from escaping souls. A series of huge but dead terebinth trees broke out of the ground like skeletal hands reaching for heaven. They lined a path toward the doors.

Now, this was more like it. Heracles looked at the residue of fungus on his fingers and rubbed them together. He shrugged and licked the rest of it off his skin, then stepped into the river. He was not going to wait for Charon's boat to take him across. He wasn't afraid of any of this. He was the mighty Heracles, son of a god. Half god, half man.

He dove into the current and cut through the water with minimal effort. Getting out on the other bank, he continued on toward the hound.

When he arrived at the huge bronze gates, Heracles could see that they were engraved with sculptures of intertwined human bodies all the way up the entire thirty-foot height. They were like a locked mass of human flesh trying to escape bondage. And he could see that these were living sculptures! They were moving, writhing human forms that could not break free.

"Ho Hurrah!" Heracles laughed. He looked down into the three growling snouts of Cerberus, who looked more wolf than dog. Its hair was long, black, and wild, its teeth dragon-sharp and three times as many. The beast was twice the size of Heracles, who could now see that its tail was a living angry serpent ready to strike.

Heracles belted out another laugh. He was thinking what he would have given to have his club right now.

The canine pounced.

Heracles raised his left arm instinctively. It was wrapped with the lion skin.

Two dog jaws clamped down hard on his forearm. But their teeth could not penetrate.

And fortunately, Heracles was right-handed.

He gave a side-winding punch on the third head so hard it knocked the thing unconscious. Ripping the other jaws from his arm, he launched the beast onto the ground.

But the beast's teeth were still locked on the lion skin, and his action had yanked the skin from Heracles's body.

He was now vulnerable.

Pulling the adamantine chain from his shoulders, Heracles wrapped two ends around his fists.

He crouched defensively, facing the dog.

It was not as stable with one of its heads unconscious. So it backed up protectively.

Looking down, Heracles saw the lion skin beneath the paws of the hell hound. No chance to get it back.

Cerberus attacked again.

Heracles raised the chain in front of him as the monster's teeth clamped down hard at his face.

The force pushed him to his back on the ground, knocking the wind out of him.

The two sets of chomping teeth held tight to the chain. He could smell and feel the animal's hot rancid breath on him—and the sting of serpent bites to his legs from the dog's venomous tail.

The dog's jaw was like a vise. So Heracles jerked the chain as high as his arms could go, raising the two conscious heads, and flung the dog's body over his head with all that was in him.

The snarling beast flipped over Heracles and onto its back on the ground. Heracles heard the thing whine with some pain, but the teeth were still gripping the chain.

So he pulled back with the quickest jerk he could and all his force. The chain came free. The sound of multiple teeth shattering assured Heracles that he had accomplished his goal.

He rolled around and up to his feet to see the beast writhing in pain. Two bloody mouths now possessed only half their teeth.

But now the third head had revived. And it was angrier than ever.

Heracles felt his right leg falter and become limp. His hamstrings and calf burned from the targeted serpent bites.

Releasing the chain from his left hand, Heracles swung it, wrapping it around the mad dog's neck.

The other two heads whined in defeat. But the mad head was not going to stop.

Heracles looked overhead. He was below one of the terebinth trees with its dead groping branches.

He had one chance. The barking dog ran toward him. Heracles threw the chain up over a branch six feet above him. The chain looped the branch and fell back down. He jumped up—just as Cerberus was pouncing.

Grabbing the chain, Heracles fell back down to the ground. The chain pulled the chomping dog's neck up and away from Heracles's face.

It gasped for breath, hanging with all its weight on the chain. The serpent tail could no longer reach Heracles. And the mad dog choked out.

Heracles let the thing fall to the ground in a heap. He would use the chain to secure it and bring it back to his benefactor alive.

But first he had to catch his breath and wrap up his wounded, limping leg.

Then he would prepare for his climactic final labor.

CHAPTER 27

Alexandria

The sun god Ra arrived soaking wet at one of the side gates of the city, where he was secretly let in by the hippo goddess Tawaret. He was exhausted from his lengthy journey through territory occupied by enemy armies. Though humans could not see or hear him in the heavenly realm, the gods of Greece had the city surrounded and were patrolling the area as well. So he'd had to crawl on his belly at times and wait for hours before he could move. His final path was to swim across Lake Mareotis to get to this gate on its outer bank.

Ra met with Amun, Horus, Montu, and Osiris at the western wall. They faced Zeus and his brother Hades, who stood together in Hades's frightening underworld chariot below. In Egypt, Osiris was the counterpart to the Greek Hades, god of the underworld, Lord of the Dead. His green-skinned body was wrapped in white linen cloth. He wore an elongated Egyptian atef crown and carried a crook and flail that hosted occultic power. Like Hades, he could summon the awesome denizens of the underworld. Their face-off in the midst of the necropolis threatened a battle of the living dead.

But it was the appearance of Ra on the battlement that had clearly unsettled the Olympians below.

Ra whispered to Osiris, "Go retrieve Serapis and the Canaanite deities. I want to make a show of force that will humble these barbarians."

Osiris left them.

Ra turned back to his besiegers and exclaimed, "Surprised to see me?"

Zeus took no pains to hide their espionage. He demanded, "Where is Set?"

"I left him in the coils of Apophis, who decided to show up on our Nile journey with a little chaos to spoil your plans. I make no pretense. I was lucky to get away. But I am afraid you will not have the benefit of my betrayer, the mightiest of warriors, on your side."

Osiris made his way to the Serapeum in the western district nearby. It was a temple for Serapis as the city's patron deity that rivaled that of Ptah's in Memphis. A large quadrangle plaza surrounded by colonnaded walls. Osiris marched up the rampway of the elevated mound that created an artificial "holy mountain." The large courtyard hosted the temple at one end and two large obelisks by animal pens for sacrifices at the other end of the pavilion.

When Osiris entered, he was surprised to see so many humans filling the entire premises engaged in rituals and prayer. It threw him off. He knew they would be praying for the city and success, but he had never seen this many before.

He saw Serapis, Anat, and Resheph drinking deep of the blood of sacrifices at the altar outside the columned temple.

He drew near to some of the worshippers and heard their prayers. They were not prayers for the empowerment of the divine defenders of the city. They were prayers for their defeat.

Out on the western battlement, the principalities continued their face-off in the unseen realm. Ra looked down from the wall, still confident despite their loss of Set. But at least the Greek gods didn't have him either.

Zeus said, "It's over, Ra. We are here to negotiate peace."

Ra replied, "You are here to force unconditional surrender and total subjugation."

"Well, yes, that too," Zeus admitted. "But unless you want mass destruction and the total incapacitation of the most important harbor port for the whole of Egypt, you had better consider our terms."

Ra said, "We still outnumber you, and we are still secure behind these walls."

Zeus grinned maliciously. "Are you sure about that?"

Ra looked to Amun for assurance.

Amun had none to give. He muttered, "He said that when we assumed you would arrive safely with Set."

Zeus gave a distinct two-handed whistle that carried on the wind into the city.

A dread filled Ra. He and the others looked around the outside walls for an approaching ally, maybe a creature of some kind.

But there was nothing.

The Greek armies remained in their camp resting and doing chores around the grounds.

Ra said to Zeus, "A dog-whistle for Cerberus? Wait until you meet our underworld pet, Ammut."

The Egyptian deities glanced confidently at one another. Ammut was called "Devourer of Souls," a hybrid animal of hippopotamus hind, forequarters of a lion, and head of a crocodile. It was a ferocious beast that easily equaled the fierceness of Cerberus, the three-headed hound of Hades.

Ra discovered that Zeus was not in fact dog-whistling for Cerberus when the solar god heard a return whistle behind him in the city.

The gods turned to see on the street below them Serapis and the Canaanite gods Anat and Resheph dressed in armor and standing over the remains of Osiris and Ammut.

A wheelbarrow contained the dismembered body parts of Osiris in his white linen wrap, now deep-red with blood. The young goddess Anat stood with a diabolical grin, her body drenched in the gore. She shouted out, "Oh, mighty Ra, we have a royal puzzle for you to put together. Set had told me that fourteen pieces was the number, am I right?"

In the founding myth, Set was said to have cut his brother Osiris up into fourteen pieces out of jealousy for the throne.

Ra said nothing. As for Ammut, the fierce beast's snout was chained shut and his legs tied up on a pole like a pig for roasting.

Serapis slapped his hand on the whining mutt and said, "I suspect the Greek gods would be more interested in *eating* Ammut than *meeting* Ammut."

Ra felt a chill run through his flesh as he realized that Serapis, Anat, and Resheph had double-crossed their Egyptian citizenship for their Greek overlords.

The gods of Egypt were now in the hands of a coup with the mutineers in their midst splitting them from their fellow divine generals inside the city. They were surrounded and infiltrated.

They were defeated before they could fight.

• • • • •

Antiochus Epiphanes had been waiting anxiously for the arrival of the Roman delegation to his camp in Eleusis outside the city walls of Alexandria. Finally, the moment he had been waiting for, the answer to his request for affirmation sent through his own ambassadors to Rome.

He had received word from his ships guarding the harbor and had done his best to make the meeting a pleasant experience. He made the soldiers clean up and present themselves in columns of order as the envoy came through camp. The cavalry stood at attention, armored horsemen and their steeds gloriously displaying Seleucid pride.

Antiochus had put on a special purple toga he had brought along to express cordiality with Rome as well as purple socks in his open-toed sandals. On his newly cut hair, he wore his portable golden wreathed crown reminiscent of Apollo's own. He had brought with him two of his King's Friends, Timarchus and Heraclides, as well as his generals, Apollonius, Seron, and Lysias. At the king's request, they all wore togas and stood in an expectant line at attention in the open agora that Antiochus had repurposed for this meeting.

Newly appointed senate consul Gaius Popilius Laenas approached Antiochus with two fellow politicians representing the Roman Senate. They were guarded by a small cohort of fifty legionaries. In his sixties with cropped gray hair, Popilius wore a senatorial toga with red stripes. He carried a walking stick and a folded tablet made of bronze.

Antiochus had known Popilius from his time as a hostage in Rome and smiled widely as he approached. When he did not receive a smile in return, a foreboding feeling came over him. He reached out his hand to greet the consul. "Popilius, how good to see you. May I invite you to a delicious feast I have prepared in my private tent?"

Popilius did not answer, and he did not reach out his hand in greeting. Instead, he offered the writing tablet to Antiochus. "Read this first."

Surprised and off-balance, Antiochus opened the bronze tablet and read. It was a Senatus Consultum, a decree of the Roman senate with binding authority. It stated that Rome had just won the battle of Pydna, which finished their long wars with Macedon. They were no longer distracted and were free to focus on their interests in Egypt. They commanded Antiochus to cease and desist from all hostilities with Ptolemy and return to Syria within a fortnight or consider himself at enmity with Rome.

The decree was shocking and direct. If Antiochus ignored this command, he would find himself at war on two fronts, Egypt and Rome, something he could not sustain. But immediate and total withdrawal would make him look weak to the Ptolemies and other enemies. He wanted to figure out how he could strategically withdraw and save face, so he told Popilius, "I will call my friends into counsel and consider what I will do."

Popilius stared at him, his expression unsatisfied. Then the consul held his stick out and stuck it into the sand at Antiochus's feet. He walked slowly around the king, drawing a circle in the sand as he went.

Returning to face Antiochus, he said in a cold tone, "Before you step out of that circle, give me a reply to lay before the senate."

Antiochus looked with shock into Popilius's eyes. He could see that the consul was completely sincere and resolute. At that moment, Antiochus realized that his hopes and dreams for expansion of his hegemony over the South, his plans for owning the riches of Alexandria were all crushed into hopeless defeat. All the years of wars with Egypt were a complete waste of time and resources. And there was nothing he could do about it. He had no opportunity to negotiate or even save face. He either submitted to Rome or fought a war with her. A war he could not win.

Swallowing hard in his dry throat, Antiochus said with a humble voice, "I will do what the senate thinks right."

Now, finally, Popilius smiled. He offered his hand to shake. He asked jovially, "Now where is that meal you promised? I'm famished."

It amazed Antiochus how ruthless to her opponents Rome could be and yet how promptly just and fair to her clients.

As Antiochus led Popilius to the banquet tent, the consul commented, "You are not looking well, Antiochus. You seem—gaunt."

Of course he was getting gaunt. Antiochus had been eating less lately to avoid his intestinal pain, which by now had become relentless. He cringed at the sharp pain in his gut.

On the way to the banquet, his Samaritan general Apollonius stepped up beside Antiochus and whispered, "My king, I have received word from Menelaus in Jerusalem. There is a revolt in the city. The high priest Menelaus is confined in the Akra fortress under siege by other Jews. He requests your help."

Antiochus's blood boiled with rage. He had just been humiliated into submission by a bullying Rome, and now this. He felt like he wanted to take out his frustration on someone, something, anything.

"Gods damn those Jews," Antiochus muttered. "They never got rid of their Ptolemaic affections or their ridiculous religious exemptions they extorted from my father. They think they can rebel and become independent. I think it's time that godforsaken den of thieves learns a lesson about who is king."

•••••

In a secret dungeon below the Serapeum, Zeus, Hades, and their turncoat allies, Serapis, Anat, and Resheph, began the process of interrogating their Egyptian captives, Ra, Amun, Horus, and Montu. The Egyptian gods were strung up naked with their arms and legs spread out in an X formation against the walls. Osiris would not be a problem, lying as he did in pieces in a wheelbarrow. Ammut was still hogtied over in the corner of the stone-walled prison, his ravenous mouth chained shut. The other Egyptian gods on the north side of the city above would not even realize what was going on beneath their feet until it was too late.

Ra, now with human form, had already had his skin flayed from his body by the deft handiwork of Anat's blades. His angelic musculature was bloody raw, and the Watcher was moaning softly beneath his tightly-gagged mouth. His painful screaming during the flaying had annoyed Zeus, like fingernails down a piece of slate rock. It took a cunning mind to figure out the right torture for beings who could not die but could feel pain through supernatural weapons and devices. Unlike humans, their angelic flesh could regenerate with preternatural healing. But even that required some time—and it required connection to their heads. They were, after all, created beings.

Zeus had become impatient with Ra. "I must say, your endurance is quite impressive. You have earned your title as the Egyptian king of the gods. I will even let you return to your throne as my puppet king. But only if you tell me why you have made it so easy to take the city."

It had bothered Zeus that Ra had foolishly boasted about outnumbering the Greek gods, yet they had only posted four Watchers on the western walls, four on the eastern wall, and Sobek alone to guard the harbor. With the sheer number of Egyptian divinities in the pantheon, that was like inviting them into the city—no doubt for some kind of ambush.

Ra glared silently at him.

Zeus said, "I understand why you would not have shared your strategy with the Canaanite deities. After all, they are foreign hybrids, and they *did* betray you. Still, it was a bit rude if you ask me."

Ra remained quiet.

Zeus stepped back and nodded to Anat, who withdrew one of her swords and placed it at the chest of Amun.

"Now, if I remember correctly," Zeus said to Ra, "your mythology of the underworld is a rather creative one. Your Egyptian Book of the Dead says that souls are judged before the throne of Osiris, Lord of the Dead. But since Osiris is a bit incapacitated at the moment, I think it's time for my brother to take over."

Hades grinned as he raised his battle kilt and pissed on the parts of Osiris in the barrow.

Zeus continued, "It is now time for you to be judged by your own tradition. And we will start with your next-in-command, Amun. Or is it Amun-Ra? Whatever the case, *you*."

Zeus could see Amun become more agitated with fright as he stared into his eyes. "Now, that tradition says that the heart of the judged must be cut out in order to weigh it for justice."

He nodded at Anat, who rammed her sword into Amun's chest and cut downward to open a large gash. He screamed in utter agony.

She stepped back. Hades plunged his hand into Amun's chest cavity and ripped out his heart. Amun went unconscious with the loss of his vital organ. But he was not dead. And the heart still pumped with its muscle memory.

Zeus walked over to the hanging Horus and plucked a feather from his head. He handed it to Hades, who held the feather in one hand and the heart in the other.

Zeus said, "Now according to your narrative, the heart is weighed against Maat, the feather of justice, on the scales of judgment."

Hades began raising his hands up and down as if he were the scale rendering judgment.

"If the heart weighs less than the feather, the individual allegedly is free to roam the Field of Reeds paradise in Duat. Which does not sound as impressive to me as our own Elysian Fields of Hades, but they're just made-up stories anyway."

Hades kept moving his arms up and down in indecision.

"But if the heart weighs more than the feather of Maat, well, that is not good for the individual, you see, because that means he is deemed impure."

Hades now slowed down the balancing until his hand holding the heart "outweighed" his hand holding the feather.

"Surprise. Your heart is too heavy. But surprise to me when I found out that your Book of the Dead proclaims that heavy hearts are eaten by Ammut."

Hades moved over and unmuzzled Ammut, whose voracious mouth could not help but grind with desire to eat the heart that Hades handed to it.

He chomped it twice, then gobbled it whole like a starved alligator.

Ra, Horus, and Montu all whimpered in fear. They knew what that meant.

Zeus leaned in and whispered in Ra's ear, "You will tell me or I will feed your hearts to this freakish mutant, cut all of you up into pieces, and distribute you to the four corners of the earth."

Ra's eyes went wide with panic. Their immortal bodily pieces would continue to live, but without the head attached, their flesh would not regenerate, and they would live eternally in a prison of perpetual dismemberment.

"If you tell me, you will all retain your positions here in service to me. It's your choice."

Zeus gave a toothy grin as he waited for Ra to speak.

Ra's croaking reluctant voice broke the silence. "We have a circle of magic in the center of the city created by Heka the god of magic, Isis, and the Ogdoad."

Zeus knew the Ogdoad as eight primeval deities of chaos and creation. Together with Heka and Isis, they could bring up primordial darkness and waters that had the potential of swallowing the Olympians into the Abyss. Or so the rumors went.

Zeus asked through clenched teeth, "And how do we break that circle of magic?"

Ra did not get a chance to speak because Serapis flew against the stone wall behind Zeus with such force that the wall crumbled and the foundation shook. The otherwise muscular bully had been overwhelmed by something far more powerful than he was.

Zeus turned to see the divine daemon Sammael in the entrance, flanked by the Roman gods Jupiter, Mars, Pluto, and Neptune, the Roman equivalents of Zeus, Ares, Hades, and Poseidon. They looked similar as well. The Romans were masters of absorption and subversion.

Anat dropped her swords to the ground in immediate surrender. Hades and Resheph bowed their heads, averting their eyes in submission. Zeus felt his face freeze in shock.

Sammael shook his head with disappointment, clucking his tongue. The Watcher of Rome was not a physically impressive specimen. He was six feet tall, thin and lean, not muscular. His visible gender was androgynous, unclear whether he looked like a feminine male or a masculine female. He liked to blend boundaries and defy the separations of creation. He was bald, pale-skinned, and his body was full of tattoos that seemed to move with occultic animation. His reptilian lapis lazuli eyes blinked sideways. He wore a long purple robe over his royal trimmed Roman toga. His mighty power was based on his forensic knowledge of Torah and legal standing that he had once had in the heavenly court of Yahweh.

He was the Adversary, the satan. He had strategically become the god of the Roman world that was now on the rise of its Republican glory. The power that Sammael and his pantheon exuded was palpable. Zeus felt his own legs go weak. But he managed to stay standing.

Sammael spoke with measured authority. "I am afraid your siege of Alexandria is at an end. It is time for you to return to Syria."

Zeus tried to sound strong. "And what do you offer me in return?"

He knew he could not fight Sammael and the Roman pantheon successfully. And adding the Egyptian pantheon into the conflict would insure total defeat and destruction.

Zeus felt Sammael's eyes judging him for his audacity. The Roman Watcher stepped over to Ra and looked at the suffering captive. He couldn't help but sniff the smell of rotting flesh, his forked tongue flicking in the taste.

"This is what I offer." Sammael said. "I will *not* flay you all like this and cast you into the Abyss for Apophis to consume."

Zeus looked nervously at the other Olympians. No complaint was forthcoming.

Sammael continued, "Egypt is under my protection. Rome needs her grain to survive. There will be no negotiation."

He turned back to Zeus. "Why aren't you looking for the Chosen Seed back in Judea? That is your responsibility."

Zeus sighed. "There has been no sign of the archangels anywhere in Judea."

Sammael sneered with disdain. "Have you bothered to search Jerusalem, the *City of David,* the city of the Seed?"

"With respect, that would be a more difficult siege than Alexandria. The enemy's own fortress."

"Is Yahweh enthroned there anymore?"

"No," Zeus admitted.

"Well then, go and take it, you moron."

Sammael turned and began to leave. He gestured with his long, bony finger. "Release them, take Jerusalem, and do a little destruction. It may flush out the archangels."

Zeus bowed in obedience.

Sammael and his principalities left without even giving a glance back at the Greek king of the gods.

Zeus turned to his comrades. "This stays with us."

CHAPTER 28

Jerusalem

Sophia hummed a psalm to herself as she finished double-checking two sacks of necessities for her and Judas. It had been three weeks since Jason and his Ammonites had besieged Menelaus inside the Akra fortress. The siege was still ongoing but had now become complicated by hasidim Jews, who began fighting attack-and-retreat skirmishes with Jason's soldiers in the streets outside the Akra. There were reports of Ammonite squads venturing out into the residential areas in search of food.

Mattathiah and his sons had asked for a meeting with Jason to plead for the safety of non-combatant citizens. If Jason overthrew Menelaus and became high priest again, surely he would need the support of the other priests or he could not effectively rule. So Mattathiah wanted to convince Jason that the priests were concerned about the people. But Mattathiah had another reason for going. His temple duties were over, and he wanted the assurance of safe travel for his family to return to his hometown of Modein.

Sophia smiled to herself when she considered the similarities and differences of her new Jewish world from her old Athenian one. Priests were respected in Jerusalem as teachers were in Athens. And their wealth was somewhat similar. But Jews were an earthy people compared with Athenian Greeks, who prided themselves on abstraction and reason. Even the spirituality of Judaism was unexpectedly earthy to her. Their rules and rituals, laws and obligations were not restrictions that bound them but embodied performances connecting them to a transcendent Creator.

Greek philosophy on the other hand sought to grasp the underlying order or structure of the universe, what they called the Logos, to attain transcendence—salvation through knowledge. In essence, to attain their own godhood. It was as if the Greeks were seeking a Logos they did not know while the Jews had a loving relationship with that Logos. A father, not an abstraction. A shepherd, not a syllogism. A savior and redeemer, not a tool of power and oppression.

And yet, Sophia could not deny that corruption found its way into the priesthood as much as it had the academy. Human nature was inescapable. But it was not ungovernable. Despite the human frailty of her new cultural home, she felt a freedom from spiritual slavery of both mind and soul.

Sophia was interrupted in her thoughts by a hard pounding of her front door. She froze. Someone was trying to kick the door in. The security bar held at first. Another pounding, and it cracked.

It's midday! she thought, stunned. Who could be so bold as to attempt a break-in in broad daylight? She glanced around for something to reinforce the security bar. If she could grab the dining table and push it up against the door…

Another pounding made her jump. Then she heard voices of multiple men outside laughing and jesting crudely. She stood still like a gazelle ready to leap away at a moment's notice.

This couldn't be happening. Not here. Not to her.

But it did happen. The door crashed inward with the force of a man's body weight. The man stumbled inward, steadied himself, and looked up at Sophia.

He was an Ammonite soldier dressed in leather cuirass and brass helmet and carrying a short sword. Behind him, she could see the entire street was filled with other Ammonites breaking into other houses.

This couldn't be happening. Not to her.

The soldier, a young and handsome one actually, with red hair and fair skin, said with a malicious grin, "I'm so sorry, ma'am. But why didn't you answer the door?"

She hesitated. Women's screams out in the streets shook her. She couldn't breathe.

He took a step closer to her. She backed up.

"Where's your food?" The Ammonite looked her up and down with a sinister smile.

This couldn't be happening. Not to her.

Sophia pointed toward the kitchen. "All we have is over there."

But he didn't go to the kitchen. He didn't even look in that direction. He moved closer to her.

Her back was up against a pillar.

And he was right up to her now. She could feel his breath on her.

"You know what? I'm fighting to free you from your oppressors. I think I deserve some gratitude." The Ammonite reached up and pulled some strands of hair from her face.

This was happening!

Sophia spun around the pillar out of his reach and ran for the stairs. She felt him catch her by the hair and yank her backward. The pain made her yelp. She slammed to the floor.

Rolling to her knees, she scrambled for the door.

He caught her again by her robe.

She fell to her face.

He pulled her back into the courtyard area and ripped off her robe, leaving her linen tunic, which was now hiked up her legs to her thighs.

Sophia saw his rabid eyes look down at her as he started to pull his own tunic up. She kicked at him until he grabbed her legs and spread them, placing himself in between them. She flailed and tried to hit him.

He punched her once, and she fell back, barely conscious, too confused to do anything more. He leaned toward her and hissed, "You don't look like a Jew. What are you, a slave?"

Sophia heard another voice say, "She's my wife."

Through blurry eyes, she saw her assailant fly off of her with a blunt force.

Pulling her tunic down, she sat up to see Judas pounding the Ammonite's face into a bloody pulp.

The violence of it was overwhelming. It certainly helped to relieve the terror that had filled her whole body.

Finally, Judas stopped pummeling and turned to her. "Sophia, are you okay?"

She nodded and croaked out, "It's about time you got back."

He was at her side, stroking her face with his bloody hand. "Forgive me, my love. Please forgive me."

She saw him look behind her out the door. Turning, she saw several Ammonites just outside the entrance watching them with shock.

Judas drew his sword and was out the door in seconds, crashing into them with the force of a war elephant. Two went down, and one drew his sword. But he didn't hold it for long as he was cut down in a flash.

Judas shouted back at Sophia, "Go hide! Now!"

He returned to his battle. Sophia ran up the stairs to the roof. She didn't know where else to go. She didn't want to hide blind in the darkness somewhere, not knowing what was happening. She wanted to see.

Reaching the roof's edge, she looked down to see Judas exchanging sword blows with three other Ammonites. Those were odds an elite Royal Guard could handle however experienced these Ammonite mercenaries.

But what he would not be able to handle was the number of Ammonites who had turned to see Judas and were now beginning to circle him in the street.

At least thirty of them. Ammonite soldiers preparing for revenge.

"Dear Lord, no," prayed Sophia. "Adonai, give him the strength of Abishai." Abishai had been one of David's *gibborim*, or mighty men, who had killed three hundred Philistines in one battle.

Whether or not God heard her prayer for such a miraculous victory, she could see below that Judas was ready to try.

"Judas!" she whispered in silent painful resignation.

And then a loud shout came up the street from behind the Ammonites. It was a war cry.

And there was no mistaking who gave it. Big John the Fortunate.

Behind him were Judas's three other brothers, all bearing weapons, Simon and Jonathan with swords, Eleazar carrying a spear with an extra-large blade.

John swung his mighty hammer at the first men in the circle. They flew into others like broken toys. Within seconds, the brothers were inside the circle beside their brother, facing off against their assailants, the original thirty now reduced to twenty-five.

Bad odds for the Ammonites.

Sophia was oddly unfazed by the violence now. She felt herself transfixed as she watched the brothers defend each other with the force of a small army.

John's war hammer was invincible, smashing bodies and skulls. The swordplay of Judas, Simon, and Jonathan cut down Ammonites like they were standing still. And Eleazar's spear never left his hands as he wielded it with slicing fury.

"There you are, wench," came a gruff voice behind her. Sophia turned to see one of the Ammonite soldiers, a huge, ugly one, emerging from the stairwell onto the roof.

She turned back to the street and yelled, "Judas!" He glanced up at her.

She jerked around to see that the ugly Ammonite had dropped his sword and was approaching her, drooling with his disgusting mouth open, laughing to himself about whatever he was fantasizing of doing with her.

She heard Judas below her yell out, "Sophia! Jump!"

She turned to see him ten feet below holding his arms out to catch her.

She didn't have to think. She trusted him fully and jumped.

Judas caught her in his arms, absorbing the force till she felt the ground.

She was still looking up at the huge Ammonite above when she saw Eleazar's spear pierce him through his engorged belly. He screamed in pain and launched backward on the roof.

Sophia shook her shock out, and Judas helped her up.

She looked around to see the four other brothers standing there looking at her smiling, their bodies covered in blood and gore and all the Ammonites dead at their feet.

"Good jump, Sophia!" John said joyfully.

Simon added, "I wish my wife trusted me as much."

John rustled Simon's hair affectionately, which was not accepted with the same feelings by Simon.

Judas said, "We need to get our families to Modein."

"We cannot leave!" came a voice from behind them. Sophia looked to see Mattathiah panting from his running.

He said through huffed breaths, "It turns out that Antiochus is not dead, and he is approaching Jerusalem right now with an army."

"He is here to crush Jason's rebellion," Judas said. "If we can help him, we may not suffer as collateral damage."

Simon barked, "We must get to the city gates to make sure Jason does not close them!"

Mattathiah said, "I will alert your mother and wives and then our neighbors."

Their father managed to return to a trot as he headed to his own home. The brothers left Judas with Sophia. As he held her in his arms, she looked up at him and said, "Go. I am safe now."

"I will not leave you," he said.

"No one is coming back here, Judas. Jason's men will all be at the gates." Sophia gestured at the sprayed blood, broken door, and overturned possessions that were the result of the fighting. "I will clean up this mess, then go join your mother. Now, go."

Judas kissed her, and his look told her he didn't want to leave. But he followed his duty and ran off to catch up with the others.

CHAPTER 29

Judas caught up with his brothers as they ran to the western Valley Gate, the largest gate most likely to be used for Antiochus's arriving army. Hundreds of hasidim were joining them as they all expected the Ammonite forces of Jason to attempt to secure the gates to keep Antiochus out.

To the surprise of them all, there were no Ammonites to face at the gate or wall. The large, reinforced oak wood gates remained open to receive the arriving king.

Judas heard one of the arriving hasidim yell out, "Jason's army has fled through a northern gate! They are no longer in the city!"

A wave of hurrahs went up through the crowd.

Someone else yelled out, "Put away your weapons! The king is coming!" Everyone did so and knelt in submission.

At the head of the train was the *apantesis* committee, a group of a dozen of the ruling elders of the city who had ridden out to meet the king in submission and escort him back behind the walls.

Judas turned to see Menelaus arrive hurriedly with a small contingent of Seleucid soldiers from the Akra. They had finally left their fortress confines now that the besiegers had fled. The high priest would receive the king with gratitude, humiliated though he was by his inability to put down Jason's revolt.

The welcoming parade was followed by a battalion of hundreds of infantry, then six war elephants. Dozens more of the pachyderms were left outside the walls as they were more conducive to field warfare over city. Next came hundreds of Seleucid infantry, a company of cavalry, and then King Antiochus and his general on horseback. After that came several more divisions of horsemen and infantry followed by archers.

Greeting the king, Menelaus led him through the city streets back to the Akra fortress. The Hasmonean brothers followed with the crowd after the train. The elephants were left outside the gate.

When they arrived at the Akra, trumpets announced the king. His parade stopped before several troop formations of temple guards and Seleucid soldiers lined up outside the fortress.

From his distance a good block away, Judas with his brothers could see King Antiochus talking with Menelaus. The high priest was no doubt telling the king his own twisted version of what had happened here. The fraud lied with every word he spoke.

Eleazar said to the watching brothers, "If the king sends some forces after Jason now, he can easily catch him."

The counsel between king and high priest went on for several minutes. Judas could not always see them at this distance as the crowd jostled with everyone trying to get their own look at the king.

"I can't see a thing!" complained Jonathan, the smallest of the brothers by several inches and almost a foot shorter than Big John's towering height.

"Here you go," said John. He hoisted his younger brother up on his shoulders.

"That's better!" Jonathan exclaimed. "You should be my war elephant!"

Judas commented to his brothers, "Menelaus has been violently opposed to the hasidim, but the hasidim aided him during the siege."

"Do you think this could finally mean a truce between them?" John asked hopefully.

"You are too hopeful, brother," said Simon. "And there is no leader of the hasidim with which to negotiate a truce."

Then they heard the trumpets blow a distinct sound.

Judas knew that sound too well. "That's a call to war."

A commotion began near the king. Infantry had surged around him and were now pushing outward.

Jonathan yelled from his perch, "It's an attack! The Seleucids are attacking the hasidim!"

"They're not all hasidim," shouted a confused John.

"They are killing everyone!" Jonathan reiterated. "Everyone!"

"Why?" shouted John. "It doesn't make sense."

"Let's go," yelled Judas, just in time as a mob of Jews were pushing their way trying to escape.

The brothers ran through the streets and zigzagged back to their homes to get their families.

"Meet at father's!" shouted Judas.

They split up. Judas ran full-tilt through the streets, yelling at people he passed, "Run for your lives! The Greeks are killing everyone! Run and hide!"

He knew many of them didn't have a chance.

But he and his family did. They had planned ahead.

Arriving at his home, he burst inside at a run. The broken door had been propped against a wall, the furnishings restored to their place, and the floor was clean. The two travel sacks they planned to take to Modein were sitting on the dining table.

"Sophia!" he yelled out. "Are you still here?"

She emerged from the bedroom, a folded tunic in her arms. She tucked it into the open mouth of one sack as she said calmly, "I was just about to walk over to your father's home."

She took a closer look at Judas, noting the perspiration on his face, the heaving of his chest from running so hard. "Judas, are you all right?"

"Yes—no!" Judas hurried into the bedroom, where he pulled from a chest an additional sack in which he stored his light armor with his extra weapons. "I am all right, but the city is not. Grab your sack. We're leaving now!"

"Why? What is happening?" Sophia asked with concern.

Hurrying back out, Judas snatched one of the two travel sacks, tossing both sacks over his left shoulder with one hand while he gripped his sword in the other. "The king's forces are killing Jews indiscriminately. Menelaus must have lied to him."

He didn't need to say more. Sophia was already grabbing the other bag. She knew enough about Menelaus to know what he might do. They had talked of it. Killing every possible opposition was no doubt in his mind a way to consolidate power. He was using the chaos of civil war to aid his goal. Menelaus had voiced his motto often. *Never waste a crisis.*

They all met at Mattathiah's home with their wives and children. A dozen of them anxiously standing in the courtyard carrying bags, dressed for flight in heavy cloaks. Judas noticed that Eleazar the scribe was not with them. More importantly, neither was Mattathiah.

"Where is Father?" Judas asked his mother,

"He will be here shortly," she replied. "He has a plan."

"What plan?" demanded Jonathan. "We can't hide forever. They'll go house to house."

"I won't be good at hiding," said Big John.

"We can't use the horses to escape," Judas said tersely. "We'll have to go on foot."

Jonathan said, "Even if we sneak out one of the small gates, they have forces patrolling the walls by now. We'll be picked off."

"We'll have to go through the tunnels," said Eleazar.

"Exactly," said Mattathiah. Everyone turned to see him coming in from the back followed by a middle-aged woman with slight graying hair and a pleasant face they all knew.

"Solomonia!" shouted Jonathan.

She was followed by her sons, seven of them, with ages a few years behind the Hasmonean sons. They had young wives and several children. They had grown up with Judas and his brothers in Modein. Solomonia was widowed, her husband having died last year from a bad heart. But they were also a priestly family who had been close to Mattathiah and Hannah over the years. There was no explanation needed. Mattathiah was saving them with his family.

"What do you mean, tunnels?" asked Sophia.

Judas explained it to her. "There is a network of tunnels beneath the temple and city that only some priests know how to access."

A revelation dawned in her face as she looked at Mattathiah, who placed a comforting hand on her shoulder. "Sophia, I went to the Antiochene quarter and tried to get your father and family to come with me. He told me that they were going to stay under the protection of the Greek administrators of the gymnasium. He said to not worry for them, you are with your husband now."

Judas saw that Sophia was holding back tears with determined will power. He wrapped his arms around her, but she pulled back and proclaimed, "I will not be an impediment to the safety of this group. You heard what my father said. Can these tunnels lead us to safety?"

Judas said, "Some of them lead out of the city and into the surrounding valley, far enough away to avoid detection."

Mattathiah said, "The Seleucid forces have pushed their attack down toward the southern and western portion of the city. That leaves the eastern side of the temple open. If we can make it near the temple mount, I know several access points to the tunnels."

Simon said, "We are a large group of over thirty. We will not be able to hide our journey."

Judas said, "That is why we must leave right now in the middle of the chaos before they lock down the city. If we move swiftly on the outside, we should be able to make it to Modein by morning."

He turned to his father and whispered, "Where is the old man, Eleazar?"

"In the scribal residence in the temple," said Mattathiah. "He wanted to pray there during Jason's siege against Menelaus."

Judas shook his head. *The old man still believes in divine intervention.* He said to his father, "I can pick him up on the way out."

He gave one last glance at Sophia to see that she was holding up. That she was fully cleaved to her husband with all her heart. She did not disappoint him.

CHAPTER 30

In the thick of the night, Judas led his family of twelve and Solomonia's family of fifteen through the back alleys of the city toward the temple. They moved the entire group as quietly as possible, trying not to bring attention. Even the children had been sufficiently quiet and obedient. The sounds of marauding squads of Seleucid soldiers were not far away. They had to move quickly.

Mattathiah was leading them to a hidden door on the east side of the temple. This would lead them upstairs into the temple colonnade that ran around the entire courtyard. Then they would have to make their way to the western side of the temple to the Hall of Hewn Stones. Once inside, the elaborate high priest's chair could be moved to reveal one of the secret access points to tunnels beneath the temple and city.

They were within a hundred yards of the outer temple area wall when they were halted in their tracks by a squad of Seleucid soldiers blocking their route in the street ahead of them.

There was about thirty of them. Judas and his brothers drew their weapons. They could take them, but if they drew the attention of others, they would surely be caught. They had women and children with them and could not move with any real speed.

One of the Seleucids noticed them and pointed their direction, yelling a warning. The other soldiers turned to look at the escaping families.

This is it, Judas thought.

But just as soon as the Seleucids turned toward them, the military unit was attacked from the right by a squad of Jews dressed in armor and dark clothing to blend in with the night. Pockets of resistance seemed foolish to Judas against the overwhelming numbers and discipline of the Seleucids. But there would always be some who tried the impossible.

It was just the diversion they needed. Mattathiah led them down an alley to the right and ultimately around the fighting that now allowed them to find the small hidden passage that led up a flight of steps to the temple area.

They stayed hidden in the shadows of the outer colonnade that wrapped around the entire temple area. Inside the court, some temple guards could be seen patrolling the area. Most of the force had been conscripted by Antiochus to do his bidding in the city.

Judas whispered to Simon and John, "I'm going to get old Eleazar. Meet me inside the Hall of Hewn Stones."

Nodding, the brothers led the couple dozen family members cautiously along the shadows of the outer corridor on their way to the other side of the complex. It would take them some time to get there. Time enough for Judas to join them with the elderly scribe.

Judas ran ahead to the scribal quarters on the north of the building colonnade. Stairs led down to the residence of the temple scribes.

A damp hall led to the quarters lit by torchlight. Poking his head into the doorway, Judas saw about twenty or so scribes unable to sleep because of the turmoil outside the temple. Nobody in the city was sleeping.

Judas whispered, "Eleazar."

He saw the old man turn to see him. He was in a simple woolen robe and tunic. Good. They could slip out quickly.

Eleazar joined him in the dark hall. Judas whispered, "I have the whole family and that of Solomonia. We are escaping through the tunnels beneath the temple."

"I'm not going," replied Eleazar.

"What do you mean, you're not going?"

"I said I'm not going. I want to stay with my brother scribes and face our fate together."

"But we planned for this," complained Judas. "We need to go to Modein now. You are not safe here."

"I'm not going," reiterated Eleazar. "I am too old to run. I have finished my race. But you have not. So, go. Bring your family to safety. I will be fine."

Judas could not believe what he was hearing. "Eleazar, you have been family for my entire life. We are not going without you."

"Young man, you are not my elder. I am yours. And I expect some respect."

Judas knew he was right. He had no authority over the old scribe.

"I don't think the temple is in danger," Eleazar continued. "King Antiochus may be a beast, but he's no fool. He will rob the temple treasury like he did before. But he will not kill those who bring him the treasures."

"He is killing citizens indiscriminately in the city," Judas argued.

Eleazar resigned himself. "I have lived a full life. I have served the Lord with all my heart, mind, soul, and strength. I am not afraid."

"You warned me about the evil that was coming, and now you want to stay when it comes? Running isn't cowardice, Eleazar. Survive to fight another day."

"You should go, Judas," the old man replied. "The prophet Daniel foretold all this. 'The people who know their God shall stand firm and take action. And the wise among the people shall make many understand, though for some days they shall stumble by sword and flame, by captivity and plunder. When they stumble, they shall receive a little help so that they may be refined, purified, and made white.'"

Judas stared into Eleazar's steely eyes. He knew he would not change the scribe's mind. The old man had accepted his fate in the hands of God. Judas embraced him and felt the return of a heartfelt love. He whispered into Eleazar's ear, "Take care, old friend. Have hope."

Eleazar pulled away and looked at Judas with tearful eyes. "Have faith. Then fight another day."

Judas knew the sincerity of his mentor but wondered if he could ever have faith again. If he ever *did* have faith.

He ran off into the shadows.

Back up the stairs and into the courtyard, he followed the colonnade around the perimeter to avoid being seen by the priests and guards in the courtyard.

But when he reached the Hall of Hewn Stones, he pulled back around the corner. Just ahead, a contingent of seven temple guards were loitering around the entrance to the hall.

Of all the luck.

Judas glanced across the colonnade to see a large walled garbage collection pit. Mattathiah and Simon hid in the entrance to the pit, gesturing to Judas.

He slipped over to them unobserved by the guards. Inside the pit were huddled the rest of the two families.

"We need to take out the guards before we are spotted," Simon whispered,

Mattathiah shook his head. "They are brothers, not enemies."

"We won't kill them," Judas agreed,

Eleazar whispered, "What should we do?"

Judas looked into the darkness of the garbage area. There he saw faces of men, women, and children looking at him in the moonlight, frightened, hoping for salvation.

There was only one thing Judas could do.

"Get ready. Don't wait for me." Judas walked around the corner toward the guards. He heard his father whisper angrily after him, "Judas!"

He whispered back, "I won't kill them. But don't wait for me."

Then another voice whispered his name in the wind. It was Sophia. He turned to see her a few yards behind him, eyes pleading.

His heart was pulled to her. But he whispered, "Follow my brothers."

Resolutely, Judas pivoted from his beloved back to his duty. He approached the guards, who were standing around casually talking to one another. A few noticed him.

But when he drew his sword, one of the guards whistled. The rest turned to see Judas, then drew their own weapons.

"You are trespassing the holy temple!" one of them called out. "Who are you?"

Judas didn't respond. He was upon them in moments.

The guards were not skilled warriors. They looked young, inexperienced. Menelaus was undoubtedly using his best soldiers to help the king in the city. The one to the far left was a scrawny one, his sword seemingly too heavy for him. He raised it in defense.

Swatting it away, Judas hit the kid in the head with the flat side of his blade, knocking him silly to the ground. The others shouted and prepared to fight.

Judas bolted down the passageway past the fallen kid.

They took up chase.

Judas knew exactly where he was going. He just hoped that his brothers had moved quickly enough behind him.

He ran past several torches lining the stone arched hall.

When he turned the corner of the next hallway, he was at the exit door to the Tyropean Valley. As he had expected, it was guarded by another troop of seven temple guards. Judas knew this diversion was the most immediate way to draw all attention away from his family. So he made the sacrifice.

Dropping his sword, Judas walked up to the biggest guard who looked like the leader and fell to his knees, hands behind his head.

He heard a voice behind him. "Arrest this man! He attacked us!"

Then he felt a hard hit on the back of his head, and everything went black.

•••••

When Judas awakened, he was in a cell of an underground jail. He rubbed his head from the pain of his arrest. He knew where he was. He had seen this place when he was younger. It was the temple jail that was located a couple flights beneath ground level of the temple. It was a large enough facility to house a hundred or so prisoners and was created for priestly infractions or crimes. They preferred to police their own than to hand them over to the city authorities.

Getting up, Judas gripped the iron bars on the door of his single cell It was about six feet square, enveloped in cold, dank, and wet stones. He looked down the cell block. A few other prisoners were there for who knew what crimes against the temple.

Two guards were playing some kind of dice game beneath a double torchlight. One of them, another young lad who looked barely old enough to be a guard, turned and saw him. "How's that noggin of yours? Suits you right. Heard you put up a good fight."

He returned to his game. Judas sat down on a wooden bucket turned upside down, nursing his head. *Put up a good fight.* They should be thankful he hadn't. He could have killed them all.

He saw none of his family down here, so they must have made it to the secret entrance in the Hall of Hewn Stones. Hopefully, they were already exiting the tunnel system and on their way to Modein.

He had done what he had to do. If that meant trading his own freedom, maybe even his life, for thirty family members and friends, including women and children, so be it. He just hoped Sophia understood his decision.

Judas didn't know what his fate might be. He hadn't killed anyone, so the temple guard itself wouldn't execute him. But he had made a fool of the guards. He would at least get flogged. Would the Seleucid forces interfere in the temple regime? His identity as a former member of the king's Royal Guard would not bode well for him. Execution was not an unreasonable possibility for Seleucid "justice."

He was glad his family was safe. It had been worth it all.

A noise down the hall alerted the two young guards. Judas saw them look up. One demanded, "Who are you? What are you doing here?"

He heard the sound of their weapons clanking on the ground.

Then he saw the two guards backing up with their hands in the air until they were against the wall outside of Judas's cell.

In front of them stood Big John, growling, his war hammer in hand. Behind him were Simon, Eleazar, and Jonathan, their swords drawn.

John turned to see Judas, and his monstrously angry face turned into that of a happy puppy. "Judas! There you are, you reckless boy."

John held out his free hand to the shaking guards. One of them dropped the keys into his massive palm, visibly trembling.

"Thank you." John opened the cell door.

Judas stood in shock. "How did you …?"

Simon said, "Think about it, Socrates."

John added, "We knew you would get arrested, so where else would you end up?"

Judas stood frozen in confusion. "But how did you get in here?"

"The tunnels beneath the temple," Jonathan said. "They go everywhere."

"Well, do you want to go with us?" Simon demanded sarcastically. "Or would you rather stay?"

Judas shook himself out of his stupor and jumped out of the cell.

John herded the two guards into the cell and locked them in. He tossed the keys on the table out of reach. "We won't presume on the justice of these other prisoners."

The two guards sat on the floor in defeat. The Hasmonean brothers found their way back to their secret tunnel access for their late-night hike to the village of Modein.

CHAPTER 31

Apollonius stewed with anger as he rode his war steed beside King Antiochus, who was mounted on a white stallion, in the waning light of dusk inside the Akra fortress. That sleazy Jew Menelaus rode with them along with Philip the Phrygian, appointed by Antiochus to be the new governor of Jerusalem. Apollonius considered Philip to be even more barbarous than Antiochus in his sentiments toward the Jews. Which pleased Apollonius just fine.

They were protected by a hundred infantry bodyguards and thirty horsemen, the finest of riders. They led a group of fifty or so servants cloaked and on foot. They were on their way to the temple.

The fortress gates creaked open, and the company walked out into the streets. The city had been secured and locked down. There were hundreds of civilians lying dead in the streets from the slaughter that Antiochus had ordered. But residents were now under curfew, so there was much that was not getting cleaned up.

Philip, unfamiliar with the customs of the Jews, said to Antiochus, "Your majesty, should you be out in the open like this? There are still hasidim fighters we haven't yet cleansed from the city."

Menelaus answered him. "Look around you, Philip. Who do you see?"

"No one," he answered.

"The Sabbath has just begun," explained the high priest. "Everyone is settling in for their Sabbath meals. We do no labor of any kind from sunset to sunset."

Philip was not following.

Apollonius helped out. "That includes no fighting as well."

"It's a religious conviction," said Menelaus. "No working to honor God's commandment. No exceptions."

"Even if they are under attack?" asked Philip.

"Even if under attack," repeated Menelaus. "The hasidim—the most fanatically devoted Jews—believe their god will protect them as they obey him."

Apollonius smiled as he spoke to Philip. "Tonight will be a successful one for exterminating all opposition."

Apollonius had noticed the high priest had shifted his language from "us" to "them." Menelaus was no more of a believer than Apollonius. Yet the priest had managed to bribe his way up to the highest spiritual authority through cunning deception.

Jews. Scheming deceivers. The Samaritan general had plans for that snake one day when Antiochus turned his back long enough.

The gate of the temple closed behind the large party. They walked their horses followed by foot soldiers and servants across the large Court of the Gentiles over to the inner temple building.

The clip clap of hooves on the stone pavement rang in Apollonius's ears until they arrived at the Beautiful Gate of the inner temple. Dismounting, they led the soldiers and servants inside.

Seleucid soldiers were already all about on the walls and guarding each courtyard.

The first "Court of Women" they entered was a cross shape with storage rooms in each corner. They walked up a huge marble semi-circular staircase to the next courtyard that hosted a large stone altar of sacrifice next to slaughter pens of goats, sheep, and cattle. Apollonius saw a bronze laver of water to the right on top of sculpted oxen.

As much as he despised the privileged claims of the Jerusalem temple, it was more impressive than the Samaritan temple on Mount Gerizim of his people. Enough to be envious of.

No priests or Jews of any kind were in their way as Apollonius, Menelaus, and Philip followed Antiochus up the steps of the final inner temple. This was made of limestone with two huge bronze pillars guarding the twenty-foot cedar wood double-doors that opened to the Holy Place.

High above them, the crowned edges of the temple were gilded with gold. There would be much booty to plunder here.

They walked through the Holy Place that hosted various pieces of furniture and tools, including the golden table of showbread, the golden incense altar, and the large golden lampstand with seven lit lamps.

Antiochus turned to Apollonius. "I want all these gold and silver implements. Make sure they also strip all that golden trim on the parapets outside. I want it all."

Apollonius turned to his lead soldier and gestured. A handful of soldiers started to gather all the trophies together for transport out of there.

Apollonius looked at Menelaus to see how he was taking the fleecing. The high priest spoke to the soldiers with a smooth tongue. "There are more gold and silver instruments in the side rooms as well."

The king said to Menelaus, "Give me one of your sacred scrolls. The first one. What do you call them again?"

"Torah," Menelaus said,

"Yes, that's right. Give me a Torah scroll."

Menelaus nodded to a priest who was now beside him. The underling ran off into a side room to retrieve the item.

Antiochus stood before the large purple curtain with embroidered cherubim on it. Menelaus gestured to two priests who had arrived. Together, they pulled back the veil.

Antiochus saw inside the square room. He looked up at the erotic sculpture of cherubim embracing. He looked over at Menelaus and pointed at the sculpture with a confused crinkling of his brow.

The high priest shrugged and said sheepishly, "There is much mystery to the spiritual world."

"Burn it," Antiochus ordered. Menelaus swallowed his outrage.

The messenger priest arrived with a scroll and handed it to Menelaus, who handed it to Antiochus.

The king looked at it with curiosity. It was wrapped in leather. Unfurling it, Antiochus did the same with a silk cloth until he saw the parchment. He held it by the two long wooden handles on each end and walked up the incline into the Holy of Holies.

He moved around, looking up and down. Then to Menelaus again. "This is your god's throne room?"

The high priest nodded.

Antiochus puffed his chest out, "There is nothing. The Jewish god is nothing."

He continued looking around thoughtfully. He pointed up at the entwined cherubim and added, "But this, this is something. I can celebrate this. Bring me one of the servants of Aphrodite."

A soldier led one of the cloaked servants forward and up the stairs. When she reached the top, she shed her cloak to reveal herself a temple prostitute of Aphrodite adorned in see-through peplos, bracelets, necklace, and anklets, her hair tied up with a wreath.

Antiochus raised his finger to draw her. She came. He undid her peplos brooch and let her garment drift to the floor, leaving her naked.

He handed her the scroll and said, "Unroll it on the floor and lay on it."

She obeyed. Apollonius glanced over at Menelaus again to see that this was a little too blasphemous for even him to enjoy. But certainly not too much to protest. The priest looked slightly off to the side.

Every whore has a price.

Antiochus lifted his battle kilt and got on top of her. He kissed her violently and began to have his way with her.

It was an uncomfortably long time before the king was done with the harlot. Apollonius thought that Antiochus was most likely impotent and faking it.

The king stood up, breathing heightened from his activity, and brushed his kilt down. He waved for the prostitute to get up. She put her clothes back on and returned to her group down in the Holy Place.

Antiochus turned to Menelaus and pointed to the other cloaked servants of Aphrodite. "These are the new priestesses of the temple. Make sure you give the rest of them good rooms. My men will want a good time while they guard this divine toilet. Now let us go check your treasury."

On his way out of the temple, Antiochus stopped at the altar of burnt sacrifice and stared at it. He walked up and down as if mentally taking measurements. He said nothing, but after more thoughtful moments, he marched onward toward the stairway into the Court of Women.

They approached a side gate in the court that led down to the temple treasury. Soldiers had arrived in the courtyard with wagons for hauling out loot.

But Apollonius hesitated. He looked over at Antiochus as they awaited the opening of the large doors that led to the stairwell. If he were honest, he would admit that he had a touch of anxiety in what they were about to do. He had never forgotten a fantastical and frightening story he had heard ten years ago when Apollonius was governor of Coele-Syria. This was just before Antiochus took the throne while Seleucus IV was still king over Seleucia.

The king had heard there were vast riches in Jerusalem's temple, ripe for his taking. So he had commanded Apollonius to send the King's Friend Heliodorus to Jerusalem and confiscate the money. This was ostensibly so the king could pay his own taxes to Rome.

Heliodorus had returned empty-handed with a message of terror. He claimed that when he had entered the temple and approached the treasury doors, he had been confronted by an angelic warrior on horseback who wore armor and wielded weapons, both made of shining gold. His brightness was blinding. The warrior struck Heliodorus, but instead of dying, the officer fell to the floor paralyzed and dumb. It wasn't until the high priest at the time, the righteous Onias, made sacrifice for him that the enchantment was lifted.

Heliodorus was so shaken that he had converted to worship of their god and did not take the gold and silver from the treasury. Of course, it was most difficult to believe such a tale. But the thing that had disturbed Apollonius was that Heliodorus was willing to face the wrath of the king and accept execution for what he had experienced. Seleucus didn't kill him, but only because he believed the story as well.

Apollonius had never forgotten the words Heliodorus spoke to them. "For he who has his dwelling in heaven watches over that place himself and brings it aid, and he strikes and destroys those who come to do it injury."

Those words haunted his mind like a curse as Apollonius and Antiochus walked down the stairs to stand before large, reinforced oak doors guarded by several temple soldiers. Apollonius tried to maintain his confident and powerful stature as he glanced fearfully down the hallways. No golden-clad angelic warriors on horses. He told himself he was being foolish to let that old tale get to him.

Menelaus used his key to open the lock, and the doors swung wide. Suddenly a flash of golden light hit the general's eyes. He felt his stomach drop and his breath huff in surprise.

But it was not a golden spirit of vengeance. The large stone room before them hosted a pile of gold and silver in torchlight unlike anything Apollonius had seen before. He entered with Philip behind Antiochus and Menelaus.

Silly superstitious lies, he thought to himself. *I should never have believed Heliodorus.*

The pile of gold and silver must have been thirty feet in diameter and ten feet high, touching the very ceiling. It looked like a garbage dump of precious metal objects, instruments, and vessels all cast in either silver or gold. There were chests and bags of coins, piled ingots. Any form that Israelites had offered to the temple for their religious devotion.

These Jews are a greedy lot, thought Apollonius. *What a pleasure to dispossess them of what they do not deserve.*

Antiochus was in awe. He exclaimed, "There must be close to two thousand talents of silver and gold in here!"

The soldiers with wagons waited outside ready for orders to start transferring this wealth to the coffers of their king.

Everyone waited as Antiochus paced slowly around the pile to get a good look at it. Something caught his eye away from the horde. Something in the corner of the wall. He walked over and picked it up. It looked like a golden sword handle. But instead of the handle being connected to a long blade in a sheath, it ended in a dark, bulging leather pouch. Strange.

Antiochus opened the latch of the pouch and pulled it away from the sword handle. A ten-foot-long flat blade unrolled onto the floor like a scroll. The king held it up and touched the blade. It seemed like a sword blade, but it was flexible like a whip.

Antiochus looked at his comrades. "Have any of you ever seen anything like this?"

Everyone shook their heads or mumbled no. Including Apollonius, but his interest was piqued. "May I see it, my king?"

Antiochus gladly handed it to him. Apollonius felt the metal. It wasn't gold but something else entirely. *Could this be the heavenly indestructible metal adamantine I have heard about in Greek legends?*

He examined the leather sheath. "It has the name 'Rahab' etched into it."

Apollonius knew that as a common nickname for the ancient sea dragon of chaos. He stepped away from everyone, moving the strange weapon around to see the blade wriggle like a snake. Then he snapped it like a whip at the pile of gold. A small explosion of coins showered them all.

"Wow!" exclaimed Antiochus. "Now, that is the strike of a deadly serpent. What do you make of it, Apollonius?"

"I don't know, your majesty. I've never seen any metal so flexible and yet so strong. In my opinion, this whip-sword is a weapon of great power."

"Then keep it," said Antiochus. "If anyone has any use for it, you do."

"No, your majesty. It is not necessary."

"It is my will. Take the weapon and see if it can be of use to you." Antiochus quickly turned to the others. "But don't any of you get any ideas and start begging for gifts."

Everyone else stood uncomfortably still, not wanting to display any kind of reaction for fear of the king's wrath.

Apollonius wrapped the sword back up into its leather sheath.

Antiochus picked off the pile a teraphim idol of a Semitic goddess and stared at it, nodding his head over some idea he had.

He looked at Philip. "Figure how much gold needs to be set aside to gild a statue of Zeus Olympius on his throne. Make it about eighteen feet tall like the one I have in Babylon and put it on a platform in front of the altar of burnt sacrifice in the courtyard above. There is a new owner of this conquered house."

Apollonius saw Menelaus's eyes widen just enough to reveal another difficult political situation he was now in.

The high priest cleared his throat nervously and suggested, "Your majesty, may I suggest an alternative that would accomplish your purposes with more effectiveness and allow you to keep more of the wealth."

You mean, loot, thought Apollonius with a smile.

The king raised his brow, waiting.

Menelaus cleared his nervous throat again. "Well, *I* have no problem with an image of Zeus, but you may have less resistance from *other* Jews if you consider syncretizing with a more local deity."

"And what would you suggest?" queried Antiochus.

"For instance, you have Zeus-Amun in Egypt and Zeus-Belus in Babylon as a means of syncretizing the Greek king of the gods with those nations' patron deities, am I not correct?"

Antiochus nodded his head, thoughtfully listening.

"Now, contrary to popular belief, many Jews do not worship one god alone."

Antiochus said, "But I thought your god commands it."

"Well, yes, he does, technically. However, throughout our history, many of us have had a difficult time giving up certain Semitic gods and with them certain kinds of images."

Antiochus was becoming agitated, "Get to the point, Menelaus."

"Forgive me, your majesty. Baal-Shamem is still worshipped among many as the high god of the land along with his consort and sister, the warrior goddess Anat. And *massebot*, or standing stones, is a way that Semitic peoples worship their gods. You don't need to waste all that gold on an image of Zeus. You merely place standing stones on the altar that represent Baal-Shamem, the equivalent of Zeus, and Anat, the equivalent of Athena. Two seven-foot-tall stones would fit easily there."

Antiochus considered the advice.

Menelaus added, "You might find yourself with rather substantial support among many Jews."

Antiochus was nodding his head in agreement now. He asked, "But not these hasidim, these so-called holy ones?"

"I am afraid not, sire."

Philip offered up, "But they have no leader and no organization. They hide amongst the populace like scattered rats."

"What say you, Apollonius?" Antiochus asked. "You have been quiet."

"Your majesty, I confess I am not impartial in this matter. I support the decision that allows me to kill as many Jews as possible."

Antiochus laughed. "Ha! I knew I could rely upon my loyal Jew-hater Apollonius to advise me with honesty!"

Antiochus thought some more as he fiddled with the teraphim idol in his hand. Finally, he said, "These Jews have been the bane of my existence. And I am fed up. They are the only ones, *the only ones* in my kingdom who have special treatment. They have for too long abused the privilege my father gave them of avoiding complete Hellenistic reform for the sake of their petty laws and taboos. The whole world is changing, transforming into a Hellenic future of inclusion and progress. *The whole world*—except them. They want to stay stuck in their backwards cult of tradition, exclusion, and bigotry. They claim their bachelor god is sole imperator, emperor of all, who chooses them and hates everyone else. They offend every single pantheon of power that exists. They haven't been able to physically revolt because they are a weak, pathetic people. But they don't have to. They revolt in their hearts every day as they refuse to acknowledge other gods, other kings, and authority. Their revolt is much deeper than a war of insurrection. It is a rebellion against humanity itself."

Antiochus threw the teraphim onto the gold pile. "Curse them. And curse their god. Philip, create the image of Zeus Olympius on his throne that I talked about. Apollonius, finish your purge of the city. Hunt down as many of these fanatical hasidim as you can with their families and exterminate the vermin. You and your forces will represent my presence in the city. Menelaus, you and I will come up with some new laws of worship that will be required under penalty of death. If the Jews don't want to change and progress with the rest of the world, then I will force them to."

CHAPTER 32

Hera stood beside Zeus in the heavenly realm of the Holy of Holies in Jerusalem. She sighed impatiently, looking around the empty square room of limestone covered with cedarwood paneling. She thought of sprucing it up with some Corinthian pillars, marble floors, and a nice golden throne to remind her of her home on Olympus. She missed that snow-capped sacred mountain terribly. It was such a superior temple compared to this primitive outhouse. This was even a step down from the Syrian house of Baal on Zaphon that they had occupied. She felt all this was so beneath their Greek glory as king and queen of the gods. It became a dark portent of their declining future.

Finally, the other gods started to arrive. Poseidon, Athena, and Ares entered the temple, each dragging several chained and unconscious angels of God behind them, ten in all. They were beaten bloody, all of them, bodies broken into pieces dangling on the line of chains.

Poseidon bowed and said, "My brother, these were some of the heavenly host surrounding the temple when we got here."

"The others?" asked Zeus.

Ares spoke up. "They fled after battle. A few dozen of them. We cornered them in the Valley of Gehenna."

"But no archangels," said Poseidon. "Not a sign of them anywhere. And apparently haven't been for a long while."

"It appears you've already interrogated them," said Zeus, "Or should I say, trampled on them."

Poseidon nodded, grinning. "They wouldn't give anything up."

"Stubborn mules," complained Zeus. He sighed. "Put them below. I'll have Hades bring them into his underworld."

Poseidon handed all the chain lines to Athena. She gave him a dirty look but reluctantly took the chains and dragged the ten angels out of there.

Zeus mused, "I don't understand why it was so easy to take the city and temple. It had all the marks of an ambush. But no archangels and no ambush."

Hera said, "Maybe they learned a lesson from what happened to Michael in the Babylonian exile." That ambush had been a particularly glorious, though temporary, victory for the Babylonian pantheon.

Poseidon offered, "Then why would they not simply assemble more archangels here?"

Zeus concluded, "This could very well be confirmation of my contention that the seedline of the Chosen One is lost." He saw Demeter and Persephone entering and added, "Let's see if the others have found anything."

Demeter and Persephone approached Zeus emptyhanded. They had been sent to Bethlehem, the birthplace and location of Samuel's anointing of King David. Demeter announced, "We found nothing."

Then Artemis, Apollo, and Hestia entered. They had probed the city of Hebron, where David was anointed king over Judah after Saul. Apollo proclaimed, "Hebron shows no sign of heavenly host whatsoever."

Finally, Hephaestus, Aphrodite, and Hermes entered, announcing, "We scoured the forests and caves of En-Gedi. If there are any archangels there, they are better at hide-and-seek than David was from Saul."

Gaia and Dionysus had slipped in late, the former too lazy to go searching and the latter too drunk.

Hera was still furious over the disappearance of her Nemean Lion and Artemis's Ceryneian Hind. She had heard from others that the Lernean Hydra had been mysteriously wounded, and now Hades's hound Cerberus was also missing. Something very strange was going on. But she dared not bring this up to everyone because of her suspicion of a plot among them. She still believed that Zeus and the gods were secretly trying to weaken the goddesses step by step.

But then, why Hades's hound? If anything, he would be in on it as one of the three high gods.

Or maybe not.

Even though he was Zeus's brother, Hades had been complaining for centuries of being left out of Olympus and feeling like a prisoner in the underworld.

It just didn't make sense. Hera couldn't see how the dots were connected. She would wait until she had firmer evidence. For now, she would continue her own plans and seek to undermine Zeus's authority.

The king interrupted her thoughts. "No sign of a messianic seed anywhere in Judea. Michael and the archangels are absent. Yahweh's city and throne are empty. Israel has been completely abandoned by Yahweh."

Poseidon offered, "It seems that Hellenism has sufficiently compromised the faith of the Jews. We have complete control of the temple now."

"I would not presume such confidence," said Hera. "Occupying the temple is not enough."

"What are you talking about?" complained Poseidon.

Hera answered him, "To achieve total subversion and control, we must transform the *worship* of Yahweh into worship of *Zeus*."

She saw Zeus thoughtfully nodding his head in agreement.

Everyone's attention was turned to Hades, who entered the Holy Place pushing along what appeared to be a captive.

When the two were close enough to see who Hades had in tow, the other Olympians cringed in repulsion at the ugly humanoid monstrosity. It was completely naked with pale, wrinkly white skin, dirtied as if it had been buried in the earth. Its splayed hands covered its sensitive mole-like eyes from the light around them.

Hades shoved it down at the base of the Holy of Holies.

"What is that ... that *thing*?" asked Hera in horror.

"This is Molech, the Canaanite god of Sheol, their underworld."

Poseidon quipped at Hades, "And you complain about your underworld?"

Hades ignored Poseidon and walked up to Zeus, pointing at his feet where a large, flat stone had a rectangular impression in it. "This entire time that we have been in this room, none of us realized what was right at our feet."

"What?" demanded Zeus.

"It is called *Even ha-Shetiyah*. The Foundation Stone."

"And that is?"

Hades turned to Molech. "Tell them."

When Molech spoke, he had a raspy, wheezy voice like one might expect a mole creature to sound having spent its life underground. "It is the center of Jerusalem, the navel of the earth."

"Foolishness," said Zeus. "Everyone knows that the Omphalos Stone is the center and Delphi, Greece, is the navel of the earth."

"Not in their Jewish provincial geographical ignorance," said Hades, smiling.

Molech added, "It is the resting place of the ark of the covenant of Israel with Yahweh."

"Which is clearly not here," said Zeus.

Hera could see that was the source of the rectangular impression.

"But that is not all it is," said Molech. "It is also a cover to the pit that descends into the Abyss below, which leads to Tartarus."

Hera noted that Zeus was clearly more interested now as they all were.

"Poseidon, lift it up so we can see."

Poseidon stepped up, but stopped when Hades said, "You can't."

"What do you mean, I can't?"

Hades gestured to Molech to keep explaining. The mole god said, "It is supernaturally sealed with the signet ring of King Solomon, the son of David, Israel's Anointed One."

"We will see about that," crowed Poseidon as he bent down. Grabbing the edges of the rectangular flat rock, he lifted with all his might.

It wouldn't budge.

He tried again, spewing breath and turning red. But the rock would not move. He stood, both shocked and embarrassed as he was one of the mightiest of the Olympians.

Molech said, 'Solomon received the seal from Michael the Archangel, Prince of Israel. He embedded it into the stone. It is said to imprison a myriad of demons in the Abyss and that only in the time of the end shall it be opened by the Angel of the Abyss, Apollyon."

"Who is Apollyon?" demanded Zeus.

"I don't know," said Molech. "The Angel of the Abyss, I suppose."

Hera saw Zeus give him a scolding look.

Hades jumped in. "If we could find a way to remove that seal, we could unleash the powers of Hell."

"So you think you are Apollyon?" demanded Zeus. "Be my guest."

Hades tried to lift the stone and only made himself look foolish to the others. Hera wondered if there was any way she could use this to her benefit.

Zeus contemplated the possibilities, then concluded, "Hades, try to find out how to break this seal. In the meantime, I need some of you to return to Mount Zaphon and some of you to stay and help me build my throne in this garbage dump. Then we will persuade the Jews to give up their absent landlord and embrace a better future."

CHAPTER 33

Modein, Judea

Judas stood with Sophia and his brothers at the front of the synagogue watching the Modein Gerousia council take place. Mattathiah was the most respected priest in their town of a thousand people. He led the meeting that was currently attended by many of the villagers as well, including some of the wives and mothers. The synagogue only held a hundred, so the high turnout of over two hundred resulted in an overflow of citizens into the streets. Many craned their necks trying to hear the deliberations inside.

Mattathiah and the council of twelve wore fine robes of distinguished status at the front of the open sanctuary area. The old man had just calmed the crowd down after one of the men expressed his fear of Seleucid soldiers invading their city.

"Please! Please!" Mattathiah said. "We are not unconcerned about this matter as a council. But we must be careful to stay level-headed and not panic."

The complainer, a young, nervously energetic man, was clearly a hasidim in his sentiments, and he seemed to be at the end of his patience. "But Mattathiah, the king's army killed ten thousand people and enslaved ten thousand others! Twenty thousand Jews enslaved or murdered without discrimination! And many of those were civilians!"

Mattathiah said, "Yes, we as a council agree that was an unforgivable atrocity. And we are seeking redress through legal channels afforded us as subjects of the king."

"Through Menelaus?" the hasidim man responded with incredulity. "A corrupt usurper of the high priesthood! He's a Friend of the King. He's no friend of ours!"

The murmuring crowd rose in agitated agreement.

"Agreed," Mattathiah said. "But we must respect the office even if we do not respect the office holder. We are not a lawless people."

Many in the crowd expressed agreement with the elder. But another man yelled out, "How much oppression are we supposed to stomach just because he is king?!"

Someone else yelled, "When do we stand and fight?"

Mattathiah responded, "We are to obey the king in all things *unless* he commands us to violate our holy covenant with Yahweh. And only then do we have cause to resist."

The first protestor responded, "Resist the tyrant!"

Mattathiah continued, "Consider this carefully. The Seleucid attack was on Jerusalem *alone* in response to what King Antiochus thought was an insurrection. Now he knows it was not. He knows it was a political struggle between Menelaus and Jason for control of the priesthood. No small thing. But that was several months ago now, and Antiochus has left the city in the hands of his general Apollonius, who has not sent his forces into the rest of Judea. They have stayed only in Jerusalem, and the roads have been free of any troops. As a rural town, we are not a target. We are in no immediate danger."

Again, the crowd exploded in mixed reaction.

Judas had new respect for his father. Over the past month, they had had their conversations and family debates. With Judas's desire to start a family with his new wife, he had felt the pull in his own heart back to his tradition and heritage. The Sabbaths, rituals, and dietary laws by which he had previously felt constrained now gave him a sense of belonging to a community. He was no longer the rootless individual stoically standing alone, the delusional master of his own fate. The covenant and sacrificial system rooted the Jews in their God while the feasts and Torah rooted them in the Land of Promise. Torah, temple, and Land. Heaven and Earth.

Another man stood. Tobias was a priest with similar stature as Mattathiah but of a different mind. Gray-haired, he had a strong voice that commanded authority. "I see that we are a divided people. Some of you want to be left alone. Others want to fight. But how will you fight? With your shovels and pitchforks and a few swords against a mighty army of trained warriors? You will not survive, your family lines will end, and Israel will be no more. Is that what you want?"

Someone yelled, "We are slaves to a pagan king!"

Tobias said, "Yes, we are subjects of the Seleucid Greeks. But so is most of the world. Look at it from a different perspective. Hellenism has opened up the world to trade and education. Israel has risen out of poverty and starvation. Jerusalem has become an international center of commerce, economic growth, and political influence. And all because of Greek language, philosophy, mathematics, science."

The heckler shouted again, "What about their abominable gods?! What do they give us?"

Some in the crowd laughed in agreement.

"That is not fair," said Tobias. "Many of our fellow Jews even in this village have adopted Hellenist customs without conflicting with our traditions. Many of you still retain some Babylonian influences from the exile. Beside this, Syrians, Persians, Egyptians have all adopted Greek culture in public life while maintaining their religious practices in private. I contend that Hellenism transcends religious, ethnic, and national boundaries with a peaceful diversity of cultures blended in an inclusive unity that does not have to change the core substance of our religion."

Judas knew these arguments well. He had learned them himself in the gymnasium and at symposiums in Antioch. He knew both sides. He had to speak up. He approached the podium up front with raised hand. He was acknowledged by the elders.

"Brothers and sisters, you know me. And you know about my background. That these past three years I have been a commander in the Royal Guard of King Antiochus himself. But I have returned to live out the covenant of my family and forefathers. Let me first say that I believe Tobias to be sincere in all that he says. For I too once believed this way."

Judas looked over at Tobias with concern, then continued, "But I am here to tell you that he is mistaken."

Hellenists in the crowd grumbled with offense.

"I agree with my father that we should not be in danger if we mind our own business out in the rural areas. King Antiochus is concerned about Jerusalem. He does not concern himself with small targets." Judas saw his father beaming with new pride in his prodigal son returned to the fold. "But as for Hellenism, that is a more pernicious enemy. For while it presents itself as merely cultural, economic, and educational but without religious demands, it is in fact an all-consuming, all-demanding religion that worships many gods."

Murmuring and arguing broke out in the crowd. Judas looked into the midst to see Sophia watching him with pride along with his brothers. Her conversion to Judaism and their talks had been critical to his repentance.

"The tolerance of other religions that we see in Hellenism is philosophically rooted in *polytheos*, the worship of many gods. On the surface, this belief appears to allow for us to worship our one living God, Adonai, and others to worship a pantheon of gods."

Someone yelped, "Your Greek learning has made you a philosopher! Speak in simple terms for us commonfolk!"

More laughter relieved a bit of the tension in the room. Judas himself could not help smiling as he went on, "The Hellenic king only demands that we pay his taxes, obey his authority, and not interfere in the freedom of others to worship their gods. But our King in heaven has told us, 'Hear, O Israel: The Lord our God, the Lord is one. You shall have no other gods beside me.'

"Now, it is true we have all benefited from the economic and educational advances of Hellenism. I have learned in the gymnasium and been entertained at the theater. On the surface, these things are not wrong in and of themselves. But behind them are deeper foundational hidden beliefs and values. And those values come from an ultimate authority. Our ultimate authority is Ha Shem, our one God. The ultimate authority of Hellenism is her many gods. In the end, they will demand worship. Maybe not in the beginning. But in the end, the gods of all systems will come for their sacrifice."

The Hellenists and hasidim in the crowd all voiced their agreement or disagreement with his words and once again had to be calmed down by Mattathiah. Judas returned to his place beside his loving Sophia, who rubbed his back with affection and held his hand in support.

More debate ensued of the same arguments repeated from different people in different words. Judas knew that nothing would be solved today. They would have to keep trying to wake up the people.

But how to do so without inciting a mob?

On their way back to Mattathiah's home with the family, Sophia called Hannah over to walk with them and pulled Judas's arm closer in her own. "You spoke with wisdom in there today, husband. Better be careful or you may be called upon to become a leader."

They shared a smile. Judas queried, "Why do I get the feeling that you are about to ask me something?"

Sophia squeezed him tighter and glanced at Hannah. Judas looked at Hannah. "Mother, what are you two conspiring about?"

"It was your wife's idea."

Judas looked back at Sophia, feeling like a prisoner of the two women on each side.

Sophia said, "Your father has argued that the troops of Antiochus are rooted in Jerusalem and are not spreading out into the countryside."

"Yes."

She went on, "So there is a group from Modein going to Mizpah to pray for the peace of Jerusalem."

Mizpah was well-known in Judea for having a large prayer building where people had traveled to fast and pray for divine guidance over many centuries. It was a sacred location where the prophet Samuel had called the people of Israel to repentance and a return to Yahweh. Yahweh had granted a great victory there over the Philistines.

"That was cunning, quoting a psalm of David," said Judas. The psalm calling to *pray for the peace of Jerusalem* was commonly invoked by pilgrims ascending to the capital city for festivals. "How can I say no to a pilgrimage of prayer?"

"You have said so yourself," Sophia replied with a grin. "I am your smart *and* godly wife."

Judas shook his head contemplatively. "I would be happy for us to participate. But Father was just asked to meet with some hasidim in another town for counsel and advice. We brothers will be accompanying him."

Sophia would not take no for an answer. "Your father is letting your mother go, and Solomonia's seven sons would join us as well. They will be more than enough protection, and several other husbands are going as well. It's only ten miles away."

"It's halfway closer to Jerusalem," Judas complained.

Sophia became facetiously quizzical. "My memory may be playing tricks on me, but who was it who said he was not worried about our rural towns being in danger?"

Judas sighed. Caught on the horns of his own dilemma. As his father had stated, there had been no reports of any Seleucid troops on the roads in their area.

Sophia became serious, "Husband, Jerusalem is not all I want to pray for."

Judas looked into her eyes with sudden empathy. She was still not pregnant and had even expressed despair to him at times.

"Of course you can go." He kissed her. She kissed him back and hugged him tighter as they walked on.

Hannah said with a smile, "Without your beloved Sophia, I fear the monster you would have become."

Judas smiled back, scolding, "Mother!"

Sophia and Hannah had packed their belongings in a couple of satchels and mounted their donkeys for the trip to Mizpah, a short day's travel to the east. Judas had given his own exhortation of protection to their armed guards. The group of several dozen men and women with a few older children left early in the morning to seek Adonai on behalf of their village, their holy city, and God's people.

After the first five miles, the group stopped at a well on the route to take a short break and water their horses and donkeys. Sophia stood with Hannah and Solomonia, stretching their legs before the last miles of the trip.

Solomonia, an effervescent woman, said, "I confess, with seven sons I am going to be praying at Mizpah not merely for Jerusalem but for patience."

The women laughed together. Solomonia added, "They are all so strong-willed. I just thank the Lord they are godly young men."

She stopped when she saw that Sophia was tearing up. "Oh, Sophia, forgive me! I am so thoughtless. I don't mean to …"

"No," said Sophia. "It's perfectly all right."

Hannah butted in. "She is pregnant."

Solomonia's eyes went wide with joy. Sophia's went wide with surprise.

"How did you know?" she asked.

Hannah smiled. "I could tell you were going to Mizpah to thank God, not beg him."

"Well," said Solomonia. "You will soon know the great joys *and great pains* of children." They all shared another laugh. Solomonia got serious. "You will be a good mother, Sophia. I can tell."

Hannah pulled something out of her cloak and handed it to Sophia. She looked it over in her hand. It was an amulet, a small piece of silver that had Hebrew writing on it. It was attached to a silver necklace. On one side she read a verse from the scroll of Numbers.

> *May YHWH bless you and guard you. May YHWH make his face shine upon you.*
> *YHWH lift up his countenance upon you and give you peace.*

It was a common blessing they used, and it was special in that the Tetragrammaton, the very name of their God, was inscribed in it. Sophia would never say the name out loud as was the tradition. But just seeing it filled her soul with a chill of hope and God's presence.

She turned it over to see a curse on the other side.

> *May YHWH curse Lilith the night demon and her serpent. May they make their resting place far from you.*

The Jews believed that the Mesopotamian demon Lilith would sometimes come and steal away the breath of babies in the night. They believed that the amulet would protect them with Adonai's favor.

Sophia clutched it gratefully in her hands and embraced Hannah with tears.

"Lady Sophia," came a quiet male voice.

Sophia looked up to see Havim, a man in his early twenties, lean and handsome. He stood with his pretty young wife next to Solomonia. Behind him were his six brothers of varying ages down to preteen. Sophia had gotten to know them in Modein.

"God bless your child," Havim said softly. "May Adonai watch over you."

Solomonia looked embarrassed at the interruption. She said to Sophia, "I am so sorry. I didn't think to look behind me to find my little bear cubs following." She gave a scolding look at her son. "And listening in where they shouldn't."

"Sorry, Mother."

Solomonia said to her sons, "You had all better keep this a secret. Do you hear me?"

They nodded with fearful obedience.

Sophia laughed. "It's okay, Solomonia. I will tell Judas when we return. I'm sure my secret is safe until then."

The three women burst out in laughter with joy and much hugging before they continued on their pilgrimage to Mizpah.

CHAPTER 34

Jerusalem
15 Kislev, Year 145 of the Kingdom of the Greeks
December 6, 168 BC

It had been several months since Antiochus had taken control of Jerusalem from Jason's forces. The king had left its security in the hands of Apollonius. But recently, the general had received word from the king that he was coming and to raise a small army for a new plan he had conceived. Apollonius had dutifully obeyed and now returned to Jerusalem at the head of a mercenary division of Mysians, Greeks from the far west of Asia Minor, twenty-two thousand strong. These lion-hearted warriors were experts with the spear—and well paid. The rising sun cast an orange glow like fire on their bronze armor.

The *apantesis* committee, including the city elders and Philip the Phrygian governor of Jerusalem, met the Samaritan commander and escorted him into the city. Apollonius despised them all and just wanted to start implementing King Antiochus's decrees. Six thousand soldiers stood ready outside the city gates, a contingent of five hundred guarded the inside of those gates, while over fifteen thousand followed Apollonius into the city and up to the temple mount at the top of the hill.

It was the Jewish Sabbath. No one was about their daily work, and few were in the streets. In a few hours, the temple would fill up with residents for the morning sacrifice performed by the priests. A barbaric ritual in Apollonius's eyes, but it helped keep the human sheep in line.

And what he was about to institute would at least Hellenize the ritual with some civilized sophistication.

Apollonius met a Seleucid battalion of five hundred from the Akra fortress who were guarding the temple gates. He left five thousand soldiers stationed in and around the Akra and led the rest of ten thousand through the gates and into the open courtyard of the temple mount. They immediately took positions beneath the colonnades surrounding the entire temple area. They would watch over the masses who were about to be let in for the morning sacrifice. The entire populace had been encouraged to come for an important announcement from their king.

Apollonius and Philip dismounted their horses beside the temple building. Apollonius adjusted his brass general's helmet with long horse-haired plume. It was cumbersome to him but necessary for identification to his men. He brushed off his red chlamys cloak that hung over his muscle cuirass of bronze with red battle kilt. He checked the handle of his sword in its sheath and pulled a special two-foot-long ornate golden scepter from his horse pack, its embedded gems sparkling in the sunlight. This represented the king's royal authority.

He looked at the rows of cataphract cavalry lined up on both sides of the temple, five hundred in number. They were heavily armored elite shock troops normally used to break through enemy lines. Horses sported heavy chainmail. Their riders wore scales and on their heads another helpful piece of equipment. Full-face bronze and iron masks ornately engraved as human faces projected an absolute unity in look and purpose.

To the eyes of an opponent, the riders in their masks were without human emotion, ruthless in their duty, and unchanging. An army that existed for one thing—to destroy without mercy. Apollonius chose to use them here to impress upon the citizens their need to obey without hesitation the difficult commands they were about to be given.

Philip walked beside him in his governor's garb of green woolen robe. The two men approached the Beautiful Gate, where they were met by Menelaus in his high priestly outfit. This consisted of a multi-colored checkered apron over his bright-blue tunic with a sash and that goofy awkward breastplate of symbolic gemstones. To Apollonius, the silly tall, white turban with golden plate on the priest's forehead and tinkling bells on his hem made Menelaus look and sound like a buffoon.

The two leaders followed the priest through the Beautiful Gate, its gigantic bronze doors cracked open for single passage. The entire temple building had been locked up all week as sculptors and artisans had prepared a Hellenistic addition to the altar inside. Yes, things were going to change around here. But knowing the ram-headed stubbornness of these Jews, Apollonius had prepared for contingencies.

Their best bet had been the king's support of Menelaus as high priest. As they walked up the steps into the inner courtyard of the altar, Apollonius watched Menelaus with amused contempt. He was such an easy tool. He was helping Antiochus implement all his prescribed changes. And considering what those changes were, this fool in front of him was a religious fraud.

But that had always been the way to force change upon uncivilized peoples and their barbarism. Gain the allyship of the cynics within their midst, the ones who hated their tradition but were too cowardly to cut themselves off from the herd. Then buy off those secret apostates to help inspire "change" and "progress." It was a winning strategy throughout history. And Jews were no different from anyone else.

Apollonius asked the high priest, "Menelaus, where did you house those servants of Aphrodite that were sent to you?"

Menelaus pointed over to some quarters on the side of the temple walls. "My lord, we used some empty residence quarters and furnished them quite comfortably."

Apollonius saw several of the temple prostitutes accompanying Greek priests and guards into those rooms. "Good. I will want to visit them before too long."

They now stood before the large tent that had been erected around the stone altar in the courtyard. The workers pulled down the tenting to reveal a most beautiful and glorious image. Apollonius, Philip, and Menelaus gazed up at a golden-gilded statue of Zeus seated on his throne before the stone altar. The statue was eighteen feet high, seated on a fifteen-foot-tall platform of stone to match the height of the altar, allowing Zeus to watch over his sacrifices. The statue's platform stones extended forward to partially encircle the altar of sacrifice like rock arms embracing the hearth.

To Apollonius, it was truly awesome. And truly worthy of worship. Inside the temple in the Holy of Holies, they had also placed a smaller ten-foot statue of Zeus standing beside King Antiochus Epiphanes, equal in height. King and god, patron and daemon guardian.

The sound of a shofar trumpet echoed from a distant corner of the temple. The three leaders made their way back to the Beautiful Gate to get ready as the throngs of Jews began entering the outer temple area for this glorious new day.

It had taken an hour for the temple grounds to fill with thousands of worshippers. Apollonius stood on the steps of the temple with Menelaus looking out onto the sea of wretched humanity. Mindless sheep following the clown shepherd standing beside him.

He could see that the crowd was unsettled by the presence of the military, his soldiers creating a wall of protection before the steps of the temple, his horsemen on his left and right, and thousands more not-so-hidden in the surrounding colonnades. His own herald trumpeted, and the crowd settled somewhat in anticipation.

As he spoke, Apollonius projected his voice. The acoustic design of the temple grounds worked well to amplify his words.

"People of Judea, I am Apollonius of Samaria, Mysarch and general of King Antiochus IV Epiphanes." He raised the royal scepter. "I carry the authority of the king himself with his very words. Hear now the decrees of the king's Edict of Unity. First, the king declares that the annual tribute collected from the temple treasury will be eliminated."

The tenor of the crowd became positive. Some even applauded with gratitude. But the Samaritan general was only beginning.

"The tribute will be replaced by a land-tax to be levied directly on all agricultural production."

The optimism of the crowd lulled. As if they were not sure they had heard him right.

"As for your temple cult and its liturgy, there will be significant changes that are required by the king to bring this region under proper Hellenic democracy. It is time for all peoples to come together and embrace the future. We must unite and leave the past behind. Civilization must advance or we will be overrun by barbarism."

The agitation began again as Apollonius pulled out a royal scroll of parchment and unrolled it to read the decrees.

"The following decrees are being sent by messengers to all towns in Judea for immediate publication. By the authority and power of King Antiochus IV Epiphanes, the following decrees are made for all those under his sovereign rule in all Judea and Samaria. Whoever does not obey these laws shall be put to death!"

A hush went through people. They could not believe what they were hearing.

But they had better believe it.

"First, all rituals and taboos that alienate and divide amongst the peoples are hereby officially illegal under pain of death. This includes among other things the heinous procedure called circumcision, the mutilation of the male member. Also, all food restrictions against pork, shellfish, reptiles, and other creatures are null and void. The king declares all foods now clean to eat as one desires. If anyone is caught abstaining from eating these foods, they will be punished with death!"

The crowd grew more agitated. Apollonius whistled. His cavalry moved forward a dozen steps until the crowd became quieted with fear.

He continued, "All special festivals and days that separate and divide the people are hereby declared illegal under pain of death. This includes all Sabbaths and feasts of Passover, Yom Kippur, Purim, and others. Anyone caught celebrating any prohibited festivals and days shall be put to death by order of the king.

"As for this temple, it has now been officially rededicated as a temple of Zeus Olympius!"

Now the crowd began to rise in fervor. This was going too far for them. Apollonius gave a large swinging hand gesture to his soldiers all around to be prepared.

The mammoth Beautiful Gate was opened by a dozen priests. Those closest to the temple gates could see the new altar of Zeus deep inside the inner courtyard. Several Greek priests had slaughtered a large pig that they now placed on the altar before the huge, glorious golden image of Zeus.

Apollonius announced, "Thus King Antiochus Epiphanes, God Manifest, changes the appointed times and seasons to accord with his will. Whoever does not obey these laws of the king shall be put to death!"

With that, a wave of violence broke out in the assembly of Jews. Some shouted, cursed, and became unruly. Pockets of others tried to back away or leave the temple in self-preservation. They looked to Apollonius like an angry horde of insects. And he knew he had to stomp on them or they might sting him. Rebellion had to be strangled as soon as it started or it would grow to unmanageable volume.

Apollonius gestured to his trumpeter, who then blew the order to advance. The cavalry moved slowly forward, pushing the Jews back. Soldiers came marching out from the colonnades, shields up and spears out, a long line of force that circled the entire audience.

More Jews sought to exit the temple grounds. Hundreds were trampled in the panic. Those fleeing were allowed to leave.

The pressing line of spearmen kept moving, protecting themselves from thrown rocks with their shields. Some Jews drew weapons of swords and axes.

Several platoons of fifty soldiers were released into the mass of civilians to hunt down those resisting with weapons or rocks. They cut down the protestors with ease and without remorse. Women screamed. Blood flowed onto the pavement. Bodies piled up beneath the ruthless hacking blades and piercing spears of the Seleucid soldiers.

There were many accidental casualties of innocent women and men being slaughtered along with the rebels. But to be frank, Apollonius cared nothing for the collateral damage of unintended victims as they sifted through the wheat for the tares. As far as he was concerned, there were no real "innocents." Those Jews who sat back and allowed others to do their dirty work were just as guilty as those they did not stop. And those who "peacefully" engaged in their rituals of "chosenness" and religious supremacy had the same seed of vile hatred of non-Jews in their hearts that bore the fruit of insurrection. As far as the general was concerned, he wanted to kill them all. He just needed an excuse, or he would get into trouble with the king.

Now was his opportunity to try the new weapon he had been practicing with. The whip-sword named Rahab was latched to his belt. Withdrawing the blade, Apollonius let it dangle behind him as he walked down the stairs and pushed past his guard to enter the fray. Four bodyguards followed him, but they had to back away as he swung the whip-sword at several Jews. One of them was severed in half by the blade hitting him mid-section. Another had his arm cut off.

Apollonius felt his bloodlust rise within him. Bursting out in maniacal laughter, he swung the otherworldly blade over his head and snapped another head off. He felt energized. He felt like a god.

Numbers of Jews around Apollonius fled, creating a widening circle without targets for his whip-sword. He stopped, catching his breath and looking around him to see that the masses had been sufficiently suppressed. Most had fled. Many others had been cut down. The pavement all around was filled with the bloody bodies of the slain. Women wept, clinging to their loved ones. Apollonius saw priests and scribes running out, trying to help the wounded. His soldiers had secured control of the area.

Peace and order had been returned.

Apollonius marched back to the stairs to meet Philip, who was awaiting the general's command.

"Clean this up," Apollonius said. "And prepare yourself for more law and order. We have a lot of work ahead of us."

"Yes, my lord," said Philip.

"And you can start by arresting any who refuse to follow the Edict of Unity. Men or women. If they circumcise, if they keep Sabbath, if they refuse to eat pork, arrest them."

Philip nodded in submission and left to discharge his duty.

Apollonius looked past the Phrygian to see Menelaus standing on the stairs, trying to look stoic. But the general could swear he saw tears streaming down those rancid cheeks.

Weep for the slaves you lost. And for the sheep you no longer have to fleece for their wealth.

Apollonius wondered how it had gone for Andronicus, the general of the regiment appointed for Samaria. Andronicus was announcing the same changes at the Samaritan temple on Mount Gerizim that Apollonius had announced here. That temple was to be renamed Zeus Xenios, or "Friend of the Nations." He wondered how many Samaritans Andronicus had been forced to kill to enforce the peace there.

Apollonius suddenly remembered that there was one last thing he had long wanted to do. One of the differences the Samaritans had with the Jews was their Scriptures. Samaritans only accepted the Pentateuch, the first five books of Moses. The Jews had added dozens more corrupted scrolls to their canon. They could not stop their insatiable lust for spiritual control. Though his own religious devotion as a Samaritan left something to be desired, Apollonius had to admit the Jew Menelaus was right about one of his annoying repeated platitudes: *Never waste a crisis.*

So the general decided to use this opportunity of crisis to its fullest.

• • • • •

Eleazar the old scribe had been weeping for so long he had become too exhausted to weep anymore. When the massacre of the citizens had begun in the temple, he had wanted to go out with the other scribes and priests to help the wounded. But the chief scribe had forbidden it. Eleazar was too old and frail. He was commanded to stay with a handful of others to watch over the temple library.

The library was beneath the temple where it was cooler and drier, making it an optimum location to store the hundreds of scrolls they had accumulated over the decades. Scrolls of Scripture, but also other important literature of their period. Eleazar had a significant hand in the collection as that was one of his passions. But now he felt as though he had been imprisoned with the documents while his people were being butchered outside.

Eleazar and his fellow librarians had been praying ever since the bloodbath began. Now they paused at the sound of approaching footsteps, wondering what next terror was in store for them.

They heard a battering ram pounding on the door. Within a few hits, the oak door burst open. A slew of Seleucid soldiers entered followed by their leader, Apollonius the Samaritan Mysarch.

The scribes stood helpless before the soldiers. What were they here for?

Apollonius looked over at the diamond-shaped wooden shelves that lined the library. His gaze landed on Eleazar, who stood in front of the others.

"Which scrolls are your Scriptures, old man?" the general demanded.

Eleazar felt a wave of dread hit him like a tsunami. He gestured to the three closest bookshelves. "These three mostly. What is your intention?"

He felt Apollonius's malignant stare. Then the general responded, "Come and see."

He turned to his men and ordered, "Just take them all."

Twenty or more soldiers entered and snatched scrolls from their resting places, stuffing them in large canvas sacks they had brought with them.

Another scribe yelped out, "Be careful! Those are sacred."

The general gestured toward the scribes. "Get them out of here."

Eleazar and his comrades were grabbed and brought up the stairs to the Court of Women, now surrounded everywhere by Seleucid guards. The Abomination of Desolation, the image of Zeus, had been set up on the altar of Adonai with unholy sacrifice, the regular burnt offering had been taken away, and the sanctuary was overthrown. The entire temple was being trampled underfoot by the presence of these Gentile idolaters. How much worse could it get?

Then Eleazar saw how much worse. Their sacred manuscripts had all been carried up to the open Court of Women and thrown onto a pile in the middle of the courtyard. At the general's command, the scrolls had been set afire.

"No!" screamed Eleazar. He tried to run to the pile, to rescue a scroll, any scroll that he could. Tripped by a soldier, he fell forward to the pavement, a sharp pain in his elbows from breaking the fall.

"No!" he cried out again, crawling toward the scrolls. His hand grasped at a scroll in vain delusion of saving even one of them. But his hand was burned in the flames. He withdrew it, screaming in pain, clutching his wounded hand to his chest. It was red and blistered from the heat.

As the fire consumed the parchments and tablets, Eleazar looked at Apollonius with fury from his collapsed position on the ground, and cursed him, "May Adonai visit you with his flames of judgment for violating the Word of God."

The general's eyes went wide with mock surprise. He looked to the other cowering scribes, five of them. "This decrepit old man has more courage than the lot of you." He turned back to Eleazar. "I thank you for giving me an idea."

Apollonius ordered the closest captain, "Arrest these scribes." The five Jewish men shook with fear. Eleazar got back up to his feet proudly, protecting his burnt hand.

"Captain, I commission you to take your company and do a search of the temple mount. Arrest all scribes, confiscate all scrolls, and consign them to the flames. Then investigate the entire city and countryside, all its synagogues, to find any other portions of their Scriptures—*and burn them all*."

The captain bowed. "Yes, my lord."

Apollonius concluded, "I will take this command to the rest of Judea. If King Antiochus wants to stop the spread of xenophobic division, this hatred of foreigners and their gods, there is no better way than eliminating the disease-ridden source."

Eleazar was shackled with irons. His eyes filled once again with tears of anguish. His dream of gathering the Scriptures together for his people, all the years of his hard work had just been torched by a monster in one moment, one command.

He stared into the future of suffering for his people, the rest of the 2,300 days as the prophet had foretold. Israel's transgression had brought her own desolation. And now God's people were going to be refined and purified by fire.

In the heavenly realm of the inner courtyard, unseen by the humans, Zeus drank from the blood of the swine that had been slaughtered on the new altar before the Jerusalem temple. *His* altar, *his* temple now. Zeus Olympius.

He felt the power of idolatry surge within his spirit. He felt mighty and invincible. Worship was empowering. The city was now his. He sauntered into the temple to find the gods and goddesses celebrating with unspeakable acts on each other. As usual, Hera was not there. She hated their orgies.

"Gods of Greece!" he announced. They stopped, some of them in the middle of violent pleasure. "I do not want to be a killjoy, but we have much ahead of us if we want to maintain the stronghold we have on Yahweh's land. It may be the actual secret to withstanding the advance of Roman hegemony. He who holds the Creator's territory holds the key to world domination."

Athena spoke up. "My king, are we not content to maintain our negotiated status with Rome? Sammael is a mighty Watcher. Roman armies are virtually invincible. And their recent conquering of Macedonia does not bode well for Greco-Roman relations."

"That is why I want you all to pack up for a trip. To the Black Sea in the north."

"The Black Sea?" complained Poseidon. "Right now?"

"Yes, right now. I have been working on a plan, and the time has come to reveal it to you all."

Poseidon complained, "Can it wait just a little? We are a bit occupied at the moment with an important celebration of your enthronement."

Zeus grinned. "Well, Hera isn't here, so why not?" He moved to join them.

•••••

Beneath the temple mount, Hera found Hades sulking in the dark, empty chamber of the temple treasury. "There you are, Dark Lord. Always in an underworld of some sort."

Her attempt at wit fell flat on him. Hades glared up at her from his seated position on the floor. He looked pathetic. "I can't bring myself to see what they do to Persephone up there. What *she* does to *them*. I love her too much."

"Indeed, you do." Hera sat down beside him on the floor. "Those of us who love too much are the ones who suffer the most."

Hades looked over at her and lightened up. "I guess you do understand—with Zeus and all."

"Hmm. I do." Hera paused strategically. "Hades, may I ask you a personal question?"

"What?"

"Do you know what happened to Cerberus?"

He shook his head. "At first, I thought he had just wandered away on his own. But when I returned to Cape Tainaron, I found blood on the ground around the gates he was guarding."

Hera tried to be as casual as possible in her fishing expedition. "What do you think could overpower a mighty threshold guardian like that?"

"I don't know." Hades looked truly confused. He really wasn't in on it.

Hera decided to spring her trap. "Do you think it might have something to do with … Zeus?"

Hades looked at her. "Zeus? Why? Do you think?"

"Well, he has treated you so poorly. Keeping you out of the Olympians. Making you take the most difficult job of guarding the underworld. I mean, it's almost like he is setting you up to fail."

Hades looked genuinely flabbergasted. "Do you really think so? I have sometimes wondered the same myself. But then I doubt."

Hera put on all her charm. "I don't know. I mean, you are the most intelligent of the three brothers over sky, earth, and underworld. Zeus has his thunderbolt and Poseidon his physical strength. But if you think of it, you are the biggest threat to Zeus's greatness. Maybe I am wrong, but I have heard Zeus say more than once that 'it is a good thing Hades is in Hades.' I always wondered what that meant, but now I can see it. You not only have the intelligence and wit to lead the Olympians but the sobriety. And that helmet of yours could equal out the odds."

"Yeah, I guess you're right," Hades replied, looking less unhappy.

"Well, just between you and me," said Hera, "I only want to see you get what you deserve. And I think you deserve more than the underworld. But that's just me."

Hera deliberately left her suggestion ambiguous so Hades would interpret it with his own ambitions. His posture had risen in confidence. His disposition was no longer depressed. She could see his puny little mind was starting to wonder. *Trying* to wonder.

She thought she had better stop while she was ahead. She felt good about this meeting. She had accomplished her purpose of sowing a seed of discord within the triumvirate of the three brothers.

CHAPTER 35

Modein

Judas sat with his brothers as his father oversaw a meeting of the hasidim being held in the synagogue of the village in the late-night hours when most were asleep. There were just over sixty of them, and they had met without the Hellenists because they were not trusted. Word had arrived about the holocaust of innocents in Jerusalem by the king's general Apollonius and the outrageous institution of Zeus worship.

"But that is not all of it," said the messenger. Jacob was a gruff trader merchant who had returned from the holy city just today. "The king has made an edict that we are not to obey our covenant obligations: circumcision, Sabbaths, kashrut."

The men were silent in disbelief. He added, "Under penalty of death. He calls it the Edict of Unity."

Silent unbelief turned to complaints and laughter of scorn. Division and oppression in the name of unity. Someone in the group voiced the obvious conclusion. "Mattathiah! Is that not the justification you claimed worthy of revolt?"

Mattathiah paused, then admitted reluctantly, "Yes."

Judas could see his father thinking through the implications. Some of which Judas was no doubt also thinking.

Jacob went on, "The king has sent messengers to each town to herald the new decrees."

The strongest member of the hasidim, an ex-soldier named Joab, spoke up. "There are hasidim in every town and village throughout Judea. But we are not organized. We need to create a network."

Mattathiah added, "And we need a leader, a strong arm to unite us, or we will be scattered to the wind."

Joab looked over at Judas. "Judas, you have military experience as a commander in the Royal Guard. You know Seleucid battle strategy better than any of us."

Judas shook his head. "But I was a Hellenist. Too many of you hasidim consider me unclean."

"Not all of us," said Joab.

"Enough to cause division and destroy the unity we need to achieve real victories. We need a leader who is above reproach. Someone with impeccable reputation and widespread respect as a spiritual ruler." Judas looked at Mattathiah. "I nominate my father."

The response was a resounding murmur of agreement. But Judas would spend no more time on this second priority. He could only think of one thing right now. "My wife and mother are late in returning from Mizpah. They should have returned two days ago. As important as this meeting may be, they are my immediate priority."

Judas began to make his way out of the synagogue. His brothers followed him along with three other hasidim and family members who had participated in the Mizpah pilgrimage. Judas nudged his way through the crowd until they were all outside the synagogue.

Judas turned to Eleazar. "You will stay with Jonathan and Father."

Eleazar protested, "I am just as good a warrior with my spear as any of you with your swords and hammer."

Judas looked at him with stern eyes. "That is why you need to stay here. I won't take all the best with me and leave the town unprotected."

With a sigh, his younger brother accepted his charge. Jonathan affirmed him with an arm on his shoulder. Judas looked around at the other hasidim who had joined the brothers. "Simon, John, and I will ride to Mizpah with these others. Get your horses and weapons and meet at the city gate as soon as possible."

· · · · ·

Jerusalem

Antiochus sat on his ornate throne before a crowd of a thousand Jews in the outer grounds of the temple mount. The throne rested upon a large temporary wooden platform constructed at the side of the temple with the rest of the temple grounds stretching out before him. The king's patience was wearing thin. He leaned over to Philip and Menelaus sitting on his left. "Where in Hades is Apollonius? He is the one who convinced me to come all the way here. I am about ready to get up and return to Antioch if he doesn't arrive soon."

Philip kept his eyes on the crowd, looking for any unrest. "I am sure he will be here any moment, your majesty. The general is most loyal."

Antiochus noticed the Seleucid soldiers lining the entire colonnade of the temple mount. A thousand of them. A battery of a hundred cavalry each on both sides of his platform. He did not want a riot and resultant massacre to inconvenience his plans.

"Here he is," said Menelaus.

Antiochus looked to his right to see Apollonius rushing up the steps. "Your majesty, please accept my deepest apologies for my tardiness."

He hurriedly took his seat at the right hand of the king. Antiochus frowned. "You had better have a good reason or I have a mind to punish you with these Jews."

The general's face tightened with shock. "Please, your majesty, allow me to explain."

Antiochus smelled him. "You reek of smoke." He saw dirty smudges on the general's face and hands.

"Again, forgive me, your majesty. I was delayed because I caught a group of Jews violating your Edict of Unity by secretly observing their Sabbath in a cave outside the city walls."

Antiochus's interest was roused. "What did you do?"

"I burned them all alive in the cave."

Antiochus raised his brow, impressed. "Men, women, and children?"

Apollonius nodded solemnly.

"Oh," said Antiochus. "Well, in that case, you are very forgiven." He smiled at the thought. "Philip was right. You are most loyal. Now let's get this torture going."

Apollonius stood up to speak to the people. He gestured for the trumpeters, who silenced the crowd with their blowing.

"Hear, O Israel, your king sits enthroned before you, Antiochus IV Epiphanes, God Manifest, ruler of the Seleucid kingdom! He is here to preside over the punishment of those who would not obey his Edict of Unity!"

They had chosen to perform the torture on the temple mount to impress upon the Jews just how serious the king was about his demands. They must transfer their fear of their god onto a fear of their king.

At the other end of the long platform were multiple instruments of torture set up for the day in clear sight of all those below.

The first defendant was brought out by two temple guards, chained in neck, hand, and foot manacles. The goal was propaganda. Showing the heavy chains of justice upon criminals to instill fear of lawbreaking in the audience.

Antiochus recognized this one. It was that very old scribe he had sometimes seen in Antioch. The man was pulled up before Antiochus's throne.

The king asked, "What is your name again?"

"Eleazar, your majesty. I am a scribe of the temple."

"How old are you?"

"Ninety years of age, my lord."

"Ah, yes, I remember you. Hearty constitution for an old man. And you have a good reputation around my court." He saw the old man protecting a bandaged right hand. "Why would you be here?" His question was sincere.

The old scribe replied, "Because I would not eat swine's flesh."

Antiochus shook his head. He could not believe the stubbornness of these people over the most petty of things.

He asked the scribe, "You do realize that you are about to be tortured and executed for disobedience to my Edict?"

"Yes, your majesty."

"You are willing to die for simply not eating pig meat?"

"Yes, your majesty."

Antiochus squinted his eyes, trying hard to understand the reasoning. "Have you ever tasted pork?"

"No, your majesty."

Antiochus laughed incredulously. "Then you are missing out on one of the most glorious flavors of meat created by the gods." He said with a light heart, "I would go so far as to argue that bacon is truly divine. Is it not wrong to hate that which is by nature good?"

"You are correct, your majesty, when you say that creation is good. But the Creator has also given his people his divine law, which commands us to separate ourselves unto him by what we eat and do not eat."

"That seems arbitrary," remarked Antiochus. "And why is such a menial thing like food such a heinous sin to this god of yours?"

"The heinousness of disobedience lies not in the nature of the profane finite offense but in the nature of the holy infinite God who is offended."

Antiochus considered this curious perspective. There was some sense to it. "But if this Supreme Being of yours is truly watching over you, then surely he would excuse any transgression that arises out of compulsion."

"We still choose who to obey. And he will surely judge *you* for your sin of compulsion. I am not in the dock, your majesty. You are."

Antiochus glared at him. *The nerve of this feeble miscreant.* This pathetic little old Semite was defying the sovereign power of a mighty Greek king with such vile contempt. Antiochus thought of slitting the Jew's throat himself.

Instead, he gestured to a guard standing over a table with some of the sacrificial offering meat on it. Swine sacrificed at the altar of Zeus.

"You will eat it!" the king said.

The guards held the captive's head and forced open his mouth. The guard with pork in hand forced a piece into his mouth, and they shut his jaw. But the moment the guard stepped away, the old man spit the meat out onto the ground.

Antiochus ordered them to rack the ungrateful bastard on the Wheel. The guards took the old scribe over to a large solid-wood wagon wheel eight feet in diameter. Its edge was gilded in bronze. The wheel was attached to an axel that could be rotated by a handle large enough for two to operate.

The guards removed Eleazar's chains and tore the clothes off his body. They tied his hands and legs to leather straps that stretched his body out into the shape of a human X. He faced the wood, leaving his back, legs, and buttocks exposed for lashing.

Another temple guard took a scourge to Eleazar's naked body. The whip instrument contained multiple leather straps ending in tips with pieces of metal and bone embedded in them. Each strike ripped through flesh and bone, eliciting a cry of agony from the victim.

It only took a dozen lashes to shred the old man's back and legs into bloody pulp. Antiochus could hear the weak groans of pain from the captive with each hit. It was amazing to him how enduring this old man was. And how resolute. Hearty constitution indeed.

The flogger stopped and looked to Antiochus, who nodded.

The guard said to Eleazar, "If you will eat the pork even now, you will be released and forgiven by the king."

What Antiochus did not see was that the temple guard showed Eleazar a piece of beef hidden in his hand. Dropping his voice to a whisper, he pleaded, "Eleazar, just say that you will eat. I will give you this piece of kosher beef, and you can pretend you are eating pork when you are not. Outward obedience with inward defiance."

Eleazar struggled through his pain to whisper back, "You would have me sin greater by inspiring others to sin through my deception. Young man, we will all die and one day be judged according to what we have done."

The guard shook his head to the king. The captive would not repent. Antiochus shouted to Eleazar, "What do you have to say to this god who allows you such meaningless suffering?"

Eleazar prayed to God in heaven, "Be merciful to your people, O Lord. Make my blood their purification and take my life in exchange for theirs."

It was all so foolish to Antiochus. Absurd even. That this fool would rather suffer and die a miserable death than eat a mere piece of meat. Antiochus had often put down madmen who threatened the order of society with their ravings of lunacy. Perhaps this was an entire culture of madness. Chaos that had to be wiped out in order to purify the Hellenist order.

If he had to kill every last one of these Jews to keep peace, unity, and tolerance, then that is what he would do—gladly. And for the gods.

Antiochus gave the order to finish the scourging unto death.

· · · · ·

Mizpah

The ten-mile trip to Mizpah had been gut-wrenching for Judas. He had originally assumed the late return of the pilgrims was not unusual. That they would probably be home any day. But as he got closer to the town with no sign of the Modein company on the road back, his dread grew stronger. He prayed silently to Ha Shem for the safety of his wife, mother, and all the other village members who had accompanied them.

Under the moonlight of the late evening, Judas could see they were in visual distance of Mizpah. He detected plumes of black smoke rising lazily against the dark night sky. One glance at Simon and John and they kicked their horses into a race for the village gate.

When the six members of their party arrived, they were greeted by a bedraggled crowd of no more than a hundred survivors.

"What has happened here?" asked Judas.

One of the villagers, a heavy-set man with fear in his eyes, said, "The king sent soldiers with a new command called the Edict of Unity. All Jews are to stop our religious practices. Those who vocally refused were arrested. Those of us smart enough to lie said we would obey the king. So they spared us."

"Edict of Unity." repeated Judas. This was the same news the merchant Jacob had brought to Modein. "You are referring to the new decree to halt circumcision, Sabbath, and all our dietary restrictions."

"Yes, but it is more than that!" the villager added vehemently. "The king has set up an altar to Zeus in the holy temple. He says we are to sacrifice unclean animals to the gods."

Judas could not believe what he was hearing. "That is complete desecration of our covenant with Adonai."

"Abomination of Desolation," exclaimed Simon. "Just as Eleazar warned us."

"They'll get to Modein eventually," John said somberly,

Judas asked the villager, "What of the Modein pilgrims? Are they still here?"

"They were all taken to Jerusalem."

Judas gave a dark look at Simon and John. They all turned their horses and bolted eastward.

• • • • •

Jerusalem

Menelaus felt uncomfortable sitting beside King Antiochus. He had wanted to distance himself from the king's public presence so that he could not be as easily tied to the punishments the king was overseeing right now on the temple grounds. But Antiochus had ordered him to be there. Menelaus was just glad he didn't have to sit beside that monster Apollonius on the other side of the king. He despised the Samaritan general and knew the general despised him. Next to Menelaus, Philip the governor expressed vocal curiosity of their new defendants.

A Jewish family of seven young men and their mother was paraded before the king and his "court" of officials. Their ages appeared to be from their twenties down to their teens. And they were all handsome. Especially the youngest ones. Menelaus could feel a desire for them rising within his loins. What a shame if those pleasant looks and physiques would be disfigured and unusable for his pleasure.

Well, there were plenty of other fish in the sea for his appetite.

"And what is your name, mother?" asked the king.

"Solomonia, your majesty. These are my sons whose father has died."

Antiochus said, "You have all been charged with disobedience against my royal Edict of Unity. You will not eat pork, and you will not participate in sacrifices to Zeus Olympius. What have you to say for yourself and your sons?"

The eldest son stepped forward. He was well-built, almost like a soldier. His eyes were dark and serious under a furrowed brow. "Your majesty, my name is Havim. I am the eldest, and I will speak as the male responsible for our household. You speak the truth about us. We will not defy the divine laws of our God. But do not suppose that torture will accomplish your purpose in us. For through severe suffering and endurance, we shall have the prize of piety and shall be with God, for whom we gladly suffer. But you are a tyrant, and because of your bloodthirsty idolatry, you will one day experience the divine justice of eternal torment by fire."

Menelaus was shocked by the bravado. He glanced over at Antiochus to see him red-faced with fury. The king shouted out to the guards, "Bring out my executioner and give this insurrectionist the full course of treatment! And make his family watch!"

Stripping Havim's garments off him, the guards dragged him up to the platform of various torture devices. They tied him on a rack spread-eagled.

The executioner came out to meet his victim. He was a hairless man, bald without eyebrows or eyelashes. He was muscular with Ethiopian features, but his skin was pale white with light-blue eyes. An albino. He looked like a wraith, a spirit of death. It took a special kind of creature to perform some tortures. A heartless demon. This one acted with speed and efficiency as a hunter might skin his prey.

First, he scalped Havim's head with a sharp dagger, ripping his beautiful black hair from his skull. Then he cut out the young man's tongue.

Menelaus saw the mother weeping but forcing herself to watch as though this would maintain poor Havim's human dignity in the midst of such humiliation.

Menelaus knew what the full-course treatment was that Antiochus had referred to. That was why he closed his eyes. He didn't want to see what happened next.

But he heard it. He heard the screams. The sound of the executioner's axe chopping off each of the victim's hands and feet. Then the sound of sizzling as the executioner carried the poor soul over to a fire and threw his victim's body into an iron pan large enough to fit a man.

A breeze carried the sickening smell of burning human flesh to the nostrils of everyone on the platform. Menelaus wrinkled his nose at it. Fortunately, the screams did not last long before they were cut short in horrible death and the body was taken away.

The next son, in his early twenties, was chubby with a round, happy-looking face and rosy cheeks. The young man's eyes were penetrating blue and seemed to haunt Menelaus with their sadness. Antiochus ordered him to state his name.

"Antonin."

"And will you also refuse to eat the pork?"

"I will," he said. "And you will not refuse the judgments of divine wrath in the afterlife. You accursed wretch, you dismiss us from this present life. But the King of the universe will raise us up to an everlasting renewal of life because we have died for his laws."

Menelaus rolled his eyes. *Am I to sit through seven of these pious lectures? I don't have the patience.*

The king gestured to the executioner. "Flay him. See if he retains his confidence then."

The young man was brought up to the rack and tied down. The otherworldly executioner then took a sharp blade and began to cut the skin from the screaming lad.

Menelaus closed his eyes again at the gruesome scene. But he gradually peeked out more and more until he was watching the entire final act of horrifying torture. It was interesting how the more you watched, the more you could stomach until at last it became more a matter of curiosity than horror. Even the screams of the victims became less repulsive.

They did deserve it, after all. The penalty for treason against the throne was justifiably execution. And this was only the tip of the pyramid of how many other Jews were defying the king and causing chaos in society.

As agents of chaos they would be made the example.

In his late teens, the third son gave his name as Guriah. Another waste of a handsome boy, so innocent-looking with his slim, muscled arms and legs and smooth, beardless face. When he got his chance to speak, he too turned down the pork. He thrust out his tongue and raised his hands in offering as he pronounced arrogantly, "I received this tongue and these limbs from heaven. In obedience to Adonai's laws, I freely give them up as my brother did. And from Adonai, I hope to get them back again."

This one the guards lashed to the wheel. The executioner broke every finger, toe, elbow, and knee. Every joint on the lad's body he disjointed with his instruments. Even the vertebrates of his back. The cracking bones could be heard in the crowd below, who by now were becoming restless with the suffering. Soldiers moved in with raised pikes and shields to keep the mob from becoming unruly.

But Menelaus noticed the mother never wavered from watching every detail of torture performed on each of her sons. Her face was reddened and drenched with tears, but Menelaus could see a conviction in her that shook him. She appeared to be encouraging each son, rooting them on to their deaths as if those deaths were meaningful. And the young men's references to the afterlife and judgment seemed to come from a sincere belief that they really would get their bodies back in some new kind of way. They really believed in a future resurrection.

By the time the fourth sibling was dragged forward, the sun was getting high in the sky. Menelaus felt his eyelids getting heavy. He had eaten a meal shortly before they had begun, and now he was feeling the effects as his body craved a nap. He struggled to keep his head up so the king would not notice. He barely heard a name. Eleazar? Elijah? He felt a dizziness engulf him in a twilight where he heard distant screams of agony that blended into crowd rumblings and sounds of chopping, frying, and sizzling.

An elbow nudged him in the side, awakening him. Philip's elbow. He had dozed off and missed the fourth son. Who was up now? The fifth. Menelaus felt a second wind as he watched what must have been a boy no more than fifteen give his name to the king. "Eusebon."

This one had long, dark hair, a square jaw, and a cocky self-assurance like one of those boys in the gymnasium who looked both smart and athletic. Like he had it all. And he had it all to lose. It was tragic.

This time the king decided to make it even more absurd. He said, "Eusebon. What if I only gave you one bite of pig? That would be all you have to take to fulfill my command. Just one tiny little bite. Not even a mouthful."

The young lad seemed as strong in his resolve as his older brothers. "O king, I would not trade eternal life for a mere bite of food. I cherish the hope God gives of being raised again by him. But for you there will be no resurrection to life, only resurrection to judgment."

There it was again, thought Menelaus. *Resurrection They were obsessed with it*. He had been a priest his entire life and had rarely ever heard of the concept of resurrection. Isaiah, Ezekiel, and Daniel had used the word, but as a metaphor for the return of the twelve tribes back into the land of Israel. Some had claimed their return to Jerusalem under Cyrus had fulfilled that metaphor while others claimed not all twelve tribes had returned, but only Judah, Benjamin, and Levi. The other tribes had been dissolved into the nations with the Assyrian exile. And only their future Messiah would unite them all into one in the land.

Either way, resurrection was a creative and prophetic symbol, not a physical reality. Where did these fanatics get such ideas?

Suddenly, Antiochus raised his hand to stop the guards. He pointed to the sixth son, barely into puberty. This one disturbed Menelaus because he reminded the high priest of himself at that age, angular face with piercing eyes and large, thin nose, his whole life yet to be lived.

"And what of you? Will you eat?"

"O king, my name is Hadim. I am younger in age than my brothers, but I am their equal in will. Since to this end we were born and bred, we ought likewise to die for the same principles. And we six brothers have paralyzed your tyranny with our piety. Is this not the start of your downfall?"

Antiochus sighed, then spoke to the executioner. "Do them together. Let's get this over with."

The guards brought the two boys up to the wheel and tied them, one on each side of the outer bronze tread. But this time, they were laid with their backs to the tread and their hands and feet pulled behind them. They looked like two scorpions on opposing sides of the wheel.

Some guards brought coals from the fire of the frying pan and placed them beneath the wheel structure. One of them punctured the youngest in the belly with a red-hot iron. His intestines spilled out.

The wheel was then turned to roast each of the brothers slowly and painfully because of their obedience to their god.

Menelaus saw the king clutch his own abdomen with his secret pain. The high priest knew of the malady. It was some kind of intestinal disease that Antiochus had struggled with for a long time. He tried to hide it, but sometimes it was so obvious to anyone who watched him closely that he was suffering bowel pain. The irony did not escape Menelaus. Antiochus was suffering a longtime torture as he tortured others.

But now, the king turned to the last son. Marcellus couldn't be more than ten years old. This one was very desirable to Menelaus, so bright and hopeful with his large puppy-like eyes, big ears, and cute overbite. He reminded Menelaus of his grandson Joseph. The playful-looking little boy looked so out of place in this scene of misery and pain. The king had gone all out with an outrageous offer as though playing a game of dice and betting everything to try to win against these poor commonfolk with wills of iron.

Surely, this simple, frail child would break.

"Young boy, I want to make you an offer," Antiochus pronounced loudly. "I will swear an oath on my throne that I will make you a Friend of the King, make you rich beyond your wildest dreams, and give you a public office where you could do well for your people. All you have to do is put aside your ancestors' restrictive rules that you live under and swear allegiance to your king. You will save both yourself and your mother."

The boy remained silent. The king spoke to his mother. "Solomonia, talk some sense into your boy. He is a mere child with his whole life ahead of him. He could do more good for the Jews than all his brothers put together."

Solomonia stared at the king incredulously. She turned to the boy and told him, "Do not fear this butcher but prove worthy of your brothers. Accept death so that in God's mercy I may get you back again along with your brothers."

Menelaus saw Antiochus turning red with anger again.

The boy finally spoke up. "O king, you are a bad man. You do not obey God. But I will obey him. God is our heavenly father, and he is punishing our people for disobeying him. That is why you are able to hurt us. But one day, God will hurt you, and I will see my brothers again. We will all be happy together. But not you."

Antiochus screamed out, "Shut this little putz up! Throw him in the flames."

The guards moved to grab the boy, but he eluded their grasp. Dodging around the guards, he ran up the stairs of the platform. The executioner reached for him, but he was too slow a lumbering giant. Marcellus dodged him as well.

Then Menelaus realized that the boy was not trying to escape into the crowd. He was running straight toward the large bonfire of flames by the frying pan. Diving into the fire, he cried out in pain. He rolled around, his reflexes trying to protect him. But he did not leave the fire.

Within a minute, the boy stopped moving in the coals and lay still as his flesh was consumed by the flames.

Menelaus could not believe his eyes. How could such a young child have such firm convictions? From where did he draw his thoughts if not from his mother? He concluded it was a family of madness. The madness had spread like a disease to all of them as it had done to so many of the Jews who refused to obey the king.

He heard Apollonius lean into the king and ask him, "Your majesty, may I execute the woman with the special sword you gave me? You will be amazed with its elegance."

Antiochus waved him on. The general got up and descended the stairs. Solomonia stood erect as if to defy Apollonius and everything that had just happened to her sons.

The general stood six feet from her and pulled out his whip-sword. The blade unrolled to the ground like a dragon's tongue.

Apollonius swung the blade over his head in a circle.

And he cracked the whip-sword and stole the life of his victim without a second thought.

Valley of the Rephaim

Judas, John, Simon, and the three other men from Modein were within a mile from Jerusalem when they came upon a squad of twelve Seleucid soldiers coming their way, obviously some kind of area patrol.

Simon whispered, "Should we fight? We can take them easily."

"No," ordered Judas. "Let me talk to them."

They were in a valley, and it was too late to run. It would only make them look guilty. They would have to talk their way out of this one. Judas cursed himself for not bringing Jonathan along. That lad could talk circles around these officers and bamboozle them. But Judas and Simon would have to do this on their own without their smooth-talking younger brother.

Judas had stopped his men. The soldiers approached within fighting distance, their hands ready on their weapons. The leader, a shifty-looking devious man, called out to them, "Who are you, and what is your purpose?"

Judas had to think fast. "We are residents of Jerusalem returning from a journey to Mizpah. It is a common prayer pilgrimage for us Jews."

Partial truths were the most effective lies.

But the shifty leader did not look gullible. He said, "You look more like armed men on a mission to me."

Judas acted surprised. "These are dangerous times, sir. We arm ourselves for protection against highway bandits."

He was relieved that the soldier did not appear aware of the attack on Mizpah.

The leader stared into Judas's eyes as though trying to assess if he was lying. He demanded, "Where are your women?"

"Back in Jerusalem. We heard that there might have been some trouble at Mizpah so we didn't want to risk bringing them."

"As a matter of fact, there was trouble at Mizpah. Why didn't you mention that?"

"Yes, so we discovered when we arrived. Thankfully, it was long over by then."

The shifty leader smirked. "I think we will escort you back to the city in custody and see if these women of yours will corroborate your story."

So he *didn't* believe Judas.

Judas glanced with a carefree expression at the rest of their party as though they had nothing to hide. He could only hope the others were as good at acting as he was. He knew his brothers would follow his moves, but he didn't know the other men well enough to assess their reactions.

They remained quiet as Judas shrugged. "We are in your custody, sir. Lead the way."

The soldiers surrounded the horse party and began to escort them to Jerusalem. Judas had no idea what they were going to do now. Their lie would eventually be found out, so should he take a chance now and attack?

His question was answered by a shout down the road. Another Seleucid official was approaching with a squad of soldiers.

When they met in the road, the other leader pronounced, "Lieutenant Erasmus, I am Captain Apelles. I have been commissioned by General Apollonius to gather your troops to my own for a mission."

"But Captain, we are on patrol. We have these men in our custody."

"What have these men done?"

Erasmus became agitated. "Well, they haven't officially broken a law. But they have given suspicious answers to my questions that I need to investigate."

Judas slumped in his seat and smiled innocently, doing his best to appear unimpressive.

The captain looked them over, then turned back to the lieutenant. "You will have to let them loose. My matter is more pressing."

"May I ask what your orders are, sir?"

"We are to enforce the king's edict in several towns and villages, starting with …" He looked at his assistant who was looking at a map. "What was the name of that stupid town?"

"Modein, sir," said the assistant.

Judas felt his stomach drop. He glanced surreptitiously over at John and Simon, who glanced back fearfully.

"Yes, Modein. We need your squad to complete a full unit of fifty. And even that is sparing due to the number of troops needed in Jerusalem."

So Antiochus's forces were spreading out into the rural areas now. No one was safe.

Judas saw Erasmus staring at him with suspicious eyes. "You are free to go."

Did the observant shifty lieutenant notice Judas's discomfort?

"Wait a second." Raising a hand, the captain addressed Judas. "Do you Jews know where Modein is?"

Judas tried not to sound too interested. "Yes, Captain. We know the area."

Apelles waved his assistant forward. "Atticus, bring that map to this man."

The assistant jockeyed his horse up to Judas. The captain said, "Our map was terribly drawn by someone who barely knew what he was doing. Can you confirm these details about the location of this first city, Modein?"

Judas looked at the scrawling on the parchment. It wasn't very good, but it was close enough to get the soldiers to Modein. He chuckled as he lifted it up to show the captain and lied. "You are correct, Captain. Your mapmaker barely knew what he was doing. Or confused some villages in his memory."

He pointed to Modein on the map. "This is where Lydda is. Not Modein. Modein is much further south here."

Judas gestured on the map to where there was nothing in reality. "When you get into this area, just follow the large wadi ravine through here, and it will lead you to Modein down here."

It would in fact lead them to nowhere. Or rather, if the soldiers kept going, it would lead them to the coast, thus bypassing the neighboring villages as well as Modein itself.

This was only a tactic of delay. Judas knew the commander would eventually find his way. He just hoped to be back in time to protect Modein and the other villages from danger.

"Thank you for your help," said Captain Apelles. "You are a loyal subject of the king."

Judas smiled and nodded. The captain continued down the valley toward his destination to nowhere, leaving Judas and his companions to begin trotting toward Jerusalem. Once the soldiers were totally out of sight, they kicked their horses and raced to the city as fast as they could.

· · · · ·

Jerusalem

Sophia and Hannah had been waiting in the dungeon below the temple mount all day. They had been thrown into a cell with several dozen other women, many of whom had infant sons in their arms. Their new companions had been kept down here for days and were all filthy, hungry, and scared. Sophia had quickly found out that most of these women were here because they had circumcised their sons since the Edict of Unity had commanded them not to. Others had been circumcised before the Edict, but such details were not important to the abominable one, King Antiochus Epimanes. Antiochus the Mad.

Of their own party, they had not seen anyone since the soldiers had shoved the captives into the jail. Solomonia and the four other women in the group—a grandmother, mother, and two teenaged daughters from the same family—had ended up in another cell while the men and boys had been pushed down a separate passageway.

One thing was certain. Infants or not, the women were going to be punished together for their defiance of the king's decrees. So when they were released from the iron cells and herded up the stairs into the temple mount area, Sophia said a silent prayer for strength and protection. Hannah held tightly to her arm. They didn't want to get separated in the chaos.

Sophia could hear her mother-in-law whispering the twenty-third psalm of David. She joined her.

> *Even though I walk through the valley of the shadow of death,*
> *I will fear no evil,*
> *for you are with me;*
> *your rod and your staff,*
> *they comfort me.*

More women joined in their recitation. A soft, whispering chorus united in prayer.

> *You prepare a table before me*
> *in the presence of my enemies;*
> *You anoint my head with oil;*
> *my cup overflows.*
> *Surely goodness and mercy shall follow me*
> *all the days of my life,*
> *and I shall dwell in the house of the Lord*
> *forever.*

They were herded up to an area just outside the temple near a large platform that hosted fires, a rack, a torture wheel, and other instruments of torture. Sophia could see bloody carnage left from previous inflictions. She could smell the odor of burning human flesh. A shiver of dread filled her. She felt nauseas as she looked down to see blood on the pavement at her bare feet.

At the far side of the huddled prisoners, Sophia spotted the other women and girls who had been part of the Modein group. Only Solomonia appeared missing. Turning, she looked behind her into a crowd of local residents who seemed beaten down in spirit. She searched the crowd for Judas's face. For any of her family. Big John would be a big comfort right now.

Hannah whispered to her as if she read her thoughts. "Even if our husbands have figured out our absence and are on their way, we must trust in the Lord for our salvation."

Sophia held her belly protectively and pulled out her amulet to clutch it with hope.

> *May YHWH bless you and guard you; may YHWH make his face shine upon you.*
> *YHWH lift up his countenance upon you and give you peace.*

On the right side of the platform was a court of some officials. Sophia could see King Antiochus, the high priest Menelaus, and two others she did not recognize. One was dressed as a high-ranking military officer, the other a governing official of some kind.

The women tried to comfort their infants. Most were awake and crying for attention or milk or comfort. Sophia could see the king was bothered by it all and wanted to get this over with.

He spoke to the women. "You are all here for violating my Edict. None of you will eat foods that I have declared clean. Others have circumcised your sons in direct defiance of my orders. You refuse to Hellenize and insist on raising traitorous families who will one day defy me as well. I have ordered that those of you with infants have your infants hung by rope from your own necks and all of you to be cast down from the walls of Jerusalem."

Sophia and Hannah grasped each other's hands tightly. A disruption of verbal shock and crying broke out amidst the women. As Sophia looked at her mother-in-law, she felt her head spinning out of control. Even the crowds behind them voiced opposition.

The Seleucid soldiers all around them advanced with force to make sure no one got out of line. Voices in the crowd cried out, "Mercy! Injustice! Abomination!"

When the crowd had calmed somewhat, Antiochus stood with red-faced rage and shouted, "I will tolerate no more sedition! Submit or die! Progress or die! Hellenize or die!"

He turned to the guards around the women. "Bring them to the wall."

• • • • •

Outside Jerusalem

Judas and his men reached the southern Fountain Gate of Jerusalem from the Kidron Valley. There they spotted a commotion of crowds further down the valley on the eastern walls of the city.

A group of people crossed their path on the way to the commotion. Judas shouted out, "Hello, there! What is going on?"

One of the women turned back, weeping. "The women! The women in prison! At the walls of the East Gate!"

Judas looked at Simon and John, and the brothers all sprinted toward the East Gate, the others just behind them.

When they arrived, they witnessed a horrifying sight. At the bottom of the ravine below the forty-foot-high walls of the city lay a blanket of bodies. Women. Bloodied and crushed by the fall from the wall high above. Some residents were already pulling out their loved ones to carry away and bury. Others knelt or lay prostrate and wept. Other women wailed with mourning.

Judas began shaking. Racing ahead, he jumped off his horse. Simon and John followed, the other men as well. He walked amidst the bodies looking for Sophia or his mother.

But what he saw made him stop dead in his tracks. A grisly atrocity. All around him, many of the women had infants tied to them by ropes around their necks, also dead.

What kind of evil mind would spawn this gruesome massacre? What kind of beast?

Judas returned to looking for Sophia.

"Please, Adonai," he whispered. "Please let her not be here. Please let her …"

He froze, shouting, "John! Simon!"

He raced to where two bodies lay on top of others.

Sophia.

Mother.

His knees buckled with grief, his head swirled with dizzying shock. And he wept.

Sophia was on her back, lying on top of another woman. She hadn't hit a rock like many others. She didn't even have blood splattered anywhere. She looked as though she had just fallen peacefully asleep. Her hands clutched her necklace at her heart.

More curiously, his mother was lying on her stomach right next to Sophia, her hand outstretched and palm on Sophia's abdomen. She must have survived the fall long enough to crawl over to her daughter-in-law and place her hand on her belly.

Mother had a heart of gold and a will of iron. Even in death, they could not stop her.

Arriving, John and Simon got down with Judas, holding him to keep him from collapsing in grief. They silently shared their pain with one another for what seemed an eternity.

And then it struck Judas. Sophia was clutching a necklace. He hadn't been aware she possessed such a necklace.

Reaching down, he gently opened her frozen grip finger by finger until he pulled out what was in her palm.

A small silver amulet.

One side had a blessing from the Torah.

> *May YHWH bless you and guard you. May YHWH make his face shine upon you.*
> *YHWH lift up his countenance upon you and give you peace.*

On the other side was a curse.

> *May YHWH curse Lilith the night demon and her serpent. May they make their resting place far from you.*

And then he knew. Sophia had been pregnant.

She had not even had the chance to tell him. To share their joy together. And now they were forever apart.

Forever.

"No!" he screamed to the heavens. "Nooooooo!"

His eyes moved back down to the top of the walls where Seleucid soldiers looked down upon their diabolical deed like demonic Watchers. They had killed them. Killed his mother, his wife, and his child.

King Antiochus had killed his mother, his wife, and his child.

CHAPTER 36

Pontus, Scythia

Heracles traversed the southern shore of the Black Sea four hundred miles north of the Seleucid capital of Antioch, Syria. This was the region of the Scythians, fearsome nomadic horse warriors whose barbaric society had gained a reputation among the Greeks for its peculiar cruelty. The Greek historian Herodotus had described some of their bizarre savage practices. They scalped their enemies and used their skin to cover their quivers. They drank the blood of their first human kills and drank wine from the skulls of their victims. There had been rumors of cannibalism. Scythians bathed in the vapor of burning hemp and smoked the leaf called cannabis to commune with the dead. They tattooed their bodies, sometimes in totality, and wore leather and animal skins like that of leopards.

Their equine culture centered around the horse. They valued the horse more than other humans. They sacrificed horses to their gods and ate their flesh. Heracles figured they probably had sex with the animals. They were supreme on the flatlands of the steppes because of these powerful, swift beasts, and their expertise with archery was unparalleled.

They were known for the uncivilized practice of using some of their own women as soldiers in battle, training them equally in both horsemanship and archery. This distortion of nature had spread amongst the various Scythian tribes over time until it bred a unique separate tribe of exclusively female warriors who had concluded they needed no men at all except for breeding. They were called Amazons or Amazonians, and they had a reputation of being fierce "man-killers" in the Pontus region.

The Amazon tribe was Heracles's next target. His task was to capture the belt of the Amazon Queen, a figure shrouded in much legend. Well, Heracles was used to that himself. He chuckled. This was going to be fun.

Entering the port city of Sinope, Heracles disguised himself as best he could as a burly deckhand for one of the merchant ships. He wanted to gather some intelligence on his target warriors to assess their strengths and weaknesses. Even though they were all women and therefore their weaknesses obvious and manifold, one should never underestimate their enemy.

Heracles entered a crowded tavern near the harbor. Walking deeper into the noisy establishment, he shrugged his wide shoulders to create a deferential posture and decrease some of his height. He found an open spot at a small table where a sailor sat alone. The man wore a ragged tunic and a bandana on his bald head.

Heracles stepped up to the table. He wiped his brow, having rubbed dirt and oil into his skin earlier, and scratched his messy hair. "Do you mind if I share the table, friend?"

The sailor looked up at him, clearly impressed by his size. "What would you do to me if I said no?"

Heracles felt off-guard by the comment. He wasn't sure what to say.

Until the sailor grinned widely and slapped his arm. "I'm just playing with ya, big fella. Take a seat. Name's Mago."

"Alcides," said Heracles, plopping onto the bench as if exhausted from a hard day's work. Alcides had been his birth name.

"From Thebes, are you?" Mago asked.

Heracles was surprised again.

"Ah, it's your accent. From Tyre myself, but I've been all around the Mediterranean. What brings you so far north?"

"Oh, just off-loading a shipment of oil from Cyprus," Heracles replied. "The captain just paid us all off, so how about a couple rounds on me?"

Heracles flagged a beer wench down. They saluted each other and drank. After three more beers, Heracles asked his new friend, "So what do you know about the Amazons down by the steppes? Is it true they are a tribe of only female warriors?"

"Aye, that they are. Greeks call them the Daughters of Ares. They worship Cybele, the Anatolian mother goddess."

"How do they reproduce? Are they all like Sappho from the isle of Lesbos?"

Heracles had read Sappho's poetry. She was obsessed with women.

Mago laughed. "I imagine many are. They don't much like men. They recruit women from the normal Scythian tribes around them."

Parasites off the broader population, Heracles thought.

Mago stopped himself and laughed. "Ha! There's a contradiction of terms: 'normal' and 'Scythian.'"

Heracles laughed along. He was enjoying himself. They drank another beer. Heracles could drink any man under the table. And this Phoenician's tongue was getting looser with more alcohol.

Mago continued, "But they do breed at times with other Scythian tribes. They find the strongest specimens and mate with them. Then they return to their tribe to give birth and raise them as Amazons."

"What about male offspring?"

Mago looked around, then leaned in to whisper, "They kill most of them. Others, they castrate like eunuchs. Makes them more feminine. They use them as servants. They put collars on them like dogs."

Heracles felt his face go wide with shock.

He muttered, "Barbaric."

Mago mused to himself, "Women can be ruthless."

"I hear they are expert horse riders and archers," said Heracles.

"Oh, yes!" Mago belched. "You don't want to face them on the steppe. They can outride and out-shoot any man. They can turn around and fire behind them with deadly accuracy while being chased."

"But are they strong?"

"Ah, the rumors are they are as strong as men. But they use composite bows. The force of the arrow is five times the pull. They cut off their right breasts so they can use their bow with more accuracy."

"What a shame," said Heracles. "I love breasts. Are they beautiful otherwise? Exotic?"

He couldn't help but get aroused thinking of seeing a beautiful Amazon woman in action—with one large left breast.

"They say their queen Deianeira has the beauty of a goddess."

Heracles started fantasizing about Deianeira and what he might do to her. *Deianeira. Queen Deianeira.*

Mago broke him out of his daydream. "Her name means, 'Man Destroyer.'"

Well, that was a fly in the ointment.

The sailor continued, leaning in again like a woozy drunken conspirator, "But her champion warrior Aristomache, I hear she is not Scythian. Comes from Gath. They say she is eight feet tall and has killed hundreds of men." He looked nervously around again. "They say she has giant's blood."

Heracles raised his brow in interest. He had been told by his father that he too had giant's blood. Would he finally find a worthy battle opponent in this world of puny men? Would he find an equal to mate with? He hoped this giantess was not too ugly.

Mago went on to say that rumor spoke of at least several hundred women in this tribe of Amazons. Then he fell unconscious to the table, out for the evening. Heracles belched, feeling he could drink another ten beers. The poor sucker sailor was so inebriated he probably wouldn't remember their discussion. Which was good for Mago's sake because then Heracles wouldn't have to kill him to protect his cover.

The night was still young, so Heracles traveled inland to the steppe, the large arid plateau where the Amazonians traveled. He chose this hour so as not to be seen approaching his prey. The shining stars above lit the hard-packed dirt as he jogged. It was colder here than on the coast, and it would be a lot hotter in the daytime due to the wide-open desert expanse. Nothing much grew on the steppe, which made it inhospitable for agriculture but perfect for the nomadic Scythians and their Amazonian offshoot.

Heracles found the Amazonians encamped at the edge of the forest that led to the Pontic mountains beyond. They likely held hunting parties in the woods, bringing home meat to smoke and store. He saw dozens of yurts, large, round, and elaborate tents of hides popular in Asia. The sailor had mentioned that the tribe was strongest on the flats of the plateau. Heracles looked out into the expanse and then at the forest, thinking through his strategy. He would need one more night to prepare his plan of attack. During the day, he would sleep in the forest.

CHAPTER 37

Modein

The funeral procession for the martyred families of Modein was done communally in a ritual mourning for seven days. The three other men who had accompanied Judas and his brothers had found their own slain family members. Two were the father and older brother of the mother and two teen daughters pushed from the city wall. The grandfather as well as grandmother had been among the slain.

The third hasidim had three male family members—an elderly grandfather, brother, and nephew who like Solomonia's sons had refused to renounce their faith in Adonai. These victims had all been dumped in the Valley of Hinnom, Jerusalem's cursed valley once used for child sacrifices to Molech.

The six comrades had purchased two large carts to bring the bodies back home for burial, including the elderly scribe Eleazar. The bodies of those executed, including Solomonia, had been in far worse condition than the women thrown to their death from the city wall. They had each been savagely tortured, shredded, shattered, dismembered, and burnt all because they would not forsake their religious covenant with Adonai.

For some victims, they could not find all the pieces. They brought what they could find. They met several cohorts of Seleucid soldiers on the grim journey home. To Judas's surprise, they were let pass unhindered. Perhaps the soldiers considered the sight of such grisly remains would convince the populace to submit to the Edict.

Judas's female cousins and other women neighbors prepared the bodies of Sophia, Hannah, and Eleazar for Mattathiah and his sons. First, they washed the bodies, then used herbs and spices and anointed the bodies with oil before wrapping them in shrouds for their burials. Their bodies and those of the other martyrs were placed in wooden coffins and walked in procession through the main street of Modein followed by residents dressed in sackcloth as mourning clothes.

Judas led the procession, but his mind was lost in the Abyss. He could barely hear the women wailers behind him or the flutes playing funeral dirges at the back. He didn't care for any of it. He didn't care for anything anymore. He had nothing left to live for.

He watched his father closely. Mattathiah had wept and wailed at first. But now he was leading the funerary rituals with somber face. How could he be so stoic? His wife of thirty-plus years had been taken from him. She was a woman of God, loving, kind, a true helpmate who had borne and raised five sons. She was the finest example of a wife and mother that Judas had ever seen. How could his father have any composure at all? How could he move on?

Mattathiah had told Judas it was because he knew he would see Hannah again. And that if Judas truly believed in the God of Abraham, Isaac, and Jacob, he would know the love of a heavenly father that surpassed all earthly love. That without the love of God, our human love had no hope, no endurance beyond the grave.

It was all pious delusion to Judas. But he wanted to believe it.

The coffins were buried in graves of the necropolis outside Modein's city limits. The living participants would all be considered unclean for seven days because of their connection with the dead during the funeral. Therein, they would mourn together in households until the seven-day period was over.

Family and friends surrounded the gravesites of his mother, his Sophia, and their child. Because he did not know the sex of his unborn child, he called it Ariel, a name that could be used for male or female. More importantly, it meant "Lion of God."

Eleazar was buried with them in the family plot. He had been family to them. Mattathiah read Psalm 91 as the coffins were lowered into the ground.

> *He who dwells in the shelter of the Most High*
> *   will abide in the shadow of the Almighty.*
> *I will say to the Lord, "My refuge and my fortress,*
> *   my God, in whom I trust."*

Judas became completely unaware of his family around him, his father and brothers, and everyone else. He felt all alone in the cosmos. His attention spiraled inward like a tunnel shrinking in around him. He began to think of his beloved and the love they had shared. A love that had been taken from him before it could bear fruit. The times of happiness together, laughing, eating, praying, making love. The memories assaulted his mind like torture.

All of it, taken away. Destroyed.

Then Mattathiah's reading brought Judas back to the moment as the words of the psalm now had strange new meaning for him. Though they were spoken as words of comfort, he felt them as barbs of mockery.

> *Because you have made the Lord your dwelling place—*
> *   the Most High, who is my refuge—*
> *no evil shall be allowed to befall you,*
> *   no plague come near your tent.*
> *For he will command his angels concerning you*
> *   to guard you in all your ways.*
> *On their hands they will bear you up,*
> *   lest you strike your foot against a stone.*
> *You will tread on the lion and the adder;*
> *   the young lion and the serpent you will trample underfoot.*

> *"Because he holds fast to me in love, I will deliver him;*
> *I will protect him, because he knows my name."*

They were all just platitudes to Judas. Empty platitudes. Delusional expressions of a vain hope. A call to protection that had never come for his beloved Sophia. Or for his mother or his mentor and countless others. Devout followers who had sought God and received suffering. He had tried to save them, but he had failed. But at least he tried. Where was God?

They recited the Kaddish, another prayer of mourning. Judas didn't bother to recite with them.

> *May He give reign to His kingship in your lifetimes and in your days, and in the lifetimes of the entire Family of Israel, swiftly and soon...*

And on and on. *Yeah, right.*

When the time came for the tearing of their clothes to express their heartbreak, most people would symbolically tear a corner of their tunic. Judas grabbed his cloak and ripped it almost completely in half.

He felt his arms shaking with pain and rage. His big brother John put his arm around Judas, but he pulled away. There was no consoling him.

He led the others in grabbing a handful of dirt to toss onto the coffin, reciting, "May she rest in peace."

All go to one place. All are from the dust, and to dust all return. Now that was one promise of God he believed in.

After the family, the other mourners, dozens of them, dropped in their handfuls of dirt and recited their meaningless lie. *May she rest in peace.*

Then Mattathiah gave the final blessing, a phrase that cut through Judas's heart like a dagger.

> *The Lord bless you and keep you.*
> *The Lord make his face to shine upon you and be gracious to you.*

Judah Maccabee - Part 1: Abomination of Desolation

The Lord lift up his countenance upon you and give you peace.

Judas reached in a pocket of his cloak and squeezed the amulet he had found in Sophia's hands. *Bless you and keep you? Give you peace?*

He could stand it no more. When everyone returned to their homes to gather for the funeral banquet, Judas took his sword and walked out into the desert alone. It was night by now, and nobody had seen him leave, so chances were they would not know where to look for him.

He walked for as long as he could before the cold of the desert night chilled his bones. He made a fire and listened to the sounds of the world around him. Insects, birds, wolves. He could swear he heard the howling of the demon creatures of the wilderness. Mocking Satyrs laughing like hyenas. The demon Lilith whispering as her serpent slithered around him. The *siyyim* and *iyyim* of wraiths and spectres chattering in the cold breeze.

He took handfuls of dirt and rubbed them into his hair and body.

All are from the dust, and to dust all return.

He felt a deep, gnawing hole burning through his soul. He howled with misery into the darkness. Up at the blinkering stars above.

Judas awakened in the morning beside the smoking embers of his fire. He grabbed ashes to rub into his face.

All are from the dust, and to dust all return.

He stared into the smoldering remains of the fire for what seemed like a lifetime that went by in an hour. When he came out of his stupor, it was night again. He began to shiver with the cold. But this time, he didn't bother to start a fire. He wanted to suffer. To feel pain.

By the morning, he felt a fever coming on. He sat until evening again. The hunger was nothing compared to the thirst that parched his throat.

And now he made his decision. The time had come. He had nothing left to live for. His love had been murdered. His faith stillborn. There was nothing left for him to do but end it all.

Taking out his sword, Judas got on his knees. He placed the blade to his belly. He would fall on his blade, and by the time anyone found him, he would be long dead and in Sheol. Would he see his beloved there? All he knew was that he would never see her on earth again.

And then he heard a sound. The wind howling in his ears. No other noises. No insects. No creatures of the wilderness. Only the sound of wind. It struck him. Even when he felt as if there was nothing, there was the wind like spirit flowing all around him. The words of his mentor Eleazar came back to him.

"Even when it seems that Adonai is nowhere to be found and nowhere to be heard, even when we think that he has abandoned us, he has not. He is still sovereign and secretly working his will and purpose in and through every event of history. As in the days of Elijah, sometimes, Adonai is in the silence."

In the silence.

In the pain.

The challenge that Eleazar had made to him: "How long will you try to live between worlds? You cannot ride two horses. Your people need you."

The words of the scripture that Eleazar had read from the scroll of Esther now made sense like never before: "'Then King Ahasuerus said to Queen Esther and to the Jew Mordecai, 'See, I have given Esther the house of Haman, and they have hanged him on the gallows, because he plotted to lay hands on the Jews.' Then he sent letters by mounted couriers saying that the king allowed the Jews who were in every city to gather and defend their lives, to destroy, to kill, and to annihilate any armed force of any people or province that might attack them, children and women included.'"

Eleazar pleading with Judas: "Is this not a word for us this very day in which we live? Is this not a word for such a time as this?"

Judas dropped the sword into the dirt and collapsed to the ground in a fetal position, weeping like never before. He had thought he had no more tears left to shed with the loss of his beloved. But now he found a flood of pain exiting him like a broken dam.

And a backwash of grace flowing back into his soul.

CHAPTER 38

Pontus, Scythia

Heracles had taken a complete night to prepare for his attack on the Amazonian tribe of female warriors. Their encampment on the edge of the forest provided him cover to spy on them. But the talk he had had with Mago, the heavy-drinking Phoenician sailor back in Sinope, had provided him the most helpful information he needed to plan his attack.

He had decided to hit them with a ruse focused on one of their weaknesses, their fetish for horses.

He wore his Grecian battle kilt and open leather sandals but went bare-chested and carried no weapons. He crept like a silent panther along the forest line, concealed in the brush in the middle of the day.

From his vantage point hidden in the foliage, he could see the entire tribe worshipping at a stone shrine they had placed just inside the tree line. The shrine was a large, black angular-shaped rock that apparently stood in as an image of the goddess Cybele. In front of the rock, a horse had been sacrificed.

Heracles had seen that kind of strange black rock before. The kind that fell from the sky and were worshipped by other tribes in Thrace. He chuckled to himself how these women needed some good Greek education in logic. They were worshipping an earth goddess whose spirit was encased in an image that fell from the sky god.

He didn't dwell on the thought because he was too transfixed by their fully naked bodies writhing and shaking in ecstatic dance before their deity. Ah, yes, some of them did have one breast cut off. But not all of them. Others were more fully endowed. Pity that so many were so ugly. There was a variety of skin and hair colors, but the majority were pale-skinned and red-headed. He usually liked red-heads. But what surprised him was the hair that had been artificially colored to be greens and blues and yellows. Some of it shaved off on half the head. Others had their hair cut short to the scalp. The only women in Greece who did that to their hair were prostitutes, thespians, and mad women.

What a waste to see so many of them degrade themselves.

Pulling himself away, Heracles stole back over to the horse pen, guarded by a single woman. He slipped up behind her and broke her neck like a twig.

A simple wooden fence with a gate corralled hundreds of horses of all kinds and colors, brown, black, white, spotted. All of them were mares. Heracles huffed. *They are really going to ridiculous lengths with this female obsession.*

Some of the horses neighed and jittered as if they had felt his contempt. He crouched and petted the nearest horse, the largest in the troop, a black Percheron standing seven feet to the shoulder. Lean, majestic, female, and meticulously groomed. This was probably the ride of that giant warrior Aristomache—if she wasn't a mere legend.

Heracles smiled to himself. This would be *his* ride!

There were no saddles. Amazons rode bareback or with blankets and no stirrups. But there were simple reins woven from horsehair.

Creeping up to the gate, Heracles gently lifted it, moving it to the side. The horses did not seem to care. They were well trained.

He returned to the Percheron and lashed together as many horses as he could lead by their reins.

Mounting the Percheron, he yelled at the top of his lungs, kicking the horse's ribs and leading a stampede out of the corral.

His horse broke into a full gallop out onto the steppe. Four others trailed him, Heracles holding their reins in his left hand and the mane of his ride in the other.

Horse thievery would surely draw the wrath of the tribe after him.

The corral emptied behind him. But as he was speeding out into the open, he saw the women running after their horses to stop the chaos he had created. It would not be long before they were clothed, mounted, and on his tail. He only had a small head start.

Heracles kicked the horse and yelled louder, his laughter belting out at the fun of it all. This horse could really run. He felt the wind blowing his hair.

Within a mile, he glanced behind him and saw a force of fifty already on his tail.

And they were gaining. His multiple horses were slowing him down.

He had to get to the spot on the steppe where he had left his lion skin and club before they caught up with him.

He felt a rush of wind past his ear. An arrow. They were close enough to fire on him. And they had good aim.

He didn't have much time left.

And then he saw his skin and club on the ground ahead where he had left them.

Heracles slowed the horse to a canter and jumped off, more arrows whizzing by him. There surely would have been many more missiles had he not stolen the prize steed, one they would not want to risk harming. He slapped the horse's hind, and it took off.

Running to his skin, he draped it over his shoulders with the large maned head as his helmet. He picked up his club and laughed. He couldn't help it. He so enjoyed the energy of it all.

He crouched into a battle-ready stance.

The first Amazonians arrived, halting a hundred feet out. They waited until the rest of the tribe had caught up with them, at least a hundred strong.

Heracles didn't see an eight-foot-tall warrioress with them. But whoever was leading them, a small black-haired woman, gestured, and they approached him cautiously, sweeping out in a long line. As they got to within fifty feet, their formation began to curve and encircle him. They didn't present any arms. They were trying to figure him out.

Heracles was noticing their strange clothing. They wore leather that was embroidered with flamboyantly colored designs. Some had pointed conical hats with flaps. All of them wore leather pants, something he had never seen women wear before. It must have been their need for leg protection since they virtually lived on the backs of their horses.

But with these outfits and their haircuts, the overall impression he got was that these "female warriors" looked like they were trying to be like men. Like they had rejected their own femininity. Not all of them, thank the gods. There were still some worthy of lusting after.

Heracles grabbed his lion skin close as the circle of riders began to move around him to his left. At first, they walked their warhorses, then they trotted. Then their gait picked up to that of a canter.

They yelped with screams and noises that sounded like hyenas and other desert animals.

The leader drew her bow, and they all followed suit as they continued to canter around him in circumambulation.

He knew what was coming, and he got ready.

They all drew arrows and nocked them, aiming directly at him, waiting for the command. And trying to terrify him.

He laughed.

The leader yelled out, and they all released at once.

Heracles pulled his lion skin around him tight and lowered his head so the lion's skull covered his head.

He felt the sting of a hundred arrows hit him at once all around his body—and bounce off into the dirt.

Lifting his head, he shouted, "Ho hurrah! Try again!"

The leader and many others were looking at him in shock. They had not known about the impenetrable hide of the Nemean Lion.

The ground was littered with broken arrows. Heracles knew they had special arrowheads called trilobates that had massively damaging triple edges. Others had barbs that broke off in the body. Still others were poisoned with viper venom. None of them had any effect on the Nemean Lion skin.

The leader yelled. They drew again, nocked again, and released again. Heracles protected himself again with the lion skin. The arrows bounced off and broke again.

They did it a third and a fourth time. Heracles could see the frustration in their faces grow into hysteria. Their yelping became more agitated. They were clearly used to getting their way.

When the leader saw they were getting nowhere with repeated missile launches, she finally signaled. The circle began to tighten. They were drawing in closer to Heracles to attack him directly.

That was exactly what he had wanted them to do.

Putting away their bows, the Amazons pulled out wicker crescent-shaped shields that protected their side facing their enemy. They drew small bronze battle-axes with a pick-like point at the other end.

They got closer and closer as they continued to gallop in their circle of death around him. They were twenty feet away now.

Suddenly, the horses began to fall like a ring of dominoes. They had stepped into a circular covered pit that Heracles had dug the night before in preparation for this moment. The pit was only four feet deep and about four feet wide, big enough to bring down the horses, break their legs, disable them, and deliver the female warriors onto the ground—and into the hands of Heracles.

They tumbled and rolled around him. He cast off his lion skin, clanked his heavy bronze wristbands together, and readied his club. He paused at first. He had never fought women in battle. It wasn't natural. He was used to protecting women, providing for them, and making love to them. This was bizarre, and it caused him to hesitate. He saw one that was gorgeous with her red hair and pulpy lips getting up from her fall at his feet. He wanted to grab her and kiss her. But when her pointed axe end pierced his foot, he bellowed in pain and came to his senses.

These weren't normal women. They were wild banshees possessed with a demonic hostility. They did not want to make love with him. They wanted to make war.

So he gave them war.

Pulling the axe head from his foot, he used it to cleave the girl's head in half. He used his club to swat the others away like flies. It had surprised him how truly light in weight women were. He knew that already, but only in the context of making love, not in battle. They flew in the air like kicked cats. But he had to give it to them that they were relentless.

They must really hate men.

But they couldn't match men. Their horses made them equal in speed to males, and their bows gave them equal killing ability from a distance. But in up-close hand-to-hand combat with a man, they were useless. Sure, Heracles was preternaturally strong, but it still felt like he was beating children to a pulp as opposed to the battles he had had with male warriors.

He felt a strange sense of sadness. He hated to see the beautiful faces and bodies of the gorgeous ones go to waste as he crushed, mangled, and demolished them.

It wasn't right. Women shouldn't be warriors. It was both so easy to kill them and so hard to go against nature.

When the dust settled, he stood there, barely having broken a sweat, looking down upon the tragic waste of life around him. A hundred broken, bloodied female corpses, some of them even beautiful in death.

Heracles limped around to see if there were any victims he had to put out of their misery. He was interrupted by a bellowing high-pitched scream. He looked up. Outside the ring of death, he saw two of the Amazonians escaping on horseback. Good, they would carry the news back to their queen.

They passed by the source of the annoying ear-piercing shriek. It was a very large woman marching toward him. A large and imposing warrior in light chainmail with javelin in hand and shield strapped to her back. It had to be one person and one person alone. Aristomache, the queen's champion.

Heracles wondered if she was going to demand her horse back.

So the rumors were true. She was easily eight feet tall. He could see tattoos of animals all over her body. She was abnormally muscular for a female and homely looking, to be honest, with her shaved head and tall lanky legs. She wore a leather cuirass that crisscrossed her chest and left her breasts exposed. In her case, she had chopped off both breasts in her Amazonian pride and seemed to be sporting her chest scars like a badge of honor.

It struck Heracles as grotesque. Inhuman. Well, he shouldn't complain. He was only half human himself. They were two of a kind.

One thing he was sure of. He would never have sex with this thing. He would have to kill it.

His distracted thoughts were broken by her raising her javelin and launching it at him with deadly force. He turned to his side and caught the missile in mid-air. Okay, maybe not *deadly* force.

He felt a sliver from the birchwood piercing his hand. Tossing aside the javelin, he dropped his club and limped out of the circle to meet his opponent without a weapon. It wouldn't be fair to match her equally. He had to give her an advantage.

He bit his palm to pull out the sliver that had lodged there.

By the time they met, she had pulled her crescent shield off her back and was protecting her scarred torso while handling her pointed axe in her right hand.

Heracles looked up into her eyes. They were raging red with fury like a mad she-wolf.

He said, "You need a strong man to keep you in your place."

She yelled at him. Or rather, screeched.

She really *was* tall.

But like most giants, her swing was slow and her gait cumbersome.

She swung with a grunt of force. He used his bronze wristband to deflect the blow.

Again, she swung. Again, he deflected with his bracelets.

Within several moves, he had easily figured out the cadence of her fighting form.

It was undisciplined.

She grunted and swung again.

This time he dodged it, limped to the side, and grabbed her axe arm as she fell off-balance.

Taking her arm, he spun around, leaning into her to use his lower center-point as a lever against her height. He flipped her over his back.

She landed with a thud on the hard ground.

He snapped her wrist, and she dropped the axe in pain.

Looking up at him, she began to scream that high-pitched screech that appeared to be her attempt at a war cry. Instead, she sounded like a bitch hyena in heat.

And she wouldn't stop.

So he punched her face with full force.

His hand went through her skull into the dirt.

The screeching stopped. His ears felt relieved.

Walking back for his lion skin and club, he returned to pick up her body and carry it back toward the camp.

The midday sun blazed above, its blanket of light burning everything. A circle of buzzards was already descending to begin picking the defeated carcasses of their flesh.

Heracles limped away, leaving his mess to be cleaned up by the scavengers and insects of the desert.

When he arrived at the edge of the forest encampment, he was greeted by the other hundred or so Amazonians lined up with shields and presented weapons.

He didn't stop in his gait. He didn't even hesitate. He just kept walking right up to the camp with the dead giantess in his arms, blood still dripping from her crushed skull.

A wave of terror flooded their faces as they noticed their dead champion.

He reached their line. They simply parted in awe and let him walk by.

He walked through the camp past a line of silent and terrified witnesses.

Heracles could tell which tent was the queen's own. It was the largest, most decorated one in the camp. Unblemished goat skins and woven camelhair with treated crimson red leather entrance flaps fronted by brass censers and a line of torches.

He walked past the two armed guards and entered the tent unmolested.

The interior was lit by several openings in the ceiling canopy, creating pillars of light cutting through the shadows.

Heracles stopped when he saw the queen sitting on a portable carved wooden throne waiting for him.

He felt stunned by her beauty. The first thing he noticed was her bright-red hair. This wasn't artificial color like the others he had seen earlier. This was long, flowing locks of natural wavy red unlike anything he had seen before. Her skin was pale with freckles, and her eyelids were painted with Egyptian-like kohl liner, giving stark contrast to the whites of her eyes. The intensity of her bright hazel-green irises penetrated his soul. He felt exposed to her. Drawn to her pouting pale lips.

Her crown was an elaborate headdress made with golden antelope antlers in honor of the Greek goddess Artemis. A long green satin robe draped a curvaceous figure he would kill for—including cleavage that implied two full breasts beneath the flowing gown. Thank the gods royalty did not perform the gruesome mutilation of their beautiful bodies.

The shining satin came together beneath a large golden belt that sported a huge buckle like that of Ares, the god of war. Sizable rings of gold in her ears and around her neck with gem-studded bracelets all reinforced her royal pedigree. To Heracles, she was a goddess like Cybele, who deserved the two male white lions chained beside her as throne guardians.

Heracles stopped ten feet from her. "Queen Deianeira, I believe this is your champion."

He dropped the corpse on the floor at his feet. The lions growled. He wasn't afraid. In fact, he took off his lion skin and dropped it to the floor, puffing his mighty chest out just enough to peacock his muscles.

She flinched with a shivering fear in her eyes.

He looked past her to a large obese female figure hiding in the shadows behind the throne. "Cybele, leave us."

The queen looked behind her, wondering what he was looking at. But only he could see. And then the Watcher was gone.

The queen asked, "Who are you, and why have you come here with such devastation?"

"My name is Heracles, and I want your belt."

She looked confused. "You killed half my tribe for my belt?"

"Well, now that I'm here, I see something else that looks good for the taking."

Heracles waited to see if she would cringe in fear. But she remained proud and unmoved.

He said, "I warn you now that the more you fight back, the more you will get hurt."

The queen looked him up and down with hungry eyes. "Are you an idiot? You think I would resist that?"

She gestured toward his physique, ending on his manhood. "I want your seed. And I am going to give you the most intense experience you have ever had in your life."

Heracles grinned. "Oh, it's going to be more than one experience." He stepped toward the throne to get it started.

CHAPTER 39

Modein

Big John stood with his father and brothers in the agora marketplace of their village along with hundreds of other residents. They watched the Seleucid official Apelles dressed in his military outfit ordering obedience to the decrees of King Antiochus, guarded by his unit of fifty Seleucid soldiers.

The Hasmonean brothers wore their priestly robes on order of Apelles, as did the other priests in the village. The few weapons of the community were ordered confiscated and placed in a guarded shed, but the priests were allowed their butchering axes and daggers in their belts for sacrifices. John had hidden his war hammer against a stone wall of the synagogue nearby should the need arise.

Apelles had marched into their town with the unit of soldiers three days ago in the middle of their town funeral. It was just after they had discovered Judas had disappeared into the desert. John knew his brother's grief was too great for him to bear and that he wouldn't allow anyone to help shoulder that burden.

Simon had taken the lead among the brothers, which was understood and acceptable to his elder sibling. It had always concerned John that Simon looked so much older than he was because he seemed to carry the world on his shoulders. His heavily creased face never seemed to smile.

John was the firstborn and a strong warrior. But he also knew that he did not have the leadership acumen nor strategic mind to lead the family when Father was gone. John's only desire was to one day become a mighty *gibbor* warrior, like King David's mighty men, the gibborim of old. A man received the designation of "gibbor" for mighty acts of valor in battle. Everyone considered John a gibbor already, but he had never had the opportunity to prove it in real combat. So as far as he was concerned, he was not one yet. But he was content to be the muscle supporting the mind of his smarter brothers as they followed their father's patriarchal lead.

Simon, however, was not so content. Though he was second-born and surely worthy, his younger brother Judas had the natural charisma and passion that seemed to draw others to himself. Even within the family, everyone knew Judas was the dominant, and John knew that had bothered Simon to no end.

But Judas was gone, drowning in his grief. And no one knew when or whether he was coming back. Though many feared the worst, John held out hope. The old scribe Eleazar had put so much into Judas all these years. Even though the Hammer was a prodigal son, he had the Word of God implanted into him, and John knew it would take root one day. He prayed this was the day. He prayed Judas was not dead. That he would return.

The commander Apelles stood before a stone altar in the center of the agora with his lieutenant, a sleazy looking man named Erasmus. Immediately upon their arrival in the village, the soldiers had been ordered to build the altar with the name of Zeus engraved upon it. Bronze censers around the marketplace and at house entrances were also required for incense offerings to the gods.

Those censers, poles with small burning plates on top, were currently filling the air with the stench of some godawful perfume and spices used by Greeks. It made the Jews cringe in revulsion. Noxious fumes for noxious gods.

Soldiers currently heaped scrolls of Scripture onto the altar that they had confiscated from any volunteering them in obedience to the king. These were set aflame with a torch. Apelles used the moment for instruction. "From this day forward, any additional copies of Torah that are found in a Jew's possession will be immediate cause for execution!"

John looked at his brothers. They smirked with defiance, having hidden multiple Scriptures while handing in old copies of scribal practice and accounting drafts.

"Come and take them," whispered Eleazar.

"Shhh," ordered Simon.

Apelles continued, "In addition to your new daily sacrifices to Zeus at this altar, there will also be a special sacrifice on the twenty-fifth day of each month in honor of the king's birthday!"

John shook his head in disbelief. Not only had this demon king Antiochus stopped the daily sacrifices in the holy temple—the only acceptable location for offerings—but he replaced them with an altar of abomination to Zeus. As if that were not enough, he was now forcing the Jews to make sacrifices to that same idol in every village along with the king. It was abominable on every level. John was ready to fight to the death against this idolatrous tyranny. All his brothers were as well. They were simply waiting upon their father for the order. Then they would launch with the fury of an army of avenging angels.

But Mattathiah was quiet as he stood beside the Seleucid officials, signaling his position as the town's most respected priest.

Apelles had some soldiers bring a squealing, squirming white pig up to the altar. An unclean animal that no Torah-observant Jew would dare sacrifice. Abomination upon abomination.

As the soldiers held the pig down on the altar, Apelles shouted, "This first sacrifice will be a swine, but the king will graciously allow you other animals for sacrifice as well: goats, sheep, even birds."

Apelles turned to Mattathiah and announced, "Mattathiah, you are a leader, honored and great in this town and supported by sons and brothers.

Now, be the first to come and do what the king commands. As all the Gentiles and people of Judea and those left in Jerusalem have done."

John knew that Apelles had previously spoken with his father about the sacrifice, offering him special honor as a Friend of the King along with silver and gold to make him and his sons rich should he carry out the sacrifice.

Mattathiah stepped forward and looked around the marketplace as though looking each and every individual in the eye with stern warning. He then answered in a loud voice, "Even if all the nations that live beneath the rule of King Antiochus obey him, as for me and my household, we will continue to live by the covenant of our forefathers! We will not desert Adonai and his Torah! Come what may!"

The crowd began buzzing. The Hellenists booed him. The hasidim applauded. Trouble was brewing. Apelles looked like he was about to explode. His glare contemplated the most painful punishment for Mattathiah.

Then a single priest stepped out from the crowd and shouted, "I will perform the sacrifice!" It was Tobias the Hellenist. The compromiser.

Of course, thought John.

Tobias walked up to the altar where the soldiers held down the pig and withdrew his sacrificial knife. He slit the pig's throat. Its squealing was swallowed up in gurgling blood that spurted out all over the altar. The soldiers backed away from the mess.

At that very moment, several things began to happen that jumbled together in John's observation. First, he heard the sound of an individual marching toward him from behind. He turned defensively.

It was Judas! He was returning from the desert in his sackcloth with his skin covered in dirt and ashes. He looked like a spirit wraith of the underworld intent on a mission.

Judas saw John's war hammer against the wall and swept it up without a second thought.

"Judas!" John called out. But his brother passed him by without so much as a glance, his eyes set like steel on the agora.

Secondly, John saw Mattathiah pull out his butchering axe and bury it deep in Tobias's neck. The wounded priest froze in shock.

Mattathiah yanked the axe back out. The priest fell to the ground like the pig on the altar, his life blood spurting from his gaping wound.

Judas was still yards from the altar.

With an eye for political opportunity, their youngest brother Jonathan began chanting, "Phineas! Phineas! Phineas!"

The crowd joined in.

John knew the story of Phineas because his father had told it many times to his sons. Phineas had been the righteous priest who pierced through a pair of idolatrous fornicators in the wilderness camp of Moses, both the man and the woman. That single act stopped the disease that Adonai had brought upon Israel for their idolatrous intermingling with the Midianites and their god Baal.

Apelles still stood near Mattathiah, looking stunned at the sudden turn of events. Spinning around, the priest hit the commander with the bloodied axe. Simultaneously, Mattathiah also pulled his dagger, plunging it into Apelles's belly and up into his heart. Death came quickly for the Greek commander.

But now the soldiers had begun to move.

So did the hasidim in the crowd. They fell upon the soldiers with a vengeance.

Simon yelled for the brothers to attack. They launched out with their butcher axes.

Apelles's lieutenant Erasmus had drawn his sword and was about to cut Mattathiah down. But Judas had reached the altar. Swinging John's massive war hammer, he crushed Erasmus's skull, launching him to the ground dead. For good measure, he then wielded the hammer to pulverize Apelles's head.

The chanting of "Phineas" did not wane as the Jews fought. It was their battle cry for holy strength.

John first used his axe, then took a sword from a soldier and used both to hack down one after another of the enemy. He was moving so fast and with such deadly precision his brothers had to get out of his way. Heads, hands, legs all came off in his fury of justice. By his own count, he thought he might have killed half of the soldiers himself. He would be careful not to crow afterwards.

It did not take long for the battle to be over as the Hasmoneans and hasidim overwhelmed the Seleucids. They jumped the soldiers before many of them could respond, took their weapons, and used them against their oppressors. Seleucid shields, swords, and spears were all used to bring judgment down upon their own heads.

The blood flowed in the street.

And all fifty Seleucid soldiers were killed to the man.

By the time the dust had settled and they took their body count, only nine Jews had been slain in the melee.

Barely a rise in his heartbeat, John stood next to his brothers, who heaved and panted from the fight. They had found their way to each other and had instinctively formed a protective arc around their father, who now stood upon the bloodstained altar and raised his butcher axe high.

"People of Modein!" Mattathiah shouted out. "Let us start a wave of justice that will sweep through the land!"

The crowd cheered.

"But know this, though we have total victory today, Antiochus will send a thousand men down upon us in response! We must leave this town to protect it! All those who are zealous for the Law and the covenant, join me and my sons now, and we will organize a resistance!"

The zealous hasidim in their midst cheered. Finally, they had a savior to lead them. Finally, they would fight back.

Mattathiah spoke with seething strength, "Grab the enemy's weapons as your own. Suit up with provisions and say your goodbyes to your families. We meet on the north side of town at sundown. Our destination will be the hills of Gophna in the north, where we can hide and prepare!"

Again, cheers of agreement resounded. The people began to clean up the bodies of the dead soldiers for burning and burial. Some had already started to dismantle the altar and take down the censers. There would be no evidence that the Seleucid unit had even made it to their out-of-the-way rural town.

Mattathiah stood with his sons and embraced Judas with all his might. John smiled at the reunion and embraced both of them.

Mattathiah said, "Judas, I know not what you think. I only know what you did. You came back." He grabbed the head of the hammer, which dripped blood and gore. "Today, you have earned your righteous name amongst your brothers."

"With *my* hammer," teased John, grabbing it back.

"You are truly Judas Maccabeus. The Hammer of God."

The brothers laughed and agreed together.

But Judas said, "No."

They became quiet.

"I repudiate my Greek name. I am no longer the Hellenist, Judas Maccabeus. I am the Hebrew, Judah Maccabee."

John cheered along with his brothers. Even Simon seemed more accepting of his sibling rival.

And John knew that his world had changed forever.

CHAPTER 40

Mount Hermon

Hera led the goddesses up the slope of the ancient cosmic mountain in the land of Bashan, the Land of the Serpent. Down below in the valley, she could see a deadwood tree in the unseen realm. Hundreds of feet in circumference, it rose into the air almost as high as they were at nine thousand feet. This world tree was the most ancient Mother Earth goddess named Gaia after whom the Greek goddess Gaia was named. She had once thrived in the spiritual realm on the souls of the human dead. Her branches reached to heaven and her roots into Hades. She had been a significant influence in the region until the ascension of King David had shifted the axis mundi of the spiritual world from Hermon to Mount Zion. Her gnarly, withered corpse was a monument to her once-majestic presence. Hera thought she could be a powerful ally if they could ever revive her.

The goddesses passed the ancient limestone stela near the summit, kissing their hands to touch it as they passed. Engraved on the stone was the oath made in primordial days by their forefathers the Watchers. When they came down from heaven, they had solemnly vowed to one another in an insurrection, "According to the command of the greatest and holy god, those who take an oath proceed from here." The "greatest and holy god" in this diabolical vow was not their Creator, Yahweh, but El, the old high god of Canaan. And this was his mountain.

Zeus had called an assembly of the gods here for a major announcement. Eleven of the twelve Olympians were present: Zeus,

Poseidon, Apollo, Hephaestus, Dionysus, and Hermes. Athena, Aphrodite, Demeter, and Artemis had arrived with Hera. Persephone, Hestia, and Gaia joined with Hades to fill out the assembly.

They stood around a large bowl-shaped pit, "the threshing floor of El," just outside the ruins of his ancient temple. These pits were a common source for humans to commune with the gods. This cosmic mountain had long ago been conquered by Mount Zion. But its importance would never be forgotten.

Hera wondered why they were meeting here instead of Zaphon. Did Zeus want to shift his holy mountain back to Hermon? Was he being nostalgic?

Zeus said to his gathering, "I have called you all here in memorial of our predecessors, the Ancient Ones."

He was referring to the original two hundred Watchers who had left their heavenly abode to mate with the daughters of men in the days of Jared. They had come down to earth at this summit and had sworn the oath of commitment to the deed. Their progeny had been the giant Nephilim, gibborim of old.

Zeus continued, "Please do not take any of this personally. What you are about to see is a demonstration, *not* a criticism of any of you."

The gods and goddesses looked quizzically at one another as Zeus whistled toward the temple ruins.

In response, a mounted warrior walked a large black Percheron horse from hiding. Hera could see he was wild-haired, bearded, and bare-chested with a battle kilt, sandals, and bronze wrist bands. He appeared to be able to see and hear the gods in the heavenly realm. Hera was no longer surprised. The pieces were coming together.

The gods and goddesses were aligned in a semi-circle in council. The strongman arrived, got off his horse, and bowed in worship to the assembly.

They all watched with baited curiosity.

Hera could now see that the three-headed hound Cerberus was leashed and walking behind him. The gibbor released the dog. It ran to its owner, Hades. He grabbed the leash and petted the animal's heads. He made it sit before him.

Ares came next from the ruins, leading the obese Amazonian goddess Cybele, completely naked except for a large rope draped around her neck that appeared to contain hundreds of human scalps. Hera despised the primitive gods and their raw simplicity.

Zeus gestured to the strong man, "Olympians, meet Heracles."

Hera muttered, "How original."

"I named him after my mythological prototype."

Hera rolled her eyes.

Zeus continued, "As you can now see, I gave him several labors in order to demonstrate to all of you his capabilities."

Ares shoved Cybele to the ground at the feet of the assembly. Her bulging fat shielded her from the fall and bounced around her like whale blubber. She was like an overturned turtle who could not right herself.

"You pig!" Gaia yelled at Ares, waddling over to her earth sister to help her up.

Zeus said, "Those are the scalps of the defeated warrior tribe of Amazons. The belt Heracles wears is that of their queen."

Hera could hear Ares mutter to himself, "Women warriors. Hardly impressive."

Heracles had returned to his horse where he pulled off a set of golden antlers.

"Those are my Ceryneian Hind's antlers!" Artemis huffed. "He killed my Ceryneian Hind?" She began to shine brightly as her anger boiled.

"Calm down, Artemis," said Zeus. "I told you I was not attacking you. I was merely choosing dangerous tasks of the highest difficulty."

Artemis looked to Hera for some kind of affirmation or command. Hera gave her a scolding look, and she shrank back.

Heracles then took off his lion pelt and tossed over the antlers.

Now Hera exclaimed, "My Nemean Lion!" She glared at Zeus with contempt. "So it was you all along."

Now she had to hold back her own shining rage.

That damned Zeus *was* trying to hamstring their powers.

Lastly, the muscular warrior threw a large burlap sack to the ground. It opened, and one of the heads of the Hydra rolled partially out, drawing expressions of surprise from everyone. Chattering erupted, but Zeus shushed them.

Heracles stood proudly, wearing his confiscated belt of Ares. Hera could see he was going to keep that one for himself.

Zeus explained, "My dear family, what you see before you is a new breed of Nephilim."

More shock and chattering erupted again.

Hera exclaimed, "You can't be serious!"

Zeus gave her a dirty look, reminding her of his warning.

She didn't care. The risk for going along was far greater than any beating he might give her. She said, "You know full well that mating with humans will get us all imprisoned in Tartarus."

Poseidon joined her. "She is right, brother. I don't want to find myself in company with the Ancient Ones."

Those Ancient Ones were Watchers who had also revealed forbidden knowledge to humans from sexual perversion to war to occultic secrets. Distorted by Greek myth into the Titans, the Ancient Ones had been imprisoned in the deepest, darkest dungeon of Hades until the judgment.

Zeus said, "I am well aware of the danger."

"I think it is a little bit more serious than mere 'danger,'" replied Poseidon.

Hades added, "And if you are counting on the promise of Yahweh that he will not flood the world again, there's always the fires of Sodom and Gomorrah to look forward to."

They were all too familiar with the result of the second incursion of Watchers that had bred the Nephilim clans of Canaan called Anakim and Rephaim. Joshua followed by King David had wiped them out as the Seed of the Serpent.

"Who did you mate with?" Hera demanded. "Is she still alive?"

In ancient days, many women had died giving birth to these hybrid monstrosities.

"See, that's just it," said Zeus. "I didn't mate with anyone. I asked Prometheus to look into the science of the primeval days. Not everything had been revealed, you know. And we have experimented a lot in the thousands of years since then."

"Prometheus!" Poseidon exclaimed with disgust. "Always starting fires!"

Hades added, "I wondered where that trickster had been hiding."

Hera had always considered the Watcher Prometheus a traitor since he was too favorably inclined toward humanity. This could help her case against Zeus.

The king of the gods continued, "Prometheus found a way to use the flesh of an earthly body, in this case one of the first Nephilim after the Flood, and duplicate it without using sexual intercourse."

Hera interrupted. "Is that parthenogenesis? Asexual reproduction?"

"Similar," said Zeus. "It's a genetic replication process. And Prometheus manipulated the physical substructure so Heracles would not be a giant in size but would still retain his power."

"So who is this replicant from?" asked Hera.

"Prometheus went to Uruk and excavated a primeval tomb from beneath the Euphrates River. He found the body of Gilgamesh, Hero King of Uruk."

A hush went through the assembly.

Hera blurted out, "You replicated the body of the mighty Nimrod?"

They all knew the story. Many of them had been there. Gilgamesh was first of the Nephilim warrior kings born of the Sons of God after the Great Flood. A divine/human hybrid, he had ruled Uruk and had gone mad in a search for eternal life. He had ended up adopting a new identity as Nimrod the mighty hunter, King of Babel and the Land of Shinar.

"Yes," said Zeus. "And I did it without sexually penetrating daughters of men. So technically, I have not violated our sexual taboo."

They all considered his words.

Hades voiced his doubts. "Still, I think it violates the heavenly/earthly separation."

Zeus ignored him and kept going, "Think of it. Now that you've seen his power, imagine what we could do with an army of these Nephilim. We could take Greece back from Rome and return her to her former glory. We could rule the earth."

"And you think these creatures will obey King Antiochus without mutiny?" Artemis demanded with incredulity.

Zeus gestured to Heracles, who kneeled and vowed, "I serve the will of the gods."

Gaia butted in with a horrendous cackling laugh. "The spirits of the dead Nephilim before the Flood now wander the earth. Living Nephilim are earthly creatures with Watchers' blood. What makes you think they won't unite and turn on us?"

"Nonsense," complained Zeus. "They will not turn on us."

All the gods glanced at each other, looking for agreement, contemplating dissent.

To everyone's surprise, Hera agreed with Zeus, stepping into the center near Heracles. "They will not turn on us."

Even Zeus was bewildered. Was she finally submitting?

Without losing step, Hera drew her sword and in one graceful swipe chopped off the head of Heracles. The body stood for moment as if not sure what it should do before it collapsed to the ground, blood squirting from its arteries.

Zeus's face turned shining-red with rage. Electrical current began to swirl about him.

Hera stepped back, and all the goddesses surrounded her protectively. Shields raised, weapons drawn.

The male gods responded accordingly, drawing together and sporting their weapons for Zeus.

The entire location began to glow like fire with the rising intensity of the gods.

Zeus yelled like thunder, "How dare you defy me! This is treason!"

Hera responded, not with anger but with stern chastisement, "It is not treason, Zeus! You think Yahweh will not judge us for this? If you think you can find a loophole in his Law, you are a bigger fool than I thought! You risk the imprisonment of us all for your juvenile schemes of power!"

The lack of aggression in the male gods suggested that they were not entirely disagreeing with her. That they thought she might have a point, and that point had consequences for them all.

Hera continued, "Consider this. In your pursuit of this Nephilim army, you have taken your eyes off the true enemy. You are deluded if you think you own Jerusalem."

"I do own Jerusalem," crowed Zeus.

She replied, "The Jewish apostasy was our power over them. But there is a growing movement of hasidim rebels who will not bow the knee."

Zeus protested, "Antiochus will kill them off."

Hera glanced around the other gods. "Has no one told him?"

They all looked guiltily unaware.

"Again, you are too obsessed with your plans to notice that the hasidim have started an insurgency. They are organizing."

Zeus's face flushed with shock, then embarrassment.

"By trying to force them to violate their beliefs or die, you have created a martyr's army of resistance. You have inspired repentance. Their faith is rising."

Zeus appeared so caught off guard that the only response he could return was anger. He started to buzz with shining current again and said in a low tone, "You and all your goddesses. Get. Off. My. Mountain."

"You need us, Zeus," said Hera.

He didn't respond. He only stewed in his thunderous swirl of energy.

As the goddesses backed away, Hera announced to the male gods, "Let it be witnessed here that we are not rebels. This is not a mutiny. Zeus is casting us off because of our opinions and advice. We remain loyal to the cause and seek to protect the pantheon from imprisonment in Tartarus. That is not treason. It is patriotism."

Turning, Hera led the goddesses off to find their own headquarters—for her next planned step of treason.

• • • • • •

For Part 2 of this novel set, get Judah Maccabee: Part 2 – Against the Gods of Greece (Chronicles of the Watchers, Book 5). https://godawa.com/get-judah-part-2/

Sign up for Godawa Chronicles Updates at Godawa.com to be the first to hear about new releases, special deals, and articles on strange things in the Bible.

• • • • •

If you liked this book, then please help me out by writing a positive review of it where you bought it. That is one of the best ways to say thank you to me as an author. It really does help my sales and status. Thanks! – *Brian Godawa*

More Books by Brian Godawa

See www.godawa.com for more information on other books by Brian Godawa. Check out his other series below.

Chronicles of the Nephilim

Chronicles of the Nephilim is a saga that charts the rise and fall of the Nephilim giants of Genesis 6 and their place in the evil plans of the fallen angelic Sons of God called "The Watchers." The story starts in the days of Enoch and continues on through the Bible until the arrival of the Messiah, Jesus. The prelude to Chronicles of the Apocalypse. ChroniclesOfTheNephilim.com. (affiliate link)

Chronicles of the Apocalypse

Chronicles of the Apocalypse is an origin story of the most controversial book of the Bible: Revelation. A historical conspiracy thriller quadrilogy in first century Rome set against the backdrop of explosive spiritual warfare of Satan and his demonic Watchers. ChroniclesOfTheApocalypse.com. (affiliate link)

Chronicles of the Watchers

Chronicles of the Watchers is a series that charts the influence of spiritual principalities and powers over the course of human history. The kingdoms of man in service to the gods of the nations at war. Interwoven with Chronicles of the Nephilim. ChroniclesOfTheWatchers.com. (affiliate link)

Theological Thriller Novels

The *Theological Thriller Novels* series by Brian James Godawa is a series of standalone novels that explore good and evil, human nature and God. Some are modern, some are fictional, some are a blend of fiction and history. Sins of humanity are depicted in the novels with honesty and accuracy. Therefore they are for mature readers because the power of redemption in a story is only as great as the accuracy of depiction of the evil from which characters can be redeemed. TheologicalThrillers.com (affiliate link)

Get Judah Maccabee – Part 2: Against the Gods of Greece.

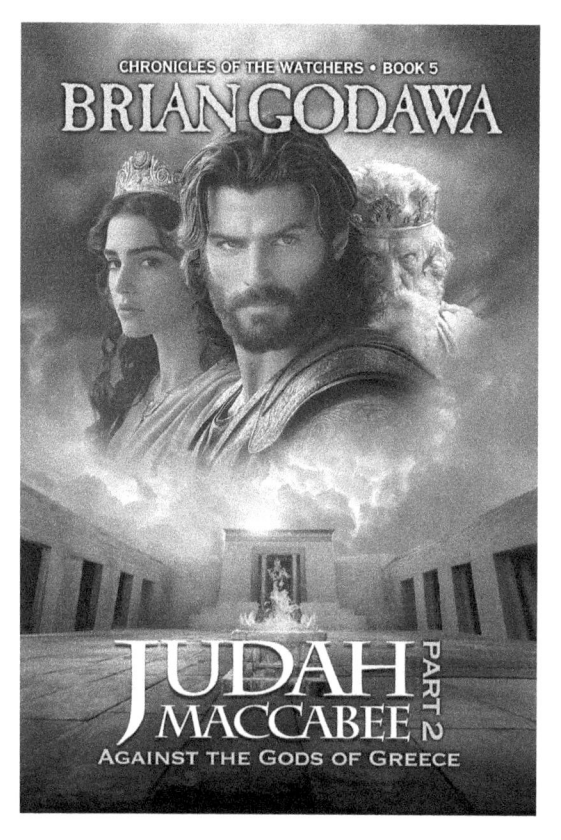

The Conclusion to This Novel You Have Read.

Supernatural epic novel about the Abomination of Desolation predicted by the Bible prophet Daniel. Jewish warrior Judah Maccabee fights a Greek tyrant. The story of Hanukkah in the Apocrypha. Biblically faithful spiritual warfare novel. Part 2 of 2.

Available for purchase in paperback, eBook, audio and large print.

https://godawa.com/get-judah-part-2/
(affiliate link)

Get the Book of the Biblical & Historical Research Behind This Novel.

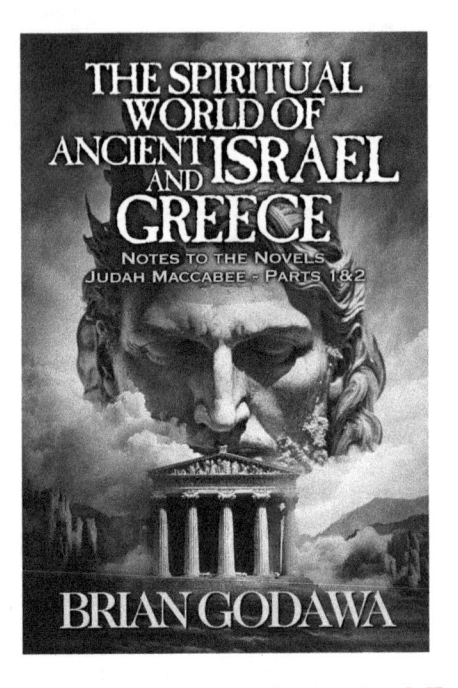

Learn the Story Behind the Historical Fulfillment of Daniel's Abomination of Desolation and More.

If you like the novel set *Judah Maccabee: Parts 1&2,* you'll love discovering the biblical and historical basis for the fascinating, mind-bending story of what happened between the Old And New Testaments.

Available for purchase in paperback, eBook, audio and large print.

https://godawa.com/get-spirit-world-greece/

(*affiliate link*)

GREAT OFFERS BY BRIAN GODAWA

Get More Biblical Imagination

Sign up Online For The Godawa Chronicles

www.Godawa.com

Updates and Freebies
of the Books of Brian Godawa
Special Discounts,
Fascinating Bible Facts!

ABOUT THE AUTHOR

Brian Godawa is a respected Christian writer and best-selling author of novels and biblical theology. His supernatural Bible epic novels combine creative imagination with orthodox Christian theology in a way that transcends both entertainment and preachiness.

His love for Jesus and storytelling was forged in the crucible of worldview apologetics and Hollywood screenwriting, as he began a career in movies and eventually expanded into the world of novels.

His first novel series, *Chronicles of the Nephilim*, has been in the Top 10 of Biblical Fiction on Amazon for more than a decade, selling over 400,000 books. His popular book *Hollywood Worldviews: Watching Films with Wisdom and Discernment* is used as a textbook in Christian film schools around the country. His movies *To End All Wars* and *Alleged* have won multiple movie awards such as Cannes Film Festival and the Heartland International Film Festival.

He lives in Texas with the most amazing wife a man could ever pray for and is accountable to a local church. He reads too many books and watches too many movies. He knows, he knows, he should get out more.

Find out more about his blog and his other books, lectures, and online courses for sale at his website, www.godawa.com.

Blank Page

Blank Page

Blank Page

Blank Page

Blank Page

Blank Page

Blank Page

Blank Page